Stor...

He tried to scream and all he knew was water. Something huge and wooden brushed over his head and he felt this was the hull of the boat. He pushed away and the whole sea heaved and vomited him out and he was in a mass of black water, then down again, and his breath sucked in water. His clothes were dragging him down and he clawed at his boots, his shirt. Then he was above water, sucked air, and saw the black cliffs were closer and the water walloped against them, then he was down again.

Then from somewhere in front, he saw a light.

A weak yellow light which glimmered and blinked. Something landed on his back, and Richard twisted over. It was Legris. Richard went to help him, then he saw the man's head loll to one side, his tongue protruding through his teeth. More water took him and Richard struggled to the surface and Legris was gone. But the light was still there. Yellow, perhaps brighter, still winking. Fighting for breath, he struck out towards it. And the blackness swallowed him.

By the same author

TREVANION
FIRE AND SHADOW
HOMELAND

Storm Within

David Hillier

WARNER BOOKS

A *Warner* Book

First published in Great Britain in 1995
by Warner Books
Reprinted 2000

Copyright © David Hillier, 1995

The moral right of the author has been asserted.

A CIP catalogue record for this book is
available from the British Library.

ISBN 0 7515 1068 8

Phototypeset by Intype, London
Printed and bound in Great Britain by
Clays Ltd, St Ives plc

Warner Books
A Division of
Little, Brown and Company (UK)
Brettenham House
Lancaster Place
London WC2E 7EN

To my mother

With special thanks to
Lorraine for her love and support
and to Tony and Barbara
for their encouragement

Prologue

HE SAW THE HORSE BEFORE he heard the sound of hoofs. A huge white stallion which sprang out of the night, muscles bunched, rushing headlong from the wood and up over the downs, its rider calling out, his voice high and harsh in the crisp night air. Richard felt his stomach tighten involuntarily, even before he saw the horseman's face. He wished he could turn away or lower his eyes, but could not. If only . . .

Then the horse leapt closer, and the man rose high in the stirrups, his gaze fixed on some far point of the horizon, and his thick red hair streamed behind him, ablaze in the moonlight. It was him, just as Richard remembered him, except maybe his face was older, thinner. Was he wounded? The horse was running faster now, faster, and now the beating of the hoofs was all around them, drumming on the soft grass of the downs, and faster still. But behind them, suddenly, the night was swallowed in blackness. A great black shape, monstrous, darker, thicker than the night, was pursuing the rider. It moved swiftly, silently over the downs, consuming everything in its path, gaining on the horse with every breath. Richard wanted to call out, but his tongue was thick with horror and would not move. What was this black shadow? In only a second the horseman would be lost. Didn't he know what pursued him? Couldn't he feel it? And then everything was black at once, and the horse and rider were swallowed into the night and Richard at last flung his tongue free of his jaw and yelled. Too late. Too late.

The great scream woke him with a jolt. But it was only after some seconds that he realised he was staring at the swollen cracks in his bedroom wall and the wind was creaking in the rooftops above. Richard Tremaine shivered. His nightshirt was drenched and clung to him. His head ached savagely. Even in the dim light of the moon, his hair glowed the same colour as the rider's, the colour of rust, of brass, of burnt copper. He tipped himself out of bed, ducked his tall frame under the eaves, and jabbed the windows open. The damp night air ran over him, soothed him. He sucked in a deep, cool breath. From afar the voices of the night porters – guttural, German – rose up with the clanging of the barges on the river. He realised thankfully that the house below was quiet, and he prayed no one had heard him. The last time, Herr Fluss had come banging on his door, and Maria was scared out of her wits. If it happened again, he would have to move.

Why always that dream? Richard pulled off his shirt and let the chill air dry his chest and thighs. How many times had this image of his father come to him? Always the same. Always riding, wildly, hopelessly, into impenetrable blackness. And always, at his heels, this other thing, this unknown horror, that pursued him. And always Richard called out, too late.

Richard flung himself back on to the mattress. From across the city, the bell tolled four. He knew he would not sleep now before sunrise, and as he lay there, he wished with all his heart that things were not as they were.

He was still awake when the messenger rapped loudly at the door a little after six and Maria the serving-girl came swearing and cursing up four flights of stairs with a letter signed simply Charles R.

Richard felt his heart race a little as he read the summons.

The letter was from Charles Stuart, the second of that name to claim the crowns of England and Scotland. Charles who was at this moment in exile, a monarch in name only, who spent his days boating on the Rhine, scheming and plotting for his restoration, and begging for a living here, in Cologne.

Richard folded the note and slipped it into his shirt.

And I am his loyal servant, he thought. His square, gaunt jaw twisted into a wry smile which perhaps betrayed the irony of the situation. Then suddenly he remembered the dream and the smile faded. Just as my father before me.

PART ONE

STORM GATHERING

October 1654

Chapter One

RICHARD HAD SEEN THE KING only twice in the last month, and then at a distance, so that he had begun to wonder why he had followed Charles to Cologne at all. At least in Paris the exiled royalists had been treated with some respect. In Cologne their reputation for poverty and loose morals and failure hung about them like a whiff of the plague and Richard had been forced to pay gold – too much gold – to secure even his miserable lodgings.

But now everything was different.

Now Richard sat in the cramped chamber which had been grandly termed the Privy Council. And across the table sat none other than Charles Stuart himself, eldest son of Charles the Martyr, King of England, Scotland and Ireland, so close that Richard, had he wanted, could have reached over and touched the faded silk tassels hanging from the King's doublet.

It must have been only for a few seconds, but Richard's sole impression was of the King's dark brown eyes studying him intently. Perhaps, he thought, within those eyes there is something of the mystery of royalty yet. From Charles' padded gloves there rose the scent of jasmine and cloves, rich, intoxicating. Then Richard saw the King's lips curl slightly, perhaps from amusement, or maybe nerves, and the plump man next to the monarch spoke and the spell was broken.

'Richard Tremaine, thank you for obeying our summons at such short notice.' The man had round, pouchy eyes and a pompous, nasal voice. Richard would have

7

immediately disliked him if he hadn't known this was Sir Edward Hyde, the King's chief minister.

Richard nodded politely, and went to reply, but Hyde was already introducing the other men crowded round the table. James, Marquis of Ormonde, Henry Wilmot, Earl of Rochester, and Sir Ralph Fielding, Colonel of the King's Horse. Richard had often run errands for Rochester, and knew the others by sight. After all, in exile there was little to distinguish lord from commoner. He looked at Rochester now questioningly but the older man avoided his gaze. In the background Hyde was still describing each person in tedious and unnecessary detail. He was just about to embark on a further introduction – on the state of England under Oliver Cromwell, the Lord Protector – when Charles placed a hand on his sleeve.

'Thank you, Edward. Let us proceed quickly.' Charles Stuart spoke rapidly, as if he too were irritated by his minister's mannerisms. He glanced at Richard and the same smile, half-formed, flickered on his lips. 'No doubt you are wondering why we wish to see you at all?'

Richard coughed. 'It is not for someone like myself to question your wishes, Your Majesty.'

'Quite, quite. But I will give you an answer notwithstanding.' Charles' voice was soft and betrayed his youth: he was only twenty-four. 'It concerns your father, you see.'

The words echoed in Richard's head. An image came back. The horse. The rider. But he recovered himself quickly: 'My father? He died almost nine years ago, Your Majesty.'

Charles nodded. 'Yes, or so we believe. But perhaps you have never heard the full ... circumstances surrounding his death?'

8

So we believe. Those words would haunt Richard in days to come, but for now he was too taken aback to give them much thought as Charles gestured to the man farthest to his left.

Sir Ralph Fielding was old now, in his fifties, with a grey, grizzled moustache and cheeks which had grown heavy and too pink. But in his heyday he had been one of the finest cavalry officers of his generation. And one of the most implacable. Richard had once billeted with a captain who served under Fielding at Hornridge Castle. The captain had described to him how the Parliamentarians had refused to surrender. So, when the castle fell, Fielding took no prisoners. None at all. The Parliamentarians, and even some of the King's men, had called it butchery. But when Richard challenged him, the captain had only shrugged. If there had been more men like Colonel Fielding, he remarked drily, perhaps the Royalists would not have lost. Now Sir Ralph wiped his mouth with the back of his hand and began to speak.

'You weren't with us at the end, were you, boy? After General Fairfax broke the King's armies at Naseby and Langport, we knew it was only a question of time before we too were destroyed, try as we might,' he added, glancing deferentially at the King. But if Charles bore any resentment about those days, he gave no sign, and Fielding continued. 'So General Hopton led us into the West with the remains of our cavalry and waited. No one knew what would happen. I remember your father sent you ahead to France, Richard. It was just as well. On the second of March Fairfax broke out of Launceston and almost trapped us in Bodmin. We escaped by the skin of our teeth. And our men ran. *Ran*. All they could think of was saving their own wretched necks. It was pathetic.' Fielding paused for a second and stared at a stain on the table. Hyde fidgeted with his quill. Then suddenly Fielding looked up and caught Richard straight in the eye. 'Hopton spent two days hiding on the moors with our army. But not us, your father and I. Hopton had given us a *duty*.' Even after all these years, Fielding's voice glowed with pride. 'We still had the treasury for the King's army in the West. It was with us at Bodmin. God knows we were short of money in those days – none of us had been paid for months – but Hopton had managed to hold it in reserve, gold mostly. It was our one asset, he said.' Fielding paused and licked his lips. 'A little under five thousand pounds.'

Richard raised his eyebrows. It was a vast sum.

'Five thousand one hundred and thirty-six pounds, to be precise,' Hyde interrupted. 'I helped collect it, remember.'

'A little under, a little over, what does it matter?' snapped Fielding. 'The point is it's enough money to raise an army and we couldn't let it fall into Fairfax's hands. Hopton told us to get it to the coast and shipped to France.'

'So what happened?' Richard leaned forward. His curiosity was overpowering. Fielding's face darkened.

'As I said, we left Bodmin in chaos. There were only six of us – myself, your father, and four troopers we could trust. We had a hellish journey. The horses were almost done in and all the time we expected the enemy to break upon us. Your father knew the land well, and that night somehow he managed to get us across country to his home – your home.' Fielding looked at Richard. 'Chynoon, I think it was called.'

'Yes.' Richard tried to keep his voice level. Chynoon. He could still remember the Great Hall and the sunlight slanting in through the oriel windows. His mother calling him from upstairs . . .

'When we got there the place was almost deserted,' Fielding continued. 'We were exhausted, the men wanted us to stay and rest, but we didn't dare. The next morning we set out at first light. But we were too late. We'd only gone a few miles when a squadron of cavalry caught us coming through the woods.' He paused. His eyes glinted. 'It was a vicious thing. We didn't know how many there were, or if we had any hope; the wood blocked our view and we were fighting one to one through undergrowth and mire and in and round the trees. There were soldiers everywhere and people shouting and the flash of powder. We were desperate. Your father fought like a madman. I was wounded in the side – a sword thrust – I thought I was killed. When I came to, everyone else was dead or dying except your father.'

'You mean he wasn't killed?'

'Michael Tremaine, killed?' Sir Ralph glanced at him quickly. 'He was unscathed! He propped me up against a tree and told me to stay there and I'd be all right.' Sir Ralph chuckled grimly. 'Of course, I didn't believe him and cursed him to hell. "I've got to go on," he told me. "With luck, I'll make Tresillian." We still had the gold, see, and we thought there were more of them nearby. So he strapped the horses together and left.' Fielding reached for his cup and drained it noisily. 'The enemy didn't find me, as you can see. But Michael Tremaine never reached Tresillian.' He settled the cup on the table. 'That was the last anyone saw of him.'

There was a pause, and drunken shouting arose from the street outside, then Charles coughed politely.

'We always believed your father was lost in action, a

11

worthy end to one so loyal. But yesterday a merchant brought me this letter from England.'

At this Hyde produced a crumpled sheet of paper, cleared his throat theatrically, and read:

'To my sovereign King,
    Recently I have found evidence pertaining to the whereabouts of a chest, which formerly belonged to your blessed father's Army in the West. This chest contains a large sum of coin and gold. I humbly beseech you to allow me to recover this chest and restore it to Your Majesty. Send a man I can trust to the Three Lords, Tregony, in Cornwall, on the night of October 25th. Let him be called Peter Upton and come alone. Your loyal servant.'

Hyde looked up and explained, 'The sender gives no further name.'

Charles tapped his fingers lightly on the table in front of him. His dark eyes were bright now and the same half-smile played with his face. 'Do you understand now why I have summoned you?'

'Your Majesty?'

'Tell me, Tremaine, you have followed me since your father's death, have you not? Nine years in exile is a long time. Why have you never returned to England and made your peace with the enemy?'

Beneath Charles' casual manner, Richard could detect a probing will. It irritated him that the King was only interested in his loyalty when money was at stake. He met the King's gaze in full.

'Return to what, my lord? I have no family. My mother was killed, as you may know, and our lands were confiscated. I have a sister, but since she now supports the Lord Protector, I have never communicated with her. Besides,' he added, his voice growing stronger, angrier, 'my father served you with his life. He made me swear to do the same. Isn't that reason enough?' Charles stared at him a few seconds longer, then gently nodded his head.

'Well said, well said. I wish I had titles or lands to give you in return, Tremaine.' He shrugged: 'But someone I can trust must go to Tregony and meet the person who wrote this letter. It seems that of all my people, you have the most personal involvement in the case, wouldn't you say? Rochester speaks highly of you.' Again Rochester avoided Richard's gaze, and Charles added: 'Sir Ralph volunteered himself, of course, but he is too well known to the enemy. If they were to catch him, they would offer no mercy. Whereas you . . .'

Charles trailed off.

Whereas I would be expendable, Richard thought. 'My lord king,' he said out loud, 'I would be honoured.'

'Splendid, splendid.' The King gave a brisk peal of laughter and grinned at the Earl of Rochester as if he had won some private wager. 'Sir Edward will give you letters of introduction. One of our agents will meet you on the coast. I believe you might know him – Samuel Dowles?'

Richard smiled, in spite of himself. 'He was a good friend of my father's.'

'I believed as much.' Charles returned the smile, a little mischievously. 'Dowles will introduce you to the gentry who are still loyal. If you find the gold, they will put it to work.'

'Sire?'

Charles tutted as if Richard were a slightly slow pupil, but there was no concealing the excitement on his face.

'Don't you see, Tremaine? Five thousand pounds

13

would transform our fortunes utterly. We could raise an army with this. My intelligence informs me that the West is ripe, the people are desperate for freedom!'

Desperate. There couldn't be a better word. In 1648 the West had risen for the King and a week later the women of the West had buried their husbands and sons. Richard wondered if Charles had considered this. But the King's face was majestic, and indifferent.

As Richard walked back through the crowded streets towards his lodgings, he frowned grimly to himself. This whole affair had the reek of treachery about it. Everyone around the table had known they were probably sending him to his death. A spy's death in some seedy dungeon or strung up on a temporary scaffold for the crowd's amusement. And yet, despite it all, he could not suppress the wave of excitement which broke inside him. At last, after so much waiting and idle scheming, there was the promise of action and the chance to return home, even for a day or two.

Herr Fluss was in the dining room with Maria, finishing his breakfast of bacon and bread. He pushed his great bulk back in his chair and scowled at Richard. 'So,' he asked sarcastically, 'your audience was a success, Master Tremaine? You are made a knight?'

Richard ignored his tone and bowed gracefully.

'I will be leaving you today,' he announced grandly. 'And you can find some other poor soul to squat in your miserable hutch.' He cast a wink at Maria and saw her suppress a giggle, then he strode upstairs and began to pack his few belongings into his battered portmanteau.

No, it was not the homecoming he had dreamed of. But it would be a homecoming, nevertheless. He fastened the straps and hefted the bag on to his shoulder. And already, in the back of his mind, there stirred a memory he could not quite capture, of the fresh smell of the sea air, and wind on his face, and the laughter of a girl, far away.

Chapter Two

JEAN PERRET WAS A SWARTHY-SKINNED man with a thick black thatch of hair. He squinted at Richard, shielding his face from the cold, wet wind which blustered in across the harbour. It was a week later and Richard was standing on the quay at St Malo in Brittany.

'So you're the King's man, eh?' Jean Perret spat and scrutinised the letter clutched in his hand.

'What difference does that make to you?'

The Frenchman smiled and rubbed his fingers together expressively: 'Royalty costs more.'

Richard had already decided he didn't care for Jean Perret, but Hyde had recommended the man personally and he forced himself to remain civil. 'And you can get me to England without being observed?'

'We leave as soon as the wind changes. Last trip of the year.' Perret glanced across the harbour. Already many of the boats had been laid up for the winter, and even in the harbour the sea was grey and chopped. 'October's a bad month. No one else will take you.'

Richard considered his options. Jean Perret's fee was far greater than the few coins Charles had granted for the journey. Not for the first time, he cursed, and explained this to Perret.

Perret smiled. 'Perhaps I will take pity on you, *mon chevalier*. When we sail, there will be work to do, below decks, that should cover the difference. Roublais will see you are fed.' He spat again. 'Though the food may not be to your taste.'

The *Marguerite*, as her bright red and gold lettering

16

proclaimed her to be called, was a small, stubby merchant ship of about fifty foot. She carried two masts, both square-rigged with two sails apiece, and a broad, pot-bellied hull. The *Marguerite* was packed with Breton salt which Perret was shipping to the pilchard factories in Cornwall, and she sat heavily in the water. On board, the acrid tang of the cargo impregnated everything. Within an hour, Richard's clothes were stiff with salt, and his tongue puckered with the sour, sickly taste. When Roublais, the mate, brought Richard a bowl of beans for his evening meal, he understood Perret's remarks about the food: all he could taste was the stink of salt that left his mouth dry.

As they sat in harbour waiting for the wind to change, Richard's thoughts returned again and again to England. It had been nine years. He remembered his father's messenger riding into the yard, telling him to leave immediately, and the confused, hasty journey to the boat. And then the weeks spent skulking in the Channel Isles, hearing of Hopton's surrender and the King's final defeat, but never any news from his father, not a word. He had been seventeen years old.

Once, the dream came back to him, and he woke in the cabin shivering with a foul, salty sweat and listened to the water splash against the hull and the gulls crying. At other times, he would stalk the deck impatiently and try to remember happier days. Images came to him of breathless summer afternoons, the corn thick in the fields, the hedgerows humming and brimming with flowers. Or that last winter when his mother had left and he and Rebecca had spent their lessons in the library, with the fire banked up, and in the afternoons had gone running over the headland to the sea.

Rebecca Penmarris.

He could still remember her jet-black hair and her

17

dark, proud eyes. When he last saw her, she had just turned fifteen, and he wondered what she would be like now. Probably married, with three children and another on the way, he thought grimly. Time changes us all. When he closed his eyes and tried to think of her, the pictures were faded and dull. They were never as real as the rider in the night, and the black shapeless horror which pursued him.

On the third morning, Richard woke, his head buzzing, and realised something was different. Suddenly in a panic, he staggered up the stairs and fell with a bang on to the deck. Jean Perret stood over him laughing and said something harsh in Breton. The wind was fresher and the deck heaved and swung beneath Richard's face. He got carefully to his feet and shook himself. On all sides the sea stretched out sullen and blue and cold. The ship pitched again and he put out a foot to steady himself. Jean Perret laughed once more. 'The wind has changed, *mon chevalier*!'

The sky was a full blue, filled with the wind which bowled across the sea and threw itself around the merchantman. Only in the far south could Richard make out a low strip of land, and above it a ragged flag of cloud lowering in the sun.

'How long have we been sailing?' he called across, but Jean Perret turned on his heel and marched aft to where Roublais was holding the wheel.

Richard shook himself and managed to reach the gunwales without slipping and stood clutching the rails. After the fug of the cabin, he sucked the damp sea air greedily into his lungs, and straining forward he watched the blunt prow of the ship as it pushed and shoved its way through the black slabs of water and sent the thick white foam running down the sides of the ship.

18

He was still looking at this when he felt a hand on his arm.

'*Elle roule, mon chevalier, elle roule!*' Jean Perret winked as if his words had some significance. Close up, his breath stank of sour beef and salted fish.

'How long will it take?'

'Before you see your beloved *patrie*? Two days with this wind, maybe less.'

'And if we see the English Navy?'

'*Ça fait rien.* We are just a poor Breton merchant, and you,' again the wink, 'you are my own son.'

Richard wondered if he should regard this as an honour and hoped there was no family resemblance. 'This would be the first time a Breton had red hair,' he remarked.

Jean Perret seemed amused by this and slapped him on the back. '*Alors* . . . Now, at least, you can earn your keep, eh? Boissard has need . . .'

Perret's familiarity annoyed Richard and he felt himself stiffening under the pressure of the Frenchman's hand. But the scent of the sea quickened his nostrils and he laughed in spite of everything.

'As you wish, Monsieur Perret.'

Boissard was a fat, amiable man with soft, watery eyes. He was hopelessly addicted to sweetmeats, toffees, fudges and the like, and he sucked at them incessantly while he told Richard what do do. Most of his teeth were soft and blackened. They must have hurt horribly. For the rest of the morning, Richard worked the pumps in the hold while Boissard offered him advice and sucked his sweets. It was foul, greasy work, and Richard realised the hull must be continually letting water, for as fast as he heaved at the pumps, the level of water in the hold stayed the same. The stench from the bilges was overpowering. It was fat, fetid and sharp. At first, Richard tried to keep his mouth shut, but then the exertions of the pump proved too much and he swallowed great mouthfuls of the thick foul air, and with every pull of the pump he cursed Jean Perret and Boissard and Charles Stuart.

After what seemed an eternity, Boissard grew tired of his sweets, and tapped Richard amicably on the shoulder.

'Midday, *mon seigneur*. You rest now.'

Richard clambered on to deck. His head was dizzy and the fresh gusts of wind and dazzling sunlight stabbed his eyes. One or two of the other sailors smiled at him, though not kindly, and he chewed his ration of bread and pork in silence. Then Boissard ordered him back to work.

'In God's name, Monsieur Boissard!' muttered Richard after another hour or so. The knots of muscles in his arms and across his back ached dully. 'Am I the only one on this ship who can work?'

Boissard smiled and revealed a row of treacly teeth. 'Come, another two hours and Legris will take your place. Do you remember the great wars? I will tell you about my time at the Battle of Rocroi . . .'

So for the next hour Richard listened to Boissard recount the manoeuvres of the imperial troops and the charge of the French and the boom of the cannon, while he forced water from the ship's bowels. Boissard had a soft, rambling voice which would have trailed on interminably had one of the crew not poked his head in:

'English frigate over starboard bow!'

Richard stopped.

'What will happen?'

Boissard spat out a lump of toffee. 'It is nothing. Keep pumping, I shall go and look.' He heaved his bulk off his seat and lumbered up the steps. Richard stayed still. From above, he could hear voices muttering in Breton. The ship creaked and slapped through the sea, and he wondered if Hyde was right to trust these people. Then Boissard stepped back into the hold, momentarily blocking the light.

'What is it?'

'*Hein!* You are not working. It is nothing. A naval frigate, about five miles off.'

'Are they coming closer?'

'We do not know, they seem to be keeping pace with us. Probably just put out from Jersey.'

Richard's mouth tasted sharp and he swallowed awkwardly. 'Well, what does Monsieur Perret say?' He kept his voice as casual as possible, but Boissard caught the expression in his face and laughed, a girlish, sweet laugh.

'You worry too much, my friend!'

Richard swore angrily and was about to push past the Frenchman and storm on to the deck, when he realised that if Perret meant to betray him, he would do so in any case. He bent down and seized the pump handle and pulled, concentrating all his anger, his frustration, on his work.

An hour later another sailor appeared at the hatch and told Boissard that the frigate had dropped over the horizon, then he added something about the wind which Richard did not catch.

That night Richard no longer minded the stench of the cabin. He slept deeply and he knew nothing until the clanging of a bell shook him to his senses and he staggered out on deck. The force of the wind smacked into his body and he noticed that the strip of cloud in the south had swollen to a broad, heavy wrack. Before, the *Marguerite* had bucked and sprung across the waves, but now she drove through the sea, as if she were impelled by a stronger, sterner hand. Richard saw her sails had been reefed, but even so she was making more headway. He spied Perret standing with Roublais at the wheel, but the Frenchman ignored his call. Swearing under his breath, Richard climbed the ladder on to the bridge. 'Monsieur Perret!'

'In the name of God, *chevalier*, do you not know better than to talk to the captain at the wheel!' Roublais shouted, with such venom that Richard stopped in his tracks. He could see now that Perret wore a grey, earnest look. His black eyes were squinting at the sails. 'Get back on deck!' This was accompanied by an expression in Breton which Richard could not translate.

It was evident from the anxious way the men went about their tasks, and the way the ship plunged across the waters, that the weather was worsening. Richard could see Perret muttering to Roublais and the latter nodding grimly. About half an hour later, the captain ordered the sails to be trimmed again. The crew worked feverishly, crawling up the ratlines and along the yardarms, and reefed the sails until they were mere squares of canvas. But still if anything the ship cut through the waters more quickly than she had when fully rigged. Richard noticed Roublais was taking the ship's log very often now, and he stood hunched over his readings, shaking his head.

Going into the aft cabin, Richard found a half-eaten stump of bread and tore at it. Then Boissard called him below decks again, and Richard was glad of the chance to do something useful. This time he was not alone, but worked with the man called Legris, who said nothing.

'The captain seems concerned, doesn't he?' Richard asked Boissard.

'He does?' Boissard fished out a toffee from his little leather pouch and examined it before popping it into his mouth. It was some minutes before Richard realised this was the only reply he was going to get. The water had a full, dull sound inside the boat and the waves thumped against the hull. Now, as each wave hit them, the ship would slow violently, lurching them forwards, as it sledged uphill through the water. Then when it reached the peak, it would dip suddenly and plunge downhill, and the timbers would shudder and judder violently and loudly, so that the hull was full of the beating and screaming of timbers and the pulse of the ship through water. In the confined space the air was more thick and acrid than ever and Richard fought back waves of nausea. He pulled on the handle stubbornly, trying to ignore the mounting sickness and the pitch and roll of the ship and the sharp reek of Legris's unwashed body above the foul tang of the salt. They worked like that till noon, and by then Richard's stomach was cramped and bilious. Then two other sailors relieved them. When Richard gained deck, the wrack of cloud now hung over the entire sky.

The sea had swollen to monstrous proportions and the boat's two sails seemed puny and inconsequential. The swell came in huge shifts of water, thirty, forty feet tall, teethed with white, hissing foam, which towered over the ship then suddenly slid down behind it, lifting her effortlessly and plunging her forwards. And the *Marguerite* would scream down into the trough, with every fibre of her being thrumming and shaking against the rush of water. Richard clung to the shrouds. His fingers were so cold he could feel nothing – no texture, no sensation – but the tick and hum of the ropes running through his arms. Across the sea, as far as he could see, the tips of the waves glinted crisp and white.

'*Elle roule*, eh?' Richard realised with a start that Jean

Perret was behind him, his feet splayed wide on the deck, his short stocky body clothed in a shabby oilskin.

'What is happening?'

'*Merde!* The wind has shifted to the west. I should not have tried the crossing, monsieur.'

'Where are we, can't we turn back?'

'No, our only hope is to run before the storm, that way we may yet reach England.'

'England? Is it far?' Even as he uttered the words, he felt the ship heave beneath his feet and he hung on the shrouds.

'Maybe. With this cloud, we have no way of telling.' Perret fell silent and continued to look at him.

Richard wondered why the Frenchman was suddenly being this frank, then he realised. 'You're trying to tell me we may not make it, aren't you?'

Perret put his hand on Richard's shoulder. The wind suddenly punched across the deck and Richard lost what he said. Then the Frenchman turned and was gone, up the ladder to the bridge.

Richard would never forget that day. Although it was still afternoon, the cloud so smothered the sun that the sky had a perpetual look of evening and lowered threateningly overhead. The horizon dissolved into a thick grey wall of cloud. Richard could not guess how fast they were going, for the sea itself was moving and running so quickly that he lost all sense of distance. Time itself took on an unreal quality. Once in a while, Perret would bark orders at the crew or Roublais would pay out the ship's log, but how often Richard could not tell. The sea, the sky were vast, unchanging on all sides. Only the wind changed, and it bred and multiplied in the air and stormed over the ship in terrific multitudes.

They were working the pumps hard now. One hour on and one hour off and Richard took his turn gladly, willing himself to work harder. None of the sailors talked, even among themselves, and whether Richard was on deck or in the hold the only sounds were the thump and judder of the boat in the sea and the roar of the wind and the screech of the rigging.

Night fell like a stone and plunged them into darkness. Still the pumping continued. The *Marguerite* seemed more sluggish and was no longer riding the waves. Every now and then the waves would rise up and break over the gunwales and pound the deck, and the little ship would strain beneath the mass of sea and then drag itself upright. On his next rest from the pumps, Richard clambered on deck and found Boissard sheltering in the lee of the cabin.

'Any news, Boissard?'

The man's plump cheeks were grey and sullen. 'How should I know, *anglais?*' he snarled. 'Who knows? Not even our blessed captain!' He went to spit, but then a great wave smacked over the side of the ship and for a moment everything was lost in the rushing of the water. Richard saw Boissard lifted bodily and sent sprawling across the deck. He flung his own hand out and missed the lip of the door. The deck pitched like a roof and he slid and scrabbled on the wet timbers for a handhold which was not there. Boissard had grabbed his foot and was calling in a high, squeaky voice. The ship jumped in the sea and there was a ferocious snap as it hit the waves and banged the breath out of Richard's body. The next moment, he felt a strong hand haul him by the shoulders into the cabin, the door yawing wildly in the wind. It was Roublais.

'*Merde!*' the Breton swore and lurched back to the door. 'Stay there!' he called over his shoulder and slammed the door shut.

Richard did not know how long he lay there. The

cabin seemed like some stifling box flung giddily through space and smacking into the sea over and over. Eventually, he sat up and took a deep breath and coughed until he felt himself be sick. He wiped the hair out of his eyes and realised his fingernails were splintered and clotted with blood from clawing at the deck. Then there was a crash and the boat shuddered and slowed, water came spurting under the door.

Richard leapt to his feet. A sudden panic seized him and he tore at the handle, but the weight of water clamped the door fast. There was another lurch and a bang and miraculously the ship leapt free and sprang over the sea and the door flew open and Richard stumbled on to deck.

It was carnage. The deck was a mass of ropes and shattered wood. Instinctively, Richard looked up and saw to his surprise the sky directly above him. The mainmast had gone. All that remained was a shattered stump, jutting through the deck like a broken finger. Shrouds and rigging were flung across the boards and two men were hacking at these with axes. Then another wave hit them and five, six feet of water sluiced over the deck. Richard clung to the doorframe. He did not see how the sailors could have survived, but when the waters subsided he saw the two men still there, wrapped in ropes, working frantically.

The *Marguerite* steadied for a moment, and Richard seized the chance to bound up the ladder on his left and clamber on to the aft deck. Roublais and Perret were there. He half expected Roublais to shout at him, but the man simply pursed his mouth. 'I told you to stay below, *chevalier*.'

'What? And go to my grave in that box? I would rather drown fair and square.'

Neither man said anything. The *Marguerite* was

tossed into a great wall of water and clung there twisting and turning on the swell. Perret and Roublais strained at the wheel. The timbers groaned angrily. Richard jumped forward and the three of them wrestled against the wind and the water. Somehow the *Marguerite* scrambled over the wave and rolled down the next one, though her movements were heavy and lifeless. Then Perret grabbed him by the collar: 'The pumps, *chevalier*! The pumps!'

Nodding dumbly, Richard floundered down the ladder and into the hold. Inside was a cramped, stinking hell. Only Legris was there, his body sour and battered, and he looked up blankly when Richard entered.

'Boissard – is he not here?'

For the first time, Legris spoke: 'He was with you, *anglais*.'

That was all. Richard remembered feeling the hand on his ankle. The thin, shrill cry. Then he too bent to the pump and the two men pulled in silence. And after every two pulls, as regular as the pounding of a drum, came the heave and smash of the ship and then the smothering weight of water would drop over the deck above.

Richard did not think they had pulled for long when the hatch swung open and Roublais shrieked into the hold: 'Land! Land!' Then he was gone.

It took Richard a moment to realise what this meant, but Legris was already clambering out of the hold.

They clung desperately to the ropes on deck. At first Richard could tell nothing, then he noticed that in addition to the noise of wind and sea and boat, there was a new sound, a harsh, ugly sound, of water breaking and crashing. Straining over the starboard side he could make out a black tear across the horizon, and

27

he realised with a shock that this was a cliff face. Then a wave rolled up beneath them and tipped the whole boat on to its side, and Richard was swallowed into the sea.

He tried to scream and all he knew was water. Something huge and wooden brushed over his head and he felt this was the hull of the boat. He pushed away and the whole sea heaved and vomited him out and he was in a mass of black water, then down again, and his breath sucked in water. His clothes were dragging him down and he clawed at his boots, his shirt. Then he was above water, sucked air, and saw the black cliffs were closer and the water walloped against them, then he was down again.

Then from somewhere in front, he saw a light.

A weak yellow light which glimmered and blinked. Something landed on his back, and Richard twisted over. It was Legris. Richard went to help him, then he saw the man's head loll to one side, his tongue protruding through his teeth. More water took him and Richard struggled to the surface and Legris was gone. But the light was still there. Yellow, perhaps brighter, still winking. Fighting for breath, he struck out towards it. And the blackness swallowed him.

Chapter Three

WHEN HE WOKE, A SEAGULL was crying outside his window. Then the soft autumn sunlight splashed his face and he opened his eyes. He was in a small bare room, painted white, with a fire burning in the grate. An oddly familiar painting of a lady cradling a dove hung on his right. Somehow, he had been here before.

Suddenly his memories of the storm rushed back. His head spun, he gripped the sheets in both hands as the crash of ship and sea and rock cascaded around him. Was it real? The jagged pain which ran across his shoulders told him it was, but how had he got here? Where was . . .?

The truth struck him.

He was in one of the guest rooms at Chynoon, his old home.

Richard sat bolt upright. His thoughts spilled over in a confused tumble. How could he be here? Did they know who he was? He was about to turn himself out of bed when the door swung open.

The man who stepped into the room was extraordinary. He would have been remarkable for his height alone, for he stood well over six feet tall and possessed a broad, muscular physique which seemed to fill the room. But it was his face which startled Richard.

The man was completely bald and had a coarse, leathery complexion like a cow's tongue. His eyes were dark, almost opaque, and glared out from beneath two huge bushy eyebrows which were twisted upwards at the ends like horns. His cheeks, jaw and nose were

29

broad and heavy. As soon as the stranger saw Richard was awake, his mouth creased into a broad smile.

'Ah! You have returned.' The man's voice was low, gravelly, grained with treacle.

Richard did not know what to say. He must have been recognised. He coughed, tasting the sea water in his throat.

'Returned, sir?'

The man stood closer. He extended a huge hand in greeting.

'Returned to the land of the living,' he explained. 'We feared you might not come back.' Richard sighed in relief, and clasped the man's hand gratefully. So no one had identified him – yet. The man continued: 'I am William Moreton. And you are in Chynoon, my residence, in the county of Cornwall.' His words were grave, even.

Richard had known that his father's estates had been sequestered, like those of many royalists. Doubtless Moreton had bought them fair and square from the County Committee, but even so Richard felt a wave of resentment choke up inside him. He squeezed the man's hand hard. Moreton smiled benignly.

'I see your strength returns. You are blessed, truly. Of all the crew, you were the only one who was spared.'

There was something about his tone, although it was warm and honeyed, which chilled Richard. He had a sudden image of Perret, his mouth and eyes open, floating over rocks, the current picking at his flesh and hair. He shuddered.

'Plucked from the sea, and so I had you conveyed here.' Moreton's sugary tones dragged him back to the small white room. 'You are ... English?'

Richard tried to read the intention behind the words. The question seemed genuine enough. Presumably

Moreton knew nothing about him then, nothing for certain? Richard answered carefully.

'Yes, thank the Lord. My father is a merchant's agent, based in St Malo.' His voice was coarse and raw from the sea. 'He ships salt and spirits to England. I was overseeing the cargo.'

'You are not Catholic?' Moreton's eyes narrowed, though his voice lost none of its charm.

'No. No.' What was it that Richard sensed at this? 'My family are all Presbyterians. I trust you are also, sir?' He gazed at Moreton with what he hoped was suitable conviction. To admit he was an Anglican would, he knew, betray him as a royalist in all but name.

Moreton's eyes pondered him for a minute, then his great cow's tongue of a face relaxed. 'We shall get word to them immediately. They will be overjoyed. May I have their names?' He coughed, in mild embarrassment. 'I am obliged to give the names of all seafarers to the Committee. There are many spies about. Spies of the enemy.'

Richard returned his gaze and managed a casual smile.

'Of course. My father is John Ferrers, of St Malo. My mother died when I was a child.'

Moreton closed his eyes as if in contemplation. 'Then you must consider she is with the Lord even as we speak, Master Ferrers. And you, what is your christened name?'

'Richard,' he replied. 'Richard Ferrers.' Then the salty bile rose in his throat again and he fell to hacking and rasping. Moreton drew back, an expression of mild concern on his face.

'Talk no more! You must rest. I will call one of the maids to wait on you.'

31

Richard watched him retire and wiped the tears from his eyes. Then he slumped back into the bolster and stared at the ceiling. He wondered how long it would take the Committee to discover that John Ferrers, merchant of St Malo, did not exist. A week at least, he guessed, even if they could send a message across the Channel immediately. He closed his eyes, and the images returned to him. Of the waves, and men screaming, and an endless dragging through shingle and sand, and water running over him. He found himself drowning again and woke in a panic, with water splashing over his chest. He looked up.

A woman in her late twenties was bent over him, a bucket by her side, rubbing his chest with a wet cloth. With a shock Richard realised he was stripped quite naked. The woman was intent on her task and did not notice he was awake. From where he lay he could see she was quite attractive, with strong, broad cheekbones, full lips, and dark hair which hung in ringlets. Gradually, methodically, she worked the cloth down his chest and across his belly. It felt coarse and warm on his skin. In spite of himself, he felt himself becoming aroused. The woman gave a small gasp, of amusement maybe, and glanced up.

'I see you are feeling better, Master Ferrers. Hold still, will you?'

Keeping her eyes on him, she reached down and applied the cloth expertly until she was sure he was rubbed quite clean, and then continued down over his thighs and calves. 'Forgive me, but I am under instructions to scrub you clean for supper tonight.'

Richard shook his head and grinned.

'What's your name? You are one of the maids?'

The lady laughed so that the curls of her fringe shimmered. 'Goodness, no! I am Ursula Moreton, William's wife.' She laughed again at the look on his face. 'Do not be ashamed. We are all God's children, are we not? Why should you wish I were a maid?' She arched her brow. 'Especially when so few maids are maidens?'

Richard was lost for words, and decided the best he could manage was an awkward smirk. He was a guest in this lady's house, after all.

Ursula shot him a knowing look, then carried on with her work. Richard watched her. She was not tall, but she had a strong, full figure, which hinted at pleasure, and he found her movements satisfying to the eye. She finished her scrubbing and tugged the sheet back over him, then she set the pail of water on the floor and wiped her hands smartly on her apron. She cast an eye at his outline underneath the sheet.

'I see you have relaxed again, sir.'

She stifled a grin and he felt she was about to say something, when suddenly the old manor bell rang out, as crisp and clear as it ever had. Ursula bit her lip and, casting him one more look, made for the door.

'Wait!'

She turned on the threshold: 'I am afraid I must leave you, sir. There are clothes in the press in the corner. We shall eat towards sunset.'

There were so many things Richard needed to ask. But the door had already slammed behind her and she was gone.

Richard waited until her footsteps receded down the stairs, then swung himself out of bed. His frame felt bruised and battered all over, and he set his feet gingerly on the floorboards, flexing the long muscles of his thighs and calves. Moreton was right, he was blessed. And how he had not been recognised, he didn't know. He offered up a silent prayer of thanks and, still naked, went over to the window. From here, he could look down on the herb gardens and stables to the rear of the manor. He felt his heart racing in anticipation.

It had hardly changed. Below him the gravel court was bordered on the left by the red-brick stable buildings. His father had built them when he was still a boy. A stablehand was grooming a tall black mare in the entrance and whistling while he worked, and with a rush, Richard remembered seeing his mother's horse held in the same place, when she had come back from a jaunt, and hearing the stableboy whistling then, and the soft slap of the brush on the horse's flank. He looked quickly across from the stables to the low wall which lined the back of the court. On the other side lay the herb garden and behind that, misty in the late afternoon, the orchard.

He dressed quickly, his fingers shaking. He felt sure someone would recognise him as soon as he stepped outside, but what else could he do? In any case, he had to attend supper, and that would be the worst time to be unmasked, he thought grimly. He imagined the expression on his hosts' faces when – *if* – they discovered his true identity, and gritted his teeth.

But when he pulled his hair back in a queue, and donned the heavy capotain hat Moreton had provided, he realised that although he had not exactly changed beyond all knowing, there was less of the young Richard Tremaine in his face than he had expected. When he had left Chynoon, he had been a full-faced youth of seventeen. Over the years, his cheeks had thinned and revealed a taut jawline and high, angular cheekbones, burnt by the continental sun. Even his sharp blue eyes had altered. They were older now, and sterner, except when his face cracked with laughter.

Nevertheless, Richard knew he must leave the manor as soon as possible. This was no longer his home, he told himself bitterly. Now his duty lay elsewhere. He thought of Samuel Dowles, the King's agent. Dowles had been expecting him at a cove farther down the coast. Presumably he had heard of the shipwreck, but would he guess it was Richard's ship, and that Richard had survived? For a moment Richard toyed with the idea of going to Dowles there and then. Perhaps if he left secretly, he could reach Dowles' house by nightfall. But he quickly dismissed the idea. His sudden departure would arouse the worst suspicions. William Moreton would sound the alarm, the country would be swarming with troops and informers. No, he told himself, I must be patient.

Richard had left St Malo on October the 13th, and he calculated today must be the 16th. That gave him more than a week before he should be in Tregony to meet the person who had written to the King. Dowles must wait until tomorrow. Then maybe he could slip away and back again, if need be, without being seen.

Richard went to the door and looked out. His room opened on to a small landing halfway down the main stairs. He remembered it well.

To his right, the stairs continued up for another flight then let into the north wing of the house, giving access to the North Tower and the suites of main bedrooms and guest rooms. To his left, they ran down to the rear corridor which formed the backbone of the house. At the bottom of the stairs, on the left, lay the kitchens, scullery and bakehouse, larder, pantry and cool room, and farther along, the door to the yard, and then his father's beloved library. On the right of the corridor lay the Great Hall, and beyond that the old south wing of the house and the servants' quarters.

Richard stepped cautiously on to the stairs. It hardly felt as if he had been away. His fingers trembled on the banister. He was halfway down when the door from the kitchen flew open and two maids burst into the corridor below, laughing at the tail end of a joke. Richard froze, then they caught sight of him and stared up with nervous grins.

'I beg your pardon, sir,' said one of the maids slowly.

Richard stared. He did not recognise either of them.

'Is everything all right, sir?' the girl asked. Then the other pinched her and she started to giggle.

'Yes. Yes,' he replied, quickly regaining his composure. 'And who are you?'

'Bridget,' bobbed the girl, 'and Daisy,' indicating her friend.

'Charmed to meet you,' said Richard with mock gallantry, and the two girls curtseyed and scurried into the Great Hall, banging the doors behind them.

Richard watched them go. Above all else, at this moment, he wanted to explore Chynoon alone. Oddly, the house was bigger than he remembered it, bigger and airier, familiar and yet no longer homely. But his nose was not deceived. The scents and smells had not changed at all, like the vivid imprint of his memories, and crowded upon him. The heavy musk of oak panelling and musty hangings. The scent of boiled ham and crisp bread wafting from the kitchen. The smell of damp by the doorway on to the court. Richard went straight to the library, his father's favourite room. He was about to turn the handle, when he heard people talking inside and cursed under his breath. He would have to wait. He turned left, to the door leading on to the court, and heard its familiar creak as it swung open. He crossed the courtyard briskly, savouring the fresh air on his neck and forehead, and gained the herb garden.

Here at least he was alone. Seeing the plants laid out

in neat ordered rows, he had a sudden feeling of calm. He used to play here, with his sister Susannah, many years ago. He bent down and crushed a braid of rosemary between his fingers and felt the scent invade his nostrils. There was the sound of a shoe on gravel, and spinning round, he saw the curve of a lady's back walking away from him. The lady was dressed in grey velvet and in her hand she twisted a white flower . . . Then she rounded the corner and was gone.

It was his mother.

Richard stared at where the figure had been, not daring to believe his eyes. His heart was pounding, he felt giddy. Then he leapt up and was running towards the gate. But when he got there, the path was empty. To his left, under the apple trees, dusk was gathering and only the faint scent of burning oak hung in the air.

Richard stayed for a long while, not trusting his emotions, watching the evening settle over the manor. Had he really seen his mother? A memory of his mother, like a lingering scent of perfume? Angrily, Richard forced his speculations into the back of his mind. This would do him no good.

He crossed the yard to the kitchen. Billows of smoke and steam and the din and clang of pans came through the open windows. He peered in. Six women, young and old, were busy at work. He did not know any of them. Nor, when he looked over to the stables, did he recognise the two men scrubbing out the stalls. It was a relief, but strange nevertheless. He had expected at least some of the old servants to remain. By the side of the stables, four hounds lay basking in the sun. One of them noticed him, and flicked its head, and growled.

As he went inside, he spotted Bridget the maid carrying an armful of linen. The burden was too bulky for her and the top sheets were about to overtopple when she tripped on a ruck in the carpet. She gave a little cry and Richard steadied her and caught the linen before it hit the floor. Bridget giggled nervously, and began, 'Oh, master . . .' then stopped and straightened herself briskly. 'Oh, Master Ferrers, I didn't realise it was you.'

Richard studied her. She seemed tense, nervous. He smiled. 'It's all right, I won't bite, you know.' He expected her to respond but when she didn't, he asked: 'Bridget, is there something wrong?'

She shook her head violently. 'No, sir! I am in a hurry, that is all.' She made to leave.

'Wait.' He caught her arm gently. 'I was wondering, were you here, before the war?'

She looked at him nervously.

'Really, master, I must go.' Richard shrugged and let her go and watched her disappear down the corridor as quickly as she could. But she hadn't been here, he knew, nor had any of the servants, as far as he could tell.

Chapter Four

THE GREAT HALL WAS ALREADY busy when Richard
arrived, and the clatter of plates and platters and
the scent of candles and woodsmoke greeted him
from the doorway. He stopped to let one of the maids
go past and took in the scene.

The Great Hall was the largest room in the house. It
was at least fifty feet long, and rose the height of two
storeys to a lofty ceiling, on which satyrs, nymphs and
cherubs gambolled and frolicked, forever frozen in their
state of ecstasy in the cool white plaster. They gazed
impassively on the gathering below, and their little
limbs cast ugly shadows in the candlelight. Some of the
guests were already seated around the great oak table
his grandfather had commissioned, pewter and silver
glittering in the lights of the candelabra. Servants
hovered in the background, bearing dishes, trays,
bottles of wine. Behind them long burgundy curtains
obscured the Hall's fine oriel window. Richard remembered the view westward through the trees. On his
right, high in the north wall, stood the old minstrels'
gallery, empty and disused, he guessed, since his
father's time.

'Ah, Master Ferrers!' Richard realised with a start
that William Moreton was talking to him, and forced
himself to smile. 'Welcome!'

Moreton had risen from his great seat at the head of
the table. 'Here, be seated!' The three chairs on the right
of the table were empty and Moreton beckoned to the

middle one, then indicated the woman sitting opposite:
'My wife you already know, I believe.'

Ursula smiled impishly. 'You are recovered, I hope?'

Richard pulled back his chair. 'Quite fully, my lady.'

'Mama, is this the man from the sea?' Beside Ursula,
a youth in his early teens was fidgeting nervously. He
had a high, plaintive voice and wide, staring eyes which
contrasted with his pinched cheeks and pale, luminous
skin.

Richard raised his eyebrows. Surely she was too
young for such a child? Ursula must have caught his
meaning, for she kissed the boy on the forehead and
said: 'Stepmother only, I am afraid. Stephen is William's
son by his first wife.'

Moreton muttered something which Richard didn't
catch and then gestured to the far end of the table,
where a man in clerical dress sat. 'And this is Dr
Thomas Masters, a man of God,' Moreton announced
gruffly. 'And his wife Sarah.' Between Dr Masters and
Stephen Moreton sat a young woman, who nodded
politely.

The two made an unlikely couple.

Thomas Masters was a powerful, remarkably thickset
man in his early forties. He had coarse black hair which
he wore clipped short in the severe style favoured by
the Puritans. Because of its coarse texture, his hair stood
up in little quiffs and combs, like pig bristles. His nose,
his jaw, his mouth, all were thick-featured. But his eyes
were small and black, and added to his porcine appearance. Even seated, Masters gave the impression of being
surprisingly muscular, as if he had been crammed into
his clothes. His neck was short and squat and bulged
over his collar and his biceps and forearms seemed to
strain out of their sleeves. He grunted a greeting at

Richard and then returned to tearing his bread. His fingers were thick and blunt.

Sarah Masters, on the other hand, was a rich, ripe fruit. She had a round, heart-shaped face with a small neat nose and mouth. Her skin glowed with a sweet vitality that showed in the flush of her cheeks and shoulders which, surprisingly for a Puritan, she wore uncovered. She smiled enthusiastically at Richard now, and he guessed she must be no older than twenty-one.

He nodded at them both: 'Delighted to make your acquaintance.'

Masters scowled and there was a short, awkward silence while he stabbed his bread in his soup.

'Is he the man from the sea, Mama?' asked Stephen again.

'Yes, dear,' said Ursula hurriedly and patted him on the head. William Moreton glowered at him to be quiet. There was another tense silence which was only broken when Richard coughed and indicated the empty chairs on either side. 'Are you expecting other guests, sir?'

Moreton's face became amiable: 'This seat on my right is for my eldest son, Oliver. He is not with us tonight, I regret. And the other—'

'—is mine, I believe.'

Richard turned around. Behind him stood a young woman in her early twenties. Rich hair, the colour of chestnuts, fell in a tangle of curls and twists over her shoulders. She was tall, almost as tall as him, and clad in a slim grey bodice and skirt. Her neck and cheeks were smooth and fine, and he would normally have admired these. But it was her eyes which captured him. They were of a piercing hazel, almost green, which seemed to cut him to the core. 'I hope I didn't startle you?' She studied him intently. 'Master ... *Ferrers*, I

41

believe?' She arched her eyebrow, as if she found his name as ludicrous as he did.

Moreton coughed gruffly. 'Master Ferrers, please meet Susannah Tremaine. Miss Tremaine is the daughter of the former owner of this house, the royalist Michael Tremaine.'

It took Richard a moment to understand what Moreton was saying. He stared at Susannah dumbly, while she curtseyed gracefully, almost mockingly, and took her seat.

Moreton had said she was Susannah Tremaine. His sister. The words rang in his head.

He had never seen her before in his life.

'Are you all right, Master Ferrers?' It was Ursula. She leant across the table.

'What?' Richard shook himself. 'I'm afraid I haven't got over my accident, my lady. You must excuse me, my thoughts were elsewhere.' Fortunately at that moment the maids began to serve the main platters of salt beef and pork and his consternation was lost in the general hubbub. A servant brought a pitcher of wine and Richard gratefully filled his glass and felt the rich red liquid trickle down his throat. He stared into his drink and remembered his father reading Homer to him: 'Over the wine-dark sea . . .'

'You have had a near escape, sir.' Susannah's voice tripped into his ear, oddly echoing his own thoughts.

'Yes.' He turned to face her, and was dazzled again by the colour of her eyes. 'I am afraid the rest of the crew were not so lucky.'

For some reason this seemed to amuse Susannah, for she pursed her lips slightly. 'You think you are lucky to come here?' she asked quietly. But William Moreton had overheard her.

'No one is lucky, Susannah, you know that, only

blessed or damned. Only the devil needs luck.' He leaned forward, and tapped Richard on the arm.

'As I was just going to say,' Susannah replied deftly. 'If you had not interrupted.'

Moreton's eyes regarded her suspiciously but his lips creased into a smile. 'As you say, Susannah.'

'I was admiring your garden earlier, sir,' said Richard by way of a distraction. 'You have a delightful collection of plants.'

Moreton nodded at Susannah. 'I have to thank the previous owners – Miss Tremaine's parents. They have provided for me comfortably.'

Richard felt himself smart at this. In contrast, Susannah seemed to take no offence.

'They are my pride,' continued Moreton insensitively, 'rather like my wife, Master Ferrers. They can be enjoyed by all, but picked only by me, or else they will lose their bouquet.' He rested his hand on his wife's neck and began to caress her flesh. 'Do you understand?'

Richard looked him straight in the eye, trying to restrain his mounting anger. 'Yes sir,' he replied.

'If you pick a flower, it will die,' continued Moreton deliberately.

'Indeed.' Richard forced his voice to stay amiable. His head was seething. What was this man implying?

Suddenly Moreton smiled broadly. 'You must forgive me if my thoughts seem a little strange. Since the fall of the Commonwealth, there are many men who owe loyalty neither to the Lord nor to their masters. Is that not true?'

He kept his hand by Ursula's cheek.

Richard nodded. 'These are godless times, sir.'

'Yes!' Moreton's voice flashed. 'Never a truer word!' He raised his glass. 'May you be blessed!'

Awkwardly, Richard followed in kind: 'And you also, sir.'

'May you be blessed!' The other diners had picked up the toast and raised their glasses in turn.

Moreton drained his wine and smiled, then turned his attention to his wife. The guests returned to their food, and Richard breathed a sigh of relief. Susannah tapped him on the shoulder. 'So, will you stay long, sir?' She winked conspiratorially and something passed between them then, that instant, in the meeting of their eyes.

He smiled back. 'Until I am rested and can arrange for transport back to St Malo.'

'That may not be for a while. I hear the Channel is impassable.'

'Then maybe I shall stay.'

Still smiling, she sipped from her glass, revealing high cheekbones to good effect, enjoying his gaze. Richard could not help himself. Susannah certainly bore a resemblance to his sister, in her colouring and height, but that was all. His sister had been a warm, quiet girl, whereas this woman whose eyes flashed over her wine glass was extraordinarily ... *vivid*. That was the only word Richard could think of. Vivid as only exotic birds, or the fresh juice of fruits, or the essence of tropical flowers can be. He could almost feel the throb of her body through her clothes.

'Tell me, madam,' he said, 'have you lived here since a girl?'

He watched her intently. Perhaps the skin over her cheeks quivered a little, but that was all.

'When I was a child, yes. But then the war came and I have not been back since.'

'The war?'

'Yes, I went with my mother to Lembury Castle. Do you know it, Master Ferrers?'

He spoke carefully. 'Only that it was besieged by Parliament.'

Her face paled. 'My mother was killed there.'

'I see.' An image of his mother, smiling and waving from the upstairs window, came to him. He was quiet for a while, and he did not realise she was speaking again.

'. . . plucked from the sea?' she was continuing. 'Just like that cunning man Odysseus,' she added with gentle irony. 'I hear he had red hair also.'

He managed a smile. 'Maybe, my lady. But when Odysseus came home, he found his house possessed by his enemies, and he slew them all, whereas I' – he paused, wondering suddenly if he had said too much – 'have my home in St Malo.' Behind his smile, Richard cursed himself and the wine for making him so forward. He noticed that Ursula for one seemed to be studying them carefully.

He was about to say something to her when the servants brought in fresh platters of roast lamb and duck in plum sauce and Ursula turned away, making sure Stephen was served properly. Richard noticed that for a young man Stephen Moreton seemed curiously incapable. A maid brought more wine – a rich claret – and Richard was savouring the bouquet, waiting for Susannah to be served, when William Moreton called them all to attention. There was something powerful, mesmerising in his voice, thought Richard. The room became instantly still.

Moreton looked down the table.

'Dr Masters, would you be so good as to edify our souls while we nourish our bodies?'

This must have been usual, for Richard noticed how

Masters seemed prepared and rose to his feet immediately with a nod towards the guest. Susannah shot Richard a warning glance as if telling him to pay attention.

'I treat tonight of the sins of the flesh,' began the Doctor, his squat, thick body hunched powerfully inside his black suit. His pig eyes scanned the diners knowingly. 'For nothing is more pernicious than the seeds of sin which take root within our own bodies and destroy us. Is not every one of us a walking charnel house? Pure and white on the outside but inside a mess of rotting flesh and twisting, copulating worms, writhing through the hollows of our bones, our tissues, the sockets of our eyes, the soft tender vitals of our flesh? To sin is human, maybe, but how rich and fertile is the soil on which it breeds! Even now hearing me give tongue and lips to these words, does not the flesh within your bodies quiver and tremble with excitement?' He leaned across the table to his wife. His voice was as strong and as mesmerising in its own way as William Moreton's. 'Tell me, my dear beloved, does not even the whisper of the word fornicate cause you to itch and writhe in your inner flesh? Is it not ripe for the ploughing and the planting of the seed of sin?' Sarah Masters gazed dutifully into his eyes and nodded. 'Hah! Hear me then, hear me!' Dr Masters sprang back as if he had been stung and brandished a thick, blunt finger towards the naked figures on the ceiling. 'Sin breeds in the very air around us, copulates in the dust of which we are made, does it not? How then can we be redeemed from this sin? How can we save ourselves?'

Masters paused as if expecting a reply, but none came. Richard cast around him. Susannah avoided his gaze. The other diners were chewing their food methodically and staring at the Doctor, waiting for him to continue. 'The answer is simple,' he proclaimed. 'But a great, wonderful mystery is attached. We can only be saved from the sins of the flesh by overcoming our bodies. Yes! Death, when he comes, comes through the body, following in the footsteps left by sin. So we who must live forever, who are the Lord's chosen, must free our bodies from sin. And how can we do this?' Masters spread his arms wide, his face leapt and darted to express his words. His bristles quivered with excitement. 'Does not Paul teach us himself, "Everything is permissible"? And why does he teach us this? Because he knew that sin springs first from the guilt of the mind. It is only through our wicked conception of wrongdoing that we sin, not – *not* – in the deed itself. It is through thinking things evil that we do evil. Consider Adam and Eve. Were they not naked? Did they not disport with each other night and day and commit all types of delights of the flesh with each other, and did they not live in Paradise? Most truly! They fornicated, copulated, and were in bliss. And was this wrong? Of course not! What was the sin which drove them from Paradise? Their sin was when they decided to choose wrong from right. And in their ignorance, they declared that the joy of their flesh was wrong, and hid their nakedness with leaves. And was the Lord pleased? Of course not! He cast them out of Paradise, to lose their lives in misery and suffering. So, I ask again, what must we do?'

Masters leaned forward, his thick arms resting on the table, his voice suddenly low. He cast his gaze from Susannah, to his wife, to Ursula. 'We must know that as the elect of God's new kingdom, we are dead to sin, sin is fallen from us like a dead fig leaf. We must reclaim Eden! And stand naked of sin, free of the sins of our

47

body, so that we form one flesh, the one perfect body, all joined together in a very ecstasy!' His eyes glittered beadily. 'Be of one flesh! One joy! One! One!'

Masters' last words rang in the air like chimes struck from a bell. The guests stayed gazing at him, as if his message had seared through to their very souls. Richard felt light-headed. He put his hand to his brow. It was damp with sweat. Across the table, Ursula was clutching William's hand and breathing in short, hot rasps. Sarah Masters had closed her eyes and was rocking to and fro gently in her chair. She was sighing.

Richard watched her in amazement. It was almost as if she were ... aroused by her husband's sermon. *Sermon?* He corrected himself. He had never heard a sermon like this. Masters seemed to be calling them to ... what? To fornicate. To copulate freely. In the name of religion. Richard felt dizzy. Although he had been ravenous before the meal, he stared at the last few morsels of the sweet rich lamb's flesh with distaste, as if his whole body were gorged to excess.

Dr Masters returned to his seat, and kissed his wife on the neck. She looked at him misty-eyed.

'A magnificent oration, Doctor,' pronounced William Moreton, his voice thick, syrupy. 'What does our guest think of it?' He turned to Richard.

Richard struggled with the nausea rising in his throat.

Dr Masters looked at him coldly. 'It is the very word of God, sir.'

Richard stared back. He was suddenly aware that a lady's foot was kicking him gently beneath the table. Susannah, he realised. She had her head lowered and appeared more than usually engrossed in her meal.

Somehow, her touch helped him gather his wits. 'I have rarely heard a speech of such passion,' he replied. 'I look forward to listening to you throughout my stay.'

He smiled politely and the Doctor, grudgingly but genuinely, smiled back.

Thank you, Susannah, thought Richard. But when he tried to talk to her she rebutted him with a cold look.

The gathering had fallen oddly quiet, as if the sermon had stunned them. Only Stephen Moreton seemed unaffected and chattered to Ursula, who replied uncomfortably in monosyllables. William regarded him stonily. It was only over dessert that conversation returned, about the latest taxes, and the trade with Holland, and the damage wrought by the winds. There was a ripple of anger at the taxes. Dr Masters in particular seemed incensed.

'The Lord Protector cynically commands us to pay unto Caesar, when we should be paying unto God,' he remarked.

'Aye,' responded William Moreton. 'This Cromwell sees himself as Caesar, for sure.'

Richard turned to Susannah again, but at that moment she stood up and excused herself from the table.

'I'm feeling tired,' she announced. Richard tried to catch her eye. Did she glance at him? Did her lips flicker? Then she spun round in a whirl of skirts and he watched as she sashayed elegantly across the Hall.

'She is a fine lady, is she not?' asked William Moreton, as if reading his thoughts.

'Forgive me for asking,' replied Richard. 'But as the daughter of the previous owner, is not Miss Tremaine's presence here somewhat irregular?'

'It might seem that way,' replied Moreton. 'Were she not engaged to my son.'

'Then your son is to be congratulated, I feel.' Richard swallowed a large mouthful of wine. It tasted bitter.

'She *is* very beautiful, don't you think?' persisted

Ursula, and Richard became uncomfortably aware of her gaze.

'Who am I to comment?' he replied, and busied himself with his wine.

He was relieved when supper came to an end and he could return to his room and collapse on his bed. But although he was exhausted, he could not rest. His mind was seething with questions. Who was Susannah? The flash of her eyes, the mischievous curl of her lips haunted him, and he struggled to think calmly. Where was his real sister? What had happened to her? And what was the strange atmosphere in the Great Hall, which seemed to permeate the gathering? Or was he deluding himself? More than once, Richard found odd fragments of Masters' speech ringing in his ears, grotesque, disturbing. 'Is not every one of us a walking charnel house? Pure and white on the outside but inside a mess of rotting flesh and twisting, copulating worms, writhing through the hollows of our bones, our tissues, the sockets of our eyes, the soft tender vitals of our flesh ... They fornicated, copulated, and were in bliss ... Be of one flesh! One joy!' It was a long time before he could bring himself to sleep.

He did not sleep well.

Strange, potent images haunted him. Ursula Moreton was standing over him, quite naked, her broad, handsome breasts ruddy in the candlelight. She bent down and began to rub a sauce of orange and cloves over him. The sauce was so spiced and pungent that his head reeled. He looked up and Ursula had become Susannah and she was smiling at him, petulantly, mockingly, but in her hand the cloth was red. She whispered something to him which he could not catch and then a man shouted out, 'Careful! Careful!' and he woke with a start. Downstairs the ticking of the clock in the hall was like a drum on the inside of his skull. Then he realised the man was still shouting. His voice came from the courtyard outside.

Struggling out of bed, he tiptoed to the casement and peered out. For a moment he could see nothing, then the moon spilled out from behind a cloud and the spidery figures of men, like sketches of charcoal, could be seen moving to and fro across the yard. After a while he realised they seemed to be shifting barrels or crates of goods.

Richard tried to think whether this was normal or not, but his head was buzzing and making no sense of it, he slumped back on the mattress and let his dreams take him.

Elsewhere in the house, Susannah Tremaine also was awake. She crossed and recrossed her room fitfully in her shift, ignoring the chill draught from the window. There was something about the bronze-haired stranger ... She felt herself quiver. She had not expected him to be like this. When he had looked at her over supper, it was as if he knew her, saw her as she really was. Involuntarily, her hand reached for the slim pendant of silver which hung round her neck. Charlotte Tremaine had given this to her daughter on her seventh birthday. It was her most treasured possession. No. The touch of the silver gave her new strength. She would not be foolish. He was a stranger, an outsider. She must not let herself be distracted. Suddenly another image came to her, of a tall man with jet-black hair and dark, brilliant eyes. After all, she told herself, am I not already committed to someone else? And her heart surged with an emotion which was too powerful to be either affection or regret.

Chapter Five

RICHARD WOKE THE NEXT MORNING with a crisp, pleasant feeling, as if he had come up suddenly into a fresh world of clear air and sunlight the colour of hay. He pressed his face into his bolster and for a moment thought he could detect a trace of sun-sweetened grass and fresh fields. In the joyful light of day, the dark images of the night seemed suddenly unreal and faintly ludicrous, and he dismissed them as he would a childhood fantasy. Springing from the bed, he was up and dressed in minutes. When he got downstairs the Great Hall was empty. The others were still in their chambers, he was told, and he broke his fast alone. He was tempted to linger over his food on the off-chance of Susannah appearing, but then he reminded himself sternly that he had things to do. He would not let thoughts of this strange, vivid woman distract him.

Today he must find Samuel Dowles, the King's agent.

Whether Dowles would want him to stay disguised at Chynoon, or whether he could hide him until the meeting in Tregony, would remain to be seen.

Richard smiled to himself as he imagined the shock on the old man's face when he told him where he was staying. Then, stuffing the final crusts of bread into his mouth, he left the Hall and went out through the rear door. He spied Bridget scrubbing pans in the trough outside, her face red, her hands raw.

'Tell Master Moreton I have gone for a walk along the coast. I'll be back later,' he said, and was gone before she could reply. He headed due south from the manor and was soon striding down through the fields towards the shore, feeling the spring of his body over the moist turf.

It was a bright autumn day. The sky was a glaring blue and up from the sea a breeze quickened the air and brought long-forgotten scents of seaweed and old bracken and wet ivy. Richard walked briskly. Soon he was looking down the combe to the short shingle strip and the endless roll and break of the waves beyond. His feet churned the pebbles agreeably.

He had not gone far, however, before he spotted a ragged black shape reared against a rock, which sent the water shooting up in spray. He guessed what it was and tearing off his shoes and stockings, waded out in his breeches and dragged it ashore. It was more cumbersome than he expected and it was a long time before he collapsed panting on the shingle with his prize. As he had reckoned, it was the fractured remains of a spar. All that remained of the *Marguerite*, a broken limb. Grimly, he lugged the beam up the beach until it was well beyond the grasp of the tides. Then he upended it and erected it, like an oar, in a final salute.

Richard gazed out on the crisp blue waves, and the dark spread of sea stretching to the sky, and the vast bowl of sky which rose above them all. From the horizon a ragged block of cloud, caught by the breeze, was running in across the deep. He had not particularly cared for Perret, Roublais and the others. Yet their deaths touched him nevertheless. They were men, after all. He was turning to go, when some marks at the tip of the spar caught his eye. The wood should have been torn and smashed apart by the brunt of the sea. But here, about six inches from the top, were the unmistakable scars of an axe.

Wreckers.

Everyone in these parts would see a struggling French ship as fair prey, but some were less scrupulous than others. He closed his eyes and hoped that the sailors had died while they were still at sea. Again he wondered that he alone had been saved. Was it really luck? He thought of Moreton, staring across the table. 'No one is lucky,' he had said, 'only blessed or damned.'

The bright start to the day did not last long. By the time he reached the valley leading up to Dowles' house, the block of cloud had swollen to fill the sky, and the light was dim under the trees. Richard could remember running up the path from the sea when he was a youngster. Dowles had been a friend of his father's and Richard would sit in the study while the old man read him tales and legends of the ancients. Richard's feet slapped in the puddles and mire.

He glimpsed the house as he rounded the last twist in the path. It was situated at the head of the valley, in a small hollow ringed with pine trees. The house was only of modest proportions, for Dowles had lived on his own since his wife died, but it was attractive, after the modern mode, and clad in a soft grey slate. Overhead the pine trees soughed eerily and waved their heads like sentinels.

By the front door stood a stack of logs, half-chopped, the axe still in the block, just as it would have been ten, fifteen years before. A drift of brown beech leaves crackled underfoot, and Richard suddenly felt a wave of nostalgia rise within him. With perhaps less caution than was warranted, he strode up to the door and rapped three times. He smiled gently as he imagined the look on the old man's face.

There was no reply.

Above, the trees whispered to each other and a crow

cawed and clapped across the sky. Richard looked quickly over his shoulder, as if some rustle in the undergrowth had startled him, and knocked again. He thought he could hear something moving within and put his head to the door and listened.

Nothing.

Samuel must be out on business. Or perhaps he thought Richard had been lost in the shipwreck, and had gone to investigate. Richard glanced round, undecided, then crossed to the stables at the rear. The horse's bridle and saddle still hung from their pegs – Dowles couldn't have gone far. The grey clouds began to spot with rain and the drops fell softly through the wood. Richard shrugged his coat about him and went back to the house. He didn't bother to knock again, but finding the back door unlocked, went in.

There was a breath of something in the air. A light, bitter scent, like burnt almonds. He sniffed again, but already it had melted and was gone.

'Hello? Samuel? Are you there?'

But the very deadness of his voice and the dampness of the air gave him his answer. It is strange, he thought, how we can instantly sense when a house is unoccupied. Although it was still mid-morning, the cloud outside had cast the house into a deep and silent gloom. Absolutely silent. Richard's footfalls sounded intrusively loud and clumsy on the flagstones. He coughed and jumped at his own sound.

He went through to the kitchen. On the worktop a mould of blue and grey was breeding over a crust of bread. A pan, greased with fat, lay unwashed on its side. Richard crossed straight to the hearth, but the ashes were cold and powdery and he could see it had not been lit for days. He sniffed. Beside the fireplace, a rabbit hung on a hook. Its flesh had long since started to rot and a sweet, putrid odour swelled from its body. Its greasy eyes stared blindly at him. Momentarily held, Richard stared back at them, then he snapped his head away and shuddered.

There was something . . . *here*. Every fibre of his soul could sense it.

Richard left the kitchen. The hall was windowless and for an instant the damp black interior crowded in on him, and he struggled for breath, then he found the door to the study and jabbed it open. Again the same delicate bitter odour hovered and was gone, like a spirit. But here there were signs of activity. Beside an easy chair a small table was knocked over, several books scattered across the fire-rug. He stooped to pick them up, and felt the paper damp between his fingers. Three of the books were ancient texts he remembered from his childhood: Malory's *Morte D'Arthur*, Homer's *Odyssey*, Geoffrey of Monmouth. But the fourth was not printed like the others and appeared to be a handwritten journal. Richard recognised Samuel Dowles' script immediately. Flicking to the back, he saw that the last three or four pages had been torn clean from the binding. Trembling slightly, he scanned the entries.

June 17th – John Carew arrives from London. Weather inclement. Meditated on the brevity of man's life.

June 21st – My pain returned. Rested inside.

June 22nd – Feeling better, thanks to Mrs Treen's posset, rode to Polkerris, a pleasant sight, dined with the Abbots and Mr Carew. Mr Abbot much concerned about taxes. Carew made light of it – I do not believe him!

There was nothing here of interest, thought Richard.

Merely the tedious recital of Dowles' comings and goings, page after page. He read the last entry before the missing sheets and was none the wiser:

> *September 12th* – prayed for an hour before breakfast. I must keep the example of my Lord before me.

Richard ran his fingers over the blank pages, and there, ever so slight, he felt the faint imprint of Dowles' quill, through the sheets which had been torn away. He crossed to the windows. The light was spotted and stained by the rain and the shadows of the pines, but holding the book at an angle, he could just make out the marks. They were so indistinct they were almost nonexistent. He tried a different slant, and a thin ray of sun sent them into some sort of relief. Four letters, larger than the rest, stood out. CCCL. He tried again.

He was sure of it.

There in the middle of the page, where Dowles must have pressed his quill with particular passion, or maybe in haste, the shadow of just four letters: CCCL. Beyond the glass, the rain fell in a soft velvet patter.

Did they mean anything? If they were numerals after the Roman fashion, they would stand for three hundred and fifty, he reasoned. But three hundred and fifty what? Richard paced back to the fireplace. He had no idea. Not even a clue. To the left of the fireplace, a bookcase stretched to the ceiling. He took a step back to examine it, and felt something beneath his boot.

He bent down, running his hands over the rug. There, tucked beneath the fringe, a small lump. He flicked the carpet back.

It was a man's finger.

*

Richard flung the door open and stumbled out. The daylight dazzled him, and in a sudden shock he spun round, trying to catch his bearings. Overhead the pines waved their arms in a swirl of wind and a moan ran up from the valley. He fetched up against the pile of logs and clutched himself. He was sick, giddy. The silence inside the house seemed to reach out and engulf him. There was a sudden bluster and the wind beat through the trees.

Out of the corner of his eye, something moved in the undergrowth.

He froze. His pulse was hammering in his head. His body was a deafening roar. He strained his eyes but could see no one. Beneath the pines the ground was covered with clusters of holly, brambles and grey twisted plants. Where had the movement come from?

He felt someone behind him.

Richard spun round and found himself staring at the open door of the house. Then the wind rose in the trees and he felt the wood stir with an evil malevolent breath, and suddenly he was running, stumbling and leaping, down the track.

The next few minutes lasted forever. Richard bounded down the path, feet slapping through puddles, slipping through mud. He tripped over protruding roots which writhed out from the ground. A holly bush, blistered with red, caught him in the face and he threw himself away. He turned a twist in the path and came upon a fox and vixen mating feverishly in the dirt. He pulled away, more shocked than if he had found two people coupling, for this was the wrong, unnatural season for such acts. The sky was swollen with evil and pressed down upon him. The bushes cracked behind him, and he jumped back, expecting

someone, some*thing*, to spring upon him, but instead a
fat starling burst out and scuttled through the leaves.
Richard stared at his hands. They were cut and bleeding. The air was impregnated with the rot of vegetation,
the stench of leaf mould was choking him. He stumbled
to his feet as if he were drunk and plunged down
through the valley towards the sea. Behind him – no,
he would not think what shapeless horror pursued him.

He ran on, forced himself to run, and then suddenly
the air grew light and fresh and over the next rise he
saw the sea stretched out before him, blue and black
and marbled with foam. He threw himself across the
final few yards and fetched up gasping against a rock.

He could not put words to what he had felt in Samuel
Dowles' house or outside under the trees.

At first the finger had not seemed real. It had rested
on his palm, surprisingly light, an unnatural livid grey.
It was an index finger and had been severed in one
clean stroke, just above the knuckle. He had stared at
it stupidly for what seemed like an age, then its true
horror struck him, and he dropped it violently. One
clean stroke. But that was not what affected him. There
was something else. It was nothing less than the actual
presence of evil, which suddenly overwhelmed him
and, once he was outside, rushed in on him from the
dark places under the pines.

He tried to retch but nothing came but a bitter thin
bile, reeking of almonds and leaf rot. He stayed
slumped against the rock and waited for his body to
grow still. His mind, however, would not.

What had happened to Samuel Dowles? He knew,
with sickening conviction, that the finger was Dowles'
and that the man himself must be dead. The dampness
which had clung to his house could only come from
the grave.

A hand touched him on the shoulder.

He leapt round.

'No, don't! Richard!'

She had jumped back in alarm and he realised he was glaring, wild-eyed. Then the madness left him and he recognised her.

Here. Of all places.

'Rebecca!' he gasped, breathless, suddenly happy, and stared at her.

'Richard? Is it really you?' Her voice was hesitant, as if she scarcely believed her own eyes. Her mouth flickered halfway between a smile and a frown.

'Yes.' He shook the scent of burnt almonds out of his head and let it scatter in the breeze, and his face broke into a broad grin. 'Yes. It's me.'

She had been fifteen when he last saw her, and for a moment he saw her like that now, all gangling limbs and straggly hair. Rebecca Penmarris. He had remembered her laugh when he had forgotten everything else.

And yet she had changed so much. The woman before him was no longer a giggling maid. Now she was tall and graceful and appeared almost elegant in spite of her rough woollen skirt and working boots and the tattered shawl flapping in the wind. Rebecca had a long straight nose and a fine, broad forehead and straight brows, and he realised she would look almost severe were it not for the thick black hair tumbling to her shoulders and the smile on her lips. Only her hands revealed she was a farm maid, for they were chapped pink and raw from the hours she had spent in the fields.

They took a step towards each other. Richard was breathing hoarsely and lifted his hands towards her, then hesitated and let them fall back to his sides. Rebecca thought later they should have wrapped themselves in each other's arms at once, then everything else would have been explained or forgotten. But they hesitated too long, and now they stood, poised awkwardly, too conscious of their own feelings.

Rebecca bit her lip. 'I saw you come running out of the valley. I knew it was you,' she began quickly, her voice brimming with excitement. 'Mother said you were dead. Drowned on the way to France. But I knew you'd come back.' A cold stab of wind rushed up the beach and shook out her hair, but she did not notice.

'Drowned?' He stared at her blankly and then the light struck him. It was after all almost nine years ago. 'Yes. I remember, the *Sparrowhawk* foundered off Le Havre, with all my belongings' – he had forgotten the chests of clothes and documents and books, his father's final gift – 'but I was on the *Mercury.*'

There was another slight pause, as they searched for something to say.

'So where have you been?' She smiled expectantly.

'France. The Channel Isles. The Netherlands. Belgium. The Palatinate. Cologne.' The very recital of names now seemed absurd. He grinned foolishly. 'Who cares?' He threw his arms in the air. 'Who cares less?'

Rebecca giggled nervously, suddenly no longer severe, no longer cautious. 'I always thought . . .' she began, and then joyfully clutched her shawl tight about her. 'This is ridiculous, Richard Tremaine! Ridiculous!'

'Yes!' he laughed. 'It is!'

Then at last he wrapped his arms around her and they were spinning round over the beach, laughing and whooping like two children again, their troubles and worries forgotten until they tumbled, breathless and dizzy on the sand. They lay like that, laughing, and saying they had missed each other, and telling each other a hundred things at once, while the wind buffeted them and the sand worked its way into their clothes until finally their torrent of words dried up and they grew silent again, both caught in their own thoughts. Rebecca propped herself on one elbow and stroked the hair off his face. After all these years he found her touch strange, unexpected.

'You've grown older, Richard,' she said thoughtfully, and ran her fingers over the deep lines of his forehead. 'You look like you've seen . . . too much.'

'Maybe,' he replied. 'Too much of too little, more like.' He frowned. 'We've lived like beggars for the past five years. The King's government in exile!' He sat upright and wrapped his arms round his knees. His hair glinted dully in the wind. She rested a hand on his shoulder, feeling the muscles shift beneath the skin.

'That doesn't matter any more, Richard. You've come back. You can forget the past.' She rubbed his shoulder reassuringly.

Richard stared out to sea. To the breakers combing across the beach.

'What is it? What's wrong, Richard?'

'I haven't come back, Rebecca. Not for good.'

The dampness of the beach was seeping into his bones. He got awkwardly to his feet and offered her a hand up.

She didn't take it.

'I've managed for nine years without you.' She got to her feet and stared at him, and afterwards hated herself for her aloofness.

'True,' he answered humbly. There was a scar here, he knew, but he wasn't sure how he could heal it. Yet what was he to her, or she to him? Childhood friends, he thought awkwardly, that was all. But in his heart he knew he was deceiving himself. They had been closer than that. Once.

'So you're here on *his* business, are you?' Her words startled him. She brushed the sand off her chapped pink palms.

'What? You mean my father's?'

'No, the King's.' She glared at him. 'No good can come of it, Richard.'

He felt a response burning on his lips, but she broke in: 'Things have changed, Richard. Don't you understand? People have had enough of Charles Stuart! What good did he ever do us?' Then she added, very quietly: 'I hoped you'd come home.'

'I want to, Rebecca.'

'Do you? Do you?' she asked with some vehemence. 'You are just travelling, Richard, and your journey has brought you this way.' She glanced down at his stockings. 'And look at you! You're filthy! Have you been sleeping in ditches?'

He smiled at that. Suddenly her expression was that of the bossy girl who used to scold him in the washroom at Chynoon, and catching the glint in his eye, she fell silent and bit her lip to stop herself from laughing, but there were tears in her eyes.

'No, I slept at Chynoon last night.'

Her smile withered.

'What? At the manor house, as a *guest*?'

'Don't worry. No one recognises me . . .'

'But what about your sister? How did she react?'

Richard was annoyed to feel his face redden. 'She's not my sister,' he muttered.

For once Rebecca lost her composure. She looked shocked.

'She looks a bit like Susannah,' he conceded quickly. 'But she's not my sister. Surely you've seen the difference?'

Rebecca shook her head stiffly. 'You forget, your sister

and I weren't close, not like we were. How can this be true, Richard?'

Quickly, Richard explained what had happened – the storm, the wreck, Moreton's hospitality, and then Susannah's appearance.

Rebecca was still shaking her head at the end.

'I hadn't seen much of her,' she said. 'I didn't think she wanted to be friends after so long. That was all.' Again, there was a hint of bitterness in her voice. 'So do you know who she is?'

'No, of course not!' he answered irritably.

Rebecca said nothing for a while, feeling his hurt, his anger. 'What are you going to do?'

He scowled. 'What can I do? I'm a virtual criminal, on the run. If I'm caught, they'll hang me as a spy.'

'You shouldn't stay at the manor, Richard. It's—'

'I don't want to talk about it,' he snapped. 'Besides, I'm not here on family business,' he added, as if he was trying to convince himself.

Rebecca was about to say more, then thought better of it. There's too much pain already, she told herself. She wished he would let her reach out to him, comfort him, but his stern, angry demeanour told her that her sympathy would not be welcome. Instead her face blossomed into a smile. She could still show she cared. 'My mother's going to be shocked to see you.' She hugged herself. 'You will come back, won't you? After all, I can't leave you like this!' she added glancing at his stockings. 'What have you been doing?'

He grimaced. He would not think about Samuel Dowles now, he told himself. 'Just walking,' he said.

Her dark blue eyes glinted. She raised her eyebrows quizzically, willing him to smile. 'So you say, Richard Tremaine.' He looked sheepish, and she laughed. 'Come on then, or are you going to stand here all day?'

She tugged his arm and led the way across the beach. He noticed they were not heading towards her cottage.

'Where are we going, Beckie?'

She glanced over her shoulder. 'What do you think I was doing when I saw you? I don't spend my days swanning around like a real lady,' she added, with only a trace of bitterness. 'I've got to drop by the village.'

He hesitated.

'Don't worry,' she said. 'You needn't come down, though who'd recognise you in that outfit, I don't know.' She smiled. 'Apart from me, that is.'

She headed up the path on the far side and Richard fell into step beside her.

He was, in fact, quite glad of this errand. As they walked, they had time to talk, and gradually they became less self-conscious. Rebecca wanted to know all that had happened to him and he retold his escape to France and the times since, the years of exile and plots and empty hopes. And yet, as they talked, Richard was aware of an unresolved tension which lay between them. He noticed it in little things, the slight sharpness in her voice, and the pursed frown which appeared more than once, turning her face suddenly cool, severe.

'What is it, Beckie?' he asked, as they neared the crest of the last hill. 'Aren't you pleased to see me?'

She pouted. 'Of course I am!'

'What is it then? You seem so ... reserved. Look at you now!'

'Do I?' She wiped her hair out of her face. 'No, I'm not. I'm just stunned, I suppose. You've been gone nine years, Richard,' she explained, almost as an accusation, 'And now you've come back to serve Charles Stuart, you can't expect me to be happy!'

'I'm sorry.' He felt irritated, but checked himself. 'I have a duty to perform.'

'Duty? Don't give me duty!' The word inflamed her. 'Look what happened to my father for his duty!'

'What? What's happened to Sedge?' Richard suddenly realised he had never thought to ask about her family.

She spoke resentfully, as if realising this too: 'He did his duty for the King as well, Richard. While you were in France.'

He felt ashamed.

'There's only me and my mother now.' She lowered her head. 'It's hard. We manage to keep a few cows, and I help at the manor sometimes, but the weather's been so bad this last year, we lost our wheat and half the barley.' She gave him a bleak smile. 'Sometimes I think that time we spent together has soured me through and through.'

He frowned. 'How do you mean?'

'Teaching me to read and write! English and Latin! What good did it do me, Richard?' She laughed angrily. 'Hah! Here's me, a peasant girl, reading Virgil and Horace!'

'But you enjoyed it, Beckie!' Richard's father had been fond of Rebecca. She was a bright, sharp-witted girl – too sharp, Michael Tremaine had said, to be a farmer's maid. He had insisted she was educated with Richard each morning, and had even persuaded her parents when they objected. *Persuaded?* Richard shook his head. No: commanded.

Richard was suddenly reminded of those mornings in the library while the fire cracked and hissed in the hearth. He turned to her, but Rebecca was already marching ahead, her shawl tossing in the breeze. Yes, I enjoyed it, she thought bitterly, that's why it hurts so much now.

Richard ran after her.

'I'm sorry,' he said. 'I didn't mean to upset you.'

She didn't slow down. 'I know, Richard, I know.' She stared straight ahead at the gulls tumbling across the sky. She had waited all these years. Even when she told herself that he wouldn't return, or if he did that there could never be anything between them, she had waited. Because what choice did she have? A fisherman's son who wanted her for food and clothes and breeding? His father was right, she was too good for that. Too good! The words mocked her. But now Richard had returned, against all hope, and she realised he would never even guess how she felt, and for a moment she hated him, and despised herself. 'We come from different worlds, you and I.'

'No,' he replied. 'Not any more.'

But the wind must have carried his words away, for she didn't reply and they reached the end of the field in silence. There, far below, lay the fishing port of Porthcarrick, squatting in the lee of the valley.

The village was small, and consisted of three rows of cramped cottages, a drinking-house, and two boat-sheds of rough-hewn stone. A few yards below the village, the flanks of the sheer valley jutted into the sea – two spurs of black, ragged rocks – and formed a small natural harbour. Even at high tide, these rocks were clearly visible and the rough sea churned and splashed over them and stained the water a dirty white. On the beach, four small fishing boats were drawn, their seine nets bundled beside them.

'It hasn't changed,' he said.

She pursed her lips.

'Wait here,' she told him. 'I won't be long.'

'What do you have to do?' he asked, but she was already picking her way down the slope.

Richard watched her reach the bottom and knock on

one of the cottage doors. From this distance, he could still recognise her long, straight figure. She had a slightly stiff way of walking so that her head and neck were always held high and somewhat proudly, he thought, and was surprised at the warmth he felt for her. She had been like a sister to him. Closer in some ways than his real sister, Susannah.

The thought of Susannah twisted within him and he remembered the flame-haired woman at Chynoon who bore her name. Who was she? He stared out to sea. Yet, he had to admit, Susannah Tremaine was not just mysterious. There was something about her which made his skin burn.

And now, with Samuel Dowles gone, what was he to do? There were too many things he did not understand.

I have my duty, whatever Rebecca says, he thought grimly. That much was clear.

He gazed down into the village. Rebecca was already heading back up the hill. He stamped his feet impatiently. The harsh wind had chilled him to the bone.

'All right?' he asked.

She smiled, a bright, fresh smile.

'I still can't believe you're here. I half expected you'd have disappeared when I got back.'

'What?' he laughed. 'Vanished into thin air?'

They headed away from the village, inland, along the winding tracks and lanes that criss-crossed the countryside. It was not long before Richard recognised the familiar curve of a field and the scraggy thorn bushes crowning the hedge. Rebecca grinned and pointed at the grey cottage beyond.

'Remember this?'

Richard would have recognised the lopsided hulk of her cottage anywhere. A warm pang seized him. But even from here he could see the turfs on the roof were rotten and the walls were cracking.

They were still thirty yards away when Elizabeth, Rebecca's mother, came out. She had aged dramatically since he had last seen her. Her hair had been bleached by the years and she squinted at him apprehensively, furtively, one hand crooked over her forehead. Then she recognised him and leaned over and spat on the ground.

'Look, Mother, look who's back!'

'So I can see.' Elizabeth wiped her hands on her skirt without taking her eyes off him. She had the same broad forehead as her daughter but more severe, more uncompromising.

'Mrs Penmarris, it's good to see you again.' Richard bowed, but she did not smile.

'I cannot say the same, Master Tremaine.'

Sensing her anger, Richard grew serious. 'I was sorry to hear about your husband.'

She stared at him with such bitterness that he winced.

'He followed the King,' she snapped. 'And what good did it do him? We don't want your kind here any more, Master Tremaine! Do the Committee know?'

It had never occurred to Richard that people he knew as friends might betray him. He took a step back.

'Mother!' Rebecca's voice was hurt, pleading.

Elizabeth laughed.

'Don't worry. I won't betray your master's precious skin! Not when I remember how well he treated us.'

'Mother, don't!' Rebecca urged. 'It doesn't matter now. Richard never knew.'

'Knew? What do you mean?'

Rebecca stepped forwards, between him and her mother, feeling their raw emotions. 'During the war, when my father was fighting under Hopton, we could not pay the rent. Your father repossessed our land.'

Richard stared at her. 'That's impossible! My father followed the King himself. He would never do anything like that!'

She looked at him sadly. She was too proud to reveal her own anger.

'I heard him with my own ears, Richard.'

Her words were simple, bare of all accusation. Nevertheless, Richard felt his temper rising. What did they expect him to say? That his father was a hard, callous landlord who cared for no one but himself? His own memories were not like that – would not be like that. He glared back at them. Then Rebecca put her hand on his arm.

'Richard, it doesn't matter any more. Don't you see?'

But Elizabeth stared at him as if it still did. And he was ashamed that he couldn't bring himself to apologise for his father. Elizabeth made a harsh clucking noise with her tongue.

'Still the master's son, aren't you, Richard?' Then Richard saw she had picked up a pitcher of water and was offering it to him. 'Here,' she said roughly. 'You're filthy, better clean yourself up or you'll be mistaken for one of us.'

'Thank you, Elizabeth.'

'No. Don't thank me, Richard,' she replied, with only a hint of a softening. 'Why break a family tradition?' She beckoned him inside.

Their cottage consisted of a single room, no more than fifteen feet long. It was a chill damp place, but meticulously clean and ordered. Earthenware crocks lined the far wall, containing flour, oats, meal, and on shelves above stood pots and jars of jams, spices and preserves. A large bronze washbasin lay in the corner together with a pitcher, ewer and a stack of kindling. The sole furniture comprised a straw mattress slung against the wall, two wooden chests and a cloam oven, blackened with age.

Richard had forgotten how they lived. He felt a sudden twinge of guilt. He understood the bitterness in Rebecca's voice now.

'Here, let me,' he said awkwardly, and helped Rebecca set the washbasin in the centre of the room.

She smiled gratefully, and felt herself warm towards him against all her better judgements. When she squeezed the cloth over his arms, she realised her fingers betrayed a tenderness she could not hide. She was relieved, but perhaps also disappointed, that Richard was oblivious to this. His only feeling was one of great peace.

After the events of the last few days, he would have given almost anything to stay, to call even this wretched dwelling 'home', if only for an hour. But it was too much of a risk, he told himself. If he was seen by anyone from Chynoon, it would raise suspicions he couldn't answer.

Once he had cleaned himself, he took his leave and saw Elizabeth sigh with relief. Rebecca escorted him down the hill. At first he thought it was just for companionship, but as soon as they were out of earshot she asked, none too casually: 'So, what *are* you doing for the King?'

He cocked his eyebrows in mock seriousness. 'You know I can't tell you, Beckie.'

The path dropped into a wood running up from the valley floor. Here it was surprisingly dark and the air crowded in on them. Reluctantly, Richard recalled the strange creeping evil that had hung under the pine trees at Samuel Dowles' house. It had seemed so real.

71

He shuddered and looked across to Rebecca. The less he involved her the better.

She saw his expression and turned, suddenly earnest: 'Richard, forget this King's business! What good will come of it? I'm sure if you talked to the authorities they'd grant you a pardon. Even my father—' She stopped herself. 'You could get some land.'

'What? I could rent some fields from Moreton?'

'It would be something, Richard!' She stared at him intensely. 'What life have you got as an exile?'

He didn't want to answer her. No life, he thought, and yet that was more than his pride would admit. 'My father . . .' he began, '. . . died. I can't just pretend it didn't happen. I have a duty.'

She saw the pain in his eyes. 'All right,' she whispered. 'So what are you going to do?'

He sighed. Dowles had been going to introduce him to the local gentry. 'Tell me, which of the old families are still loyal to the King?'

A branch of holly blocked their way. Rebecca pushed it back and held it for him.

'I don't know, Richard. Most people no longer care, except maybe the Roselyns.'

'Of Caerleon? Is Sir Charles still alive?'

She nodded.

Sir Charles Roselyn had fought at Stratton with his father, thought Richard, and Rebecca's father too. He would be a good choice.

Here the path left the trees and ran up through bare fields to Chynoon. Rebecca stopped and Richard paused, suddenly awkward, aware of her very close to him. Then she reached up and kissed him on the cheek.

'Will I see you again, Richard?'

'Maybe,' he muttered, aware that her question meant more than that, and that his answer meant less. How could he say that he had come back hoping to see her, only to find himself smitten by a total stranger? *Smitten?* Was that really how he felt? He was angry and confused. I'm not a child any more, he thought. We have changed, Beckie, he wanted to say. We can't live in the past. And yet he knew that if he said that, she would not believe him, and he could not bear the look on her face. In a way he did still feel something for her. But he forced those feelings back. We were no more than friends, he reminded himself. No more.

Rebecca had turned away. 'You'll be gone again before I know it, won't you?'

He struggled for words. 'I don't know, Beckie. Probably.'

Probably. The word stung her. You can be so insensitive, Richard Tremaine, she thought. As if I don't matter. But then, after all, my people never matter, do they? The lines of her jaw tightened slightly. I'll not ask you to stay again, no.

'Well,' she said coolly, 'farewell, Richard.'

He stared after her, aware of all the things he could say, but making himself stay still. Whatever I said, he told himself sternly, I would be saying it for the wrong reasons, to make myself feel better. It would only hurt you more. Even so, he stood there, hesitating, angry. But she had already turned and was melting into the shadow of the trees, like a ghost.

Chapter Six

CHYNOON WAS LYING IN THE grey light of afternoon when he cleared the last hill. Its windows glowed, warm and yellow. It was good to be home, he thought grimly, but his head still buzzed angrily with thoughts of Rebecca. They should not have parted like that. He stared at the ground and did not see that at the far end of the yard, by the stables, Susannah was swinging down from her horse, sporting leather boots and a wide-brimmed riding hat.

'Master Ferrers!' she called across to him.

Richard kicked at the gravel.

Susannah waited for a second. But when he did not notice her, she turned brusquely and it was this sudden flurry which caught his eye.

'Miss Tremaine!' he replied, forcing himself to smile. And you are part of my problem, he thought angrily. If you weren't here, would I have treated Rebecca in the same way? 'Did you have a good ride?' he asked, but his voice betrayed his displeasure.

'Yes, thank you.' Susannah patted her horse on the neck. The man she knew as Richard Ferrers glared at her. His hair glowed orange and gold in the afternoon sun, and she felt herself shiver. The stableboy tugged at her horse's reins.

'The countryside is beautiful in the autumn,' said Richard. His gaze intensified, raking her, stripping her.

Suddenly from the window of the library she saw Ursula Moreton watching them. She tensed, suddenly self-conscious, afraid. No, don't talk to me now, she thought. Not here. She shot him a smile. It was hard, unexpectedly spiteful. 'How *romantic*, just like the son of a merchant.'

Richard's cheeks burned. He went to answer her retort, but stopped himself. Not while I'm in this mood, he muttered. He turned sharply on his heel and stalked into the house.

Just as Ursula Moreton was coming out.

In the darkened corridor, Richard did not see her until she tripped and they stumbled into each other. Ursula gave a little gasp and he had a sudden impression of her full, ripe body pressed against his – breasts, warm, vulnerable stomach – and a sweet tang of perfume, like oranges, then he was apologising and helping her to her feet.

'Master Ferrers! What a pleasant surprise!' She looked at him suggestively. 'We wondered where you had got to.'

'I went for a walk along the coast,' he explained. 'I hope I didn't cause offence.'

'Of course not!' she laughed. 'We can expect you at supper tonight?' Her eyes glittered. 'Shall I send one of the maids to clean you? Or would you prefer me?' She enjoyed the confusion in his face for just a moment, then disappeared down the corridor.

Richard did not follow her. He had to be alone. Part of him still wanted to talk to Susannah – why her sudden swing of mood? – but instead he turned left to the library. He listened briefly at the door and hearing nothing, went in.

This had been his father's favourite room. As soon as he caught sight of the rich leather-bound books – russet, indigo, mahogany, cinnamon – Richard almost expected to see his father looking up from his chair by the window, some ancient text on his lap.

I always found my father here, he thought ruefully. When the messenger came announcing the outbreak of war, Richard had come rushing into the library to see his father leaning on the mantelpiece, the slip of paper in his hand. 'The King is God's anointed,' Michael Tremaine had declared, his voice thick and resonant, 'and our cause so just that those who die in it are little less than martyrs.' Richard remembered being lifted by a surge of emotion, and tears starting in his eyes, and his father smiling at him confidently. 'This is our duty, Richard,' he had said. 'Justice will be done.'

But now the room was empty.

Richard went to the cases and saw that Moreton had taken over his father's books. It was an extensive and valuable collection. Ovid, Livy, Lucretius . . . The only thing that had changed was the picture over the fireplace. His father's painting of an ancient bacchanal had been replaced with an engraving of the Crucifixion. The Lord Jesus stared down on him compassionately.

Richard ran his fingers over the dry leather spines. Cicero, Virgil . . . His father would spend hours with him, translating or simply reading aloud. 'You must hear the sound of the words to understand their meaning,' he had said. 'Man never needs to translate the noblest poetry, Richard, remember that.' And Richard had dutifully listened, his head dreaming of riding through the meadows, or chasing dragonflies by the pond. 'There is an immortality in great words,' Michael Tremaine told him on another occasion. 'When we are gone, these words will still remain, for others.'

Richard realised that his father had been right, in a way. When all his blood and flesh had returned to dust, these dusty tomes were still here, waiting to be read and turned to life. Without thinking, he reached up and plucked out the first volume which came to him. He recognised it immediately. A slim collection of Tibullus' verse, one of his father's favourites. He flicked open the front cover. Here his father would sign his name . . .

But underneath the signature, in the same spidery scrawl, something else was written, in Latin. *'Divitias filius fulvo sibi congerat auro.'* Richard would have given it no further thought, but then he saw that underneath was the date: March 3rd 1646.

Sir Ralph Fielding had said they retreated from Bodmin on the 2nd of March. Michael Tremaine must have written this the very morning they set off, before they were attacked . . .

Richard stared at the page. The black letters were so crisp and strong, they could have been written earlier that day. *Divitias filius* . . . He had forgotten most of his Latin, but then the meaning came to him: 'Let my son gather riches in yellow gold.'

The words seemed so striking. It was as if his father had reached out, through time, and whispered them in his ear.

Did he know? Richard wondered. That I would come looking for him all these years later? What was he trying to say?

But the words gave no suggestion. And what they meant, or why they had been written, he couldn't tell.

'Careful! Careful now!' The shouts startled him. Looking out of the window he saw, through the haze of evening, a group of labourers dragging a cart, laden with soil, across the yard. As he expected, the men's faces were unknown to him. In fact he knew from their outlandish voices that they were not from the region at all. Where had he heard that accent before? In the North, or East Anglia? Then one of them stepped from behind the cart and wiped his brow with his scarf, a tall, thin man with a hooked nose and grey stubble, and Richard realised with a shock that he knew him.

He racked his memory. Then the name came to him: Henry Couch, a smallholder from inland. Michael Tremaine had employed him occasionally in lieu of rent. Richard felt a strange mixture of excitement and apprehension. Quickly replacing the book, he slipped out through the rear door and followed the men across the yard. The labourers heaved the cart behind the stables, scattering a pair of sprawling dogs. Richard followed them around the corner and was startled to see that what had been waste ground was now the site of a new building. It was a long, low, brick-built shed, with windows running down its side and doors and stables at each end. Richard stared in bewilderment. Why on earth did Moreton want to build this? For the servants? From what he could tell, the servants still slept in the old south wing of the house, as they had since his grandfather's day.

The labourers dragged the cart to the far side of the building and began to shovel the dirt into an open trench. They seemed wretched and sour-faced and their only words were oaths and curses which stabbed the air. Henry Couch seemed to be the only Cornishman among them and worked sullenly by himself. The others ignored him. Richard withdrew into the trees which lay north of the house. Couch would take this way home. He waited impatiently. Overhead a wood pigeon called out, the air grew darker. It would be night soon.

Eventually the men finished, slung their tools into the cart and went their separate ways. Henry Couch gave his forehead a last wipe and came slowly towards the wood. He was on his own. He had covered about a hundred yards when Richard stepped from behind a tree.

'Henry.'

Couch stopped dead. His face snapped into an expression of horror.

'No!'

Richard didn't understand. 'What is it, Henry, what's wrong?' he hissed. 'It's me! Richard!'

The old man staggered backwards. His face was white and drawn tight over his skull. 'Forgive me! Forgive me, master! They said you were dead!' Couch began to stumble back along the path towards the manor.

Cursing, Richard ran after him. He should have foreseen this. The old man was surprisingly spry and had almost reached the clearing by the ditch before Richard grabbed his shoulder and spun him round. Couch gave a dry, desperate cry and Richard clamped a hand over his mouth. Two crows took off from the trees in fright.

'Henry, it's me! I'm alive!'

Couch's eyes bulged as if he were being choked. Richard could feel the man's spittle squirming against his palm. He swore again and jerked him back and forwards like a rag doll. 'Henry!' He hauled Couch back up the path to where a holly bush, studded with crimson, offered some shelter and threw him on to the ground. The old man gave a yelp and lay still, gasping like a dog.

'Look, it's me! Don't shout! Now, what is going on?'

'Master Tremaine! I thought you were the dead man!' Richard would have smiled, but Couch's face was still contorted with pain. 'When I saw you like that . . .'

'Well, I'm not.' He bent down and prodded Couch in the chest. The old man winced. 'Feel for yourself.

Listen,' he added in a whisper, 'You must tell no one, do you understand? No one.'

Couch nodded. 'So where have you been, master?' he asked, his voice still breathless.

'France, and Cologne, and the Low Countries.' He stopped for a moment. 'It's good to be home.'

'Why have you come back? Jessie Moyle always said you'd come back.'

Richard bent over him. 'Why do you think, Henry? Everyone wants to come home eventually.' He paused. 'What happened to my father? Do you know? Did you see him?'

Couch was seized by a violent coughing fit. He twisted over on his side and wheezed into the damp leaves. Richard looked anxiously around but could see no one in the woods. Eventually, the coughing passed and Couch dried his mouth and propped himself on his elbow.

'Are you all right, Henry?'

'It's the blasted damp.' He coughed once more into his hand and cleared his throat. 'Yes, I saw your father. The last time he was here.' He sighed. 'I remember Martha running out to me in the fields, saying the Roundheads were coming, and that very night your father rode in.'

Richard's eyes were rooted on him. 'Go on,' he said quietly.

'I didn't know your father had arrived until the next morning, but as soon as I heard, I came by to pay my respects. And there he was, sitting astride his horse with a fresh plume in his hat. He laughed when he saw me. He used to have a nickname for me. Billy, he called me, and slapped his thigh and laughed out loud.'

Richard smiled to himself. His father would have said *Cubile*, the Latin for Couch.

'Was he on his own?' he asked.

Couch shook his head. 'No, there were others – an officer, and a couple of the men.'

'You say he was already on his horse – did he ride out then?'

'Yes, just after sunrise. He said goodbye to Mrs Collins, the housekeeper, and cracked a few jokes with the men. "Where are you going, sir?" I asked. "Tresillian," he replied, "to find the King's army," and just then little Harry Jenkins, do you remember him, the stableboy, scuttered into the yard and gives master a letter.'

'A letter? Who from?'

'I've no idea. Your father read it, tucked it into his breast, then gave the call to move out.'

'Did they have any packhorses with them? Or any cases? Chests?'

Couch pursed his lips. 'Not that I remember. Travelling light now, one of them said. They hoped to make good time.'

'I see.' In his mind, Richard could picture the little troop of men riding into the woods above the house, fog lying in the dips of the hills, sun just warming the air. So, they had got shot of the gold either before they arrived at Chynoon or by the time they left. He frowned. Was that what Fielding had said? He tried to remember.

Couch coughed and wiped his face with a grey greasy cloth. 'And you're staying at the manor now, master? Does the Colonel know who you are?'

'Of course not. If he knew I'd be hung as a spy.' Richard threw the old man a warning look. 'What is Moreton like, Henry? Where are all the old staff?'

Couch clutched the holly bush and dragged himself upright.

'Moreton dismissed them as soon as he arrived. Sent

them packing without a penny. That was the year of the King's execution.' He came closer so his breath landed in sour gasps on Richard's cheek. 'Listen, master, be careful.'

'How do you mean?'

Couch hesitated. His hands were trembling. 'He fought for Parliament in the wars, didn't he? Fought a lot, they say, one of Cromwell's right-hand men.'

'Then what's he doing here, in Cornwall?'

'They say he's in disgrace. There was a disagreement, or—'

The bell rang from the house, curiously harsh and metallic in the soft evening. Richard cursed. That was the bell for supper. He couldn't afford to be late. He patted Couch on the shoulder. 'Listen, it's good to see you, old friend. But not a word to anyone, you understand?'

Couch looked at him furtively. 'Of course not, master. I'll not forget. I'll not forget.' With that he turned and walked off through the trees as quickly as he could.

Richard was not looking forward to supper that evening, but it proved to be something of an anticlimax. When he arrived in the Great Hall, only William, Ursula and Stephen were there.

'I hear you have been admiring God's handiwork, Master Ferrers?' asked William Moreton.

Richard stared at him blankly. Stephen giggled under his breath.

'The countryside,' prompted Ursula. 'I told my husband you have been taking the air.' Something rubbed against the side of his ankle.

'I was admiring the sea,' replied Richard. The views are particularly fine from the cliffs.'

At that moment the door clicked open behind him

and he guessed – no, *sensed* – that Susannah had entered. Much to his annoyance, Richard felt his body tense. He did not turn round but kept his eyes fixed on his plate. Moreton smiled: 'Good evening, Miss Tremaine. You look radiant tonight.'

Susannah smiled archly and pulled up her chair. 'You are too kind, sir.' She did look radiant, thought Richard, almost grudgingly. Her face and neck still glowed from her ride, and her hair was filled with a deep, sparkling lustre. His skin tingled.

'The sea is very beautiful,' said Moreton, returning to Richard. 'Though sometimes beauty can mislead us from truth, can it not?' Moreton regarded him intently.

'What are you discussing?' asked Susannah brightly. 'Master Ferrers looks very serious. How like a merchant!'

'Master Ferrers was telling us how he delights in natural pleasures,' explained Ursula, and this time Richard distinctly felt a small, woman's foot stroking the side of his calf. He looked across at Ursula but her expression did not change.

'Indeed, my lady,' he replied coolly, 'provided they can be comfortably enjoyed.' He turned abruptly to Susannah. 'Did you enjoy your ride, Miss Tremaine?'

'No doubt better than your walk, Master Ferrers. I try to ride every day if I get the opportunity.'

'So do I!' agreed Ursula enthusiastically. The foot stroked him again, with remarkable delicacy.

Richard coughed. 'Are Dr Masters and his wife joining us?' he asked.

William Moreton informed him that Dr Masters was delayed in Truro and would not be back until the morning.

'And Oliver?' inquired Susannah.

Richard inconspicuously put his hand beneath the table and levered the foot away.

Ursula gave a little cry. 'He is expected later,' she said quickly and patted Stephen on the head. Stephen giggled and slouched in his chair.

This must have annoyed Moreton, for he suddenly barked: 'Tell the boy to sit up properly, woman!'

Defensively Ursula put an arm round Stephen. 'Sir, he is just a child.'

The boy blinked pathetically at his father as if he didn't understand the command.

'I don't give a damn!' roared Moreton. 'He can still sit like a son of mine!'

The room was suddenly very quiet. Next to him, Richard could feel Susannah tensing. Ursula lowered her gaze and dragged Stephen into an erect posture. The boy looked sullen and fiddled with his knife. Gradually the storm passed, and William's face relaxed into his normal expression.

'I was admiring the buildings behind the stables,' said Richard at last. 'You have obviously taken care with them. Are they for the servants?'

'They are for guests.' William gave Richard a hard look. 'Now, tell me, Master Ferrers, more about your father's operation in St Malo. It interests me.'

He said these last three words with such deliberateness that Richard was in no doubt of the implication. He suspects me, he thought. Richard took a deep sip from his glass.

'My father began shipping salt back in the thirties,' he began, 'when the pilchard trade increased. He soon saw the profits to be made from packing the salt at source. This reduced the cost of cooperage by a penny in the crown . . .' Richard's account was painfully boring and meticulous, and he talked with all the

84

enthusiasm and imagination he could muster about the different qualities of Breton salt, the profits per hundredweight, the fluctuations of the market, until eventually Susannah called out:

'Enough, sir! Enough! I am afraid you would send the angels to sleep.'

'I am sorry, my lady,' he said humbly. 'Perhaps too much business is bad for the digestion.'

'Would that Dr Masters were here,' she replied, with only the faintest smile. 'So that one of his sermons might whet our appetites.' She looked across, catching the understanding in Richard's eyes, and let her mouth caress the tip of her glass. His expression changed, and she felt a shiver of satisfaction run up her back. But then she was aware of the steely gaze of William Moreton and dropped her eyes to her meal. I am betrothed to his son, she reminded herself. I cannot, must not, be otherwise. It would be the death of us all.

When Richard tried to make conversation with her, Susannah deliberately ignored him. She felt relief when eventually he gave up and they ate their meal in silence, punctuated only by Ursula's oddly suggestive remarks and William Moreton's replies. She should have felt even more relief when Richard left immediately after the meal, yet she found her eyes straying after him, and excused herself as soon as she could from the Great Hall.

She knew she must return straight to her room. Anything else would be madness. But against every judgement, she found herself pausing on the stairs outside his room, her hand halfway to the door.

If I could talk to him, perhaps he will understand, she thought. She hesitated, feeling suddenly breathless. There was so much she wanted – *needed* – to tell him.

But then she heard a servant in the corridor below

and the sound brought her to her senses and she continued quickly up the stairs. She must be mad! She was playing with fire! Susannah reached her room and flung the door shut behind her. She leaned back against the wood panelling, feeling her heart race. She couldn't believe she'd been tempted like that. The less he knew, the better, for all their sakes. He would have to look after himself, just as she did.

Susannah crossed her room and stared out into the night. Guiltily she realised her real motive was not to warn him – that was only an excuse. There was something about him which reached into her soul. There was a fire in his eyes, and something else, a sense of sorrow or loss, that she could not explain. And it was this last quality, more than anything, which made her feel that of all men, he might just understand the memories that haunted her.

In his room, Richard lay on the bed, staring at the ceiling. He needed desperately to make sense of things. He had been in England less than two days but already his plans were in wild disarray. His head reeled.

Beside his bed William Moreton had left a large leather-bound Bible. Richard had not read the Book since his schooling but instinctively, he found himself picking it up. Moreton is having an influence on me after all, he thought. He turned to the first page. *In the beginning*, proclaimed the verse. By the buttery glow of the lamp, he read the opening of Genesis as if for the first time. He did not know why, but he found great solace in contemplating the order of the universe, and knowing that beneath everything there lay a pattern, a design. *In the beginning God created the heaven and the earth*. We may not understand, but we can trust, he thought, and then was dissatisfied. Where was the order in his life? What was he supposed to be doing?

There was so much he didn't understand.

Samuel Dowles' death haunted him. Who had killed him? Why had he died? Somehow Richard knew it was because of his arrival. But why exactly? And if so, should he still go to the meeting at Tregony? He flung the book down. What else could he do?

What was harder to understand was his feeling for Susannah. Again at supper he had felt himself irresistibly drawn to her. Why did he find her so . . . *desirable*? It was uncanny; she seemed wild, vivid, so unlike anyone he had ever met, yet he felt he had known her all his life.

And what of the others? William Moreton appeared to be a moody but devout man. But Ursula, on the other hand, had the morals of a whore . . . He shut his eyes. Why did Moreton tolerate such behaviour? Surely he knew? He remembered his host's words the day before, about his herbs: 'They can be enjoyed by all, but picked only by me, or else they will lose their bouquet.' Were those the words of a cuckold? Richard didn't know.

Finally, there remained the mystery of Michael Tremaine himself. Not for the first time, Richard felt that this mystery lay at the heart of all the others. According to Sir Ralph Fielding, Richard was sure, his father had ridden on alone after the attack, with the gold. But Couch said they were already travelling light when they left Chynoon that morning. What did happen to him? And where was the gold? If he had been killed with the money, wouldn't it have been found with the body? Again those strange Latin words came back to him: 'Let my son gather riches in yellow gold.'

Richard shook his head. His thoughts pursued themselves in circles for hours, but whichever way he looked at them, he felt no wiser. He longed to close his eyes and fall into a deep, numbing sleep, but he forced himself to stay awake until the house lay quiet and he was sure the others had retired for the night.

If he was to start looking for answers, there was no better time than now.

It was, he guessed, beyond midnight when, wearing only his nightshirt, he let himself into the corridor. Without a light, the passageway was impenetrably dark, and he waited until his eyes had cleared before making his way downstairs. No one slept on the ground floor here except for a few servants in the far south wing, so there was little chance of being over-heard. Nevertheless each crack or creak seemed to shout in the silence like a gunshot. He proceeded slowly, trying to remember the uneven boards and steps from his childhood adventures. But as a child he had been nimbler and quicker, he realised ruefully. By the time he reached the ground floor, his nightshirt was damp with sweat.

Downstairs the clock – his grandfather's – rocked quietly in it casing. A quarter past twelve. Warm scents of dinner and baking drifted up from the floor, clung to the tapestries. He brushed past them and into the Great Hall. Somehow in its cavernous space he felt strangely exposed, the blank void of the minstrels' gallery behind him seemed like an empty staring eye. A few embers glowed bloodily in the hearth. There was a sudden movement, a dry, light scratching, and two mice darted off the table in front of him. Richard jumped. His heart was racing and, not for the first time, he wondered at his wisdom for doing this. What, after all, was he hoping to find? And yet every sense told him that there was a secret here, screaming to be released.

On the far side of the Hall, he eased the door which led into the south wing. This was the oldest part of the house. The servants would be sleeping at the end of the corridor and Richard went slowly. His footsteps were muffled by the thick, low walls and he groped his way forward, running his fingers over the roughcast plaster until he came to the opening he wanted. Here stairs led down to the cellar. He peered into the gloom, sniffed the air. A damp, sour aroma crept up the steps and, in a moment of unreason, he was reminded of the smell in Samuel Dowles' house. Then he mastered his instincts and plunged down the stairs.

The steps were worn and slippery with age, and as he descended, Richard had the sense of a pool of blackness welling up to meet him. He was breathing very quietly, yet in the deathly silence at the bottom of the stairs, his breath sounded hoarse and loud like the soughing of the wind. He waited for a moment until his heart slowed, then placed one hand on the cellar door.

Locked.

The door rattled slightly on its hinges.

Then he heard it.

A dull, shifting sound, like the rubbing of sacks over flagstones, from beyond the cellar door. Richard stayed stock still. His ears strained, greedy for the slightest prick of sound. There was a moment's silence; he leant his head against the door. He heard stranger sounds then: the cold roar of the stones and the chill plink of water in a gully somewhere, but then that sound again, amplified now so it was like the grating of a saw through wood. There was definitely someone – or some*thing* – moving around in the cellar. Something crunched under his feet. He reached down – it felt like crisp grains of sand – and he licked his fingers. There was the unmistakable taste of the sea.

Somewhere above, a door opened abruptly with a clunk. He heard footsteps, heavy, purposeful.

Richard had a sudden picture of William Moreton stalking through the house towards him. If Moreton came down to the cellar, there was nowhere he could hide, for the stairs gave straight on to the cellar door. Frantically, Richard hurled himself up the steps.

He gained the top of the stairs, paused for a second, and realised the door from the Hall was already opening. He veered right and plunged farther down the corridor. Behind him the yellow light of a candle was seesawing back and forth in someone's hands.

The person made no sound and Richard guessed he hadn't been seen. He stumbled forward, blindly hoping to get out of sight before the person glimpsed the pale white shape of his nightshirt. Thankfully, his hands found the deep recess which let into one of the old storerooms and he pressed up against the cold oak door, not daring to breathe.

Waiting.

The person, whoever he was, seemed oblivious to all this. The light bobbed forward to the top of the cellar stairs, then Richard heard his feet slapping on the steps. There was the heavy jangle of keys and the click of the lock, and Richard knew the person had gone inside.

Richard allowed himself the luxury of a slow, deep breath before he cautiously made his way back along the corridor to the Hall. He crossed the Hall quickly and had put his hand to the far door when in one dreadful movement it flew open of its own accord.

He was face to face with William Moreton.

Moreton was fully dressed. The light from his lantern threw his face into heavy black lumps. They stared at each other, then after what seemed an eternity, Moreton spoke:

'Master Ferrers.' Each syllable was thick with suspicion. He brought the lantern forwards, threateningly.

'I'm sorry for startling you.' Richard smiled. 'I couldn't sleep. I was looking for something to drink.'

Moreton came closer. His eyes shone darkly.

'At night, Master Ferrers, my guests must keep their beds, do you understand?' Although his words were reasonable enough, there was something awful in Moreton's leaden tone and expression that made Richard for one blundering moment wonder if he would live to see the morrow. Then the sound of hooves rang outside. Horses were clattering into the courtyard. Moreton motioned for Richard to stay still and crossed quickly to the rear of the house.

'Ah.' Moreton was back, a faint smile on his face. 'It's my son, Oliver. He is returned.' He cast one final glance at Richard. 'We will talk no more of this. Go to your room, sir, and rest in peace.' He turned away.

Cursing himself silently, Richard went upstairs. Behind him he heard the bolts of the rear door being drawn and a man's voice calling a greeting.

Chapter Seven

HE WOKE THINKING OF SUSANNAH Tremaine. Rich chestnut hair. Her strong eyes were watching him, glinting, mocking and he had the sudden conviction that she was no more fooled by his play-acting than he was by hers. He rubbed his eyes with the base of his palms and sat up. Why should she suspect him? In the cool light of day, his fear seemed baseless, yet a vague, nameless anxiety nagged at the back of his mind. He tried to track it down, but nothing came, and screwing his eyes angrily, he hauled himself out of bed.

He poured water over his head from the ewer in the corner, and hoped it would wash his dreams away. It didn't.

Reluctantly he made his way downstairs. To his surprise, Dr Masters was already at the breakfast table.

'Good morning, Doctor. I thought you were staying in Truro.'

In the harsh morning light, Masters' face was livid and sullen. His two fists clutched a loaf. 'We returned late last night.' He wrenched the bread apart and lapsed into silence.

It must have been late indeed, thought Richard. Or else you never were in Truro. He remembered the figure going down to the cellar with the candle. Had that been the Doctor?

There was a bustle as Sarah Masters came in, followed by William and Ursula. Sarah gave her husband a deferential peck on the cheek, then sat down, nervously rearranging the pleats of her skirt. 'Good morn-

ing, Master Ferrers,' she said quietly, as if she were
risking her husband's displeasure. Richard nodded
politely.

Ursula seated herself opposite, and with foreboding
Richard wondered whether there would be a repeat of
last night's charade. Masters scowled at them all and
carried on tearing at his bread.

'It's a beautiful day, Master Ferrers,' said Ursula
enthusiastically. 'Will you take another of your jaunts
this morning?'

'I hope so.' Richard helped himself to a cup of warm
ale and avoided her gaze.

'I do so admire a man who enjoys nature,' she continued.

'Better for a man to lose the world and find his soul,'
interrupted Moreton. 'Is that not right, Doctor?'

Masters said nothing. But, astonishingly, he leaned
across to his wife and kissed her full on the mouth.
Nor was it any chaste peck as she had given him.
Sarah's lips parted and she began to kiss him passionately. No one else seemed at all perplexed by this and
carried on eating their breakfast.

Richard smirked to himself. Charles Stuart would be
more at home in the new England than he expected.

Eventually Masters released his wife. 'To take what
one holds dearest and sacrifice it for the Lord, is that
not true salvation?' he asked.

But Richard's thoughts were elsewhere. He suddenly
realised what had been nagging him since he woke.
Ursula's talk of nature had reminded him of what Susannah had said yesterday, when she returned from her
ride: 'How *romantic*, just like the son of a merchant.'
And then later, at supper: 'Master Ferrers looks very
serious. How like a merchant.' It was the light, mocking
way she said 'merchant'. He had thought she was being

bored, dismissive, but it was not that at all. She was saying, 'I know your part, you are playing it *so* well.'

Richard was so struck by this that he ignored the rest of the discussion and excused himself from the table. He needed fresh air. He needed to think. One thing was clear: if Susannah had somehow stumbled upon his true identity, he was in real, immediate danger. Could he trust her? Richard forced himself to be calm. There was only one thing to do. He must speak to her as soon as possible.

But what if she does know? he thought. What then? How will I stop her from telling? He knew there was a cold, ruthless answer to this problem which others – Sir Ralph Fielding perhaps, or even his own father – would not have shrunk from.

Richard crossed the yard and walked down through the fields. He waited until he was out of sight of the manor and then cut up to the left. Here the ground rose sharply, and he toiled upwards, his body suddenly heavy, until he reached the top and the wind greeted him with a cool, fresh blast.

Below him the manor house lay in its hollow. Beyond, on either side, were the copses of beech, bare and russet now, which in the spring would be a foamy mass of green. To the right, he could make out the stables, herb garden and orchard, and then the fields, still misty in the morning air. To the left of the house, the drive ran away and disappeared in tumbling hills. And far beyond, in the distance, the great flanks of Hensbarrow Downs, cold and bleak, rose up and met the sky. Behind him, and for as far as his eyes could take him, lay the sea, vast, empty, and splashed with sudden bursts of emerald and lime and olive where the sunlight glanced on the currents. The sea shivered and rippled in the sun, catching silver here, there, on the edge and lip of waves, and from the cliffs and beach below the crash and scramble of the waves came to him.

He would never forget this view. This is my country, he thought. He pressed his eyes over the landscape, taking in its slightest detail, the pinpricks of life – the white spots of cottages, the dim brown shapes of cattle, the sound of a horse calling in a neighbouring parish.

He did not know how long he waited. One hour? Two? But at last, when he was about to give up, his patience was rewarded. The main door of the stables was pulled back, and a sorrel mare was made ready, trotting and snorting in the morning air. Richard peered down. Susannah. There was no mistaking that flame of hair, or the full curves of her figure which the tight lines of her blue riding jacket did nothing to hide. She mounted quickly, easily, then guided the mare across the courtyard and towards the open fields and deep valleys to the west of the manor. Richard watched her go, and when he was sure of her route, set off down the hill after her.

Of course, a man on foot could not overtake someone on horseback. But the fields in that area were rough, uneven, and cut across frequent hills and dips so that the going was difficult for a horse, nor did Susannah hurry, but let the mare pick her own pace. Nevertheless, by the time Richard reached the base of the hill, Susannah had already disappeared into the valley beyond, and he was breathing hard.

The valley brimmed with trees, their branches flashing with cinnamon, nutmeg, silver, hanging with great drifts of ivy. The only sound was the twitch and rustle of birds – starlings, blackbirds – in the banks of tumbled leaves. Richard descended under the trees. After the rain, the ground was slippery, treacherous, and he wondered that she had taken a horse this way.

At the bottom a stream snaked between roots, opaque and muddy. He paused, not sure of the way, then spotted where her horse had scuffed the leaves coming down the hill. Across the stream, the hoofprints were clearly visible in the soft thick mud. He followed, quicker now, breaths sharp and fast, through the maze of trees and twisted clumps of holly, hawthorn, blackthorn. The wood was silent except for the swell and ebb of the wind in the trees and the odd pip-pipping of birds. Then, just ahead, he saw the sorrel mare, tethered to an old stump, nibbling patiently at a patch of grass.

Richard stopped behind a tree and caught his breath. What was she doing here? Then, about thirty feet away, he saw another horse, a sleek black stallion, also tethered.

He crept forward.

He saw now that between the two horses lay the opening of a small bowl-like hollow set in the side of the hill, ringed with beeches. He worked his way up the side of the bowl and peered over the edge.

Beneath him, Susannah Tremaine was standing with a tall raven-haired man. Her arms were stretched round his neck, pulling him close. They were kissing.

Richard felt a sudden and totally unexpected pang of emotion, not unlike jealousy, which he forced to the back of his mind. Was this why he had followed her, to spy on her lovemaking? he asked himself bitterly. He wished he could turn away, but found himself rooted to the spot, fascinated. A flock of starlings flashed through the trees.

They kissed for a long time until at last, breathlessly, they drew apart and Richard got his first view of the stranger. He was, thought Richard grudgingly, undeniably handsome. He had a lean, hooked nose, dark eyes, which Richard guessed were blue, and a strong, rakish jaw. His crown of thick black hair was curled and seemed to boil up on top of his head. Susannah rested her cheek on his shoulder and Richard saw him whisper something in her ear. It must have been a question, for she gave a slight shake of her head and clutched him more tightly.

But this answer seemed not to satisfy the man, for he asked her again, this time more loudly so Richard caught the last few words: '. . . prevent you?'

Susannah pulled away. Her eyes were wild, emotional, her cheeks flushed.

Richard gripped his hands into fists.

'No!' Her voice was shrill, wounded. 'I can't!'

The man laughed. A dark, jagged laugh, like the sound of water boiling over.

Then he hit her with a single sweep of his hand, as if he were knocking a fly away.

Susannah gave a short, broken scream and stumbled. The man stepped forwards, his hand raised.

But by then Richard had already vaulted over the lip of the hollow and was landing in the soft leaves beside her.

'What in the devil's—' The stranger stared at him furiously.

Richard said nothing. His heart was pounding.

'Richard, this is none of your business!' Susannah cried out angrily. This was just what she had feared. 'Richard! Don't!'

Richard scarcely heard her. His eyes were fixed on the man in front, gauging him for weaknesses. The man leered at him contemptuously. He was tall, as tall as Richard, slim and wiry. His eyes gleamed like a hawk's.

'You obviously know this lady?' The stranger's tone

was relaxed, mocking. Richard's head seethed. He would not be talked down to.

'You have no right to strike her.'

'No right!' The man shouted the words, suddenly furious. 'Who do you think you are?'

I am Richard Tremaine. The words were on the tip of his tongue, fighting to get out, but he checked himself, willed himself to be calm.

'What does it matter who I am?'

There was a cold flash as the man drew his sword and held it poised in front of him. He laughed, the same jagged laugh. 'Because a man without a sword does not dictate terms, sir!' He grinned at the blade. 'This is what I respect.'

Richard took a step back. He had not expected this.

'No! No!' Susannah panicked and pushed past him. This must not happen. Her words were a rush. 'He's unarmed. He didn't mean . . .'

The man looked at her intently. 'Do you think I care?'

Then abruptly he spun on his heel and stalked away. Richard watched him go, his fists still clenched.

'No, Oliver! Wait!'

But the man had already seized his horse's reins and swung himself into the saddle. With a final, furious glance, he plunged down through the trees towards the stream.

Richard realised with a jolt that he had just met Oliver Moreton.

Susannah turned back to him. There were tears in her eyes and her right cheek was inflamed and swollen.

'Are you all—'

'You had no right to interfere!' He now saw her tears were tears of anger, not pain. He might have been killed, she told herself. Killed, for what? A stupid, foolish gesture!

'He hit you—'

She didn't let him finish. 'You followed me, didn't you?' Something in her wild, crazed expression cut him to the very quick and he wanted to seize her, pull her soft, wounded face close to his. '*Followed* me!' She threw her hands in the air.

'It's not like that.' His voice failed him.

'Why? So you could spy on me, is that it?' She came closer. Her mouth was puffy, angry, her hair was streaming like flames. Her tight blue riding jacket was smudged with the dust of leaves and dirt and lichen. 'Do you get a certain excitement from this sort of thing, is that it?'

Her words touched a raw, angry nerve. 'Don't flatter yourself, woman!'

'Hah!' Susannah ran her fingers through her hair and glared at him, and, in spite of herself, she found herself enjoying the look in his eyes. Before she could stop herself, she was saying: 'You want me, don't you, Richard? Don't you, Master *Ferrers*?'

She said his name with such sharp, taunting irony it stung him like vinegar. So, she *does* know the truth, he realised with a jolt. He clenched his jaw angrily, his eyes blazing, and she felt her blood race. Her lips quivered in an almost-smile, relishing her power. 'Yes,' she said, easily reading his fears. 'I know your secret.'

He was tempted to say 'And I know yours,' but stopped himself. This secret knowledge was one of his few advantages. He stalled for time. 'You do?'

'So what are you then?' Her eyes were piercing. 'A spy?'

'Don't be ridiculous!' He laughed and sat down in the leaves. Keep your story simple, he told himself. 'I'm from Portsmouth. A clerk by trade. My master was smuggling salt and brandy.'

'And you thought Moreton would treat you better if you were the son of a legitimate merchant?' Susannah stared at him contemptuously. And then he saw her face relax and the tension seeped out of the air. 'So is that all you are, a clerk?'

He grinned. 'Are you going to tell?'

Susannah shook her head disdainfully. Her hair rippled like a shower of sparks.

'Why should I care what lies you tell?' She began to brush the dust from her jacket with perfect indifference, but then added: 'If Oliver knew, your life wouldn't be worth a prayer. Be careful. You shouldn't have challenged him.' Almost despite herself, she flashed a brief smile, so quick he almost missed it. 'Thank you, Richard.' Abruptly she walked to her horse and pulled herself into the saddle.

'Well?' she called provocatively. 'Are you going to take root there?' He grinned at her again, and his lean, tense face suddenly came alive.

Together they walked back through the valley to the manor, she on her horse, he at her side.

'Are you really going to marry him?' he asked at last.

Susannah did not reply. Her thoughts were more confused than she was prepared to admit. They forded the stream and climbed the other side. They had breasted the top and were just breaking into open fields when she said with all the calmness she could muster:

'Oliver and I have an understanding. We will be married in the spring.'

Richard studied her intently. Her voice was firm, but why did he sense something else beneath the surface: reluctance, regret, fear? Or was that only his own wishful thinking?

'What about your guardian? Does he approve?'

'And who is my guardian? Don't you know?' She

laughed bleakly. 'William Moreton, that's who.' She registered the change in his face, then continued: 'The County Committee sequestrated the estate because we couldn't pay their fines. Moreton undertook to settle the debts if they released me into his wardship. You see, with the rest of my family dead, I'm the sole heir.'

Richard stared at her.

'What, you mean you own Chynoon?'

'In theory, yes.' A small smile spread across her face. 'Moreton has leased it from the Committee until we marry.'

'But I have heard you had a brother, Richard Tremaine. Isn't he the real heir?'

'Richard?' She looked at him sceptically. 'Richard was a delinquent, like my father. He died at sea when he fled to France.'

A delinquent – the old term of abuse. He paused: 'I take it you are no admirer of Charles Stuart?'

She shook her head. 'The once and future king? Who *is*? My father was a fool!'

Richard felt the blood rush to his head. 'So,' he asked sharply, 'you've sold your birthright to Moreton, is that it?'

It was a thoughtless question. Susannah flushed angrily. 'How dare you! I will be very happy with Oliver!'

'I'm sorry—' he began. But with a sharp flick of her crop, she cantered across the field to Chynoon.

Richard cursed, and raced after her. His temper would be the death of him. He ran across the drive and around the side of the manor.

'Whoreson! Bastard!'

Four boys were fighting on the lawn beside the herb garden. The smallest, a scraggly lad of eight or nine years old, was lying on the ground, while the others pounced on top of him, scratching, poking, pulling his hair. Richard ignored them. Susannah was just dismounting by the stable doors, tossing her hair in the breeze. He marched towards her, intent on cutting her off. Behind him, the boy wailed and screamed.

'Susannah! I have to speak with you—'

'I think you have said enough.' Her skin was flushed, angry. She forced herself to avoid his gaze, and marched towards the house.

'Please!' They had reached the rear door, and she turned abruptly. Her eyes were raw and tender and dazzling. For one impetuous instant, Richard wanted to throw his arms round her.

'Don't worry, *sir*.' Her voice blazed with sarcasm. 'Can't you trust a poor girl like me with your precious secret?' And then she tugged at the door and rushed inside.

'Bastard! Bastard!'

Across the yard, one of the boys had grabbed a fistful of their victim's hair and yanked it out in a great tawny clump. 'Whoreson!' The others pinned him down and laughed merrily.

Richard roared at them. 'Leave the boy alone!' He took two steps towards them, fists raised, and the boys scattered like a shoal of fish.

Damn her! he thought. Damn *me*! The most desirable woman I have ever met is engaged to Oliver Moreton.

Chapter Eight

IT WAS EARLY AFTERNOON BY THE time he reached Rebecca's cottage, and shadows already stretched across the fields. He did not know why he was here, other than that he craved a sense of peace and here, of all places, he would find it. He could talk to her, and she would listen, and perhaps she would understand. He knocked lightly on the door. There was no reply. His heart sank.

Maybe she would soon be back.

Richard unlatched the door and went in. The shutters cast the cottage into darkness and it took his eyes a while to adapt. Clothes lay on the bed. Pans and three plates sat unwashed on the serving plank as if Elizabeth and Rebecca had left quickly. Who was the third person who had shared their meal? he wondered idly. Then he realised that the clothes in the mattress were a man's jacket and breeches. He stared at them, strangely curious. Whose were they? Did Rebecca have a lover? Something very like resentment passed through his mind, but he shook it away. Impatiently he turned and stalked out of the cottage. If Rebecca wasn't here, he decided, he would go and find her.

For want of a better plan, he retraced the route they had taken from Porthcarrick the previous day, and it wasn't long before he found himself looking down once more on the village.

Today it was a hive of industry and the knock and clang of iron on timber rose up from the valley to greet him. A dozen or so men were sawing and trimming timbers in the clearing above the beach. Others heaved the planks into the boathouses. Women sat on the steps of their cottages, mending nets and chattering.

Richard stood and watched the scene for some minutes. The planks the men were cutting were the dark colour of seasoned boating timber, then there was a flash of red and gold and he recognised with a shock Jean Perret's painted nameplate.

The villagers were dismembering the remains of the *Marguerite*.

At that moment Richard caught sight of Rebecca coming out of the inn. She was talking to a tall, solidly built fellow with a black shovel of a beard. Then she waved him farewell and followed the path up the valley towards where Richard stood.

Richard noted that her head seemed bowed, and her movements tired. But as soon as she saw him, Rebecca quickened her pace and was smiling by the time she reached the top.

'Richard! I didn't think I'd see you again!' She gave him a happy, but pointed look, which he ignored.

'I guessed you'd be here. What are you doing?' he asked.

'Nothing much.' She reached for his hands and kissed him on the cheek. With the wind shaking his hair like a shower of brass, he had a wild, hunted look, she thought, and squeezed his hands tightly. 'It's good to see you, Richard.'

He gave a crooked smile. It was good to see her as well. He felt a profound sense of ease in her presence.

'I wanted someone to talk to, Beckie,' he explained. 'After all, you're the only person I can trust.' But even as he said this, he felt himself hesitating. After all these years, how well did he really know her? She had changed so much.

Rebecca saw him falter. Just talk, is that all? she thought, and wished she had the courage to confront him, there and then, with her feelings. But what good would it do? If he felt anything for me, wouldn't he say so? she told herself. I would only demean myself in front of him. And I won't do that, for any man. Instead she set her mouth in a harder line than came naturally.

'Are you sure you *can* trust me?' she replied sharply. 'The old loyalties no longer matter, Richard. I won't protect you just because you're the master's son.'

'I know that,' he answered quietly. 'But you know what I mean, don't you?'

Yes, she thought. I know what you assume. And this did nothing to soften her mouth.

They set off up the hill towards the cottage.

'The timber in the village,' he began. 'Do you know where they got it from?'

She shrugged. 'It was washed ashore from the storm, I suppose. Why?'

'It's the remains of the ship which brought me over,' he told her. 'It was wrecked.'

She nodded sympathetically. 'Once she ran aground she was fair game, you know that. Moreton gave them permission to take what they could. Anyway,' she took a fresh breath, 'how are you? How goes the royal plot?'

He scowled. 'Slowly. I just have to lie low and be patient.'

'That must be hard,' she commented wryly.

'Why do you say that?'

'Come on, Richard!' Now her tone was teasing. 'You've been an impatient, impetuous fool ever since I've known you!' Richard jumped at her, laughing, and she skipped away from him.

'And you were always so sensible, Beckie!'

The jibe struck her more sharply than he intended. Not as sensible as I ought to be, she thought, or else I wouldn't have waited for you, Richard Tremaine. 'Always make a joke, don't you!' she replied, as if she half meant it.

'What else can I do, Beckie? Look at the King of England! Look at me! Look at my clothes!' He tugged theatrically at his Puritan's robes, then said with a smirk: 'And whose were those gentleman's clothes lying around in your cottage?'

Rebecca was suddenly furious.

'What right have you got to go through my belongings?' she demanded.

'They were lying on your bed!' he replied. 'There's nothing to be ashamed of, Beckie! You're not married!'

Her eyes flashed, then she spun round and marched off up the hill. Richard swore and – she noted with some satisfaction – ran after her.

'It's not funny, Richard!'

'I didn't think it would upset you.'

'Why? Because you don't think I have any self-respect?' she snapped.

'Come on, Beckie, let's not argue.' He touched her on the shoulder.

'All right,' she pouted. 'I'm not a girl, Richard. I don't get hurt by cheap jibes.'

He was tempted to disagree with her, but thought better of it. They walked in silence for a while, listening to the birds in the late afternoon air and the rustle of the trees.

'It will be evening soon,' he said. 'The people at the manor will wonder where I've got to.'

'What do you think of the Moretons, Richard?' she asked seriously. 'Have you noticed anything *strange* about them?'

He let out a burst of laughter. 'You're sounding very mysterious!'

She ignored him. 'No,' she persisted. 'Listen! I tried to tell you yesterday. People are talking.'

'What about?'

'People are saying William Moreton is *evil*.'

She used the word in such a way that in spite of himself, he felt a chill enter his bones.

'People say that old Sir Anthony has come back from the damned,' she continued.

Sir Anthony Tremaine, my grandfather, Richard thought scathingly. Sir Anthony the Devil, as he was still remembered by the old folk.

'Sir Anthony?' His voice was prickly. 'That old wives' tale!'

'I know, I know,' she agreed, as if she were embarrassed herself. 'But they have a point, Richard. Moreton keeps strange friends. People who travel by night. And there's more besides. He's used several of the servants cruelly. He's thrown people out of their homes. Just like your grandfather,' she added pointedly.

Richard said nothing.

'And there's been talk they've seen the wish-hound again.'

'That's impossible,' he said. 'You know that's a lie!'

'Adam Pett saw it last week.' Her eyes were dark, earnest. 'He was coming back through the fields and he saw it running across the downs, as black as the devil!'

Richard felt something dark stir within him.

'The wish-hound,' he muttered. It couldn't be.

When his grandfather, Sir Anthony, was alive he kept a pack of hounds which would roam wild over the hills with no respect for the property or livestock of his tenants. Rumour had it that on the night Sir Anthony died, a monstrous black hound appeared and was heard baying outside the house. Calling Sir Anthony to Hell, said his nurse. He remembered as a child how the villagers had claimed the wish-hound had been seen since. And always evil came with it. He shook his head.

'Everyone knows it's just nonsense,' he said out loud. 'The wish-hound is a creature of myth. It was probably one of Moreton's dogs he saw.' He caught her gaze. 'You think I should leave the manor, don't you?'

'Yes,' she said. 'Before it's too late, Richard!'

He smiled derisively. 'So you're trying to scare me with old wives' tales and those lies about my grandfather?'

'No! I'm just telling you what people—'

'Do you think I enjoy staying there?' A bubble seemed to burst inside his head. 'Seeing some Roundhead lording it over my father's house? Who are you to tell me about it?'

'No one,' she replied bitterly. 'No one at all.'

'I won't leave,' he continued. 'Why shouldn't I stay, for the time being?'

'I didn't mean to upset you, Richard.'

He was silent for a moment, then: 'I've got to go, Beckie. They'll be missing me.'

She felt the tears pricking her eyes. I won't apologise, she thought stubbornly. Not after what he's said.

'Will I see you again?' she asked.

He was going to say no, that wouldn't be wise, but there was something in her eyes which made him stop, something which reminded him of different times.

He sighed. 'I'll come tomorrow at three or four o'clock, if I can.' So the chains of the past bind us, he thought, when everything in the present has changed.

Rebecca stood watching him go, a tall, strong figure,

moving quickly and aggressively away over the field. From his bearing today she would never have recognised the hopeful young man who had once courted her with poetry and wild flowers.

When she got back to the cottage, Elizabeth was there. She guessed what the matter was as soon as she saw her daughter's tight-lipped face.

'No good can come of that boy,' she said.

'It's all right for you to say that,' replied Rebecca sulkily. 'But he meant everything to me.'

Elizabeth snorted. 'I told you, you had best forget him. It was just a dream, Beckie. Can't you see he thinks of no one but himself? Just like his father.'

Rebecca sat down on the edge of the mattress and rested her chin on her hands. 'I wish my father was here,' she whispered. 'He'd know what to do.'

Elizabeth clucked her tongue. 'You're only saying that because you know he's always liked the boy, aren't you?'

Rebecca said nothing but sat still as a tear rolled slowly down her cheek. In spite of herself, an old line of poetry came to her, which she could not place, other than to remember Richard whispering it, many years ago: *Sunt lacrimae rerum et mentem mortalia tangunt* – There are tears in our affairs and their mortality touches the heart.

Chapter Nine

BY THE TIME RICHARD REACHED Chynoon, he felt quiet and subdued. He was thankful that no one saw him or stopped him as he crossed the yard and went into the house. Nevertheless, he only entered the sanctuary of his bedroom with reluctance. The bare white walls seemed bleak and comfortless, and a vague, indistinct melancholy hung over him. What am I doing here? he asked himself. What do I really hope to achieve?

The King seemed far away now, remote and unreal. Cologne was a city of dreams. And here he was, lodging in his father's house under an assumed name, obsessed with Susannah Tremaine. *Obsessed?* The word had sprung into his mind. He examined it again, as he might a strange sharp stone he had plucked from a stream. Her face flashed before him, half twisted away, eyes dazzling. Was that why he was staying here? To be with her?

He sank down heavily on the bed, his head on his arms. And what about trust? Rebecca had warned him he could trust no one – surely he could trust Susannah least of all? Yet when he was with her, he just knew implicitly that he could. He rubbed his face in his hands, as one who wakes, bleary-eyed, from a deep and terrible sleep.

Instinctively, he picked up the Bible from the chair next to his bed, and as he did, a thin sheet of lilac paper fell out. It had been slipped next to his bookmark.

He examined it carefully.

It was a single sheet, folded once in the middle. Its message was simple: 'Meet me after dinner in the orchard.'

His eyes leaped over the words. Susannah! She must have hidden it here.

Dropping the note on his bed he jumped to his feet and went up the stairs to her chambers. He waited outside for an instant, gathering his breath, then tapped lightly.

'Yes?' Susannah opened her door only a fraction and peered out. Her hair was still in disarray from the ride, and she had a changing robe loosely wrapped over her shoulders. He felt a sudden rush of excitement, and hid this behind a flamboyant smile: 'I would be delighted with your company later on, my lady.'

'You would?' Her face was blank and strangely pure. 'I'm sorry?'

Richard hesitated. Perhaps this was a mistake. He should have been content to play the assignation by her rules. 'This evening,' he prompted. 'In the orchard.'

Susannah's forehead knotted into a question: 'No, Richard, I don't think so.'

Richard felt as if he had suddenly stepped out on to emptiness. What if the note wasn't from her? He tried to avoid her gaze, and found himself staring at the cord of her robe, where it clung to her waist.

'I see.' His voice was barely more than a whisper. 'My apologies, Miss Tremaine.' He stepped back from the door.

'That's all right,' she answered oddly. 'You do understand, don't you?' He thought for a moment that there was a *look* in her eyes, then her door swung shut.

Richard wandered back to his room in a daze. Damnation! How could he be so stupid? He closed his door behind him and leaned against it with his eyes shut, cursing himself until at last he stood up and went back to the bed.

But the note was gone.

He peered under the coverlet, in the cracks between the floorboards, even behind the bolster and among the sheets, but there was no mistake.

Who could have taken it?

He had only been gone a few minutes. There had been no one on the stairs or in the corridor. He opened the Bible, just in case he had slipped it back inside, and was struck by something he had not noticed before, which clung to the pages: the slight scent of oranges. He sniffed again, and was reminded of his encounter with Ursula Moreton in the corridor, and the ripe feel of her body close to his.

Was it this discovery, or Susannah's cool rejection of his advances, which helped him decide his mind? Or had Rebecca's entreaties finally persuaded him? Whatever the reason, Richard suddenly felt he no longer had a place here. He must leave Chynoon as soon as he could.

Dinner was at four o'clock that afternoon. When Richard got to the Hall, the others were already there. He saw Susannah from behind, her hair tumbling over her fine, strong shoulders, and realised she was sitting next to Oliver Moreton, with whom she was so engrossed in conversation that she did not seem to notice him until William Moreton announced: 'Ah, Master Ferrers! Greetings!'

At this, Oliver broke off from Susannah in mid-sentence and turned angrily towards him.

'Master Ferrers, this is my son, Oliver.' William Moreton extended a huge hand in Oliver's direction.

Richard nodded politely. 'We met while riding today.'

He paused, then added: 'I apologise for not recognising you at the time, sir.'

Oliver's face looked as if someone had poured soiled water over it. 'We will have to get to know each other better, sir,' he replied grimly.

Richard met his gaze calmly. 'The pleasure will be mine.'

William Moreton appeared not to notice this interchange. 'And this,' he continued, indicating a thin-lipped man on the other side of Susannah, 'is an acquaintance of Oliver's: Mr Hugh Lovelace.'

Richard nodded in acknowledgement. Hugh Lovelace was morose and thin-lipped and wore his black hair in a severe, straight cut. 'You are visiting these parts, Mr Lovelace?'

Lovelace managed a smile. 'Only for a season.' His accent was brusque and dry. Richard pulled up a chair.

'I can hear you are from London?'

Lovelace coughed somewhat self-importantly. 'I perform some clerical duties for the government.'

'Master Ferrers is from Brittany,' interrupted William Moreton. 'The sea spat him out on our coast, two days ago.'

'Yes. And Colonel Moreton has very kindly offered me hospitality.' Richard looked up from his bowl. 'I hope to be leaving you soon if that is agreeable. You have already been more than generous, and—'

'Nonsense!' William Moreton perhaps spoke more loudly than he intended, and the other conversation around the table came to an abrupt halt. He gathered himself and smiled. 'Does not the Lord say: "For I was an hungered, and ye gave me meat: I was thirsty, and ye gave me drink: I was a stranger and ye took me in." ' His bald head shone in the candlelight, so that for a moment it seemed he was crowned with flames.

Then he reached forward and grabbed one of the loaves on the table and passed it to Richard.

Richard self-consciously took it and broke a piece off. Oliver glowered at him.

'You are welcome,' continued William, 'for as long as I am master of Chynoon. I won't hear of you leaving until at least the first week of November. Is that not so, beloved?' He laid a hand heavily on Ursula's shoulder and with the tips of his fingers caressed the tender skin of her throat.

'You are indeed most welcome, sir.' Ursula smiled at him suggestively and again Richard was reminded of her firm, warm body, scented with the juice of oranges.

'I have already taken *note* of your welcome, my lady,' he replied pointedly, and Ursula dropped her eyes quickly to her lap. It was as good as a confession that the lilac note had been hers. He glanced at Susannah, but Susannah held her back to him and he realised with a stab that she was talking to Oliver once more.

At that moment the door swung open and two men entered. They were clad in black and, from the mud splashed over their cloaks, had obviously just arrived. They marched across the Hall, saluting briskly.

'Sir, I am sorry we are late. The roads were passing bad.' The first man wore a proofed breastplate which he unbuckled as he walked. William introduced him as Captain Piers Standish, commander of the garrison at Fowey. He was a tall, gaunt figure with a crisp black moustache. The second man was older, and heavier, with a slightly swollen face. 'And this is Gregory Clement,' announced William, 'formerly Member of Parliament for Tregony.'

Both men took their seats, Standish unslinging his breastplate, flinging his riding gloves on to the table beside him, and slapping his hands together.

'Damn, it is cold out!' he declared, and reached for the wine.

William regarded him impassively. 'You have at least arrived in time for Dr Masters' address,' he replied. 'We missed you yesterday, Doctor!'

Dr Masters rose to his feet, the muscles in his left cheek twitching slightly in the candlelight.

'Yes. Tonight I take as my text those words from the first epistle of the apostle John.' He paused dramatically, and the Hall fell silent. Then he recited from memory: ' "He that committeth sin is of the devil; for the devil sinneth from the beginning. For this purpose the Son of God was manifested, that he might destroy the works of the devil. Whosoever is born of God doth not commit sin; for his seed remaineth in him; and he cannot sin, because he is born of God." '

The logs crackled on the hearth.

' "Whosoever is born of God doth not commit sin",' the Doctor repeated slowly, as if the words were being chewed over in his mouth. 'What does this mean? Does it mean that we can do no wrong? Out of the question! For many who were called have been lost, have they not? Many of our dearest friends, the fruits of our bosoms and loins, are now cast into hellfire and weep for their transgressions, do they not?' His gaze raked the assembly. 'How many of us know that in their hearts lies not the seed of righteousness but the gnawing of the worm of evil? Yes! We present a sweet and honeyed face to the world, but inside, what is there but the seething of the evil one? Falsity! Lies and pretence! Lies all!'

Richard stared down at his plate and snapped his bread briskly between his fingers. Susannah had fallen very still. Masters was breathing hard as if he had run a great race or bore up a huge weight.

'No!' His voice filled the Hall, boomed from the ceiling. 'Of course we can sin, of course. But only if we do not give our very souls to our cause. The devil can devour what is ours, not the Lord's. If we give all to the Lord as the good apostle says, what can there be left for corruption? How then can we be destroyed? Yet so often in our hearts there lurks the desire for self. Self! Often we desire to clutch to us some silly private thing, and in so doing clutch the very worm to our breasts! No, what are we called to do? To give up what we hold most dear, that we may love the more!' He glanced quickly at his wife, who sat, head bowed, candlelight picking out the soft curve of her neck. 'Abandon our loves!' he roared. 'Enslave ourselves to the cause of righteousness. And then we cannot – cannot – sin!'

He sat down heavily.

'Amen! Amen!' Hugh Lovelace's eyes were shining with excitement.

'Amen! Amen!' Now the others were joining in. Captain Standish grinned wolfishly and slapped the table. William Moreton banged his wine glass in unison. 'You speak from the very soul, Doctor.'

Suddenly Ursula staggered to her feet. Her hand clutched the edge of the table. 'What is it, Mama?' Stephen Moreton leapt from his chair.

'Sit down, boy!' William bellowed. Stephen hesitated and then burst into tears.

'William, please don't.' Ursula pulled Stephen to her and hugged his face into her dress. 'I am just . . . not well, that is all.' She smiled palely at the guests. 'Please, will you excuse me?'

She glanced at Richard and for an instant caught his eye.

'Of course, beloved.' William rose from the table and

kissed her chastely on the forehead. 'Stephen, accompany your mother to her room.'

'Yes, sir.' Stephen dutifully crept after her.

'How do you enjoy Dr Masters' preaching, Master Ferrers?' Oliver's voice was sharp, scathing. Next to him, Susannah appeared to be examining her plate intently. Even so, she could not entirely suppress the shiver which ran through her.

'In truth, he is very moving,' Richard replied evenly. He stared back at Oliver and then turned slowly towards the Doctor. 'Where did you learn your letters, sir?'

'In the Lord's army,' Masters answered. His fingers caressed his wife's hand. 'Under Colonel Moreton.'

Moreton's stony face was lit by a slight smile. 'Do you remember that night before Preston, Doctor?'

'Yes. And Drogheda too.' The Doctor was surprisingly quiet. Richard had known men who had fought against Cromwell at Preston and escaped. But none had escaped from Drogheda. Richard turned to Susannah pointedly: 'And you, Miss Tremaine, you were at the siege of Lembury. What do you remember of the army of the righteous? How did they treat the vanquished?'

Her face paled, but her voice was raw and inflamed. 'They raped all the serving girls. With pleasure, sir.' *How dare you ask me this?* she was thinking.

Richard understood. *Is this what I want?* he thought. *To make her hate me?*

'It was war,' commented Captain Standish. 'These things happen.' He refilled his glass with relish.

Richard was about to say something else, when he was stunned by Dr Masters' reply.

'So suffer all the whores of Babylon. Did they not already give themselves to the Usurper?' Masters' voice was proud, indignant.

'The Usurper?'

'Yes.' Masters stared at him fiercely. 'Charles Stuart and all his brood who usurped the Kingship of Heaven. Am I not right, sir?'

Richard stared at him. How could these men talk like this when Oliver Cromwell had himself usurped the throne of England? He clenched his jaws. 'Certainly,' he replied as levelly as he could, 'King Charles wanted too much power.'

'He was a man of blood!' Masters jutted his head towards him. 'Bathed in the blood of innocents. The innocent lambs who lay down on the fields of England while his licentious lions feasted on their flesh.'

'Dr Masters!' Richard stopped himself.

'What's the matter?' asked Oliver Moreton loudly. 'Are you an admirer of Charles Stuart, sir?'

Suddenly all eyes were on him. The room was roaring with tension.

'Of course not.' Richard breathed deeply. 'I was merely struck by the Doctor's turn of phrase. I had not heard the royalists described as licentious lions before.'

'My words are inspired, sir!' replied Masters.

'Yes, indeed.' Richard smiled stiffly, and gradually the atmosphere around the table eased. Piers Standish gave Richard a knowing look and drained his glass.

Susannah touched Oliver on the arm.

'Master Ferrers often speaks before he thinks, Oliver.'

Richard resented her intrusion. This is a question of my honour, he thought, not yours. But her words did nothing to assuage Oliver's feelings. He leaned forward.

'Then he had better be careful. Perhaps he will find he is like the man who ran into the lion's den thinking to escape the storm.'

*

It was late evening when Richard managed to excuse himself from the Hall and make his way outside. For the rest of the meal, Susannah had studiously avoided his gaze. What was it? Was she embarrassed to be seen with Oliver? he thought bitterly. Her fiancé? In the orchard, shadows hooded the trees, smothered the grass. Somewhere someone was burning fresh wood and he sucked the resinous tang into his lungs. Why is it, he thought, that on autumn evenings the smell of firewood is always so agreeable? He had expected Ursula to be waiting for him already and he was surprised to find the orchard empty. Had he not been so curious, he would have felt relieved.

He sighed and strolled beneath the trees. He could remember playing here with his sister – his real sister – when they were still children. Dropping stones into the well and waiting for the telltale splash ... Where was she now? Was she, like his parents, also dead? He bowed his head.

In the middle of the orchard stood a sundial. The sun had already sunk behind the house, but even so he walked to it, and ran his finger over its face. It was engraved with an elaborate pattern of apples and pomegranates. His father had designed this himself, together with the verse which ran round its rim: 'Stranger, only Heracles may seize The apples of th' Hesperides.' By the side of the dial, there lay a late apple, crisp, inviting. Richard picked it up and almost immediately dropped it: the side which had rested on the ground, the hidden side, was a mess of putrid flesh.

'All things can know corruption, can they not?'

He was startled by the voice. Dr Masters was standing over him. Richard had not heard his approach.

'Doctor, what brings you out of doors?'

'What brings you?' Masters' beady eyes glinted.

Richard wiped his hands on his breeches. 'I desired fresh air.'

'Many damp humours creep up from the earth at night,' Masters warned. 'Perhaps you would like to stroll and talk for a while?'

Richard found the prospect of such a diversion frankly horrifying. He smiled politely. 'Thank you, but no. I was just returning inside.'

The Doctor scratched his scrubby hair and bowed. 'As you wish.'

Richard strolled briskly back to the manor. Why had Ursula not met him?

'Ho! Master Ferrers!'

The voice was loud, angry, and Richard recognised with a sinking feeling Oliver Moreton. Oliver strode over from the stables and intercepted him before he reached the door. He was stripped of his doublet and his white shirt revealed a powerful but wiry physique.

'I am glad I have found you, Master Ferrers,' he began, but he was not smiling.

'Sir,' Richard gritted his teeth, 'I have already apologised for our misunderstanding. It was my mistake.'

'Mistake be damned!' Oliver Moreton smacked his hands together. 'Do you think I care for your mistakes? I would have done for you there and then if you'd been armed. Come with me now, and we'll settle this like gentlemen.'

Richard replied very calmly: 'If I thought you had a genuine argument with me, nothing would give me greater pleasure. But I have no desire to kill the son and heir of my host.'

Oliver stared as if he had just been slapped in the face, and stepped forwards. Richard thought for a moment they were going to come to blows, and stood ready, feeling the muscles tense along his arms. But Oliver checked himself. Their eyes met.

'Master Ferrers, I will have satisfaction.' His words were icily calm.

Then he spat in Richard's face.

'Oliver! No!' Susannah had come out of the house and she ran across the yard to clutch her fiancé. 'No!'

Oliver grinned.

Richard's face did not change, but he felt his self-control evaporate in an instant.

'As you wish,' he replied. 'Right now, you say?' He flicked the spittle off his face. His body was kicking with anger.

'No! Don't!' Susannah's voice was shrill, imploring. She tugged at Oliver, but he moved her aside, his face crackling with a smile: 'So the merchant's son is ready, is he?'

He strode towards the stables. Richard followed him leisurely.

'Richard, this is madness!' said Susannah. She felt totally powerless to intervene and hated herself. This was not supposed to happen. She had tried so hard, in a hundred ways she could never admit to him, to keep this from happening.

'I know,' he replied.

'But he'll kill you!'

Now it was Richard's turn to smile. 'Over my dead body, Susannah.' He took off his jacket and slung it over his shoulder, just as Oliver emerged from the stables clutching a pair of swords. Behind him stood two stablehands, their arms crossed solemnly over their chests, but their faces betraying their excitement at watching their master teach his guest a lesson. Richard ignored them.

'Here, sir,' said Oliver contemptuously. 'You choose.'

Richard took the first blade and tried it in the air. Woolwich steel, he guessed, and felt its weight in his palm. Oliver was studying him carefully.

'So,' asked Richard casually, 'if I were to apologise to you now, in front of the lady, would you call off this fight?'

'Why should I?' he gloated. 'For a guest you seem remarkably full of yourself, sir. But,' he cast a softer glance at Susannah, 'for the sake of the lady, I would accept your apology.'

'In that case,' replied Richard, 'you can be sure you will get none.' He registered the shock of surprise in Oliver's face. One of the stablehands nudged the other and winked. They were enjoying this. Good. 'Now,' he continued, 'are you sure you want to fight here, in sight of the house?'

Oliver licked his lips. 'Yes,' he muttered angrily. 'Why not?'

Richard took a step back and steadied himself, feeling the ground beneath him, taking his balance. Oliver did the same. They brought their swords down so that the tips almost touched.

Susannah glanced from one to the other, and then she suddenly hitched up her skirts and ran back across the yard to the house.

Richard did not watch her go. His entire concentration was focused on Oliver's dark blue eyes. The sword in his hand, the air on his back, these were as nothing. All that mattered was the glint in Oliver's eyes.

Suddenly he saw Oliver's pupils flicker, and leapt to one side. His blade parried the lunge even as it was starting and turned the thrust easily, there was the sharp ring of blade on blade, then he sprang back, taking his weight on to his left foot, as Oliver grunted and thrust again. He shouldn't have done that, thought Richard, he's unbalancing himself, and he dropped to his right knee, letting the force of Oliver's attack carry him forwards. The steel passed within six inches of his right ear, and he felt Oliver's immense power in the sword, then he sprang to the right, knocking Oliver's arm wide. Oliver stumbled, swearing, and tried to recover his poise. Too late. Richard ducked forwards and brought his blade to rest on Oliver's windpipe.

The two men froze. They were both breathing heavily.

Richard stared into Oliver's eyes. 'Drop the sword,' he whispered. 'Gently.'

He could feel Oliver tensing the muscles in his arm and shoulder for a sudden attack, and jabbed his own sword deeper against the man's throat. 'Don't,' he advised. 'You're not quick enough!'

'Richard!'

Susannah's scream split the air. But it was the second voice which startled him: 'Drop the sword, Oliver!'

It was William Moreton.

Richard watched Oliver carefully as he slowly, reluctantly, unwrapped his fingers from the hilt and let his sword clatter to the ground. Then Richard also lowered his blade and stepped back. William Moreton was striding towards them, his face like thunder.

'What do you think you are doing?' he roared at Oliver. 'Think of our guests!'

'Sir, it was a question of honour,' retorted Oliver stiffly. 'The man had no right—'

William struck his son across the face with the flat of his hand. Oliver did not flinch. A thick syrup of blood ran down from his nose.

'I am sorry, Master Ferrers,' continued William. 'My

son has a young man's temper. He believes that justice can be settled with the sword.'

'Don't most people, sir?' replied Richard. He handed his sword to William.

'Yes,' agreed the older man. 'Our Lord Protector among them.'

Richard bowed politely. 'I am sorry for this incident, sir. I trust you will excuse me. I will retire for the night.'

'Of course. God bless your sleep, Master Ferrers.'

Oliver glared at him.

Richard turned to go. Susannah was standing a little way back, her hair streaming, her face deathly white.

'Miss Tremaine,' he said as a salute.

She mastered herself with dignity. 'I'm glad neither of you were hurt, sir. It was very foolish of you.'

Richard raised an eyebrow but said nothing, and walked back to the house. As he passed the kitchen, he was dimly aware of the white faces of the servants pressed against the window. Oliver would never forgive his humiliation, he thought grimly. But he was feeling too exhilarated from the duel to care.

He met Bridget on the stairs. She was carrying a large ewer of water.

'What's the matter, Bridget?' he asked, for she looked preoccupied. 'Don't worry, no one's hurt.'

'Oh, it's not that,' she said, as if seeing him for the first time. 'It's Mistress Ursula. She's caught a fever.'

So her performance at dinner had not been a sham, he thought.

'Is she all right?'

Bridget pursed her lips anxiously. 'It's a wicked fever, sir.'

When Richard woke it was dark in his room. He rubbed his eyes angrily and groped for the curtain. Then he realised it was still night. Someone was shouting, no, *screaming*, outside, in the corridor. He pitched out of bed and stumbled through the door. There was confusion and people running, shouting, different voices.

'Light! Light! Someone quieten her! Mary! Mary!'

The screams were virtually hysterical. Richard ran up the stairs and a serving-boy cannoned into him. He swore loudly and pushed the boy away. 'What's going on?'

But the boy just looked bewildered. 'I don't know, honest to God!'

'Aiaiaih!'

Richard shoved past him. Two serving girls were squatting over one of the older kitchen maids. 'Come on, Mary! Mary!' they were urging, their voices halfway between reassurance and panic. Then William Moreton was standing over them.

'What in God's name?' he was bellowing.

'Ai – ai!' The older woman, Mary, was making choking noises, as if something were throttling her. Her eyes bulged horribly.

'What in God's—' Dr Masters appeared at his side, then Oliver and Lovelace. Oliver stared fiercely at Richard. William bent down and brushed the two maids away as he would flies. He hauled Mary bodily to her feet and shook her.

Abruptly, she stopped crying.

Richard marvelled at Moreton's strength. Mary was a thickset woman, of fourteen, fifteen stone, he guessed. Yet Moreton had lifted her as if she were a small child dandling on his knee.

'Mary!' He spoke to her once.

'I saw it,' was all she said.

'What, Mary?' He peered into her face, searching her.

125

'The devil,' she answered, and then more firmly: 'I saw the devil.'

Richard heard one of the girls start whispering her prayers. The skin prickled on the back of his neck. Moreton regarded her calmly.

'Where did you see him, Mary?'

She emitted a soft sobbing sound.

'In the room with Mistress Ursula.'

A terrible hush had fallen over the group. Suddenly Susannah appeared, clutching a robe, behind William.

William's voice was very measured: 'Tell me exactly what you saw, Mary.'

Mary took a deep breath. 'I thought I'd take the mistress a posset to ease her fever. I didn't knock and when I opened the door . . .'

'Yes?'

'When I opened the door, I . . .' Mary hesitated again, then her words came in a sudden rush: 'He was standing over her, tall and wicked. When he saw me, he raised his head. His eyes were all aflame.'

'What did he look like, Mary?'

The woman shuddered as if she was about to be sick. 'He was a living shadow.'

One of the girls screamed, and Moreton frowned at her to be quiet. He touched Mary very tenderly on the cheek. 'Come,' he murmured, 'there is no devil here, Mary, let us see.' Gently, but firmly, he coaxed her forwards.

'No, Master,' she was pleading with him.

'Come.' He led her along the corridor towards Ursula's room. 'Dr Masters, will you accompany us?' Masters nodded grimly, and the rest followed after them. Richard felt a strange sense of dread as they stood outside Ursula's room. Mary was evidently terrified, and had only consented to be brought back here by her fear and respect for her master. Now Moreton was speaking to her quietly, and she was shaking, then he turned the handle, and the door swung open.

Mary shrieked, and one of the girls jumped like a cat. But then they realised it was a false alarm, and the room, apart from Ursula lying in the bed, a pale, white form, was empty. Moreton waved a candle about, and the darkness receded for a moment.

'See,' he announced. 'Nothing. Dr Masters, would you be good enough to attend my wife?'

Masters solemnly knelt by the bed and touched Ursula's forehead. Richard noticed that, despite all the uproar, Ursula appeared asleep and untroubled. Masters looked up, tight-lipped.

'The lady is not well, sir.'

Moreton released Mary into the care of the maids and crossed quickly to the bed. He bent down so that his lips grazed his wife's forehead. When he came up, his face was set in an impenetrable mask.

'Mary,' he said very quietly, 'I must ask you to overcome your fears. Mistress Ursula has the gravest need of you tonight.'

Everyone looked at him. But William Moreton said nothing else and walked slowly out of the room.

'Do you think it was the devil?' Richard heard the serving-boy say.

'Hold your tongue!' William Moreton sprang back and caught the boy by the throat. He smacked him against the wall. 'There was no devil, do you understand! This is a house of God!' He threw the boy to the ground. No one moved. 'Now,' he ordered, 'Mary, get to your mistress's side, and you' – pointing to Bridget – 'help her. The rest of you, apart from Dr Masters, get to your rooms!'

127

*

Richard woke as the six o'clock bell was sounding. He lay there, in the darkness, listening to the footsteps in the corridor. He had slept badly and his dreams had been haunted by the image of a man of living shadow pursuing him through dusty rooms and deserted halls. Eventually, hearing the sounds of more footsteps outside, and the servants muttering to each other in odd asides, he swung himself out of bed, splashed water on his face and neck, and dressed. The water felt oddly repellant and he scowled at the thumbnail of light creeping out from behind the morning clouds.

It was only when he entered the Great Hall that he realised something was different. The whole manor was drowned in a strange, eerie hush. The servants huddled together in corners, whispering, and no one had bothered to unshutter the windows, which gave the Hall a peculiar subterranean feel. Richard helped himself to bread and sat chewing mechanically until he could bear the silence no longer and addressed one of the serving-boys who was aimlessly prodding the fire.

'What's the matter? Why is everyone so quiet?'

The boy looked sheepish, then got up and left the room. Richard called after him, but to no avail. But at that moment Bridget came in. She too had a subdued expression.

'Ah, Bridget, do you know what's going on?'

She came close.

'Mistress Ursula passed away this morning, a little before five.'

Richard could hardly believe his ears.

'But why, what was wrong with her?'

Bridget shook her head dumbly. 'I don't know, sir. But the fever got worse all through the night. She was in terrible pain, sir, and vomiting dreadfully.' The look

on Bridget's face made no elaboration necessary. 'Just
after four, she grew very anxious and the master dismissed us. A little later, he came out, all ashen-faced,
and told us our mistress was with the blessed.'

'What? That was all?'

'Yes, sir.' Bridget kept her eyes lowered.

'What is it, Bridget? Is there something else?'

'Oh, sir, I'm so upset!' She burst into tears. Richard
put his arms round her and held her awkwardly. After
a while, Bridget mastered herself and sucked back her
tears and began to dry her eyes on her cuffs. 'I'm sorry,
sir. It's just all so sudden. And what Mary Bohago said
last night, about the devil, do you think it's true?'

'Of course not.' He offered her his handkerchief. But
privately he wished he could be more sure.

Suddenly there was a cry from above. It echoed down
through the minstrels' gallery. A high, terrible cry. Leaving Bridget in the Hall, Richard ran upstairs. The door
to Ursula's room had been flung open and inside there
was a frightful commotion. Stephen Moreton had flung
himself on to her bed and was frantically clawing at
her coverlet – it was he who was crying and screeching
so terribly – while Susannah and Sarah Masters tried
to restrain him.

'In God's name, what is the boy doing?' William
Moreton appeared at the door. Somehow he seemed
larger, as if grief had made him monstrous. His huge
frame blacked out the scene in the bedroom. 'Oliver!'
Oliver was at his side like a shadow. 'Get the boy away!'

Oliver stepped into the room and tore Stephen off
the bed in one brutal movement. Stephen screeched.

'Mama! Mama!'

Oliver manhandled him out of the room. As he
turned outside the door, he caught sight of Richard and
stopped for a second. His face blackened with a look

of such violent hatred that Richard felt he had been struck. Then Oliver jerked Stephen over his shoulder and was gone.

Richard waited in the corridor until William emerged from the room. Richard noticed he closed the door softly behind him as if Ursula were sleeping and he did not want to wake her.

'Colonel Moreton, please forgive me, I have only just heard.' Richard bowed solemnly.

William regarded him calmly. 'Though the loss of a loved one tears at the soul, Master Ferrers, it would be selfish of me to begrudge her heavenly crown.' With that he turned and went slowly down the corridor towards his chambers.

Richard was still watching him go when Ursula's door opened again and Susannah came out. She looked haggard, her face seemed unnaturally thin and pale.

'Susannah.'

Her eyes flickered in recognition and for a moment he thought he saw the real person in her face, then her mask returned and once more he saw the woman called Susannah Tremaine. 'No, Richard, not now.' She brushed past him, awkwardly, and stumbled towards her room.

That morning a terrible grief hung over the manor. Richard felt it settle on the chairs and tables and furniture like an invisible, velvety film of dust, clogging the air, clotting the conversation of everyone in the house. William Moreton stayed in his rooms all morning and Mary brought him food and drink. By the empty tray which Richard saw her taking back, he ate and drank well. Oliver Moreton and the other men were also absent. Richard was glad, for he had no desire to encounter Oliver at this time. Instead he spent the early

morning in fitful pacings across the courtyard. He had
hardly known Ursula, yet she had seemed such a
vibrant, vigorous person, he could not believe she had
been suddenly extinguished by one night's fever. Frequently, he brooded on the lilac note left in his Bible.
Had she written it? Almost certainly. Yet was it in any
way connected with her death? An odd, amorphous
guilt troubled him like the first intimation of rain.

Eventually, his wanderings brought him to the doors
of the stables. He peered into the gloom. In the crisp
October air, the stalls hummed with steam rising from
the mulch of straw and manure. One of the stableboys
was rubbing down a horse. He stopped and wiped his
brow when Richard approached.

'That was a pretty fight last night, with Master Moreton,' said the boy, grinning.

'It looked better than it was,' replied Richard.

The mare was a magnificent young bay, tall and muscular. Richard patted her appreciatively on the flank.
Her coat was damp with sweat. He was surprised, for
it was still early.

'I see someone's already been out?'

The stableboy looked thoughtful and then bent back
to his task with renewed vigour. Richard watched him
for a while then asked, more pointedly: 'Who was it?'

'I don't know.' The boy swiped the brush over her
flanks. 'Master told me to rub her down, that's all.'

'Perhaps someone went to fetch a minister?' Richard
suggested, but the boy shrugged and didn't look up.

Richard stayed watching for a few minutes more,
then wandered outside. Again, he felt uneasily that
something was not quite right, but what and why, he
could not say.

No one else was present for the midday meal, and

Richard ate in solitary state, faintly embarrassed that he was still able to continue his daily routine when everyone else seemed indisposed. After lunch, he felt suddenly, inexplicably angry with himself, and sought sanctuary in the library.

He had not expected Susannah to be there. She was standing by the window, silhouetted in a burst of light. She looked startled. He paused in the doorway, wondering whether he should go back, but, to his surprise, her lips puckered into a weak smile.

'No, don't go. Come in.'

He closed the door quietly behind him. 'Are you all right?'

She nodded her head. 'I'm sorry.'

'So am I.'

'No.' She put down the book she had been reading. 'You misunderstand: I'm sorry for what happened yesterday.'

'There's no need. I shouldn't have interfered.'

His voice was dull. It was as if the thought of Ursula upstairs drained him of all feelings. She must have sensed this too, for she said in a hushed voice: 'This is beyond all belief, Richard.'

'Yes.'

He felt awkward and found his eyes straying to the book she had put down. Ovid's *Art of Love*. Strange reading, he thought, for a day like this.

'Come with me.'

He looked up. 'What?'

She glanced at him conspiratorially. 'Come with me now, I need to be away from here.'

'All right, but how?'

'We'll go riding.'

He paused. 'Won't Oliver think—'

'Shhh.' She put a finger to her lips. 'Please, Richard.

132

This is . . . terrible. I can't see him just now.' She seemed calmer somehow, as if some inner tension had been resolved. She looked at him, catching the desire in his eyes.

And against his better judgement, Richard found himself saying yes.

Below Chynoon the hills swept down to kiss the water in little beaches, treacherous with reefs, that rose on either side to sheer, clean cliffs two, three hundred feet high. The cliffs punched up through the sea in fat knuckles and broke the water in a plunge of white foam and wave. Richard had not ridden over these cliffs since he was a boy. Susannah cracked the side of her horse and they cantered down the valley from the manor and then broke across the first hill and out over the headland beyond. As soon as they were out of sight of the house, she tore away her hat and her hair streamed, red, auburn, chestnut in the fierce autumn sun. She found the spring of the horse beneath her exhilarating, liberating, and threw a smile back at Richard, and tore across the fields. Richard laughed, laughed as if he had no tomorrow, no yesterday. For a moment, here on this leaping, bounding horse, he was free, *free*, no matter what fate pursued.

They rode for thirty, forty minutes without stopping, plunging down the flanks of valleys and then pushing the horses up the far sides of the hills until the manor lay far behind and they came to rest at the dome of a huge headland, with the sea very vast and remote hundreds of feet below. Susannah's eyes danced in the sunlight. Her horse was blowing hard and she patted him affectionately.

The sea was a brilliant and cruel blue. A light wind hunted over its surface in crescents and smudges and

Richard felt its cool air on his face and neck and shut his eyes. When he opened them Susannah was still staring at the hard brilliant waters.

'They look so smooth,' she said. 'Like sheets of silk.'

They listened to the sheets rustle in the wind.

'You're not normally like this,' he said after a long time.

She shot him a smile. 'How would you know? How long have you known me?'

He smiled back, apologetically. 'I'm sorry. I jump to conclusions, it's a weakness.'

'And what sort of conclusions have you made about myself and Oliver?' She kept her eyes fixed on the limitless sea, but her voice was brittle.

'Only that you are betrothed, and you have his father's blessing,' he answered carefully.

'Do you think I am happy?'

'Are you?'

She didn't reply, and he looked at her.

'Why have you mentioned him unless you are not?'

A strange expression passed across her face. 'And why do I ask you, when I am already betrothed? I don't know. Perhaps I wonder how I appear to you, Master Ferrers.'

He searched for words. 'You appear to be someone very special. Even a merchant's clerk would say that.'

Her lips flickered bravely into a smile. 'I wish you were not here, Richard. Do you understand? Yesterday, when you fought with Oliver, I thought he would kill you.'

Richard smiled knowingly. 'So did Oliver.'

'Don't you see what I'm trying to say?' She stared at him intently. 'I can't afford for us to be close.'

'Then why have you asked me to come with you now?'

'I don't know.' She dropped her eyes and began to pluck at her horse's mane as if this mattered to her.

Richard watched her. The afternoon sun fell so bright it bleached her face so that it was pure and pale, a thing of transparency. He reached and ran his hand down the side of her cheek.

She looked up, and neither spoke for a long time. Richard had the sudden impression of how artificial and transient their existences were: she, pretending to be Susannah Tremaine, he, pretending to be a ship-wrecked merchant's clerk, brought together like two leaves blown by a fickle wind. She turned towards his hand, and he thought for a moment she was going to kiss him, then her lips cracked into a rich, ruby smile and she said, with deliberate innocence: 'Come, sir, or we will miss the best of the day.'

She tugged at her reins and together they descended towards the rolling fields beyond, olive green and honeyed in the sun.

Susannah had been right: the day was too good to miss, their horses were still fresh, and they rode until the sea and the cliffs were many miles behind. They talked little, merely the occasional comment about the land, or the view. Instead they enjoyed a quiet, easy companionship. Or perhaps they both knew that any conversation might destroy the peace between them. For talk would inevitably involve Oliver, and the future, and their own suspicions, and all those things over which they had no control.

Richard rode well, and it took Susannah no time to see he had been professionally trained, from the sure posture of his back, to the elegant grace of his horse's steps. Who was he? It had been obvious he was no merchant's clerk as soon as he picked up Oliver's sword. But then she had known more than that from

the moment she saw him dragged from the waves.
There was something in his gaunt, muscular face which
flared so quickly to laughter or anger that troubled yet
fascinated her. He is not at peace with himself, she
thought. But then, who am I to blame him for that?

By the time they neared the manor, dusk was falling
and a thick blue haze hung over the hills. Smoke rose
from the chimneys in slow, lazy tails, and somewhere
the satisfying crunch of an axe on firewood rang out.
They paused for a moment on the last rise, looking
down on the buildings, and Susannah wished they
could stop just there, and never return to the lives
contained in those walls. Next to her, Richard felt the
same.

'Susannah?'

She recognised the tone in his voice and knew that
if she turned to him now, they would be lost.

No, she thought. I must not.

Without a moment's hesitation, she geed her horse
down the slope. Richard stared, then with a laugh and
a flick of his wrists he raced after her and overtook her
in the last field before the manor. Their horses clattered
triumphantly into the yard, sending gravel skipping in
their path. Then the thought of Ursula fell upon them
and they reined in, suddenly self-conscious, guilty.

They dismounted in silence and led their horses into
the stable. The animals glowed in the evening air, thrilled from their final canter. Bouquets of steam bloomed
from their nostrils. Richard nodded at the graceful bay
the stableboy had been rubbing down that morning.

'Have you ever taken that mare out?'

Susannah shook her head. 'No, though I hear she's
quite skittish.'

'Is it Oliver's?'

She laughed. 'Don't be ridiculous! No, Dr Masters bought her for his wife a couple of months ago.'

Richard tried to think why Sarah Masters would have gone riding within an hour or so of Ursula's death, but came up with nothing. Perhaps she too had just wanted to escape from the oppressive atmosphere of the place. He heaved his saddle off his horse and on to the hook on the wall. Susannah was unbuckling hers and he offered to help.

'There's no need.' Susannah shook him off with a wry smile and expertly swung the saddle on to the bracket beside his.

He smiled back and said quietly: 'I've enjoyed today. Thank you.'

'Thank *you*. I needed to be away from this place.' Here in the warmth of the stable, all the feelings she had denied returned. She came closer so she was standing only inches away. She smelt the fresh glow of his body, sensed the healthy warmth of his skin.

'Perhaps we can do the same tomorrow?' he asked.

She looked up into his eyes and stroked the shoulder of his jacket. 'You do jump to conclusions, don't you?' She arched her eyebrows, taunting, hopeful.

'If you continue doing that, I will jump to one now.'

Her face suddenly became serious. Her fingers ran over his coat.

He stared at her, lost for a moment.

'Ah, Miss Tremaine! I thought I heard you return!'

Dr Masters burst through the doorway. Richard turned abruptly away and began to adjust the straps dangling from his saddle. 'Good evening, Doctor!'

Masters clapped his thick hands together. The sound echoed round the stable. 'It is cold out, no? Did you have a good ride, madam? The Colonel asked after you.' This last sentence fell heavily, almost as a reproach.

Susannah tugged a lock of her hair into place. 'Is he in the Hall now?'

'No. You must call on him in his rooms. Dinner will not be served tonight. And you, Master Ferrers?'

Without answering, Richard walked out into the fresh night air. The windows of the kitchens cast yellow pools of light over the courtyard. Normally they seemed warm, inviting. Now they were jaundiced, sickly. Behind him Susannah made awkward, polite conversation with the preacher.

Oliver was waiting on the doorstep. Richard would have ignored him, but he stood there with his feet apart, hands on hips, blocking the way. His face was the very image of injured male pride.

Richard met his gaze and held it. 'I am sorry about your mother, sir.'

'She wasn't my mother,' Oliver replied coldly. 'Do you think I particularly care?' He spat at Richard's feet, as if reminding him of his previous insult. 'But as for you, sir – you wasted no time in consoling my betrothed.'

Richard cocked his head over his shoulder. 'I chaperoned her because you were indisposed. At her request.'

Oliver clenched his jaw. A tick beat angrily in his left cheek.

'Oliver! Hello!' Susannah saw his expression and lowered her gaze. Worst of all, she was aware her cheeks were blushing, and that made her blush all the more. 'Are you well?' she managed.

Oliver's voice was little more than a whisper. 'Damnably.'

Richard judged it would be a good time to make his

exit. With a curt nod, he stepped past Oliver and left them facing each other on the threshold.

Inside, the pall of mourning smothered everything. The corridors seemed darker, mustier. The candles flickered wearily, as if unable to breathe. The clang of pots from the kitchen sounded like the tolling of a bell.

With leaden steps he made his way to the North Tower, to William Moreton's chambers, and knocked on the door.

'Who's there?'

'Richard Ferrers.'

There came the sound of heavy footsteps, then the door opened a crack, just enough to reveal one of William Moreton's eyes, bulbous, all-seeing, strangely distrustful. He studied Richard intently, as if doubting his appearance, then suddenly pulled the door back.

'Enter.'

Richard knew the room well from his father's time. He was in a small anteroom which led into the main body of the tower, where Moreton's chamber and study would be. The room was sunk in darkness except for a solitary candle. A Bible lay open on the desk. The candle was burning badly and gave off a sour smell of tallow.

'I'm sorry to disturb you—' Richard began.

'Tell me, sir.' Moreton turned unexpectedly and peered at him. 'Are you afraid of death?'

Richard was taken aback. 'I don't know.'

Moreton leaned closer, so that the flickering candle cast the pores of his face into huge relief.

'Then you don't know why you are alive. When an apple is ripe, it falls to the ground. Ursula was ripe for death, do you understand? It is not our will.'

Richard had a sudden violent memory of picking

up the apple in the orchard and finding it rotten and decayed.

'So what do you have to say to me? That you are sorry?' Moreton curled his lips into a parody of a smile. 'Sorry that I must accept her ripeness? I enjoyed her while she was on the branch, that is all.'

Richard placed his hand on the door. He felt an irresistible urge to be gone from this man.

'Colonel Moreton, I regret my sentiments must seem shallow. I have not pondered on these matters like you.'

Moreton slumped once more before the book, the audience at an end. 'Go in peace, sir. Oh,' he glanced up.

'Yes?'

'You will be at the funeral tomorrow, I trust?'

'Tomorrow?' Richard was mildly surprised. 'I had not expected it so soon.'

'The longer we delay, the more our fortitude may be tried, even when we may be certain of her joy.' Moreton licked the tip of his finger and turned the page. 'Dr Masters will officiate.'

'Dr Masters.'

'Yes.' Moreton regarded him through lidded eyes. 'Reverend Tomlin was ejected from his living for his . . . episcopalian beliefs, thanks be. As God's elect, we will provide our own service.'

Chapter Ten

I<small>T WAS A COLD, BLEAK</small> morning. It had rained during
the night and damp flags of clouds hung lifelessly
in the sky, threatening more. The wind had risen
slightly from the east and pushed sharp fingers into
their ears and eyes as they made their way across the
fields towards the church.

They were a small, wretched group. Six labourers
bore the mean boxy coffin on their shoulders. They
struggled to keep the load even and more than once the
box swayed and bobbed alarmingly, not that William
Moreton appeared to notice. He walked in silence, his
massive head bowed low, oblivious to the driving wind.
Next came Susannah, walking stiffly beside Oliver, then
Hugh Lovelace. Susannah's sharp glance told Richard
to keep away and he could only guess what had passed
between her and Oliver the night before. Richard trailed
at the back with Sarah Masters. Before them all strode
the Doctor, his face clenched like a fist.

The church of St Gregory loomed in front of them,
low, squat, ringed with the dark swirling forms of the
yews. Richard hadn't been here since a boy. Suddenly
the smell of wet earth, rich with the decay of life, rushed
back to him. When Richard's grandmother had died,
the churchyard had thronged with villagers, merchants,
craftsmen, well-wishers, members of the gentry. Even
though she had been the wife of Sir Anthony the Devil,
he reminded himself. But today it was almost empty.
The manor servants – Mary, Bridget, Daisy and the
others – huddled dejectedly in the lee of the wall. The

only other mourners were a few sombre men, some wearing the sashes of military rank. Chief among these were Captain Standish and Gregory Clement. Standish nodded sternly at them, his moustache rigid, his broad cavalry hat in his hand.

Richard noticed the entourage was not headed for the church, but crept round to the east side of the graveyard. Sarah Masters seemed suddenly overcome with grief. Making a soft, childlike sigh, she bowed her head, slowed down. Richard offered her his arm.

'Are you all right?'

She blinked up at him and bit her lip.

'Yes, I just thought . . . The crypt is so cold.'

'Crypt?' he asked, but with a horrible premonition he already knew her answer.

'Susannah has said we may use her family vault. No one has used it since her father died. What is it? What's wrong?' She suddenly caught the look in his eye.

Richard stared at her in disbelief. Susannah had no right to usurp his family's final resting-place like this, for God's sake! But what caused him to stare so was the news that his father was buried there.

Fielding had said he last saw Michael Tremaine riding off towards Tresillian. The King had agreed that no one knew what had happened to him. And Richard, like everyone, had assumed his father had simply disappeared. It had never occurred to him that his father might simply be lying in the Tremaine family vault. Why hadn't Couch said?

'Richard?' Sarah was tugging his sleeve.

He shook himself.

'Come. The others are almost there.' The dark-clad mourners had formed a group around the mouth of the vault. In their middle stood Dr Masters, scowling suspiciously. As they approached, he began to intone in a loud, blunt voice:

'Wherefore we must lay our beloved sister Ursula in the bosom of the Lord, confident in His mercy and in the perfection of her life through His grace, and eagerly looking forwards to His own visitation among us.'

Masters was conspicuously not using the service designated in the Book of Common Prayer. Richard was not surprised. Many Puritans regarded the Book as little more than popery, but neither, for that matter, was Masters using the new, official Directory of Public Worship. The absence of any formal service gave Ursula's funeral a rough, improvised feel.

Not that Richard was paying much attention to the words. The Tremaine vault was let into the side of the small hill which rose behind the church. Its doorway was a single sheet of slate, on which were inscribed the names of the departed. And there, at the bottom, in crisp, sharp lettering, he read:

'Michael Tremaine. 5th March, 1646.'

That was all.

On either side of the doorway stood small columns, fluted and crowned with sculpted apples and pomegranates, supporting a low triangular pediment, on which was set one word: *Resurgamus*. 'We shall rise again.'

Now two of the labourers blocked his view as they prised open the slab and dropped it with a dull thud on the ground.

Richard kept his eyes fixed on the slate and hardly noticed the men step forwards and awkwardly lumber the coffin through the gap. Sarah was sniffing ineffectually into a large handkerchief. Susannah was stiff and tight-lipped and steadfastly ignored him. Today she was the dutiful fiancée, he thought cynically.

'Look, now she sleeps, but she sleeps not. She will rise again, at the time appointed.' Dr Masters placed his hands together. 'Come, let us pray.' Richard followed suit.

The design of apples and pomegranates hung in his memory. Where had he seen them before? He knitted his eyebrows in an effort to concentrate on Masters' supplications.

'Have mercy on us, dear Lord. For we will live with you forever, pure and incorruptible.'

Apples. He recalled Masters' words in the orchard. 'All things can know corruption, can they not?'

And the answer came to him. The frieze on the portico of the vault was the same as around the sundial. Apples and pomegranates. And what had been the inscription on the dial? 'Stranger, only Heracles may seize The apples of th' Hesperides.'

Of course.

The apples of the Hesperides were sacred to the goddess Hera. They were of pure *gold*. Golden apples, stolen by Heracles. Richard stood blinking at the pediment. The prayer had finished and the men emerged from the vault, wiping their hands on their breeches.

Suddenly there was a shout and someone swore. Stephen Moreton came racing through the gathering. Richard stared at him. The boy's hands and face were stained with blood. Tears streamed down his cheeks and his big wide eyes were crazed and darted from side to side. 'No! No!' He nimbly sidestepped Captain Standish's outstretched arms and with a hoarse cry, leapt into the crypt.

William Moreton's face was swollen with anger. He barged past the Doctor.

'No! Let me alone! Let me—'

Moreton had Stephen by the collar and was hauling

him backwards as he would a stubborn ram. Stephen was struggling furiously. His thin arms were twisting and writhing like a spider's legs. 'Let me alone!'

'I thought you locked him in his room?' Moreton barked at Mary Bohago.

'I did, sir!'

He loured at her and threw Stephen to the ground. 'Listen, boy!'

Stephen was whimpering. Moreton bent down and struck him across the face. The mourners looked on in silence. 'Listen!' Oliver took a step forwards and laid a hand on his father's arm. He whispered something and William scowled. By this time, Stephen had clambered back on his feet. He was trembling violently as if he was about to be sick. Richard could see he was still eyeing the entry to the tomb.

'Ursula is dead,' said Moreton very firmly. 'You must leave her be!'

Something inside Stephen seemed to snap. He stood, trembling and twitching, but at these words the force went out of him and his limbs were weak, puny things again. Moreton rested his hand on his son's shoulder. 'Come,' he said quietly. 'We must go home.'

Silently, the small party walked back across the graveyard towards the manor.

Richard stayed where he was. He was filled with revulsion for these people. More than anything he wanted to be alone.

He gazed at the tomb.

So, father, he thought, you have rested here all these years, unmourned.

The two labourers had already refitted the slab and were tamping it into place. One of them looked up.

'Sad business, ehn't it?'

Richard nodded dumbly. He had nothing to say. The

two labourers regarded him oddly as they shouldered their tools and walked off.

He was still standing there when he saw her enter the graveyard. Rebecca. She was carrying a basket of pale flowers, so white they were almost luminous. When she saw him, she paused almost imperceptibly, and then, head held high, came quickly through the grass towards him. In the soft grey light, her hair was as black as crow's feathers.

Rebecca did not smile. They looked at each other for a long time, before Richard spoke.

'Hello.'

She lifted her basket slightly. 'I brought these, Master Moreton asked me to.'

He sat down heavily on the grass. 'My father's buried there.'

'Yes.'

'I didn't know.' He put his face in his hands. 'It's as if he's just died, Rebecca. God, I feel so tired.'

She put her basket down.

'I'm sorry, Richard,' she said coldly.

He looked up. 'Do you know, right until this morning, I didn't know he was dead. I expected it. But I didn't *know*.' He stared into her eyes. 'But what am I saying? Your father died as well, didn't he?'

She gave him an odd look and rubbed her hand over his doublet. 'It happened a long time ago, Richard. Don't trouble yourself.'

He stared at his feet for a moment, lost in thought. Golden apples. Why were they significant? He tried to think, but he was so confused with emotions that he found it impossible.

He looked up at her and for the first time noticed how cold and angry her face was.

'You didn't come yesterday,' she told him. 'I waited for you.'

He looked at her blankly.

'You said you'd come, around three or four.' Rebecca lowered her gaze as if she were ashamed to admit she'd been hurt.

'I'm sorry. What with Ursula's death, I couldn't get away.'

'I hear you went riding.' She gave him a withering look. 'You don't have to lie to me, Richard.'

Then it came to him. His father's signet ring. On the little finger of his left hand, his father had worn a small gold ring, with which he sealed his letters. And on the seal was stamped the motif of two apples.

'Richard?' He saw the hurt in her eyes.

'I'm sorry,' he said, feeling somehow resentful that she had this claim on him. 'Look, we'll talk soon. Once things have settled down.'

Rebecca bit her lip. 'No,' she replied. 'I don't think there's much point, do you? We can't bring the past back to life, can we?'

'No,' he muttered, his thoughts elsewhere, 'perhaps not. But you know I'll always care for you, Beckie.'

Suddenly she found him unbearably patronising. She turned stubbornly to the flowers and began to unpack them from her basket. She wished he would leave.

Richard got to his feet. Golden apples.

'Rebecca?'

'Yes?'

'Before I go, could I ask you one thing?'

She did not look up. 'It's about your father, isn't it?'

He nodded. 'Were you here when they buried him? I'm sorry, I need to know.'

Her voice betrayed none of the anger she was feeling. 'I don't remember much, Richard. There wasn't a proper funeral. Parliament's army were billeted in the house and Isaac Rogers the steward had it done quietly one night. He didn't want any spectacle, he said.'

'Where's Rogers now?'

Rebecca dipped her head. 'Just over there, behind the yews,' she said wryly. 'He died the year after.'

An idea was forming. Taking root among the dreams and clues of his thoughts.

What if his father hadn't died? Was that why Fielding had been so circumspect? Henry Couch had said his father left Chynoon travelling light. What if, instead of a body inside the coffin, there lay something else? The gold. Hidden in the one place no one would ever look? Richard's thoughts were racing. He could see how his father's mind would work. The golden apples! He almost laughed.

'Thank you, Beckie. I'm sorry to trou—'

'The wind's getting up,' she said harshly, indicating the tops of the yews. 'There's going to be a storm.' She shot him a glance. 'Go, Richard. I don't want to talk to you any more.'

She was still kneeling by the vault when he reached the far end of the graveyard and turned. She looked very pale and still, he thought, as if she were carved from marble, and for a moment a great feeling of sadness fell upon him, then the brisk wind shook him and it was gone.

What neither of them saw was the tall, dark figure standing in the shadow of the yews. Oliver Moreton was still there when Richard reached the manor. And he was there when Rebecca at last flung the flowers to the ground and shouted her anger at the wind.

Chapter Eleven

THE WIND HAD INDEED RISEN. It pulled and barged the trees and sent clouds streaming across the night sky. The moon was waning and blackness lay in deep pools beneath the oaks and beeches.

Richard pulled his doublet tighter about him and hurried his pace. At least his footsteps were drowned in the creak and crack of the trees. It did not take long before he saw the church looming out of the darkness ahead. Silent and empty, its windows staring blindly, hollow eyes. The yews whispered together.

Even at a distance, he could make out the glow of Rebecca's white flowers at the foot of the tomb. They seemed almost luminous in the feeble light.

I should not have left Rebecca like that, he thought, but he was too excited to dwell on this. But if I am right, and the gold is here . . . his thoughts ran on wildly. If I am right.

He crossed the graveyard quickly, feeling suddenly self-conscious before the blank eyes of the church.

Then he was at the foot of the vault. His fingers brushed aside Rebecca's carefully arranged flowers and traced over the marks of the chisel.

Michael Tremaine. 5th March, 1646.

The slate was smooth and clammy. He found the place where the slab was let into the front of the crypt and felt for a gap or point of purchase. There was none. The labourers had treated the stone with respect and it sat snugly in its bed, as it would till Doomsday. He tried again and broke a nail.

Overhead there was a sudden clap of air as a huge bolt of wind burst through the graveyard. Richard jumped round. The yews were dancing in the wind, swirling and writhing like things alive. He shook himself.

It wouldn't take long.

He pulled a long, thin table knife from his boot and began to work it around the slab. The blade slotted into the crack between the stone and the lintel and, very gently, he levered it backwards. The slab stuck for a moment and he felt the blade strain, then it came free, and balanced against the palm of his hand. He leant it down, taking its weight easily. The vault was impenetrable. A pit of blackness. He stooped and climbed in.

The close, damp air was smothering, and he felt for one ghastly moment as if he was drowning in blackness. Outside the tossing yews and tearing winds seemed like a different world. In here everything was close and silent and drained the very air of noise.

Richard forced his fears into the back of his mind and groped his way forward. He took two steps, then his toe caught on an uneven flagstone and he fell blindly, arms outstretched, against the far wall. He struck some object – wooden, damp, slimy – which cracked immediately, and his hands plunged into something whose texture he would never forget. Choking a scream, he dragged them out and wiped them desperately on his breeches. The smell released from the smashed coffin was indescribable. The shattered wood twitched suddenly as an afterthought and fell in on itself.

Oh God, have mercy on me.

He stared around in panic. He had not imagined it would be like this. Never. But it was too late now. He had to know. Stubbornly, he mastered his feeling of horror, and gradually his eyes overcame the stifling blackness of the pit and he could make sense of where he was. The vault was about fifteen feet long and seven feet wide, and was lined with what felt like wet, greasy bricks. On either side, and on the wall facing him, were three rows of shelves on which coffins could be laid. Those on the right side of the far wall were full. On the left side there were only two coffins, and one of them, even in this foul gloom, was obviously Ursula's. A cuckoo in the nest, he thought grimly. When they rise on Judgement Day, what will the Tremaines say to this stranger in their midst? He had a sudden vision of the grey rotting corpses clambering out of their boxes, and embracing each other with thin, bony arms.

Willing himself to bend down, he examined the other coffin on the left. There was a metal plaque tacked to its side, corroded with age. He tore it from the wood and took it to the doorway, grateful for the sweet fresh air. In the wretched light of the moon, he could just identify the first word: 'Michae . . .'

He was trembling as he knelt beside the coffin. Should I be doing this? The question had tormented him all afternoon, and now for one brief second, it fluttered in the air, but really there was no choice.

He had to know.

The lid was pinned down, but the wood was already damp and soft and came clean of the nails on the second tug.

And he saw.

Inside, arms crossed over his breast, lay the corpse.

Richard stared in horror. He could barely recognise him. The maggots had made cruel work of his face, his eyes, his hands. The coffin gave off a sweet, putrid odour which seemed to wrap its arms around him. Richard threw himself back and clawed his way to the door. He crouched there panting until the waves of nausea subsided, and then, slowly, painfully, went back to the coffin. The atmosphere inside the crypt was choking. Death rose from the coffin and forced its way into the back of his throat. Some crazed, half-sane notion had come to him of bidding farewell to the corpse, but when he looked once more at this wreck of flesh and bones – the bones he saw protruding through the cheeks, the temples – all he could do was slam the lid shut. The wood rang dully. Dust hummed in the air. Sweet, putrid dust. Richard felt dizzy and sank down on to the cold, damp floor. Soon the chill would enter his bones, he thought, and shook himself violently.

There was one other thing he must do.

Ursula lay in the coffin directly above his father's.

Gently, very gently, he tried the lid, and was relieved to find it came free in his hands, and all too soon, he was staring at the serene, handsome face of Ursula Moreton. She sleeps, he thought, recalling the Doctor, and shuddered. Soon the maggots would disport themselves on her proud, ripe body, too.

Forcing himself to be calm, he peeled back the white gown in which she was wrapped. He wasn't sure what he was looking for, but he found it before he had even begun to search: around her pale throat, Ursula wore a necklace of livid bruises.

No wonder Moreton had wanted her buried so quickly.

There was the click of a pistol behind him. Richard turned, slowly, in a daze. The doorway was blocked by the shape of a man.

'Don't move, you bastard!'

It was Oliver Moreton.

Even then Richard was slow to react. Nothing seemed real any more.

'Are you going to shoot me?' he asked casually.

'Don't move!' Oliver was furious. 'What in God's name . . .' He peered past Richard at the open coffin. 'Why, you . . .'

Oliver leapt into the vault.

'Steady,' someone called behind him, and Richard just caught the word before Oliver punched him to the ground. He doubled up and collapsed, gasping. A boot caught him clean on the jaw. His head was knocked backwards and smashed into the base of the left wall.

'Filth! Filth!'

Richard must have blacked out for a second, for the next moment everything was spinning and he was being dragged into the graveyard, and there was wind roaring on his cheek. Oliver threw him down and his face landed on the upturned slab. So cold in the night air . . . His lips were strangely wet and licked the cool slate.

'You monster!' Oliver had him by the throat again and dropped him a second time. Richard realised he was in pain, but his consciousness was so far away that he was only dimly aware.

'Steady, sir!' Another man had grabbed Oliver's arm and was holding him back. It was Captain Standish. Oliver was panting violently. 'You might kill him.'

Oliver laughed harshly.

Richard stared up at them. He tried to speak but no words came.

Oliver looked down on him with contempt. 'Get up.'

Chapter Twelve

THE GREAT HALL WAS A blaze of light. The fire seethed, the candelabra was ringed and crowned with flames. Candles burned on the table, on the mantelpiece, on the iron spikes set in the wall. William Moreton was seated at the far end of the table. He looked up when Richard entered and his eyes were like two wicks, dancing with fire.

Richard was thrust into a chair before the fireplace and strapped down with a huge leather belt that cut into his arms. The journey from the church had been nightmarish, unreal, as he had staggered and stumbled across the fields, Oliver, Standish and their companions dragging and cursing him and the tops of the trees twisting and shaking in the wind. The lights dazzled and it took him several seconds to understand what was happening.

'So! Have you no shame?' William Moreton arose from his chair and stalked across the room.

Richard regarded him dumbly.

'Great God, man!' Moreton's neck bulged over his collar. His eyes bulged from their sockets, as if they were about to explode with wrath. He bent down so that his face was only an inch away from Richard's. Great beads of sweat stood on his forehead. 'Have you nothing to say?'

'What do you expect me to say? What have I done wrong?' Richard attempted to stay calm, but even to his own ears, he did not sound innocent. The stench of the tomb still rang in his head.

'Do you wish me to spell it out, so you can revel in
the tale of your own filth?' Moreton's spittle dusted
Richard's face. He blinked. 'Was my wife not a sweet
thing, Master Ferrers? Was she not the very pith of
life?'

'Yes—'

'And was she not eaten out by death and left a poor
husk tossed to the winds of time in one night? Does
that please you, Master Ferrers? Eh?'

'No, sir.'

William straightened himself, a look of grim satisfaction on his face. 'But when poor Mary saw the devil
looming over her bed, did I believe her? No! In my
pride I preferred the wisdom of man. If only I had
listened! You are Satan himself!' His voice rose like a
blast of wind. Wind rocked against the windowpanes.
The candles flickered.

'Sir, I am not!' Richard strained against the leather
bands which held him. 'This is lies!'

'Silence! Silence!' Oliver Moreton shouted.

'Sir,' continued William, suddenly calmer. 'You are a
cunning-man, a servant of the devil.'

'This is ridiculous!' persisted Richard. 'I was ship-
wrecked. You gave me hospitality.'

'And look how you repaid me! You are a very parasite that has gnawed the rose in my hand!'

'What proof do you have?'

'Proof? *Proof!* When but half an hour ago you were
caught disporting yourself with my wife's body! Look
at you, man!'

Richard stared at Moreton in disbelief. But he had to
admit the man's accusations contained a horrible logic.

'So,' he said slowly. 'What happens next? Am I to
stand trial?'

Moreton's face was lit with a smile. 'Do you confess? To the murder of my wife?'

Richard was aware that everyone – William, Oliver, Standish, the servants – was staring at him intently.

'Of course not,' he replied deliberately. 'But yes, I agree she was murdered. I have seen the marks on her neck.' He stared at Moreton. 'Who was last with her when she died?'

Moreton punched Richard in the face. He glared down, admiring his handiwork, then turned away and murmured: 'Take this parasite to the cellar.'

Richard was unable to stand. Everything was a blur. He did not see Susannah, her face white with shock, come stumbling into the Hall, clutching her robe around her. Two servants dragged him out and down the stairs to the cellar.

The door swung open. Manacles for ankles and wrists were fitted to the wall. Then he was dumped on the ground head first and the cold stone bit into his face and the chains were snapped shut, pinching his skin, and he was left.

Back in the Great Hall, Oliver turned and gave Susannah a sharp, jagged smile.

'What's the matter? He deserved no less.' He paused, now stern. 'I saw the way he looked at you.'

But Susannah was too dazed to respond.

Oliver's done this because of me, she thought. This is my fault. I should have ignored him. I could have warned him.

Oliver placed his hand on her shoulder and turned her to face him. The relentless pressure of his eyes mesmerised her and she shivered.

And now I'm powerless.

*

Richard did not know how long he lay on the floor. The cellar was pitch dark and time had no meaning. Occasionally he would hear the thud and scrape of people moving overhead and, once or twice, a sudden burst of laughter or raised voices. But what they were saying, or what time it was, he could not tell. His head spun, his limbs were tired and sore. He had lost track of how often he had been hit, and his bruises and pains dissolved into each other. One of his eyes felt badly swollen. He tested it gingerly with his fingertips and winced. As he lay staring into space, the blackness came alive and took on solid forms and he saw before his eyes the vault again, itself a pit of blackness, and the racks of coffins, and smelled the rotting flesh.

And then he was standing above his father's corpse once more, gazing down on his death's head, and, as if in a dream, Richard saw again the dissolving flesh, the sallow bones, the hands crossed on the breast, and in that instant, piercing through his confusion with sudden clarity, he realised that the body in the crypt could not have been his father's.

His father had lost two fingers of his right hand at the Battle of Cheriton. He could remember his father had still been bandaged when he saw him two months later and how his mother had fussed over the wound and his father had sworn and damned her for interfering. Why hadn't he realised it before? It was obvious, yet in the tomb he had been so overpowered by the stench of death.

Richard pulled himself up against the damp wall. He was already numb with cold. But if that wasn't his father in the grave, who was it? And where was Michael Tremaine?

Somehow, given his current situation, this question

had an almost academic quality. What did it matter who was lying in his father's tomb? Richard had understood the look in Moreton's eye: the trial would end in only one way. He stared blindly into the blackness and waited.

He was woken by the grating of a key in the lock and the creak of the door. Then yellow candlelight fell across the floor and he screwed up his eyes.

'Richard? Is that you?' It was Susannah. She steadied the candle on the flagstones and for the first time the cellar was thrown into life. Richard could see he was surrounded by barrels, and sacks and boxes of all sizes, piled high to the ceiling. Next to him, three more sets of chains dangled from the wall. Susannah closed the door and winced as the hinges whined. She was sure that the slightest sound would bring the others running. She was trembling.

Am I really doing this? she thought. But her mind was already set. She would not let Richard die for her.

He whispered her name, and any doubts she had vanished.

'Dear God, you look terrible.' She bent over him and examined his eye, and he had a sudden heady whiff of perfume.

'I've felt better.' He shook his chains ruefully. 'What time is it?'

'Eleven o'clock.'

'In the morning?'

'No, at night.' She continued to prod and test his eye and he gritted his teeth. He was struck by the deep lines of concern which the candle threw across her face. In the half-light, her hair glowed like deep bronze. 'Oh, Richard, you are stupid! What were you doing?'

He frowned. 'I can't tell you. But will you believe I'm innocent?'

'I know you are.' Susannah continued to study his face. 'I think there's only superficial damage. Your cheek caught the full brunt of the blow.'

'Does Moreton know you're here, Susannah?'

'No. Oliver had the keys. I waited until he was asleep.'

She was taking a terrible risk, he realised. He did not wonder how she had known Oliver was sleeping. He smiled faintly. 'Thank you. It's good to see you.'

Susannah gently touched his shoulder. 'I'm sorry, Richard.'

'What will happen next?'

'Moreton will have you tried in two days. You'll hang for certain. Or . . .' She dropped her eyes. 'Moreton was talking of a burning.'

Richard swore under his breath. 'This is ridiculous! Is there nothing I can do?'

'Don't you understand, Richard?' Her voice was sharp, goading. 'Haven't you had time to work it out?'

'Work what out?'

'It was all a trap, don't you see? Right from the moment you were rescued from the wreck. Why do you think those others weren't saved?'

Richard suddenly felt very cold. 'What others?'

'The other two Frenchmen. They were washed ashore next to you. One was old with grey hair.'

'What happened to them?'

Susannah hesitated. 'I don't know, Richard, at least I'm not sure. But they were alive when we pulled them out.'

Richard shuddered. The one who was old and grey would have been Roublais.

'So what are you saying?' he asked heavily. 'That Moreton saved me—'

'—so he could murder his wife? Yes!' Her eyes flashed. 'That's just what I'm saying.'

Richard did not reply. His mind was racing back over everything that had happened since he came to Chynoon. The look on William Moreton's face that first morning. Ursula, falling against him in the corridor, pretty and nervous at dinner. The note that was left in his Bible and then disappeared. Were these all fragments in his undoing?

'Just think,' continued Susannah, 'Oliver found you at the crypt, didn't he? Yet how was William already in the Hall waiting for you? Who told him what to expect?'

'But why should he want to kill Ursula?'

'I don't know, but I can guess.' Susannah paused, then said in one deep breath: 'If Ursula's dead, what's to stop William marrying me himself?'

Richard looked at her, appalled.

'But what about Oliver?'

'Hah!' She laughed humourlessly, her voice sharp, flighty with nerves. 'You don't know William, do you? Listen to Dr Masters – do you think he has a conventional view of morality?'

'I know many preachers try to startle their audience—'

'Richard!' She grabbed him by the shoulders and shook him. 'Masters does not try to startle his audience, don't you understand? Do you think the others are shocked? Once you've been put to death, do you think Moreton will delay in joining with my flesh? Why, he will deflower me in the very sheets on which he took Ursula's life.'

He pulled her down to him, squeezing her body next to his. She was breathing heavily.

'Richard, I can't bear it. The thought of him touching me, holding me, forcing me.'

He kissed her. They were both doomed then, and he was seized by a sudden desire to taste her lips, her mouth, before it was too late.

She hesitated only for a second, then her lips parted and their mouths dissolved into each other. Her tongue began to lick and nibble at his mouth. It tasted indescribably sweet and soft. She grazed her teeth over one of the cuts on his lips, and he winced.

'I'm sorry,' she whispered. 'I'll be more gentle.'

Richard tugged at his chains. He wanted to hold her, caress her, take her warmth in his arms. They kissed again, this time more passionately. He could feel her cheek pressed against his. Her hands were cradling his neck, his throat. Against his chest, he felt the firm swell of her breasts, gently pressing through her bodice, and he arched his body against hers. She responded. Easily, she flexed herself, relishing the long, muscular contact between their bodies, forcing him back against the hard ridges of the flagstones, letting her weight rub against his legs, his thighs, his stomach.

She pulled herself away from his mouth. 'We haven't got much time,' she whispered.

'Will he really take you?'

'Yes.'

He squeezed her flesh, desperately, hungrily. The stiff material of her skirts rucked against his legs. Beneath the material, her body tensed and responded, at first in small circular movements, and then in long, powerful strokes. Her legs were astride him, lean, lithe. Richard strained his arms, and managed to edge his fingertips down her back and on to the firm, rounded curves of her buttocks. He pulled her sharply against him, and she gasped, then tore herself away and sat up, looking down on him.

'Susannah—' he began, but she put a finger to his lips. She was trembling.

'Moreton may wed me,' she said. 'But I will never be his.' Their eyes locked. Richard felt his throat go dry. His blood was hammering in his veins. Without taking her eyes from him, Susannah reached down and hoisted up her skirts. She felt a sudden thrill as she saw the expression on his face change. The sudden sense of her power inflamed her.

'There.' She smiled triumphantly. 'You see what no other man has seen.'

He raised his hand slowly, delicately. His chains would just permit his finger to touch the very edge of the thick triangle of hair which blossomed between her thighs. It was warm, springy. She eased herself forwards a little, teasingly, tauntingly, and smiled. Suddenly his fingers were bathed in a soft, wet warmth.

'You're so beautiful,' he whispered, and she glowed in his admiration. 'Come here. To me.'

She understood his meaning. She got up and stood over his head and then, slowly, firmly, lowered herself.

Lightly, very lightly, his tongue whispered over her. So lightly that the first flick was little more than a breath of pleasure. Her thighs were trembling. Her legs shuddered and he reached up and held them apart, pinning them open, drawing her more fully to him. It was as if her whole being had become the smallest, lightest bud of flesh, trembling, dancing in a flame which grew ever tighter, hotter as his tongue sought her out, sought her endlessly, nibbling and probing and teasing and sucking at her very soul – just a tongue, she told herself, it's just a tongue – until with a sudden frantic rush, she exploded into a thousand splinters of flesh, over and over.

'Please, I need you inside me,' she told him, and his body was already writhing against the chains, the chains biting into his wrists, his ankles. She reached down and laid his trousers open. Then she grasped him in her hand – firm, strong – and she was squatting over him.

Hair was tumbling in her face and she flicked it away. 'Richard,' she whispered. She lowered herself. Her thighs were wet, as if drenched in a hot, intoxicating wine, and then the tip of him nuzzled her. She stayed like that for a moment, and he felt her heat feeding down on to him. Then, inch by inch, she brought herself down, feeling him moving up inside her, slowly, relentlessly entering her. She breathed out slowly, deeply. Then she was wide-eyed and there was a moment's tender resistance. Richard flexed himself, she made a short noise, no more than a sigh, then she dropped clean down on to him. Richard gazed at her, devouring each look, each expression, as gently, painfully, he began to shift inside her. 'How does it feel, Miss Tremaine?'

She smiled and closed her eyes. 'Exquisite.' Her syllables came irregularly, between breaths. He began to push himself harder, more powerfully, and she pushed back, pinning him with the chains, flexing her strong, delicate body, meeting thrust for thrust, gasp for gasp. The candlelight rocked and swayed across the cellar. Her breaths were shorter, hotter, she felt herself grow fuller with him. Sweat was pouring down his chest, his back, and Richard fought against the chains, craving to be closer to her, deeper into her, taste her, feel her, *be* her. She was working at him frantically, grinding her hips backwards and forwards, her eyes unfocused, her hair splashing over her shoulders, her hands clutching the thin cotton of his shirt and pulling, tearing, until he felt his life boil up within her and thunder out in a great scalding cry and their faces were lost in a web of her hair and she threw her neck back and groaned and suddenly the candlelight was not leaping and the flagstones were cold and grainy and there was air on her back and thighs and she collapsed against him.

Richard could have lain like that for an age, feeling her body cool and his senses leak away into the cellar, but the next thing he knew, Susannah was shaking him and working at his handcuffs. There was a strange clink and he heard them clatter to the ground.

She smiled at him, a little mischievously. 'Didn't I tell you? I also have the keys to your chains.'

The door to the cellar creaked once as they opened it. Above them the stairs to the corridor were masked in blackness. Richard felt something pressed into his hands.

'Here,' whispered Susannah. 'Take this.'

It was a pistol. She gave him no further explanation, but went past him up the stairs and along the passageway to the Hall. He followed. The Hall was empty. Even the embers in the grate were dead and he guessed it must be one or two in the morning. Susannah turned the handle on the far side and they took the corridor which led to the rear door. Richard's skin prickled. His ears strained but he could hear nothing save the tick of the grandfather clock and the rustle of her dress ahead of him. Then the keys rattled in the lock until she found the right one, and suddenly the door swung open and a cold blast of air greeted them. The wind was bounding across the courtyard, shivering the tall beeches and clustered apple trees.

'What do we do now?' He brushed his lips against her ear. She was so *sweet*.

'We need horses. Two horses.' She smiled nervously, squeezed his hand. She was crazy to do this, she knew, and trembled with excitement.

'Is it safe?'

'The stableboys sleep in the loft, but if we are quiet . . .' She broke off. 'What choice do we have? We'll never get away on foot.'

Cautiously, they inched their way around the edge of the court, hugging the walls of the house. Somewhere an owl called. Richard held her by the wrist and felt her pulse beating.

They were next to the stables now. He strained his ears over the buffets of the wind. Nothing came from within apart from the heavy shifting of the horses. He gained the door, ducked down, nudged it open. Inside was the warm smell of horses and hay. He breathed a sigh of relief.

'Richard! Quick!'

Susannah's voice was hushed, urgent. He darted outside. She was pointing back to the house. Someone was moving upstairs. A weak circle of light drifted over a window and was gone.

'Do you think they heard us?'

Richard found a trowel propped against the wall and wedged the door open. 'Quick, the horses!'

She followed him in. Carefully they eased the stalls open. One of the horses snorted, and Susannah laid her hand on its nose and quieted it. Then they wrapped their arms around the horses' necks and began to lead them out. 'Easy, easy.' The sound of the hooves was muffled by the straw lying thick on the floor. The wind pounded against the side of the stable, the horses hesitated as if sensing the humans' nervousness, and then with an almighty snap the door sprung free and clapped against the frame. Cursing, Richard jumped to secure it, but it was too late.

'What's that?' One of the stablehands had appeared over the side of the loft. He was angry and befuddled with sleep, then he caught sight of the horses and roared, 'Stop! Stop!'

Instinctively, Richard seized Susannah by the waist and jammed the pistol into her neck. 'Quiet!' he ordered. 'Quiet!'

Susannah squirmed against him, then she understood his plan, and stopped. He felt her body pressed against his and squeezed her closer. The stablehand froze, not knowing what to do.

'Don't make a sound,' hissed Richard. 'I don't want to hurt her, do you understand?'

He backed out into the yard. Damn. They would have to do without the horses. He looked behind him. The light was no longer at the window. Then he turned and they ran towards the trees which clustered on the north side of the manor. The had no sooner reached them than the stablehand had leapt down and was rushing towards the house, shouting and bellowing. They didn't have much time.

The wood was a hostile place at night. Branches trailed in front of their eyes, whipping their faces, roots twisted out from the ground and snared ankles. Susannah had difficulty running at all. Her skirts were ungainly, cumbersome, and caught in the brambles and thorns which snaked across the path. From the manor a great cry went up, and men were shouting, running. Richard spun over a stone and stumbled into a tree, barking his shins. He swore and Susannah knocked into him. 'Come on.' Dragging her to her feet, he plunged up through the trees towards the brow of the hill. He smashed his way through a mass of holly. Susannah's skirt caught in a branch and she jerked it free savagely, gashing her hands. Then his foot sank into a rabbit hole and he felt something snap. Pain stabbed through his ankle. He was over, tears blinded him. Susannah was at his side, clutching his shirt.

'Is it broken?'

He flexed his ankle and winced. 'No, I don't think so, but something's torn.' He struggled up and balanced on his good foot. This was hopeless.

'Richard! They'll catch us soon!'

'I know!' he snapped and fell against her. 'Can you take my weight?'

'I'll try.' She heaved against him and they hobbled up the last few steps out of the wood. He tried the foot again. Pain lanced through his ankle, but it would have to do. He twisted free of her grip, and half-hopping, half-jumping, somehow blundered over the field. Susannah was with him.

'Where are we going? We'll never get away.'

They fetched up against the hedge. His breath came in sharp rasps and it was a second before he could answer her. 'If we head north,' he gasped, 'the country is wilder.'

The next field had just been ploughed and the ground was wet and loose, their feet churning it to mud. Richard gritted his teeth. Mud clung to their shoes, slowing them down. His ankle burned.

Somehow they reached the far side and clambered over the hedge, tearing skin on brambles, thorns. At the crest of the hedge the wind caught them and they heard the unmistakable sound of baying.

'Moreton's released the dogs.' Richard felt himself

grow cold and shook himself angrily. They had no chance.

'We won't make it, will we?' asked Susannah. Her voice was crisp and calm. She looked him straight in the eye.

Richard thought frantically. There had to be a way.

Then it came to him.

'Two fields away there's an old mine working,' he told her. 'It hasn't been used since King James' day.'

She looked quizzical. 'How do *you* know?'

'I saw it while walking,' he said quickly. 'It's our best hope.' He hobbled on again, ignoring the pain. 'Come on.' But she was already ahead, running across the field.

She waited for him at the far side, and they clawed their way through the hedge. 'Down here,' he said.

Susannah peered behind them, but in the inky darkness she could see nothing. She jumped into the field and helped him down the hedge, and together they covered the last few yards. Here the ground sloped downhill and the sea, curving round the headland below Chynoon, roared in the distance. About halfway down the hill, a tangled thatch of brambles and gorse crawled over several large stacks of waste long since abandoned. They clambered through the needle-sharp gorse and in the middle, still visible by moonlight, there opened a black shaft, crooked like the gap between a man's teeth. Richard went to the edge.

'The ground only drops about ten feet,' he explained. 'Then there's a passage, heading down. Can you jump?'

Susannah paused for just long enough to arch her eyebrows at him, then leapt into the hole. There was a thump as she landed. 'Can *you*?' she called back.

Richard sat on the lip of the shaft and swung himself

down. His good foot took the weight of his fall, but he still caught his breath.

'Come on,' she urged, taking the initiative. 'We need to get farther in.'

At the bottom of the shaft, a passage had been driven through the rock towards the sea. The floor was surprisingly even, for here the men had pulled carts and hoppers of dirt and ore, but the walls were jagged, rough-hewn, and the rock, being mainly shale and rotten granite, crumbled in their hands. Susannah and Richard stumbled blindly down the passage, Richard using the walls to steady himself. They could see nothing, and the only sound was the plink and drip of water somewhere ahead. Richard was worried they might step into a shaft by mistake – for he knew the men had pushed the workings deeper than this – and after twenty feet, he called out for Susannah to halt. His voice echoed down the passage.

'How's your foot?' Susannah came beside him and rubbed her hand against his side.

'It will be fine. I just need to rest, that's all.' He bent down and kissed her gently on the neck. 'You shouldn't have come with me.'

'What?' She rolled her eyes. 'Do you want me to stay and let Moreton have me? I hate him!' Susannah looked at him, beautiful, imploring: 'You could take me with you.'

She felt his lips against her mouth.

'I've wanted you to say that ever since I saw you.' And what of Oliver? he wondered. Did she hate him as well? But he tried not to think of this.

They held each other for a long time.

'What shall we do?' Susannah traced her hand down his neck and across his chest.

Richard sighed. Whatever they did, they would be

lucky to escape, but he tried to sound as confident as possible. 'Hide here today, then tonight head along the coast. We'll try to find a boat to take us to the continent.'

Of course, if they did that, it would mean abandoning the very reason he had come. Richard tried to think of the cramped council chamber in Cologne and the rich, heady scent of royalty, but they were not as real as the perfume of Susannah's dress, the press of her skin next to his. Then from some stubborn recess of his memory, his father's voice came to him.

'The King is God's anointed,' Michael Tremaine had said, 'and our cause so just that those who die in it are little less than martyrs. This is our duty, Richard.' Where was that surge of loyalty now? he thought. They were just words. But even as he told himself this, he was already realising he could not abandon his father yet. Not after seeing the body in the vault. There was a conflict here which he did not know how to resolve. Susannah felt his arms stiffen.

'We will go away,' he promised. 'In good time.'

In good time. He hoped those three words would suffice.

He leant forward and kissed her neck, her chin, her lips. Susannah sighed against him. He reached beneath her skirts and began to stroke her legs, gently, reassuringly. He was greedy for her.

Suddenly she tensed.

'What is it?'

Susannah put her finger to his lips. She was listening intently. Richard froze.

'What is it?' he mouthed to her again. Then he heard it himself. Someone was moving ahead of them, farther along the passageway. There was a crunch as a foot brushed against a loose stone, and the sound of something being set down. Richard felt his body tighten. He levered himself to his feet and crept forwards as best he could. The sounds came again – not that far away – then Richard's weak ankle buckled under him and he stumbled against a rock. Everything was suddenly still. Richard took a deep breath and called out: 'Who's there?'

There was no reply.

'Who's there? We know you're there! Please! We need help.'

'All right, all right,' grumbled an old voice. They could hear the person shuffling along the passage towards them. Richard hardly dared breathe, then out of the darkness emerged a short, stooped man with a thick grey beard, who looked more like a troll or a dwarf than a human. Richard gaped in disbelief. He knew this man. Rebecca had said he was dead.

The old man squinted up at him. 'On the run, are 'ee?'

'Yes. We need to hide.' Richard did his best to cover his face by scratching his nose. But in the almost total gloom of the mine the old man didn't seem to recognise him.

The old man sniffed the air and craned his neck forwards. 'Hmmm. It'll be light soon.' Then for the first time he caught sight of Susannah. 'What's this? You've got company?'

Richard hobbled over to her. 'We need to hide,' he repeated. Why had Rebecca lied to him? Suddenly he understood the significance of the man's clothing in her cottage. He had misread her.

The old man squinted at Susannah and cackled gaily to himself. 'You're the Tremaine girl, aren't 'ee? Need to hide? Heh! Heh!' He stopped and wiped the spittle from his mouth. 'Come with me.' With that, he shuffled off down the tunnel. 'Oh,' he called back. 'Mind the shaft. It's just here.'

Clutching hands, they followed. As the old man had said, a large shaft opened in front of them, emitting sour, stale odours. They stepped carefully round it and then the tunnel bore slightly upwards and they came to a dry, flattish area, where a small fire glimmered in a hearth. The old man was stooped down, rubbing his hands before the flames. He grinned.

'Make yourselves at home, why don't 'ee?'

And home it was. Against the far wall were slung a mattress of straw and several blankets. Next to this stood three earthenware pots, presumably containing water and food, and a wooden crate. Against the other wall firewood was stacked in neat piles and a brace of rabbits hung from a nail.

Richard smiled at Susannah and they settled next to the fire.

'Been living here for a couple of years, off and on,' the old man explained. 'Got the earth into my bones now.'

'Why?' asked Susannah with some puzzlement.

The old man liked that and chuckled to himself. But his laughter was harsh, like the rattle of nails in a bucket, and held no humour. ''Cause of I fought on the wrong side too many times. 'Cause of lots of things, I guess.' His eyes became serious and he stared at the blazing twigs for a time. 'I was with the King's army from 'forty-three,' he continued. 'That must have been ten years ago or more, I guess. I fought with Sir Bevill Grenville at Braddock Down and when we stormed the hill at Stratton. And then at Lansdowne, when Sir Bevill died. I'll never forget that. The Roundheads had us pinned on the hillside good and proper, then Sir Bevill led us up the hill into the face of their muskets.'

'That was many years ago,' said Susannah awk-wardly.

'What?' The old man looked up from the fire. His eyes were rimmed with tears. 'But daresay I won't forget.' He spat and wiped his hand on his britches and offered it, first to Susannah, then to Richard. 'I haven't been an' introduced myself, have I? Sedge is the name. I was born near here.'

The name meant nothing to Susannah, but Richard had known Sedge years before. He was Rebecca's father. Rebecca had lied when she said he was dead. Richard gripped the hand hard. Perhaps he shook it too warmly, or perhaps his face betrayed some expression of old, for Sedge suddenly narrowed his gaze.

'Here,' he muttered. 'Don't I know 'ee?'

'No. I don't think so,' Richard replied gruffly. 'I'm from Portsmouth. Have you been there?'

Sedge tutted noisily. 'It wasn't at Portsmouth I've seen you.'

Damn. Richard struggled for an answer. Even now, in this predicament, he felt strangely reluctant for Susannah to realise who he was. He coughed loudly, screwing his face into a grimace. Then suddenly, as if sensing his discomfort, Susannah came to the rescue. She fixed Sedge with a dazzling smile.

'So what happened after the war? Wasn't there an amnesty?'

What does she suspect? wondered Richard. Does she know I have something to hide? And yet, even so, she would come with me . . .

Sedge meanwhile had turned away, Richard's identity forgotten. He frowned. 'The amnesty, you say? In 'forty-six? Yes, I came home then.' He picked up a stick and jabbed it viciously into the heart of the fire. 'Home to damned lies. Then in 'forty-eight, the King's men rose again and I went with them. Parliament weren't so merciful the second time.' He sent a shower of sparks scurrying upwards from the fire. 'I fought for a long time then. Didn't fight to win, no, but because it was all we could do. The Scillies. Ireland. I saw the King at Dunbar. And still I hadn't had my bellyful of killing.'

The lines deepened in Sedge's face, and Richard understood why. At Dunbar ten thousand men had died. Sedge breathed out heavily.

'Then at last I grew tired.' He scratched his beard. 'And I came back.'

'Don't the villagers know you're here?'

'If they did I'd be dead for sure. In 'forty-eight two of them helped crush the rising. There's people as blame me for their deaths.' He spat viciously, as if all his anger were condensed into his mouthful of spittle. 'Blame Cromwell, I say.' With that he fell silent, and they sat staring at the weird shapes thrown up by the fire.

It was strange, thought Richard, how their paths should cross. To find Sedge here, of all places, after so many years. Was it coincidence? He had a sudden, unmistakable impression that there was some unseen force or design impelling him, guiding him, eventually and inevitably, though to what he did not know. He coughed conspicuously and turned to Susannah:

'Your father fought for the King, didn't he?'

Susannah looked momentarily taken aback, then nodded. 'It was a long time ago, Richard.'

'What's that?' Sedge stirred, as Richard had guessed he would. 'Captain Tremaine? Now there was a gentleman!'

'You knew Susannah's father?' asked Richard, as ingenuously as he could.

Sedge looked at Susannah almost with fondness. 'He called me and I followed. Fought under him through all 'forty-three and 'forty-four. Then he stayed with Hopton and I went with Grenville.' He stopped. 'And then when my wife couldn't pay the rent, he dispossessed her and tried to throw her off the land. A bloody fine and damned gentleman! And now you've come begging in my hole.'

Susannah shifted uncomfortably, and then Sedge suddenly broke into a smile.

'No,' he said. 'Don't fret, my dear. I don't blame you. God damn me for it, but your family wasn't all bad. I remember your brother Richard and Beckie were as close as two young lovers once—'

'Did you never see Captain Tremaine again?' asked Richard brusquely.

Sedge coughed. 'No.' And Richard's heart sank. Then Sedge continued: 'But I still remember the day he died.'

The skin prickled down Richard's spine, his thoughts of Beckie forgotten. 'When? What did you see?'

Sedge paused for what seemed like an eternity, gazing into the fire. 'It was the damnedest thing,' he began. 'It was in 'forty-six, just after Bodmin fell. I'd been with Captain Mulruhan's Foot, but by then there were only twenty of us left – twenty out of two hundred, mind – and in the night I slipped away to see Elizabeth. The next morning I was coming back over the fields, when I saw the biggest dog I have ever seen.' Sedge nodded his head for emphasis. 'A huge grey beast with gaping jaws. Came bursting out of the woods. I thought it was mad or rabid, and jumped aside, but it just ran past me, down the fields and away.'

Sedge paused again, and Richard waited patiently for him to continue.

'Anyway,' resumed Sedge, 'for some reason, shock I

think, I decided to go and look where it had gone. But when I got to the hedge, what did I see?' Sedge peered into their eyes. 'One of the King's men, stretched out on the ground. And when I got closer, who was it but Jacob Sawle?' He turned to Susannah. 'You remember Jacob, don't 'ee? Your father's servant – he was with him all through the war.'

Susannah nodded quietly.

'Was he dead?' asked Richard.

'No, but almost. He'd been shot in the stomach. I reckon he'd lain there all night. There was nothing I could do.'

'And what about Captain Tremaine? Did you see him?'

Sedge shook his head. 'No one was there, just me and poor old Jacob. He was hurting cruelly. He clutched my hand and wouldn't let go.' Sedge looked up thoughtfully. 'And you know what he said to me? His last words, mind. He pulled me down so his lips were only an inch from mine, and he whispered: *Our prince is in Avalon.*' Sedge wiped a hand over his beard. 'That was all. Damnedest thing I ever heard. Reckon the effort must have killed him, for he slumped back and was gone.' Sedge shook his head slowly. 'It's strange, but he acted like it was so important, like his life depended on it. To go talking about King Arthur at such a time! The damnedest thing!' He snorted. 'As if our prince is in Avalon or anywhere! King Arthur's nothing but a fairy-tale! Why, we had just as well put our faith in Charles Stuart.'

'Yes,' said Richard quietly.

'You know,' continued Sedge, 'I still think of that dog.'

'You mentioned Captain—'

'Hush!' Suddenly Sedge sprang up. His head twitched from side to side.

'What is it?'

'Hush!' he hissed again, and went back down the tunnel. Susannah looked anxiously at Richard. He clutched her hand. Then Sedge was back and swore under his breath.

'Who's following you?' he asked brusquely.

'The Moretons,' Susannah replied. 'We ran from the manor.'

'And led them straight here!' Sedge bristled at them. 'Listen!'

Richard strained his ears but all he could hear was the distant moaning of the wind.

'Dogs!' Sedge explained. 'Damn them!'

As if to prove his point, the sound of baying suddenly came to them, brought in snatches by the wind.

'Will they find us?' Susannah looked at him tensely.

'They will if you stay here,' said Sedge.

'But they will if we leave. I can't run,' replied Richard.

'Do you think I care?' asked Sedge sharply. 'If they find me, do you think they'll let me go?' He glared at them: 'No, even if you run for it, they'll still come here, damn you!' His eyes lingered on his few pathetic belongings. 'Damn you all! I was happy here.' He stooped over a wooden crate and took out a small leather pouch which he stowed in his jacket, then glanced up impatiently. 'Well? Are you coming, or will you rot here?'

Susannah looked surprised, but Richard already knew how the old man's gruff appearance belied his true nature. In spite of their situation, he managed a grin.

'Where are you going?'

'Down. Deeper into the mine. There's a way out,

maybe.' Sedge tightened the belt round his waist. 'It's dangerous, mind. No way for a lady.'

Susannah got to her feet, goaded by his remark. 'Well, I'm not staying here. Will this dress do?'

Sedge considered her, then shook his head.

'Give me your knife,' she told him. She stabbed the blade about halfway down the skirt and hacked away the fabric. 'There,' she smiled, pleased with her work. 'I hope this doesn't shock you, Richard.' Her skirt now came no lower than her knees, revealing her slim, muscular calves and ankles.

'That's no way for a lady to dress,' he remarked.

'Just what are you implying?' She arched her eyebrow.

Sedge muttered something and turned away. 'We'd better be going.' With one final glance round his dwelling, he led them back down the passageway. They had only gone a few feet when a loud bark made them jump. It was closer than they had expected, by the mouth of the tunnel. A man was calling, 'Hoah! Hoah, boy!'

Sedge hurried them to the open shaft.

'We're going down there?' asked Richard sceptically.

'It's the only way.' Sedge sat on the edge of the shaft, then rolled himself onto his stomach and slid into the opening. They could hear him grunting and his feet scrabbling for a footing, then a fall of pebbles which made Susannah gasp. 'Here! Over here!' came a voice from the entrance.

Richard hissed into the shaft: 'Sedge! Are you there?'

'Come on! Quickly!' Sedge's voice was hoarse, urgent.

Susannah went first, then Richard. They found the shaft was not nearly as precipitous as it had seemed, and they were able to slide and scrabble down fifteen feet or so until they came to a shallow platform where Sedge was crouched.

'The next part is difficult,' he whispered. From above there was a heavy clunk as something – a stone probably – was thrown into the tunnel. 'Is it deep?' a man was asking angrily, and Richard recognized with horrible certainty the voice of Oliver Moreton.

'Watch what I do,' instructed Sedge. He stood up, and swung his arms back and forth a couple of times, building momentum, then suddenly he flung himself forward off the ledge and into the blackness. There was a sickening silence for what seemed like an age, then a heavy, muffled *thunk* and the shifting sound of loose stones.

Richard looked at Susannah: 'Are you scared?'

'Are you?' She smiled at him. Then she stood up and he could see her concentrating as she swung her arms to and fro and leapt. He counted his heartbeats and then he heard her landing, lightly, on the other side.

'Susannah! Are you there?' But this came from above. Oliver was at the top of the upper level, and was shouting down the tunnel.

Richard climbed to his feet. A cold draught rose from the bottom of the shaft and chilled his face. He swung his arms, one, two, then heaved himself forward. Blackness rushed towards him, then the ground hit him in the stomach and he lay gasping and winded in the dirt. He looked up, breathless. His ankle was searing.

Casually, Sedge picked up a loose chipping and dropped it into the shaft. They listened and listened until a long way below there came a light rat-a-tat as the stone skipped against projecting rocks. Then nothing. 'Lucky your ankle wasn't worse.' He offered Richard a hand up.

'Susannah!' Oliver's voice echoed angrily through

the mine. Susannah looked anxious. 'Come on,' she whispered.

They had landed at the start of a lower level. Sedge led them forward quickly, away from the shaft. The mine was utterly black, and they had to rely solely on touch and the shuffling sound of the old man. The tunnel sloped down crazily, suddenly pitching at angles of fifty, sixty degrees, or abruptly dropping down a flight of rough, broken steps. The walls were streaming with water and covered in a dank, foul-smelling slime which soon plastered their clothes, their skin, their hair. Richard struggled to keep up. The uneven surface twisted and tore at his ankle and more than once he had to stifle a cry of pain. Eventually, Sedge pulled up beside an opening. Richard heard the man's breaths coming in hoarse rasps. Then Sedge sniffed emphatically. 'Can you smell it? They're smoking us out!'

In the blackness his words sounded ominous. Richard sniffed, and faint on the air came the scent of burning rags.

'Damp cloth makes the best smoke,' muttered Sedge. 'I thought they'd try this, damn them.'

The smoke was becoming thicker by the second.

'Will it work?' asked Susannah.

They heard Sedge scratch his beard. 'Not if we keep moving. But it will make the air thinner.'

Richard struggled to resist a sudden, unreasoning panic. The blackness, which was absolute, seemed to be choking him. He sucked deep breaths into his lungs. 'Come on,' he said impatiently. 'Let's go.'

'We go down here,' said Sedge, and squeezed into the opening, followed by Susannah. It was a much smaller tunnel, maybe five feet high and two wide, and it was cut almost haphazardly through the rock, jumping down in odd, unpredictable zigzags. They scrambled down it as best they could, the enclosed tunnel growing hot and stale with their breath and their sweat. A rivulet of water ran along the bottom, and they splashed and slithered through it, no longer caring how wet they got. Then Susannah felt Sedge disappear ahead of her and there was a large splash.

'Sedge!'

There was a thrashing sound. 'Can you swim?' came his voice.

Susannah felt a cold chill grip her. 'What is it?' she demanded.

'Water,' he called up. 'The tunnel's flooded.'

Susannah inched forward. The tunnel fell for a couple of feet then disappeared into a sheet of water. Clutching her breath, she forced herself into the pool.

It was much colder than she had expected, and she gasped as the water shot up her legs and thighs and froze the pit of her stomach. She kicked her feet wildly, but could not reach the bottom. Then Sedge grabbed her and Richard was beside her. She was surprised to find a strong current dragging at her legs.

'What is this?'

'The old adit,' gasped Sedge. 'They hit a stream while sinking the shaft and had to put in a drainage channel. This will take us to the shore.'

'Is it safe?'

Sedge grunted. 'With any luck the run of water has kept the adit open. I came this way once last year.'

'It's been raining heavily,' said Richard.

'Yes,' admitted Sedge. 'If the adit's blocked, or if the tunnel's too full of water, we'll rest here till Judgement Day.'

Richard felt Susannah's hand squeeze his. 'Well,' he said, 'we'd best get started.'

Sedge struck off into the blackness, churning the

water awkwardly. Susannah and Richard followed. They must have covered only five, six yards when their feet scraped against something and they found they could stand thigh-deep in water. Breathlessly, they struggled upright and waded through the half-filled tunnel. A sharp wind blew down from somewhere and soon they were chilled to the bone, stumbling over submerged rocks, stubbing their hands and heads on protrusions. Ahead of them, Sedge ploughed forward. If he ever hurt himself, or slipped, he made no sound, and his pace hardly ever varied. The water dragged at their bodies, weighing their clothes like lead, and soon they were forcing their legs forward by sheer acts of will, scrambling, wrestling with the water, hardly knowing how slowly or quickly they were making headway, until at length Richard realised their surroundings were changing.

Gradually the tunnel was narrowing and, more worryingly, the level of water was deepening. At first the water had come up to their thighs, now it reached their waists and in some places their bodies sank to their midriffs. Richard gritted his teeth and kept his thoughts to himself. Sedge would have already known this, he realised, but would not want to alarm them.

They pressed on. Now the walls were closing in on them, the roof seemed suddenly lower. Richard caught his forehead on a sharp finger of rock which drew blood. Here the water was up to their chests and they could no longer wade, but had to twist and drive their bodies forwards, clutching at rocks and ledges for handholds. Richard felt Susannah's feet against his side and he realised the water was now too deep for her and she was swimming. Then he too was swimming, struggling to work his arms and legs in the confined space. The water was moving faster, rushing in their ears, splashing over their eyes and noses.

Suddenly they found themselves next to Sedge.

'What is it?' Richard spat a mouthful of water.

Sedge spoke quietly. 'The roof dips here beneath the water.'

Gingerly, Richard put out his arm. Sure enough, the roof of the tunnel, which at this point was only a foot or so above, abruptly dropped down and disappeared into the stream.

'How far is it like this?'

'I don't know. When I came here last, the adit was only half-full.' Sedge spoke slowly, measuring his breaths. 'In a minute, I'm going to dive down and try to swim along the passageway. If we're lucky, the tunnel goes up again and there'll be air to breathe.'

No one said anything. They trod water, listening to the stream lapping against the sides and roof of the tunnel. Sedge was breathing very carefully, as if he were testing the strength of his lungs. Eventually, he seemed satisfied that he was ready.

'Follow me in a little while, but not too soon in case I get stuck.'

'How will we know if you've made it?' asked Susannah.

'We won't,' said Richard.

Sedge braced himself against the roof. 'Remember,' he said, 'swim on your back, with your face to the roof, that way you'll stand a better chance.' Then he pushed with his arms and sank into the stream. They felt the water flutter with his kick, and he was gone.

Richard felt curiously numb. A thousand thoughts flitted in and out of his mind, but each was gone before he could do more than glimpse it. His father, the tomb, the beads of sweat on Moreton's brow, the scent of almonds in Samuel Dowles' house, Susannah glancing at him across the reins of her horse. So many things. He put his arm round her and hugged her to him.

'Do you think he's got through?' she said at last.

'I expect so,' he said confidently. 'Do you want to go first?'

'Yes.' She began to feel the roof for a good diving-point.

'Susannah,' he brushed her face, 'take care.'

'Don't be silly, I'll see you in a minute,' she replied, and then with a breath was gone.

Now he was really alone. Richard imagined her slim body snaking through the water, searching the roof for air. He must stay calm. He counted to sixty and then began to prepare himself.

As soon as he was underwater, everything happened in a deafening rush. The current tugged him down of its own accord and his nails scrabbled against the rock. The roof dropped farther then he expected and for a moment he was crushed against the rock while he forced himself deep enough. Then the tunnel closed over his head and he had a sudden image of the depth of earth and stone above him. He struck out blindly, pushing himself into the flow of the water. Water was squeezing into his eyes and nose. His chest was tight, pain spanned his ribcage, swelled inside his lungs. He had a terrible premonition that any moment he would nudge against Susannah or Sedge floating listlessly against a rock. He took another stroke and another. And another. His lungs were bursting. Where was he? With a crack, an outcrop struck him on the forehead and he gasped. Water poured into his mouth, throat. He was choking. Swim on your back, Sedge had said, and Richard, suddenly remembering, flailed himself over.

Suddenly he struck air. Sedge was right. Here, where the roof rose a little, was a thin slip of air. He sucked and spluttered, then lost his position and sank again, and clawed himself back so that his forehead was pressed tight against the roof and his nose and mouth could somehow breathe. The air tasted of dust and clay. He hung there, panting, and then worked his way forward, lizard-like, along the top of the tunnel, but he made only four or five feet before the roof sheered down again and he plunged back under. He gave three strong strokes then, abruptly, broke water and came up, gasping and heaving, into daylight. Daylight! For a moment, he floundered drunkenly in the shallows, then Sedge caught him and hauled him on to a raised platform of sand. Susannah lay beside him. In the dull light she looked very pale, her hair was plastered over her face, but she was smiling.

They were in a large chamber which opened at the far end directly on to a beach. The stream came bubbling up from the adit to spread into a broad pool before running on to the sand.

Richard gazed at Susannah. Her bodice and skirt were torn and clung to her in tatters, and suddenly he felt himself desire her again, more powerfully than he would have thought possible. He seized her and kissed her on the lips. The closeness of death is the greatest aphrodisiac, he thought, and were it not for Sedge slumped quietly beside them, they would have made love again, there and then. She wrapped her arms around his neck. 'I thought I'd never see you again,' she confided, and kissed him again, forcefully.

'The hills will be watched by Moreton's men,' Sedge interrupted them. The old man's nose was gashed across the bridge and he looked tired. 'It will be broad daylight soon.'

Richard got up and waded painfully through the pool. He sagged against the entrance, exhausted beyond belief.

The tide was at its lowest ebb and before him the grey waste of sand stretched out, slick with water, grey and insubstantial in the first light which crept through the big bruised clouds to the east. A storm was in the air. Susannah shivered. Richard looked at her.

'Ready?'

She nodded and clambered to her feet. The three of them stepped on to the beach and set off northwards under the shelter of the cliffs. Richard was limping and put his arm around Susannah. 'Come on,' he said. 'If we can get away, we'll be all right. I know the gentry in these parts. They'll help us.'

She glanced at him curiously. 'You do?'

Richard avoided her gaze. 'You'll see,' he replied.

'At the far end of the beach there's a path creeps round the cliffs,' interrupted Sedge. 'If we can get there we can cut up the combe and on to the moors.'

They quickened their pace, hugging the base of the cliffs for what shelter they provided. Wind rolled in from the east, chilling them to the bone.

'Damn!' Richard pulled Susannah to the ground. Sedge was already squatting behind a large slab of rock. They had gone less than a hundred yards. Behind them, across the beach, a lone horseman was riding. Even at this distance, the figure's jet-black hair was unmistakable. Oliver. They crouched between the rocks. With a sigh of relief, Richard realised Oliver hadn't noticed them yet, but it would only be a question of time. The rocks offered scant camouflage.

'I said they'd have the beach covered,' whispered Sedge.

'What do we do now?' Susannah looked at him apprehensively.

'We can't stay here,' said Richard. 'He won't be on his own. They'll find us for sure.'

'What about the cave?'

Sedge shook his head. 'We won't make it.'

Susannah reached a decision. It was strange, but she had always felt it might come to this. She had been foolish to think otherwise, for all her dreams. She put her hand on Richard's shoulder. 'Richard, do you care for me?'

Her question angered him. 'You know I do.'

'Do you trust me?'

'Susannah, what are you trying to say?'

She chose her words carefully. 'If you left me, you could still escape.' She saw his eyes widen, and hurried on: 'Richard, what choice do we have? If Oliver has me, you can get away.'

His voice was thick with emotion. 'You said you'd come with me!'

'You know I want to!' she flared. 'But I can distract him. Look, we haven't got much time.'

He hesitated. *Could* he trust her? He stared at her intently, as if willing his eyes to see through her flesh and penetrate to her soul. Who are you? he thought. Who are you?

'If I return for you,' he said, 'will you come?'

She glared at him. 'If you don't, I'll never forgive you!'

Sedge laughed drily. 'Well? It's our best chance.'

'Will you be safe?' persisted Richard.

'You held the pistol to my head, remember? Besides, Oliver has to believe me: he needs to marry me.' Or his father does, she thought darkly. She stroked

Richard's head, tenderly, where he had been cut, and kissed him.

Richard clutched her, feeling her warm, strong body through her dress. 'I'll come as soon as I can.'

'Do you promise?'

'Yes, damn you!'

'I'll go riding every morning if I can. Wait for me in the hollow.'

She kissed him quickly. The horseman was less than a furlong away.

'Let me get clear, then go on,' she said. 'I'll tell him you abandoned me.'

With that she got to her knees and began to work her way back through the rocks, keeping out of sight. Richard watched her, still hardly believing what she was doing and that he was letting her go, freely, after all that had happened. Susannah waited until she had gone back twenty, thirty yards, then she sprang up and ran across the beach, her hair streaming in the wind. She ran fast, then faster, until the feelings in her heart became a blur. Oliver saw her almost immediately and spurred on his horse. Sedge touched Richard on the elbow. 'Come on.'

Reluctantly, Richard jerked his gaze away from Susannah. He and Sedge crept along the base of the cliff. They covered twenty feet and threw themselves into a crevasse. Richard scrambled to his feet and gazed back across the beach.

Susannah was far away from them now. She had stopped running and was standing still, a slim, delicate figure against the empty expanse of sand. The wind was tugging at her skirt and hair and she had wrapped her arms around herself for warmth. Oliver was almost upon her. He reined in his horse.

'Get down!' Sedge pulled at Richard's arm. Sunlight

was spilling across the waters in swathes of pearl. It would be day soon. Richard shrugged him off.

Oliver's horse stood in front of Susannah. He leaned down from the saddle and extended an arm to her. Susannah took it and was lifted up beside him in one easy movement. Then Oliver spurred his horse and was already riding back along the beach. Overhead a gull called and called again, his call coming back and echoing and calling again until the man and the woman had dissolved into the early-morning haze.

PART TWO

STORM OUTSIDE

Chapter One

THE LABOURER HENRY COUCH HAD lived alone the three years since his wife's death, but if he was bitter at his new-found loneliness, he would not admit it. What did a man want with a woman at his time of life? he asked himself pointedly. In any case, he would soon be leaving this world, if the Lord was willing. He sank down on the straw pallet in the corner of his hut and levered off his boots. The leather was cracked and leaking and his feet were wrapped in wet rags which stank unpleasantly. He rubbed his toes for warmth, his breath labouring in his lungs. The Lord forgive me, he muttered, and felt the dampness spread across his chest.

'Henry.'

The voice jolted him. 'Who's there?' His own voice was nervous, strained. He reached for his staff.

The door swung open. Richard Tremaine was standing on the threshold, silhouetted against the night.

'Henry! It's me, Richard.' Richard lurched into the hut and swung the door to.

'Master, what are you doing here?' Couch eyed him fearfully, his hand still clasping the stick.

'I need help.' Richard slumped to the floor. 'I haven't slept for two days.' He dropped his hands on to his knees and shut his eyes, then, hearing no reply from Couch, opened them again: 'What's wrong?'

Couch's lips scarcely moved. 'They say you killed Mistress Ursula.'

Richard sprang up. 'Damn you, Henry! It's all lies.

193

Don't you understand? Moreton killed her, so he could marry Susannah.'

'Don't come any closer, master.' Couch's fingers were knotted over his stick. 'In the love of God – they found you in her tomb.' His lips were wet with spittle and he backed away against the far wall.

Richard felt at a loss. He saw the panic in the old man's eyes and carefully lowered his hands. 'Henry, I didn't do it. I need your help, or else they'll take me for sure.'

'They said you were the dead man,' Couch muttered, as if to a third person.

'Dead man?'

'Jessie Moyle had a dream. She said you'd come back from the dead.'

Richard became impatient. 'What? That's ridiculous. Look, here I am!'

Couch persisted stubbornly. 'Jessie was certain, master. She said you were dead, but you'd come back, to reclaim your own. And then Mistress Ursula is killed and they find—'

At that moment Richard lunged forward suddenly and snatched the stick from Couch's grasp. The old man tried to struggle but Richard was too strong and batted him away with the flat of his hand.

'Look!' he commanded. 'I don't care about this woman's dreams. I'm here, I'm alive! Will you help me?'

Henry looked wretched. He was gasping painfully. 'I don't see I have much choice, master.'

'Good.' Richard patted the stick against his palm. 'And if you help me, I promise I'll be gone for good, understand? First, I need to know something: you said you saw my father the day he died. Did you see Jacob Sawle? Was he with him?'

Henry went to speak but the breath caught in his throat and an ugly cough bubbled up from somewhere deep within his chest. Richard waited until he had finished.

'Can I get you something to drink, Henry?'

Henry blinked at him through bleary eyes. There was red on his palm, and he wiped it hastily on his jacket. 'Can I sit down, master?' There was all the resentment of a dying man in that last word.

'Of course.'

Couch slumped on to his pallet. Richard inspected the contents of an earthenware jug by the door, but the water had a yellow, brackish look to it.

'Jacob Sawle?' Couch recovered himself. 'Yes. We found him in the fields. Dead.'

'And what about my father? Who found him?'

Couch thought for a moment. 'I don't know. I remember Isaac Rogers, the steward, brought his body back. They buried him quickly, 'cause of the Parliament.'

Except it wasn't his body they buried, thought Richard. 'You said a stableboy brought my father a note that morning before he rode out. What happened to him?'

'Harry Jenkins? He left the farm when Colonel Moreton took over. Someone said he was working as a carter, upcountry, but I'm not sure.'

'Could you ask, Henry? Is there anyone who might know?'

Couch shrugged weakly.

'What about the housekeeper, Mrs Collins?'

'Died the year before last.'

'Who else was at the manor?'

Couch thought again. 'No one, apart from Mrs Stephens, the cook. All the others left when your mother went to Lembury. I last heard Mrs Stephens was working for a family near Exeter.'

Richard considered the information carefully. Then he returned his gaze to the old man before him.

'When I saw you last time, I asked about Moreton. I don't think you've told me everything you know, have you, Henry?'

Couch buried his face in his hands. 'I'm just a farm-worker. I don't know anything, master.'

'No,' replied Richard. 'There's something happening, isn't there, Henry? None of the old servants have been kept on. Goods are unloaded in the middle of the night. Then Ursula is murdered under the very roof. What's going on, Henry?'

'I swear to God I don't know, master!' Couch's face was white and ghastly.

'Then why are you screaming?' asked Richard drily. 'And why when I saw you in the wood did you ask me to forgive you? Why, or by God you'll wish you were dead!'

He picked up the old man by his collar and shook him violently.

'What is it, Henry?'

'I don't know!'

'They rescued me from the storm – what happened to the others? What happened to the ship?'

Something inside the old man snapped. He began to sob uncontrollably, a terrible gurgling sound. 'What do you think we were doing when you saw us in the garden with the cart?' he wailed. 'What do you think we were doing?'

Richard eyed him sceptically. 'What are you saying, Henry?'

But now there was no stopping him. The words burst out. 'We were burying their bodies, burying bodies, don't you see? The Colonel had them killed, and gave us the bodies to bury. I picked one of them up with my own hands. May the Lord forgive me!' He waved his hands, like claws, in the air.

'Good God.' Richard released him and let him sink to the ground, sobbing. 'He killed the sailors who brought me?'

'In cold blood, master.' Couch did not look up.

'Why did no one say anything?'

'Do you really not know?' Couch's voice was suddenly scathing. 'The Colonel owns us all, master, just like your father did. Owns our very souls. Do you think anyone cares so long as they get their share of the spoils? The Colonel is in so thick with the authorities, do they care so long as it's foreign ships?'

Richard stared at him. His head was reeling. Susannah had claimed as much, in the cellar, and he had ignored her. But now, to see the look on Couch's face, to hear the tone of his voice . . . He put his hand to his head.

'Shocked, master?' asked Couch bitterly.

Yet it all made sense. As Susannah had said, he was spared so they could blame him for Ursula's death. My God, he thought, is Susannah safe there? Should I have listened to her? He punched his fist against the wall. He had had no choice. None at all.

'Henry, you've got to help me,' he said at last. 'I need to get away.'

'Don't I wish I could do the same?' asked Couch. 'We're damned, master. Damned.'

There was the sound of footsteps outside. Richard frantically motioned for Couch to stay still, and stepped behind the door. There was a light knock, then he heard Rebecca say:

'Henry? Can I come in? Is Richard with you?'

Richard pulled the door open. Rebecca was standing outside. Her face, normally pale, was flushed, her eyes wide and nervous. Richard was momentarily at a loss for words. 'How did you know I was here?'

'Why did you tell my father where you were going?' she asked pointedly.

Richard remembered Sedge's look of astonishment when he had finally told him who he was. Incredibly, the gruff old man hadn't believed him and it had taken Richard several minutes of hard talking before he was persuaded. And then it had taken Sedge several minutes more to stop hugging Richard like a long-lost prodigal son. Despite everything, Richard grinned to himself.

Rebecca saw his amusement and, perhaps in reaction, added unkindly: 'I almost didn't come, in any case.'

His smiled disappeared. 'I'm glad you did.' He laid a hand on her shoulder and steered her towards the door.

Rebecca frowned. She found his gesture cold and formal, but then she caught sight of Couch, hunched sullenly on his pallet, and understood. The less the old man heard, the better. Outside, night had fallen and here, under the trees, they could talk privately.

'What are you going to do?' asked Rebecca. She was annoyed that her voice sounded as concerned as it did.

Richard didn't answer her directly. 'First of all, is Susannah all right?'

'Why do you want to know?' she demanded. 'Yes, they believed her story, if that's what you mean, but that's hardly surprising, is it? She's good at lying.'

Her accusation stung him. 'Rebecca, I can trust her, believe me.'

'Can you? Who is she, Richard? Don't you know yet?'

'She helped me escape, Beckie! If not for her, I'd still be locked up.' He grabbed her by the wrist and stared into her eyes. 'We all have secrets, don't we? Why didn't you tell me your father was alive?'

Instead of apologising as he expected, Rebecca flared with anger. 'You don't realise what it's like, do you?' Her voice was sharp, scathing. 'Living in fear of discovery, night and day expecting the worst. I thought you were dead, Richard! Then you appear out of the blue. There were things I couldn't tell you.'

'So you don't trust me either, is that it?'

Rebecca flinched as if she had been struck. Did he really need to ask her that? 'My father says he can arrange a boat,' she said at last, painfully. 'It will take you to France.'

Richard breathed out heavily. The chance of leaving for France with Susannah was tempting beyond belief. But he was not ready yet. Not while so many things were unresolved. He steeled himself. 'Thank you, but I've made up my mind. I can't go.'

'Why not, Richard? You're not waiting for *her*, are you?' The resentment made her voice harsh.

'No, there is something I must do.'

'What, for the King? For Charles Stuart?'

No, he thought angrily, for myself. He turned on her: 'Beckie, what's happening here? Henry's just told me Moreton killed the sailors on the *Marguerite*.'

She shrugged, but her mind was elsewhere. 'Maybe. I don't know, Richard. I know nothing about it.'

'But you go to Porthcarrick all the time. I saw the remains of the ship there.'

'Since when has wrecking ever been a crime?' she asked. 'If the sea puts a ship on the rocks, where's the wrong in that?'

'But if the others were killed—'

'Richard, I told you he's evil! Why didn't you listen to me? Because you didn't want to hear, did you? Anyway,' she retorted, 'why should that bother you? We're the poor souls who have to live with him.'

'Moreton has accused me of murdering his wife. I've been used, damn it.'

'We're all used, sooner or later.' She shot him a look, but he missed her implication. 'Leave while you can, Richard. This means nothing to you any more.' We mean nothing to you, she meant.

'No,' he replied stubbornly. An image of Susannah came to him, warm, supplicating, but he pushed it away. 'I came here for a purpose, and I'll stay until it's done. I need to find out what happened to my father.'

Of all that he had said, this seemed to incense her most. She glared at him frantically, her straight, noble features contorted with exasperation. 'He's dead, Richard, don't you understand? What's the point of digging up old ghosts?'

'Because they're *my* ghosts!' he shouted back.

His outburst snapped the tension between them. They stood staring at each other, regretting.

'Look,' Richard held her hands fondly, 'I can't run away from this. You must see that.'

'But what if you get caught? They'll hang you for sure.'

'That's my choice, isn't it?' He kissed her on the forehead.

'I can help you, Richard.'

He shook his head gently. 'I can't ask that of you.'

'Then why did you want me to come here?' She looked into his sharp blue eyes, trying to read the emotions which flickered beneath their surface.

'I wanted to apologise. When I saw you in the graveyard I was selfish. I wasn't thinking of you.' He paused. 'I didn't want us to part on bad terms.'

In spite of everything, his words hurt her. Politeness instead of passion is the most wounding of all, she thought bitterly.

'There was no need, Richard,' she answered. 'I was not offended.'

He stared at her intently. Weren't you, really? he wondered. Rebecca's face was pale, proud, and he found himself resenting her composure. Why didn't she ever show her emotions? Didn't she care?

'There is one thing,' he said. 'Do you know anyone called Harry Jenkins? He was my father's stableboy.'

'Harry Jenkins?' She shook her head.

'Could you ask at the village, and anywhere else? I need to speak to him.'

She nodded, without enthusiasm. 'All right, I'll ask. What shall I tell my father?'

'Tell him if I need a boat, I'll be in touch.'

'You know where to find us, Richard.'

And with that, Rebecca turned and disappeared into the shadow of the trees.

Richard looked after her for only a minute. Then he returned to the cottage, and if he was troubled by half-formed regrets and forgotten longings, the sight of Henry Couch still huddled on his pallet drove them away. Couch was ashen-faced and breathed with difficulty.

'You're not well,' Richard told him gently.

'I know, damn you, master,' Couch replied, as if he held Richard personally responsible.

'Will you help me, Henry?' said Richard. 'Help me, and I'll leave you in peace.'

'What do you want?'

'I need to change my appearance. Do you have some clothes?'

In spite of his pain, Henry Couch managed a sickly smile.

Half an hour later Richard emerged from the hut. He was clad in the oldest rags Couch could find. His face and hands had been blackened, his hair torn with a knife and matted with dirt. His clothes stank of Henry Couch. He could smell the old man's enseamed grime, his sour sweat and phlegm. But he no longer looked like Richard Tremaine. Richard limped up the path and through the copse towards the lane. The wind was even stronger now and banged through the trees and shook the ground.

He had thought all day about what he should do. When Rebecca had offered him a boat and a quick escape to France, part of him had leapt at the chance. Perhaps if Susannah had been there, by his side, he would have taken it, and to hell with the consequences. He hated to think of her waiting for him at Chynoon – hated, detested the idea of Oliver Moreton being with her – but he had no choice. In his heart, he was resolved to stay until the meeting at Tregony. Perhaps then he would know what had happened to his father and he would be free of the past once and for all. In the meantime, his best course was to contact the local gentry, which was what Dowles would have done. And that meant he was headed to Caerleon, the home of Sir Charles Roselyn.

The wind stabbed through the trees. Richard shuddered and pulled his rags about his shoulders and wished Henry had allowed him a cloak or cape. It was six, seven miles to Caerleon as the crow flew, longer by foot, and he hoped he would make it. His ankle was still tender, but it was tightly bound and the bite had gone from its pain.

Damn Couch! He stamped his feet to keep his blood moving and clapped his arms around him. Black, curdled clouds were spinning up from the sea and clotting in the sky above him. The moon rimmed them with cold, glistening silver. This wind will blow our thoughts from our heads, he muttered to himself. He cut through the trees until he struck a lane which sank between sheer hedges, seven feet high and fringed with thornbush. He jumped down gratefully into the lee of the hedge, landing on his good foot, and carried on up the hill. His soles were wrapped in strips of rotten rag, and he padded up the lane with scarcely a sound.

The countryside was normally empty after dark, and on a night like this, Richard expected to meet with neither man nor beast. So, as he came up the rise, he was surprised to see a group of horsemen gathered at the crossroads ahead. They were dressed in heavy riding capes and sat hunched in their saddles. He thought for an awful moment they were Moreton's servants and scrambled up the hedge as quickly as he could. Then he realised that the men had stopped and seemed to be laughing and jeering at something on the ground. The thing was leaping and bounding and making strange barking noises. Richard ducked down behind the hedge and skirted along the field towards them. The men laughed again. Richard crouched behind the ruins of a hawthorn and peered over.

On the ground lay an old man. His limbs were twisted like a spider's, and Richard saw this was through no act of nature, but that the man was actually pretending to be some weird and monstrous beast and was crawling in the dirt and gnashing his teeth and yelping like a fox. This was why the men were laughing.

'Aihai hai iagh!' The man threw his neck back and holloahed to the crescent moon. His neck was as scrawny as a chicken's, his Adam's apple trembled like a bobbin.

One of the riders conjured a strip of ham from his saddlebag and dangled it above the man's snout. 'Here, Tom,' he called. 'Snap 'un up!'

He dropped the bacon and Tom snaffled it out of the air. The riders clapped and hooted. Some threw other titbits and the old man dug them out of the mud and devoured them.

Richard realised he recognised one of the riders. He was the large shovel-bearded man he had seen with Rebecca at Porthcarrick. The man seemed to be the group's leader, for he soon tired of this charade and called to the others.

'Come on, you idiots! We've got work to do. Anyone'd think you'd never seen a beggar before!' He leaned over the side of his horse and spat. 'As if this weather ain't bad enough!'

'All right, Jackie! All right!'

The others grunted, and with a few backward glances at the man scrabbling in the dirt, set off. Richard realised with relief that if they had not been delayed by this spectacle they would have run into him in the lane. The man called Tom cackled to himself and carried on eating. Richard watched him uneasily for a few moments and then squelched off across the fields until he was far past the spot. His foot rags were already soaked through and his toes were numb. He thought of Susannah and hoped she was safe. What was she feeling? he wondered. An image came to him, of her standing in her bedroom by the fire, but he tried not to linger on it. He must be patient. In a few days he would be in Tregony, and then perhaps they could be together.

An owl hooted above him. He clambered over the hedge and pressed on down the lane. He trudged for he guessed ten or fifteen minutes and then the lane forked. He couldn't remember this. The way to the left was occupied by a stream and dissolved into a muddy slurry within a few yards. The right fork had recently been filled with grits but headed too far to the north. Richard turned left and forded the stream as best he could. After twenty yards the stream trickled off to one side and the lane veered steeply downhill, snaking between the flanks of two hills. Mud lay deep and in places he found himself up to his calves in mire and cow dung and whatever other dirt had stuck to the lane. The going was tiring and his ankle nagged at him. Above, the trees moaned under the wind.

At last he reached the bottom of the hill, yet here the path disappeared into a pool of stagnant water and filth, and he had to clamber through brambles and over the hedge to work his way round. Then the lane split again. This time he took the right, and forced his way up through a narrow lane choked with broken branches and dead ferns.

It started to rain, and the wind caught the rain and shot it ferociously across the country. The puddles lying in the middle of the lane became deeper. Water forced its way through his scarf and jacket, drenched his clothes. The lane banked sharply to the left, and staggered in a rough crescent along the gradient of the hill. Now the clouds were so thick that the moon had disappeared altogether. The world was sunk into a thick, clogging blackness. The rain grew heavier. Richard began to stub his feet against stones, logs, sticks, and several times he lost his footing and tripped or slithered or jerked up against the hedge. Where was he going? In the pitch blackness, he felt he had lost all sense of direction. At length, the lane evened out and cut across another path, but where this was heading, he couldn't say. He struggled to the top of the hedge, stabbing his hands on thorns, and tried to get his bearings, but the clouds were so low and dense he could see nothing but the ridges of the nearest hedges and black smudges of trees.

Suddenly he heard horses, coming up the path from the left. The wind and rain had swallowed the sound until they were almost at his feet. He toppled off the hedge into the ditch beyond just in time as a band of three horsemen rode by. They were cavalry troopers. All wore the tight round helmets and breastplates of government issue. They pulled up at the junction, their horses snorting and stamping. 'Which way?' one of them asked. 'How should I know?' another snapped, and swore violently: 'Curse this weather!' He swung his gaze around and Richard ducked down. He had the unmistakable feeling they were looking for him. Then the third man spoke: 'Carson and Pound, you take the left track. I'll go straight on. We'll meet by the old stone. Be quick.' Without further questions the horsemen split up. Richard waited as the sound of their hooves faded into the wind, then dropped back into the lane. This was madness. He was never going to reach Caerleon at this rate. He stood undecided, feeling the rain blast him and his body shaking with the cold, and then he took the left path, the way the troopers had just come.

This time he made good progress. The path was narrow and pitted with hoofprints, but it sloped downhill and was sheltered by a low bank. Richard began to feel some of his old confidence returning. His ankle was easing now, and his pace quickened comfortably. He came to a larger, deeply rutted lane, and took a right, reckoning this was the best direction. A dense squall shivered in the pools and rivulets before him, but he ignored this and pressed on. He came to another fork and went left, bowing his head, feeling the rain pelting his back, going as quickly as he could. Then abruptly he turned a corner and found himself staring into a farmyard. The lane ended here. He had no sooner realised his mistake when the farm dogs sensed his arrival and began to bark ferociously from inside the house. He thought for a moment of running across the yard and cutting through the fields on the other side, but stopped. He wasn't even sure that Caerleon lay that way. In the farmhouse the dogs were going frantic. Quickly he withdrew up the lane. Now the rain hit him straight in the face, blinding him. Where was he going? He was gripped by the realisation that he was lost, totally lost, in a hostile country. He rounded the next bend, water lying deep in the lane now, and sank to the ground. He was exhausted.

'Ho, what is this? A poor naked wretch, as I?'

Richard jerked his head up. Out of the darkness, a thin, raggedy figure had appeared. It stooped over him, momentarily shielding him from the rain.

'Whoever you are, that bide the pelting of this pitiless storm,' the man muttered, 'are thee well?'

Richard realised with a shock that this was the beggar he had seen earlier. The man laughed to himself. It was, amid the wind and rain, a most inhuman sound. 'Come in out of the storm, heh, heh!' He gripped Richard's arm and tugged him upright.

Richard regarded him unwillingly. 'Who are you?'

'Me? Who am I? Now he asks questions, does he?'

The man bent almost double. 'Why, I am poor Tom, or I am today.' He peered into Richard's face. 'And you're a fool to be out tonight, for sure. And you're not the only one, for sure,' he added pointedly, and wagged his finger.

'How do you mean?'

'Soldiers. Servants of the evil one, riding hither and thither over the hills tonight. Say they're hunting man.' He sniffed as a dog sniffs for scent. 'About your age if I'm not mistook.' He squinted knowingly. Richard backed away.

'I'm just a traveller, like you.'

Tom laughed. 'Pray you're not like me, boy. I have no way, I stumbled when I saw. No, they'll smell you a mile off, you're not like me. They gave me food, tasty bits.' He licked his lips and came so close that Richard turned his head away. 'Who gives anything to poor Tom? Whom the foul fiend hath led through fire and through flame, through ford and whirlpool, o'er bog and quagmire!'

Richard began to shiver.

'Are you cold?' asked Tom. 'Tom's a-cold. Bless thy five wits.' His eyes suddenly took on a crazed glare. 'Look!' he cried. 'Look!' He pointed a thin scraggly hand up to the sky. 'Can you see it?'

'What?'

'The foul fiend flies in the teeth of the storm. There! And there! And there again!' He began to gibber uncontrollably. Richard stepped away and started to go back up the lane.

'Wait!' Tom called after him. 'Where are you going? Do you know?'

Richard hesitated. 'To Caerleon.'

'You won't find it that way, will you?' Tom cackled again. 'You're lost, aren't 'ee, boy? The servants of the devil will catch 'ee and put 'ee on a spit. Tasty titbits, tasty!' He clapped his hands and leapt in the air. The sky groaned overhead and a barb of lightning stabbed through the night. Tom was illumined in a sudden flash of white. His mouth was agawp and toothless, his eyes blazing. Richard saw for the first time that his head was hideously scarred, so that no hair grew on the right side, and his skull was covered by a glistening web of pink tissue.

'All right,' he said. 'I am lost. Can you take me to Caerleon?'

Tom slapped his hands together. 'Of course! Of course I know the way! Aren't all we fools the leaders of the wise, and look, you're lost!' He tugged at Richard's sleeve. 'Now lift your foot, or else your sole will be damned with mud.'

This was when the madness started. Richard would never forget his journey across the hell-strewn country-side, black with storm, blistered and blasted by the blinding winds, lanced, whipped, lashed by the thunderflash, and he and poor Tom stumbling hunched and wretched through the pelting lanes and ditches. And all the while Tom would sing to himself and cry to the winds, and real tears would stream down his face.

'Still through the hawthorn blows the cold wind. Says suum, mun, hey nonny nonny!'

Tom threw his head back and laughed like a dog, and skipped and cavorted in the mire before him. Richard rested himself against a gatepost. Lightning spat across the hills, the sky ripped and roared.

'How much further, Tom?'

'We must go deep first. Deep!'

Richard stared at him.

'O what a poor wretch is man,' intoned Tom. 'Homeless and out of doors. But a poor stick of flesh and bone, on which a few rags hang.'

Something in his words struck Richard. 'No,' he replied quietly. 'We are more than that.'

'Pray what, exactly, my *wise* man?' enquired Tom.

Richard shrugged. 'Men are more than that. We have hopes, we have loves, memories, dreams. We have duties which bind us together. We have families, friends.'

'Dreams? Why, I have such dreams, boy!' Tom rocked on his feet like a bird. 'I dreamed I deflowered the Queen and coupled with the clouds. Why, I dream I am a man – a man! – instead of this sick incarnation. We are all contagioned! Diseased with dreams. Do we care? Do we love? Do we know God and duty? How we delude ourselves, pretend these things are real. Kill, live, love, die – for what? For lies! Damn damn damn lies! Take all our civilisation, it barely extends beyond a mother's love, and what else have vixens and vipers—' Tom stopped abruptly and cocked his head to one side, then he sprang at Richard. Richard went to fend him off, but Tom knocked him to the ground, and they rolled over, scrabbling in the mud.

Just in time. At that moment the three troopers pounded up the lane at breakneck speed. The first rider spotted them and reined in his horse. The animal was kicking and prancing in the mud, ears flattened, its great hooves narrowly missing their huddled bodies.

'Hoah!' called the man. 'Who goes there?'

'Dolphin, my boy, boy! – sessa!' Tom blinked up at them. 'Have you found your prey, my lords and ladies?'

The soldier wiped the rain out of his eyes. 'And who's this?' He stabbed a finger at Richard.

'Hah! Here's one who's better than I!' squealed Tom. 'He has coupled with demons and licked their—'

'Quiet, damn you!' ordered the trooper. He peered menacingly at Richard. 'Who are you?'

Richard shook himself. 'Me?' Who am I? Now he asks questions, does he?' He paused. 'Why, I am poor Tom, or I am today.' He squinted into the trooper's face. 'And you're a fool to be out tonight, for sure. And you're not the only one, for sure.'

The trooper scrutinised him for a second and then grunted dismissively. 'The devil take the both of you,' he snapped. 'Let's go.' His companions nodded and shook their reins and disappeared down the lane.

'Let them trot by,' cried Tom after them. He stretched out a hand to pull Richard up. 'You've got a feel for it, boy!'

Richard stared at Tom's hand. It was a hideous twisted claw. Two fingers had been hacked away.

What if . . .?

'Father?' he said. 'Father, is that you?'

Tom blinked down at him, water running over his eyebrows. 'I have spawned with the devil, son. I have slept in the contriving of lust and waked to it.' He held his hand out, patiently, like some bizarre benediction. 'Forgive me.'

Richard took it and pulled himself up. 'Father, is that you? It's me, Richard.' He peered into Tom's face. Lightning glinted in his eyes.

'Aye, I'll father you. I'll lead you farther up the path.' Tom jerked his head and cantered backwards. 'Fee, fie, fo, fum!'

I must be going mad, thought Richard. Tom was disappearing up the lane, and he ran to keep up. I must be crazed, to believe even for an instant, that this man could be my father.

The lane clambered up the side of the hill and then wound along its spine for a mile or so. Then Tom gave a great whoop of triumph and gestured frantically ahead.

'There she is, the promised land!'

From this point the hill ran down into a valley. At the base of the valley, fringed with trees, loomed the shape of a large country house. Caerleon. The rain beat across the landscape in great drifts and beyond the house lay the black expanse of the sea.

Richard stared at the house for no more than a few seconds. But when he turned round, Tom was not there. He thought Tom had started down the lane and raced after him but after twenty yards, the lane ran straight and Richard could see it was empty.

'Tom!' he shouted. 'Tom!' His voice clawed up between the winds and was snuffed out by a great blast of air.

He stumbled back to the top of the hill.

'Tom! Tom!'

But the hill was empty.

Chapter Two

SIR CHARLES ROSELYN MET HIM in the library. He was a grey-haired man in his late fifties, bleary-eyed, pink-faced and furious.

'What in God's name—' he began. Richard was leaning back in one of the mahogany chairs, enjoying a glass of warmed beer from the kitchen.

'Sir Charles.' Richard put the glass down and smiled. 'I'm sorry to trouble you like this.' He gestured at his rags.

'You have no right!'

'Please sir, the servants.' Richard nodded at the door. Sir Charles glowered angrily, and then, as if he found something oddly compelling in Richard's gaze, turned and closed the door.

'My servant said you had an important message,' Sir Charles reminded him curtly. 'What is it?'

Richard got up and bowed. 'I am here on the King's business.'

'We have no need of a King, now the Lord Cromwell protects us,' replied Sir Charles suspiciously.

'I heard you were loyal to the Crown.'

'Great God, man!' exploded Sir Charles. 'Don't you know that's treason – what do you take me for? If you want to arrest me, go ahead, but I'll not help you with your silly entrapments!'

Richard shook his head. 'Sir, I am not from the Lord Protector.'

'How do I know?' Sir Charles eyed him disdainfully. 'From the way you dress, how do I know you're not just another tramp? My servants should never have let you in.' He turned brusquely back to the door. 'Now, state your business, or apply for a warrant and be damned. I still have friends on the County Committee.'

'Do you really not recognise me?' asked Richard. 'I am Michael Tremaine's son.'

Sir Charles stopped, a reply half-formed on his lips.

'Sir, you lie,' he said slowly.

'I do not.' Richard took a step forward. 'Sir, I need your help.'

Sir Charles regarded him coldly.

'Proof, sir. What proof do you have?'

Richard thought frantically.

'When I was a boy my father took me here twice. The second time you let me ride your bay charger. Cockatoo I think he was called.'

'And what did my wife say to you?'

'Your first wife was already dead, sir.'

Sir Charles's eyes gradually warmed. 'Is it really you, boy? Robert—'

'Richard. You're still not sure, are you? To think my father called you a trusting old goat.'

And then Sir Charles Roselyn threw back his head and laughed.

'So,' said Sir Charles, as Richard was forking a great mess of bacon into his mouth, 'Moreton accuses you of murdering his wife, does he?'

'*Pretends* I murdered his wife,' Richard corrected him. He chewed hurriedly and swallowed. 'But that's not why I'm here. The real matter is the King's business.'

'You say you have to be in Tregony on the twenty-fifth?' Sir Charles's eyes narrowed. 'That's the day after tomorrow.'

'It is?' Richard realised he had lost all sense of time.

'And what precisely do you have to do?'

'Someone has written to the King offering assistance. I have to meet him and assess the situation.'

'Is it safe? Can you trust him?'

Richard's fork paused just before his mouth. 'No more than you trusted me, sir.'

Sir Charles chuckled, but his eyes were grey and serious. 'What if it's a trap?'

'Then I get caught, maybe.' Richard took a swallow of beer. 'The King expects us all to make sacrifices.'

'Yes.' Sir Charles looked down at his own plate. 'And I suppose you want me to make some as well?'

Richard nodded and chewed some more.

'Look, Tremaine, I have my family and tenants to consider. If the Committee even thought I was involved . . .'

Richard waited for him to trail off. 'Just give me a horse and some new clothes,' he said, 'and enough money to get by. You'll hardly know I'm here.'

He saw Sir Charles' face flicker with relief, and thought of Charles Stuart, hundreds of miles away in Cologne, expecting such men as these to die for him.

Despite his tepid enthusiasm for the King's cause, Sir Charles was a generous host. He made sure that Richard was given a warm bath, as much food as he could eat and his choice of clothes. His one stipulation was that Richard had as little contact with his servants as possible, which suited Richard well. Here at Caerleon, all he wanted to do was rest and recuperate.

For the time being I must forget everything that has happened, he told himself, even Susannah.

Yet when finally he fell asleep that afternoon, Richard found himself back in the dark corridors of Chynoon.

He knew instantly where he was, from the oppressive sense of doom that impregnated the walls. Susannah was with him, naked, warm, entwining him in her arms. He gasped hungrily at her mouth and then she screamed and was torn from him. Someone – Oliver Moreton, he believed – was dragging her away, and Richard ran after her, but she had already disappeared down the corridor into the Great Hall. He rushed through the doors, the Hall was ablaze with candles the size of fires, and there, in the midst, was William Moreton, stern and implacable, seated on his throne of blood, which ran wet and crimson in the roaring flames, and the flames leaped and danced on the blood. Richard stopped still. He was mesmerised by Moreton's eyes, which seemed to bore into his very soul. Then, by a supreme act of will, he dragged his gaze down to Moreton's feet. There, naked and crimson, lay the bodies of Ursula and Sarah and on top of them all, proud and beautiful, he saw with a shock, Rebecca, gazing up at him through still wide eyes.

Chapter Three

RICHARD'S FACE WAS TIRED AND gaunt as he coaxed his horse down the lane to Tregony. For the last two days, the dreams of Chynoon had not left him. Every night the same weird scenes had lurked in his mind until he had begun to doubt his wisdom in sticking to this meeting at all. Susannah. He could still feel the touch of her skin against his. Was she really safe there? he wondered. He should never have left her. He kicked his heels into his horse's flanks and its hooves clattered lightly on the street.

As he reached the first houses, Richard pulled the collar of his cloak high about his face, but none of the townsfolk seemed to notice him. Not that he would even recognise himself. Before leaving Caerleon, he had cropped his hair short, in the presbyterian style, and dyed it black. Dr Masters would be proud of me, he thought grimly.

The river port of Tregony possessed one of the broadest high streets in the country. A hundred years ago it had also been one of the richest. But since the silt had choked both river and trade, the town had a pinched and hungry look. Shops were boarded up and several of the merchants' houses had fallen into decay.

It was strange, thought Richard, that this little borough had returned two Members of Parliament under the old system. At this, he was reminded of the heavy figure of Gregory Clement, slouched over the table at Chynoon. The former Member of Parliament for Tregony, Moreton had said. Was that just coincidence? he

217

wondered. Or is Moreton in some way connected with this meeting? But he did not see how this was possible and thought no more of it.

The Three Lords was a large establishment which dominated the middle of the high street. Through an arch there was a spacious courtyard with stabling for many horses and even the few coaches which attempted to journey this far south. Richard gave his reins to the boy out front and went in. In spite of himself, he felt tense, nervous. As soon as he gave his name, he would be exposing himself as the King's messenger. If Sir Charles was right, and it was a trap, it would be a confession of guilt.

The innkeeper was standing behind the bar, holding a half-finished glass of ale. He was a short, surly man with a bald head and watery eyes. Although he wore only a loose grey vest, originally white, he was sweating heavily.

'Yes?'

'I'd like a room for the night,' Richard told him.

'You would, would you?' The man grinned stupidly, as if he had cracked a joke, and revealed an alarming shortage of teeth.

'If it's too much trouble, I'll go down the road to The Swan.'

'Hah! Hah! Hah!' The man's mouth gaped open even further and he scratched himself unpleasantly under the armpits. 'Name, sir?'

Richard was aware that the conversation in the tavern had quietened and several of the customers were watching him casually. 'Peter Upton.' He glanced round the bar. If any of the customers noticed his name, they didn't show it.

'So, so.' The innkeeper wet a quill and scribbled the name in the ledger in front of him. He looked up.

'That'll be one shilling, sir.' Richard flipped him a coin. 'Frances will show you up.'

A young, rosy-cheeked girl in a pinafore bobbed out of the kitchen and curtseyed.

'Travelled far?' she asked, halfway up the stairs.

'Plymouth,' said Richard without thinking.

'Plymouth? I've got a cousin in Plymouth.' She looked over her shoulder. 'Michael Pellow, do you know him?'

'I'm afraid not.' Richard wished he had kept his mouth shut.

'Well, here's your room, sir.' Frances knocked a door open with her hand to reveal a small, white room with a simple bed and clothes-press.

'Thank you, Frances.'

She flashed him a smile. 'Will you be coming down for a drink later, sir?'

He didn't catch the look in her eyes, for he was already staring out of the window over the main street. 'Maybe,' he replied absently. 'Close the door behind you.'

Once she had left, he crossed quickly to the door and heaved the bed in front of it. Then, returning to the window, he settled down to wait. In the street below, tradesmen, farmers, wives and children passed up and down, but by the time dusk fell he had seen no one suspicious, and realised the pangs in his stomach meant he was hungry. Carefully resetting the bed, he made his way downstairs.

He was surprised how busy the tavern was. The entire ground floor, apart from the kitchens and scullery, was given over to serving food and drink. Even so, the room was filled with customers and was choked with the smell of unwashed bodies and the acrid smoke of the log fire. Here and there came the fresh whiff of tobacco, newly arrived from America. He shouldered his way to the bar and ordered roast beef and a quart of ale. Then, taking his beer, he found a seat by the hearth where he could overlook the room, and settled down.

He took in the customers quickly. Most were local; farmers, labourers, craftsmen from the town, carpenters, furriers and the like, thickly built men, with leather aprons, or thick, chapped hands. A few travellers were gathered in groups, keeping to themselves. From their dress, he took them as merchants. Of course, if they were government spies, they would look just the same. He regretted his decision to sit by himself; perhaps he should have tried to join these fellow guests in conversation. Just then Frances squeezed her way over to him with his food.

'These lads will never leave a girl alone.' She winked at him.

'Is that a boast or a complaint?' he enquired, though without his usual flare. For once, the habitual coquetries no longer amused him.

'I mightn't complain if it was a gentleman like yourself,' she said, and smiled sweetly. She could be quite pretty, he thought, and was almost surprised to realise he felt no interest at all. Has Susannah really ensnared me that much? he wondered. He swallowed a mouthful of beer.

The beef was cooked to a crisp, and he spent the next ten minutes working at it methodically but with little success. He had drunk two quarts by the time the last morsel was gone, and his head was clouded agreeably. The bar was fuller now as the last of the working men had come in, and the air hummed with conversation and laughter and the warm smell of sweat and eaten food.

'Mr Upton?'

Richard froze. The words were softly spoken and came from a man who had been standing by his side for the past ten minutes or so. Even now, the man made no effort to look him in the eye but continued to stare absently at the door. Under the table, Richard clenched his hands.

'Yes.'

'Your Christian name?' Again, to the casual observer, it would have appeared that the man was talking to himself.

'Peter.'

'Good.' The man came round to where Richard could see him and Richard almost gasped in amazement.

The stranger bore a remarkable similarity to the late King Charles. He was about forty years old, of medium build, with a slim, aristocratic face, a fine grey beard and a moustache curled slightly at the ends. Only in his demeanour was he quite unlike the sombre, sorrowful King, and his eyes glittered mischievously as he introduced himself. 'Wedlock. Pleased to meet you. May I sit?' But by this stage he was already springing into the seat opposite.

'*Mr* Wedlock?' asked Richard.

'Just Wedlock,' said the man, 'as in holy matrimony.' He pulled off his gauntlets and began to pluck at the ends of his moustache. 'I say, what does a man have to do to get served here?'

'Make friends with the barmaid.' Richard waved over to Frances. Wedlock's jovial nature made him feel surprisingly well at ease.

'Marvellous! Marvellous!' The eyes twinkled and Wedlock leaned back in his chair. 'My goodness, I've had to ride today. Impossible weather! I hear you had a damned storm a few days back?'

Richard almost laughed out loud. 'Sir, after what I've been through, the weather is the least of my worries. Now,' he leant across the table, 'what do you have to tell me?'

At this point Frances slapped two steaming mugs of ale in front of them.

'She is a fair blowse, eh?' Wedlock winked, then his face became suddenly serious. 'I have indeed stumbled upon something of *value*.'

'Go on.'

'Tsk! Tsk!' Amazingly, Wedlock wagged his finger at him. 'Not just yet. First of all, tell me who sent you.'

'The King, of course,' replied Richard irritably. 'Who sent you?'

'Why, no one, of course,' Wedlock beamed back. 'I am, as they say, a loose cannon. But come, sir, I would like to know more about you than that. What is your name?'

Richard leaned forward. 'I am Richard Tremaine, originally of Chynoon. I have been an exile these last nine years.'

'Richard *Tremaine*?' Wedlock blinked. 'You're supposed to be dead, aren't you? Do you have papers?'

'I lost them.'

Wedlock raised an eyebrow.

'I was shipwrecked,' Richard explained. 'I lost everything.'

'How very unfortunate,' Wedlock admonished him gently. 'That really won't do, will it? How can I trust you if you have no papers? My goodness, man, you could be working for that chap Thurloe.' He rolled his eyes. John Thurloe was secretary to Cromwell's Council of State and head of the largest, most efficient spy network in Europe.

'Look,' said Richard evenly. 'I am in contact with

various gentry in the area. I can provide you with guarantees.'

'I see. Yes, I will need evidence.' Wedlock suddenly shot him a dazzling smile. 'Still, at least I *like* you, Richard, indeed.'

Richard ignored this. 'What exactly do you have to offer, Mr Wedlock?'

'Just Wedlock,' Wedlock reminded him, then continued: 'During the summer I was managing a farm for my cousin, who will of course remain nameless. One day I was making my tour of the fields when my dog began to dig about in some undergrowth beneath the trees.' He drew closer, so that his chin was almost touching the top of his tankard. 'Belle was tugging at a man's jacket. It was virtually rotten with age, a frightful smell.' He wrinkled his nose, his moustache twitched. 'Anyway, I investigated, naturally, and what did I find but the body of a cavalry officer, buried in the leaves.'

'Cavalry officer?' Richard felt his skin prickle. His father had been a cavalry officer.

'King's army, you know.' Wedlock nodded his head significantly. 'One of ours. Anyway, I was going to leave him put, sleeping dogs and all that, when I noticed that a piece of parchment was sticking out of this jacket Belle had in her teeth. So I fished it out.'

'Yes?'

'It was a note, explaining where a certain quantity of gold had been buried.'

'A certain quantity? How much?'

'It didn't say. Why, do you know?'

Richard ignored this question. 'Do you know who this cavalry officer was? What colour hair did he have? Did you see?'

'Dear, no.' Wedlock shut his eyes and shook his head.

223

'I was too taken aback. Besides, the body, as I said, was in some disrepair.'

'So what does the note actually say?' Richard took a quick mouthful of beer. 'You see, my father went missing about that time. He was an officer.'

Wedlock understood. 'Ah.' His eyes were wistful. 'I wish I could help. But I have only the note, and you cannot even have that until we have agreed terms.'

'What terms?'

Wedlock twiddled his moustache. 'I am a great admirer of the Crown. Goodness knows I did my bit on the field of blood—'

'Where did you fight?'

'That doesn't matter any more. We lost, didn't we?'

Wedlock's debonair manner suddenly irritated Richard. 'What do you mean, it doesn't matter?' asked Richard. 'Of course it matters! People died! My father fought at Stratton, Lansdowne, Roundway, the siege of Bristol. He was wounded at Cheriton, and again at Taunton. God knows how many of his men died. My own mother was killed at Lembury. And you say it doesn't matter!'

Wedlock looked at him intently. 'I'm sorry,' he said quietly, and patted Richard on the hand. 'You are right, it does matter. So long as Cromwell sits on the throne in all but name, it matters.'

'Even if Charles came back tomorrow, it would matter,' said Richard. 'My family died for him.'

'So did many,' agreed Wedlock, 'on both sides.' He paused for a moment. 'I fought at Marston Moor, with Prince Rupert and the Duke of Newcastle. I will never forget the numbers killed that day. Newcastle's lambs, they called his troops – I watched while they were slaughtered.'

Richard coughed. 'I am sorry for my outburst, Mr Wedlock. You were saying . . .'

Wedlock shook himself as if he had been far, far away. 'As I was saying, I am a great admirer of His Majesty; however, I cannot afford to act from loyalty alone.' He smiled impishly. 'Perhaps I would not act from loyalty at all, if I could lift it single-handedly.'

'Lift it?'

Wedlock nodded. 'It requires some manpower to retrieve the gold, manpower which I do not have. Naturally, if the authorities got even a whiff of this they would confiscate the lot, and arrest me to boot, so this is where you come in.' He tapped his nose. 'Your colleagues will have people they can rely on. You provide me with the men and I will deliver the gold.' His eyes danced. 'In return I expect ten per cent of the value and a letter of introduction to His Majesty. It is a fair price, is it not?'

Richard smiled grimly. 'Possibly.'

Wedlock rapped his fingers on the table. 'You accept, then?'

'First, I want to see the note, together with some proof of your good faith. An introduction perhaps from some men whose loyalty cannot be doubted.'

'You shall have it, sir.'

'Then, yes, I will agree to your terms.'

Wedlock smiled a thin, happy smile. 'Good.' He banged the table. 'Frances! Two more quarts for us gallant gentlemen!'

Richard winced. 'There's one final thing, Wedlock. We will not meet here again. About four miles downriver there's a ruined mill on the south bank, by Ardevora Farm. It is quite deserted.' He made a quick guess at how long the preparations would take. 'We will meet there in three days, do you understand?'

Wedlock slapped the table in admiration. 'Damn! You take your work seriously, sir! What time?'

'As near to midnight as you can.'

Wedlock smiled and saluted him with his tankard: 'Your health!'

They drank two more quarts apiece. Wedlock was in no hurry to leave and Richard found him amiable enough company. They passed the evening with some jollity, making small talk, though never once did Wedlock say anything more about either the King's gold or himself. Richard doubted that Wedlock was his real name. Even his story about his cousin's farm sounded false. But then, thought Richard, only a fool would use his real name. Eventually the night grew late. Richard tipped over his empty tankard and stood it upside down.

'Hah! This Cornish beer is the pig's own piss,' announced Wedlock. He began to trace something – a diamond – in spilled dregs on the table. He glanced up, his eyes bright and brimming. 'I have to go and relieve myself of it now, sir, in the gutter outside. I will not be coming back. If you follow me, I will shoot you.' He winked comically. 'D'you see?'

Richard realised that Wedlock was probably not joking.

'Good man!' Wedlock staggered to his feet and slapped him on the shoulder. 'Until the next time, my *confrère*!' And with that he was gone.

Richard stared into the bottom of his tankard for ten minutes or so. The tavern was emptying now, and the voices of the other drinkers sounded hollow and raucous. He shook his head and became fascinated with the carved rose on the side of his table-leg. Then, when he realised he too needed to find the gutter, he lurched to his feet and wandered outside. There was no trace of Wedlock and he relieved himself freely against the stable, feeling the fresh starlight on his neck and the glitter of stars spinning above.

When he reached his room, he collapsed face down and fully dressed on his mattress and it was in that position that Frances, giggling and red-faced, found him half an hour later.

'Now, master,' she whispered. 'Are you going to show a girl how to serve you properly?'

But one look at him told her he was not.

Chapter Four

RICHARD WOKE ANGRILY. HIS MOUTH was caked with stale beer. He rolled out of bed and found he was undressed, tripped over his britches with a bang and swore at the empty room. He knocked the shutters open and thrust his head out.

The street was damp and fresh and misty and people were moving quietly below. A cart had come in, two men were talking, a bird darted overhead. Richard jerked himself around and reached for the ewer and drank water which tasted like stale beer. His stomach felt loose and unwell. Seeking fresh, cold air, he turned back to the window and blinked in surprise.

Riding slowly down the main street on her bay mare was Sarah Masters. He would recognise her anywhere. Suddenly his wits pricked up. Where on earth was she going at this time of day? He remembered seeing her horse in the stables at Chynoon on the morning of Ursula's death, steaming with sweat.

Snatching up his shirt, he crammed himself into his britches and hopped to the door as he slipped his boots on. He was still fumbling with his shirt buttons when he got to the bottom of the stairs.

'Did'ee sleep well, sir?' Frances was scrubbing the floor behind the bar and gave him a wink over her shoulder.

'Yes, thank you,' he replied automatically. 'Tell the boy to get my horse saddled immediately, will you? Hurry, hurry.'

'Yes, sir. Rightaway, sir,' she said frostily, and stalked off.

If Richard even wondered at her odd behaviour, he had already forgotten it by the time he reached the bottom of the town and crossed the long low bridge over the river. Sarah would have come through ten, fifteen minutes before. He guessed she had taken the road for Truro. He forced his horse up the sheer hill as fast as he could and it was sweating hard by the time he reached the top.

There was still no sign of Sarah, and he urged his mount along the brow, then down into the next hollow, still lined with mist, and up the next rise. Grey muddy water was spilling across the lane, his horse's hooves splashed in puddles. The morning sun climbed over the wrack of cloud to the east and brought the fields, hedgerows and spinneys of beech and oak to shimmering, golden life. It was going to be a fair day.

Then, at the breast of the next rise, he saw her. She was going at a steady walk and he had to rein back to stop himself overtaking her. He patted his horse gently on the neck and settled into an easy pace as they climbed the final hills before the lane slid down to Tresillian and the road to Truro.

It was at this point that Richard's head cleared with the morning mist and he wondered at his wisdom in following her at all. What did it matter where Sarah Masters was going? But seeing her like that in Tregony seemed too much of a coincidence to ignore. Richard could no more let her go than he could deny the feverish power of the dreams which haunted him nightly.

An hour or so later, Richard came down the final long slope which led into Truro. The town was settled comfortably between the hills and presented a pleasing cluster of sandstone, slate, granite and painted plaster glittering in the sunlight. Sarah hadn't noticed him throughout their journey. There was something compulsive about following her, thought Richard, and he felt a quiver of excitement when he saw her pull up outside the White Lamb and go in. He tethered his own horse across the street and followed her inside.

The windows of the White Lamb were so opaque that at first his eyes struggled with the gloom. The tavern was divided into waist-high cubicles which reminded him of the box pews of church. He found his way to a seat and it was some minutes before he could make out the pretty nape of her neck over a cubicle wall. She was sitting on the other side of the tavern in the far left corner. She was an attractive woman, he mused, if somewhat round-faced and full-bodied. If she was intending an illicit rendezvous this would be the perfect place. He was amazed that Dr Masters happily allowed his wife to ride unchaperoned. He was asking to be duped.

'Drink, sir?' The serving-boy broke his concentration.

Richard ordered a quart of small beer and some bread and cheese and settled back on the bench. After last night, he had little appetite, but thanks to the ride he found the beer agreeably warm and satisfying. Sarah Masters seemed to be drinking sherry. She's nervous, he thought, for she sipped from her glass frequently and soon ordered a second and then a third.

At this point, a group of men walked in, their spurs clattering on the floorboards, talking loudly. Cavalry troopers. Richard pressed farther into his seat, but he needn't have worried. None of them even looked his way, and he was about to relax when a young lad with thick black hair slipped in next to him. Richard scowled unwelcomingly, but the young man grinned wolfishly back and settled himself with a great deal of shuffling and banging.

'Lovely morning, isn't it?' he said, and when Richard didn't reply, slapped him on the shoulder. 'What, devil got your tongue?'

Richard turned towards him. 'Sorry, I didn't catch you,' he said coldly.

'Lovely morning, I said. The name's Jeremiah. Jeremiah Brown. Come far?'

'No.' Richard shook his head and tried to relax. 'Plymouth, on business.'

Jeremiah looked at him oddly. 'You're not one of those Brothers, are you?'

Richard laughed. 'Do I look like one?'

Just then he realised that a tall, distinguished gentleman had entered the tavern and was swiftly taking his seat beside Sarah. He saw her raise her head in greeting. The stranger wore a suit of black tailored cloth, and was obviously of some bearing. A beryl flashed on his right hand. The young man was saying something in Richard's ear. Richard looked round irritably.

'What's the matter? That your lady, is she?' Jeremiah's face lit up. 'You her pander, are you? She set up for a roll in the sack?'

Richard stared at him coldly. 'No,' he said steadily. 'She caught my eye, that's all. And if you don't watch your tongue, I'll teach you some manners.'

Jeremiah's face dropped in a parody of concern. 'Oh, I'm so sorry, sir, but there's me thinking Hugh Courtney's got a name for the women, he has.'

'Wait a minute,' asked Richard. 'You say you actually know who that is?'

The young man gave him another odd look. 'Where have you been? Everyone knows that's Hugh Courtney, the Quartermaster General, and as fine a gentleman as you could wish.' He jabbed Richard in the ribs. 'If someone's got to poke your lady, it may as well be Mr Courtney.'

Richard glared into his ale. The Quartermaster General was in charge of provisioning the government's army in the West. He was indeed, as Jeremiah had said, a man of some importance. Sarah, meanwhile, was enjoying a subdued conversation with him. He could see her looking into Courtney's face, and twice Courtney pressed her hand, as if in reassurance or complicity. They ordered a bottle of claret and the Quartermaster General toasted Sarah as any gallant gentleman would.

The troopers downed their ales and marched out of the tavern. Jeremiah ordered another beer and insisted on buying Richard one as well. Richard would have liked to refuse but was grateful for the excuse to stay put. The beer had no sooner come when Sarah stood up and brushed down her skirts and made for the door. Richard dipped his head over his beer, and when he looked up the door was swinging shut behind her.

'Look, there she goes,' Jeremiah told him. 'Quick, after her then!' He obviously regarded it all as some huge joke. As Richard reached the door he glanced back. Jeremiah had his hands to his temples and was making cuckold's horns at him.

Outside, the sunlight momentarily blinded him. Then he glimpsed Sarah sitting proud in the saddle and heading back down the main street on her own. He tossed a coin at the horseboy opposite and followed her. So, Hugh Courtney, Quartermaster General. He tried to think why Sarah would have ridden all the way to Truro to meet him, unless she was having an affair. But if she was, he thought practically, would they have met in public at all, and wouldn't she have left with him?

The road back from Truro twisted and rolled between steep, deserted hills, and he had a vague notion of overpowering her and demanding to know what she was doing. But he dismissed the idea as risky and pointless. What, after all, was he hoping to discover? At that moment Sarah took the turning back to Tregony. This made no sense if she was meaning to return to Chynoon, no sense at all. Feeling increasingly intrigued, Richard followed.

It was maybe two in the afternoon when he finally saw the town straggling down the hill above the riverbed, with the warm odour of pig dung rising off the fields, and water lying in swathes over the meadows. Sarah rode up through the town, past the Three Lords, and out on the road to the east. She had only gone two or three hundred yards when she turned off to the left and entered a clearing before a small gentleman's house set back from the lane. Richard pulled up sharp and dismounted. Treading forward carefully, he could just see her swing down from the saddle and lead the horse round the rear of the house. Going back to the Three Lords, Richard tipped the stableboy a penny to mind his horse, then made his way back up the hill.

The house was ringed by six tall beech trees and a high earthen hedge. Downstairs, the rooms were shuttered and silent, but when he crept round the back he heard the sound of horses from the stables. Peering inside, he could make out Sarah Masters' bay mare chewing a mouthful of hay. Next to it stood a large black stallion, glistening with sweat.

It was William Moreton's horse.

Behind the house lay a fallow field. Richard jumped quickly over the hedge and settled down to wait behind a tangle of blackthorn and brambles. What was William Moreton doing here, so far from Chynoon? Again, suspicions crowded into his mind, but he paid them little attention. Overhead two crows circled and drifted down the valley towards the river. A heavy cart rattled by in the lane above, the carter barking orders to his boy. Inside the house someone had lit a fire, and smoke rose lazily, sweetly scented.

When he opened his eyes, dusk was already thick on the ground. The valley was brimful with mist and the sweet scent of woodfire had gone. Confused, he struggled to stand up. His legs were stiff and cold and unwilling to respond. Damn! Apart from the bread and cheese at the White Lamb, he had eaten nothing all day, and he felt suddenly so hungry he was light-headed. He scanned the house. The shuttered windows gave nothing away. He stretched and his calves ached painfully. He pulled himself over the hedge, catching his jacket in the process, and fell into the clearing before the stables. The stables were empty.

Angrily, Richard crossed to the house. The door was locked and rattled as he shook it. Quickly, before he had a chance to reconsider, he slid his pocketknife under the sill of the kitchen shutters and slipped the catch. The window moved easily on its hinges and he tumbled in. The redolent scent of the firewood greeted him, but apart from that the house had a quiet, unlived-in feel. A half-loaf was lying on the table, and ignoring the breadknife, he tore at it ravenously and walked into the front room of the house.

It was a large room, at least twenty-five feet long, and it had obviously hosted a meeting of some sort. Seven chairs were set round in a rough circle, and on the table stood five empty wine bottles with thick sour dregs that were at least a day old. Richard went to the hearth. It was cold and speckled with tobacco ash. Crumpled among the cinders were several sheets of paper which had been discarded, presumably some time afterwards, and were consequently unburned. He fished them out.

Two of the three sheets were bare except for ink smudges and the ring of a wine-glass. But the third was embellished with a flourish of idle sketches and marks which sprouted into weird flowers and bestiaries. Someone had been bored, he thought. At the bottom the page was blank except for the figure of a huge, ravening dog. It seemed to have been drawn with particular exactitude. Each hair on its back bristled. Its jaws were agape and clad with razor-edged fangs. Its eyes blazed.

'Find anything of interest, Richard?'

Richard spun round. In the doorway stood Sarah Masters.

As naked as a peach.

He gaped at her in amazement. Sarah made a half-hearted attempt to cover the thick triangle of hair which crowned the top of her legs, but other than that she did not move. Then she asked, with remarkable calmness: 'You killed her, didn't you?'

He stared at her dumbly, hardly believing his eyes or his ears.

'Well?' She waited patiently.

'Of course not!'

'Then why are you here? To spy on me?' She smiled at him and ran her hands over her body.

He tried to avert his gaze, but found his eyes drawn to her warm, plump flesh.

She laughed lightly.

'You are shocked, Richard, I can see!' She presented

him with an elegant curtsey. 'Why should you be embarrassed, if I am not?'

Richard dropped the sheets of paper to the floor. 'Aren't you ashamed of coupling with William Moreton?' He looked at her distastefully. 'What would Ursula say?'

He expected her to blanch at that, but instead she smiled so her dimples showed, and said: 'But she was pleased for me, Richard.'

'God damn you! You say she knew?'

'Of course! We all know. Even my husband approves, wholeheartedly.' She stretched her hands towards him. 'Come,' she whispered, 'can you honestly say you object?'

Richard turned away. 'Put some clothes on.'

She did not move. 'There is nothing wrong, Richard.'

'Then how do you feel about Ursula's murder, Sarah? You have no guilt about that?'

Now she faltered. 'You murdered her, didn't you?' She set her neat, round mouth in an expression of childlike defiance. 'Are you going to kill me too? Is that it?'

'No!' he snapped. 'Don't you see? Moreton killed her. Are you so blinded by your lust?'

'No, no,' she said quickly. 'William would not kill her, she was his bride, Richard. He loved her tenderly. She was called by the Lord.'

'She was strangled, Sarah! I saw the marks!'

Sarah took a step towards him. Her breasts were soft and inviting and in the chill evening air he could clearly see her nipples puckering, erect. 'I am so cold, Richard.' He regarded her stonily.

'Sarah, I do not want you.'

She looked sweetly into his face. 'I know that, Richard, but it *entices* me.'

236

'Sarah, your husband is a man of God!'

'There is no sin for those free of sin,' she replied. 'Look, I am free of this.' She ran her hands quickly over her breasts, her waist. 'My body is no longer mine, so how can I sin?'

Richard felt confusion welling up inside him, hammering on his temples. She was so . . .

He pushed past her abruptly and stalked into the kitchen. Laughing softly, excitedly, Sarah followed.

'I traced you to Truro today,' he announced gruffly. 'That man, Hugh Courtney, why did you meet him? To contrive more whorings?'

'Is that what you think, Richard?' She sat herself on the kitchen table, by the bread, and parted her legs. 'Is it?' She began to stroke herself, softly, gently, her eyes never leaving his.

'Come on, Sarah!' He felt the blood warming in his veins. 'What's going on?'

She said nothing, but leaned back, letting her eyes close. Her fingers made a slight soft sound as they worked deeper. She sighed.

'Sarah!' He tugged her shoulders. 'Sarah, I could kill you!'

'Will you?' her voice was dreamy, sensual. 'Will you *stab* me, Richard?'

He stared at her furiously, disgusted with her, yet more disgusted with his own feelings. He pushed her back on the table, trying to ignore the sensation of her skin. 'Damn you, Sarah.' She made no reply, and he crossed the room, keeping his back to her, forcing himself not to imagine what she was doing. He heard her breaths come quickly, short, light. His body felt hot, aroused, and he had an almost overpowering urge to turn, to go to her angrily, forcefully. She moaned once, imploringly, and he gritted his teeth. Then he felt something, a slight shift of air behind him, and instinctively spun round.

Just in time.

Sarah missed him by half an inch, her arm lunging past him, brushing his jacket. Then he realised she had the breadknife in her hand, and her bare arm was already round his neck. He felt her warm breasts squeezed against his jacket and her breath moist and hot on his cheek, then the knife flashed above him and he pushed himself forward so she fell winded on to her back, and Richard fell against the sudden softness of her thighs, and her legs yielded for him warm and soft, and he hesitated, then the knife came down and he twisted too late and the blade pierced him.

He felt a blunt, hard knock in his ribcage. Sarah was staring into his face, her eyes dancing. She tugged frantically at the knife. He wondered why he couldn't feel any pain. Then he realised her blade had snagged in his jacket's padding and he clubbed her hand away. She squirmed beneath him, and he felt a sudden rush of pure sexual excitement. Then he was scrabbling for the knife and got his fingers to it and closed his fingers on the blade and there was blood everywhere, but he pinned her down with his elbow and she clawed at his face and his eyes. He stumbled off her, still clutching the bleeding knife, and then he punched her once in the face and it was all over.

Richard stared down at her spreadeagled legs and arms.

'I'm sorry,' he began.

She glared at him, her face burning with emotion. 'How can you be sorry? You killed Ursula! Go on, kill me!'

She stretched out on the floor before him, defying him with the same childlike determination.

Richard's head was buzzing, he felt a wetness in his side, and realised he was bleeding after all. It seemed only a scratch, but blood had already stained the front of his shirt and the material clung to him, hot and wet. He leaned against the table.

'Why did you meet Hugh Courtney, Sarah?'

'Kill me, Richard. I'll tell you nothing.' She was panting heavily. Her face was wild-eyed and desperate and yet curiously youthful. She was still so young, he thought, and yet so lost.

'Get up,' he told her.

'No.' She lay there, still flaunting herself, as if her shamelessness was her last weapon. 'I won't betray my cause.'

'Your cause? What cause is that, Sarah?'

But she bit her lip and stared at him fiercely.

A thought struck him.

'Do you know Samuel Dowles, Sarah?' She looked at him impassively. 'What do the letters CCCL mean to you?'

'Nothing at all,' she blurted out. 'Kill me! I'm not afraid.'

He regarded her dispassionately. 'If I let you live, you'll tell Moreton, won't you?'

'Of course.'

He jammed the knife into his belt and cursed at the pain in his hand. Then he dragged her to her feet and held her at arm's length. Now he could feel that for all her vaunting, she was trembling.

'Sarah, don't be scared.' He looked her in the eye, but the pressure of his grip didn't slacken. 'Listen. I'm not going to kill you. Tell Moreton what you like. Tell him to be damned.' He jerked her towards the door. 'But first you can find me a clean shirt and some bandages.'

Richard left her trussed on the bed upstairs. The scene of her honeyings, he thought grimly. It would take her several hours to work free, by which time he would be long gone. But even as he guided his horse away through the steep lanes, the sense of evil which had impregnated the house still clung to him. What possessed her to behave like that? She revelled in her flesh. He recalled Ursula, rubbing him with a damp cloth, and the feel of her body in the corridor. And then he remembered Susannah as well, coming to him in the cellar. Blackthorns sprawled out from the hedge-tops and snared the clouds. Had Susannah been infected with the same *madness*? He remembered the warm feel of her thighs, the sudden joy that had run through his flesh. No. She had been a virgin, he reminded himself. She was not like Sarah. He kicked his horse into a faster trot, unmindful of branches or potholes. This was madness! Madness! He felt angry, confused, and kicked his horse the harder. Soon they were cantering down the dark, narrow lanes, hooves ringing over the empty night.

He rode like that until Tregony lay many miles behind and his blood gradually cooled, and he pulled his horse back into a gentler walk.

He heard the animal just then.

Softly, in between the clip of his horse's hooves, a gentle velvet pad-pad of feet. At first he thought it was the shimmer of wind through the thorn bushes, but when he listened it was there – pad, pad – behind him, keeping pace. The hairs on the back of his neck bristled. He suddenly thought of the great dog he had found scrawled on the sheet of paper. Its jaws agape, hair erect, eyes blazing. His ears strained into the darkness. Pad. Pad. He twisted round in the saddle, looked back. Behind him the lane rose into a black funnel of hedges and stooped bushes. He pulled his horse up and cursed her for breathing heavily. Was that the sound? There. And there. The blackness seemed to suddenly explode before his eyes. Without thinking, he yelled and shook his reins and his horse bounded down the lane as if she were pursued by a very demon. She stumbled in a pothole and he was almost pitched from the saddle, then she was running on heedlessly, as if demented by the same terror which gripped her master. Air blew in his face. There was a cold breath on his shoulder and he had the sudden impression of a great black shape, monstrous, darker, thicker than the night, pursuing him swiftly, silently, consuming everything in its path, gaining on the horse with every breath. Richard wanted to call out, but his tongue was thick with horror and would not move. Then they burst out of the lane into a gap between two fields and there, across the field, stood an inn with yellow lights glinting in the windows.

Richard threw himself out of the saddle and tried to regain his composure as he walked up the steps to the tavern. He was still shaking. The same thing had pursued him at Samuel Dowles' house, he was sure. He pushed the door open and was met by six staring faces.

'What's the matter, boy?' a plump, bald man asked. 'Look like you've seen a ghost.'

Richard managed a smile. 'A quart of small beer,' he said, and reached for his purse.

It was only then that he realised his purse was no longer there.

Chapter Five

RICHARD REACHED CAERLEON AS THE sun was casting a rime of light over the fields from the east. Sir Charles was relieved to see him. He was anxious that Richard had not come back sooner and he demanded repeatedly whether he had been followed. Only after that did he show his concern for Richard's injuries. Richard for his part chose to tell him as little as possible. The business with Wedlock was problematic enough.

Sir Charles called a meeting of senior royalists that night: Sir John and Richard Arundell, and Sir John Grenville. Such gatherings were liable to imprisonment under Committee rules and the mood was tense, irritable. It was not improved when the gentlemen heard the reason for Richard's mission.

'What, the King has charged you with recovering this war chest and using it to fund a rising, here, in the South West?' Sir John Arundell looked incredulous.

Sir Charles Roselyn quickly raised his eyebrows in agreement. 'It would risk everything, would it not?'

'My job is simply to find the chest,' replied Richard, then added: 'But I know the King wishes to see a rising next year.'

Richard Arundell snorted and helped himself to a second glass of port. 'Listen here, Tremaine, a rising without support would be suicidal. Tell the King we'd need a supporting force from France.' He made a quick estimation. 'At least a thousand troops, with weapons and powder for all the men we could raise.'

'And three hundred cavalry,' interjected Sir Charles.

'Is such a force possible?' asked Sir John.

Richard raised his hands. 'Sirs, this is not my concern.'

'Is is possible?' repeated Sir John.

Richard lowered his eyes. 'Probably not.'

Sir Charles received the port bottle. 'Think what happened in 'forty-eight,' he said sagely. 'The Roundheads are too strong. We need to plan longer.'

Plan to do nothing, thought Richard to himself. He cleared his throat. 'Look, as I have said, the first thing – the only thing – is to secure the gold.'

'Listen, Tremaine.' Sir Charles leaned across the table and tapped his nose expressively. 'You speak of risings, pah! What can a party of roistering gentlemen do against a Roundhead squadron? And what about the people? Will they rise for Charles Stuart? Cromwell will never be defeated in the field, believe me.' Sir Charles stabbed the air with his finger. 'But if the body had no head, what would happen then? The King's best hope, some would say his only hope, is if the Lord Protector dies.'

Richard looked at him questioningly.

'Assassination,' Sir Charles continued. 'It's Cromwell alone who holds this country together. One knife through his chest and the whole structure would come tumbling down. But no, the King would far rather see thousands butchered on the battlefield. Have you ever seen limbs hacked and maimed, men lying with their stomachs opened? Have you heard men dying? The King reads too much poetry. He prefers the heroic failure of war, instead of the shabby success of conspiracy.'

Richard gritted his teeth. He agreed with every word Sir Charles and the others said. He felt no desire to see more people dragged into bloodshed. 'Nevertheless, the gold . . .'

'Yes, the gold.' Sir Charles reached for the bottle again. 'You are quite right. That is a separate issue. We must take this fellow Wedlock at face value, I suppose?'

'Yes, we must,' replied Richard firmly. 'But we are meeting on my terms, in a place of my choosing. There won't be a trap.' Sir Charles looked sceptical, but Richard continued: 'He has offered to provide us with letters of introduction, if I can do the same.'

'Meaning you want us to provide you with one?' Sir Charles looked at the others significantly. 'Such a letter would hang us, Tremaine.'

'I promise not to let it out of my grip.'

'But if you are dead, Tremaine, they will prise your fingers open.'

Richard said nothing. Sir Charles breathed wearily.

'Look,' said Sir John Arundell. 'You know we are as keen to help the King's cause as any man, die if we have to, isn't that right, Roselyn?'

Sir Charles nodded, somewhat grudgingly.

'We will give you these guarantees,' agreed Grenville.

'But you had better trust this man, that's all,' said Sir Charles, and drained his glass.

'And if we find the gold?'

'We'll secure it, don't worry,' replied Richard Arundell. 'Gold's gold.'

'But listen,' Sir Charles cut in. 'If this does go well, you must leave immediately. You're too much of a liability, thanks to your adventure at Chynoon. If Colonel Moreton learnt you were here, I would be arrested on the spot. As soon as you've made contact with this fellow Wedlock, you must sail for France, the day after tomorrow. I'll make the arrangements.'

'So soon?' Richard thought of Susannah. Would he be able to get word to her?

'Sir Charles is right,' said Richard Arundell. 'Leave

the gold to us, Tremaine. Just make sure you agree everything with this fellow.'

But Richard's thoughts were elsewhere. What if she couldn't come? What if Moreton kept her under guard? The idea of being spirited out of the country in two days' time was alarming.

'Did you hear me, Tremaine?'

Richard shook himself. 'I will choose my own time of leaving, Sir Charles, if it's all the same.'

Sir Charles looked sour. 'Every day you're here is a risk to us all.'

Richard met his look. 'Then you'll have to take that risk, sir. Many men have taken graver ones for the King. I will leave when I am ready, and not before.'

'What's really keeping you here, Richard?' Sir Charles peered at him. 'You mention your loyalty to the King, but if the King's work is done, surely it's in everyone's interests for you to leave?'

'Of course I'm loyal to the King,' he agreed angrily. 'Don't worry, gentlemen. I will do what's best for our cause.'

The others seemed satisfied with his answers. Of course, only he was aware of how his words echoed those of Sarah Masters, and he hated himself for his mimicry. Sarah said she would die for her cause, he thought grimly. Would I do the same?

Chapter Six

THE NIGHT WIND STRUCK THE coast in bolts and welters and shook her hair into long black plumes. Rebecca Penmarris narrowed her eyes and stared out into the foaming, heaving expanse of water. Under the moon the sea was a mass of shifting sounds and roars. Black waves roared in from the deep and unrolled across the beach in a crash of white foam and spray. The shore thundered.

Was he gone yet? Or was her mother right, was he . . . No, she couldn't bear to think of it.

Rebecca shook her head as if she were arguing with the wind. Her mother would laugh at her if she knew how she was torturing herself. But then, when Elizabeth thought of Richard Tremaine, all she saw was the son of the landlord, not the man she had known since childhood. Rebecca picked up a stone from the beach. It was white and smooth like a woman's hip. She turned it over in her fingers, and for some reason its touch increased her sorrow and made her feel more alone. She flung the stone angrily into the churning foam. The stone splashed and then was consumed in the endless hiss and froth of the shore.

Would she ever see him again? She felt angry with herself, so angry that tears came to her eyes, and she screwed them tighter against the endless wind. If only he wasn't so insensitive! He had been like a brother to her. She gazed into the blast of the wind. And what had she been to him?

She turned and walked back across the beach. When

everyone else had said he was dead, she had known he was still alive. And that certainty had consoled her time after time, as her life became bleaker, the years harder.

That dream!

She had longed for when he came back, she thought bitterly. How foolish – weak and foolish! All these years she had hoarded words and phrases, thoughts and memories, that she would share with him. 'This is how I thought of you when I was eighteen,' she would have said to him. 'Let me tell you about the flowers I picked for us. Or the poems I read when I felt lonely.' Weak! Weak! And then, when out of the blue he had appeared, had he cared for her? She drove her body through the wind. And what had she done? Wounded him, angered him, made a fool of herself.

The wind cut her to the quick and she hugged her shawl tighter. She should go back soon, Elizabeth would need her. Back to my drudgery, she thought, when I should be married, with a house of my own.

She stopped still. Damn them all! Something in the raw elemental fury of this place, the cold, bare desolation of the unlit wind over water and rock, comforted her. Comforted her, yet injured her, laid her bare to the aching chill of the wind.

Another blast of air shuddered against her, and another. Her hair writhed behind her. She sighed and trudged wearily up the beach to the fields beyond. As she did, the words of an old song came to her, of which she could remember only a few lines:

> I went to the beach and called his name,
> I sang to the sea and called his name,
> I cried to the wind and called his name,
> But my true love he has gone.

Normally she would have thought little of these words, but that night on the shore they seemed almost indescribably sad, and she would have burst into tears there and then if she had not refused to give way to her emotion. She clenched her teeth.

'Rebecca!' His voice caught her unawares. She stared towards the fields, but she could see nothing.

'Richard! Is that you?' Her pulse was racing.

For a moment, she thought she must be going mad, and then she saw him step from the shadows.

'Rebecca! It's me!' He paused. 'What's wrong?' Richard felt suddenly apprehensive. In the moonlight, Rebecca looked almost resentful. He could not know that what she resented most was her own feelings.

'Nothing.' She looked at him quietly. 'I thought you'd gone.'

'No, not yet.'

'Why? Is it the King's business which keeps you here, Richard? Or her?'

With some satisfaction, she saw him wince.

'Let's not talk about that now.' He reached a hand towards her. 'I went to the cottage, but Elizabeth said I'd find you here.'

Rebecca smiled grimly to herself. So perhaps her mother understood her moods after all.

He smiled softly back. 'Do you remember we used to come here as children?'

Rebecca felt herself stiffen at the memory.

Why am I always so defensive? she thought, and forced her face into a smile. Be nice to him, she told herself. Don't wound him, don't anger him.

'I'm sorry,' she said, almost against her nature. 'I was pleased to see you. I was worried. I didn't know what had happened.' Richard didn't respond, so she continued: 'You're right, you would take me riding here, do you remember? You were older than me, and I was only a tenant's daughter. I used to think how grand you were.' Now you're being foolish, she told herself. But instead of mocking her, Richard looked at her seriously.

'It was a different world, wasn't it?' He paused. 'Come on, let's walk back. This wind is biting.'

Why don't you say that one day we'll go riding again? she thought bitterly. But then, what would be the point of deceiving me, Richard? Why would I want to be deceived?

For the first hundred yards he walked in silence, and resentfully she fell in beside him. They climbed up the swollen bole of the hill, then cut through the wood which led to her cottage.

'Do you ever wish you could go back?' he asked abruptly.

'Go back?'

'To the past,' he said. 'When things were simpler. When you mentioned riding back there, I remembered my father teaching me. I wish he were here now!' His words came in a rush of emotion.

She put a hand on his arm.

'Richard. I know how you feel.'

'Do you?' he asked with a sudden, violent intensity. 'Do you really know how I feel?'

She felt her lip tremble. Then, before she could stop herself, tears welled in her eyes. She began to cry.

'Oh, damn this!' Richard's voice was angry, but she noticed a tenderness there. He held her by the shoulders. 'I'm sorry, Rebecca. I'm so caught up in this ... *duty*' – he spat out the word – 'that I'm not thinking straight. Please. I didn't mean to hurt you.'

She felt very awkward. Damn him, she thought, and

sniffled foolishly. He touched her on the chin and for the first time she saw his face was lined with tiredness.

'Richard, I dreamed about you coming back,' she whispered.

'I dreamed of coming back too. But things are never as we expect.' He studied her carefully. 'Are you all right?'

'Yes, don't be silly!' As if to show him, she started up the path so he had to run to follow her.

'So,' she asked after a while, 'how does your duty go?'

'Well, I think,' he said cautiously. 'I hope to conclude it tonight.' He frowned. There was something, some sense of impending danger, which made him ill at ease.

'Tonight? And then you will go?'

'As soon as possible, it seems,' he replied wearily. 'It's been a miracle I haven't been caught, I suppose.'

'I'm surprised you came here then,' she said pointedly. 'You've said goodbye already, remember?'

Richard didn't reply. For no reason he could fathom, he felt oddly guilty.

They drew out of the wood. The cottage was a lopsided black mass silhouetted against the sky.

'Rebecca,' he said impulsively, 'take care of yourself. I worry about you. If this business ends well, perhaps I can help you in some way.'

She turned and the moonlight bleached her face.

'No, thank you,' she replied. 'We're not your responsibility, are we?' Deep inside, she realised she was being needlessly abrupt with him. But why shouldn't she be? she thought angrily. If that was her only defence . . . And yet the look on his face as she turned away stabbed at her heart.

'Hah! It's the boy returned again!' Sedge's bluff voice intruded into their thoughts. The old man was standing by the cottage door, smoking a pipe. The embers glowed in the darkness.

Richard smiled, relieved at this distraction from his own feelings. He quickened his pace, creating a slight gap, no more than a yard, between him and Rebecca. To Rebecca, that yard was an unbridgeable void. Ahead, her father jabbed Richard playfully in the stomach and chest.

'Hah! You used to be shorter than me, boy!'

Richard snatched the pipe from between Sedge's teeth and laughed as the old man roared.

'Quiet, Martin! Quiet!' Elizabeth scowled at them from the doorway. She was the only person who insisted on calling Sedge by his Christian name. 'What if there are troopers about?'

Sedge grumbled amiably and accepted his pipe back from Richard. 'It's not easy, for sure,' he said. 'Moreton's men came round yesterday looking for you. None of them knew who I was, but if any of those turncoats in the village know I'm here, I'll be done for.' He spat. 'They work for Moreton now.'

'Yes,' said Richard. 'They wrecked the ship that brought me here.'

Sedge nodded. 'That's not all. They freight things for him. Goods are coming in all the time.'

Richard remembered the barrels stacked in the cellar at Chynoon, and the figures heaving them into the manor house at night.

'What sort of things?'

Sedge scratched his beard. 'Couldn't say. No one talks. But he pays well. The villagers don't complain.'

'Richard's leaving,' interrupted Rebecca. 'He came to say goodbye.'

Her tone cast a chill over their conversation.

'Is this true?' asked Sedge.

'It seems so,' answered Richard. 'There's nothing for me here.'

How true, thought Rebecca.

'Well, won't you stay for some food?' asked Sedge.

Richard shook his head. It was getting late. In a few hours Wedlock would be arriving at the mill and their business would be concluded. 'I'd like to, but I can't.' He turned to Rebecca. Her dark blue eyes caught him by surprise and for a moment he wanted to take her in his arms, but he stopped just in time. That was not how he really felt, he told himself. Not now, if he ever had. He reached into his coat pocket.

'Rebecca,' he said, 'there was one thing I needed to ask you.'

He showed her a slip of paper.

'I need to get this to Susannah, tonight. Could you take it?'

Rebecca's eyes blazed at him.

'There's no one else I could ask,' he added lamely. What he didn't say was that he had waited in the woodland hollow all morning, but Susannah hadn't come.

'You're taking her with you, aren't you?'

'If she stays here, there's no telling what Moreton will do.'

There was a terrible silence. 'You are a fool, Richard Tremaine.'

'Please, Rebecca.'

'Can you trust her, Richard? Can you?'

Sedge studied his pipe and hoped they would ignore him.

'Well?'

'Of course I can! I know what I'm doing, Beckie.'

He stared at her, willing her to understand. And then he saw a certain sad realisation come to her and weaken her anger. She smiled, wistful, knowing, and plucked the paper out of his hand. 'All right, Richard.'

'Thank you.'

But she avoided his gaze and turned to Elizabeth. 'I'm sorry I was gone so long. Have you finished yet?' She went past her mother and into the cottage.

Elizabeth looked at him grimly.

'I wish you a quick journey back to where you came from, Master Tremaine.'

'Goodbye, Elizabeth. I'm sorry,' he added, though for what he was not quite sure.

Sedge coughed. 'Eh, I'll walk with you a way, Richard.'

Richard was glad of the company.

'Don't listen to what Rebecca says,' Sedge advised once they had gone a few yards. 'It's only to be expected. She's worried about you, that's all. And maybe she's a bit jealous.'

'What? Of me and Susannah?' Richard forced himself to be surprised. 'That's ridiculous. Rebecca and I have only ever been friends. She's more like a sister to me . . .'

Sedge kept walking.

'She missed you a lot, Richard. More than was wise, I think.'

Richard didn't know how to reply. He knew Sedge was right. And I thought of her too, he thought. But life doesn't always conform to our expectations. They reached the gatepost of the far field in silence.

Here Richard's horse was tethered. Sedge turned. 'She cares for you, Richard, that's all. Who else has she got to care for? Apart from me and her mother.'

Richard heaved himself into the saddle.

'That's more than I've got,' he said simply. 'Goodbye, Sedge, and best of luck. Why not come and see me in Cologne?'

Sedge shook his head. 'No, I've done enough running and fighting. I reckon I'll stay here a while yet. Take care.'

Sedge stood in the field and watched Richard ride away until he became a black shape which gradually merged and became one with the darkness.

Chapter Seven

FROM TREGONY THE RIVER FAL wound for five or six miles through deep wooded hills until it joined the Truro River at Tolverne and then ran into the estuary and the sea beyond. Over the centuries, the river had dragged down the rich loam and clay from upstream and gradually the broad reaches below Tregony had become clogged with silt. Now, when the tide receded, it revealed a maze of mudflats and winding channels and deep pools.

On the south bank, about four miles downstream from Tregony, had once stood a prosperous river mill. But this was long gone and all that remained was an abandoned and decaying hulk. Richard pulled up a little way short of the ruin. The tide was low and the lopsided walls and sagging roof loomed black and dull against the smooth flanks of mud, silver and wet in the moonlight. He gauged the tide, hoping his calculations were right. The water should be just deep enough, he thought.

Richard crept through the trees. Wedlock was not supposed to be here yet, but he thought it best to take no chances. His footsteps sounded unnaturally loud and he thought for a second of the thing that had followed him, only a few nights before, before he forced those fears away. A heron splashed somewhere downstream, but he ignored it and peered inside the mill. It was empty. Villagers had ripped the floors out for their timber and the great grindstone had been left to tumble over and crash through the side of the house.

He leant back against the old stone wall.

Would Susannah have got his note yet? He closed his eyes and imagined her folding the paper open, her eyes following his words, her lips pursed as she decided. He no longer cared to ask who she was, or why she was impersonating his sister. That no longer mattered. She would come, he told himself. She had to. And then, if she came, they would be gone.

He picked at a piece of plaster. It peeled away from the wall and crumbled between his fingers.

Rebecca tried not to think as she made her way over the fields. If she thought too much she might tear the note into strips and go back. Damn him! The wind spat through the thorn trees, echoing her feelings. Still, she thought defiantly, I will do this, not for Richard, not for Susannah – the name lashed her – but for myself. To prove I can. I will not be weak. Then perhaps I can face up to the rest of my life. Even so, the air stung her face and her eyes smarted with tears.

She was worried that Chynoon would be shut for the night. But when she got there light was spilling from the kitchens across the yard, revealing a large troop of cavalry horses gathered before the stables. Servants were bringing out baskets of fodder, the horses were stamping and snorting impatiently. From inside the manor came the sound of men talking and laughing. Feeling suddenly nervous, she crossed to the rear door and caught sight of a maid she knew.

'Bridget!' she hissed.

Bridget looked at her apprehensively. 'Beckie! What are you doing here?'

'I need to see Miss Tremaine,' she explained. 'Where is she?'

Bridget looked at her quizzically. 'Is it to do with Master Ferrers?' she asked bluntly.

Rebecca nodded. Bridget's intuition stung her.

'Wait in the orchard,' whispered Bridget. 'If the Colonel knew about this, he'd kill me.'

I could never be a maid, thought Rebecca proudly, as she watched Bridget scurry inside. Always living in fear of my master, bowing and scraping. She made her way to the orchard, feeling the bite of the wind through her thin shawl. Yet any maid would be better dressed than me, she told herself.

It was a long time before Susannah came. Long enough for Rebecca to decide she hated the girl passionately whoever she was. But when at last Susannah arrived Rebecca felt her hatred dissolving in spite of herself. Susannah was flushed, her hair wild, and her face bore an expression of such vulnerability . . .

'What's happened?' she asked breathlessly. 'Has anything happened to Richard?'

'No,' answered Rebecca curtly. 'He asked me to give you this.' She held out the crumpled sheet of paper. Her hand was shaking.

Susannah took it and read. Richard's message was simple enough, as all true love notes are: 'Meet me at Tresillian Bridge at dawn.' That was all.

She looked up. 'Can I send him a message?'

Rebecca's face tightened. 'No. He trusts you to be there,' she added pointedly, and turned to go.

'Wait,' Susannah reached forward and caught her hand. 'I don't know who you are, but thank you. Thank you.'

Rebecca stumbled away from her, unable to speak, and ran into the woods. She would not be demeaned with the woman's gratitude! She flung herself down in the leaves and listened to her breath tearing through her lungs. Damn him!

She waited until she was sure Susannah would have gone, then headed for home. But somehow she could not face going back and confronting Sedge and Elizabeth. She wanted their pity even less than Susannah's thanks. She stopped, turned about and went back to the manor. She knew Bill Taylor, one of the stablehands, quite well. He was a gentle-natured boy, two or three years her junior, the youngest son of a tailor, and like her, resentful of his lot. She found him by the horses, carrying buckets of water. He was surprised, but pleased, to see her.

'You're busy, Bill.'

'Captain Standish has arrived with his men,' he explained. 'There's always someone needs entertaining.' He roughly tipped the water into a trough. 'What can a man do to get some peace? And how are you, Beckie?' He looked at her fondly and she felt vaguely guilty that she did not return his affection.

'Very well,' she replied almost haughtily. But Bill saw through her and laughed.

'Don't worry, Beckie, I won't think less of you for being unhappy.'

I know, but I'll think less of myself, she thought.

Just then the rear door of the manor flew open. A tall man came running across the yard. 'Bill! Don't just stand there!' he barked. 'Who's that wench you're talking to?'

He came nearer. 'Oh, it's you.' He stopped and stared at Rebecca, and surprisingly she felt herself tremble. Oliver Moreton said nothing for a moment, his brows knotted slightly above his sharp, penetrating gaze. 'What are you doing here?' he asked eventually.

'I'm a friend of Billy's,' she replied.

'How good a friend?' A ragged smile played across his lips. Then abruptly he remembered himself. 'Quick, damn you! Get the horses saddled!'

'Why, Master? I thought the men were staying?'

Oliver fetched Bill a sharp blow round the head. 'Be thankful I'm in a good mood! Get to it!'

Rebecca grimaced. She hated this casual cruelty. Yet there was something magnetic about Oliver's total self-assurance. Instead of curtseying, as was proper, she looked him straight in the eye. 'I'd best be going, sir. I'll be in your way.'

'Never, my dear. I won't forget our meeting.' Oliver grasped her poor, chapped hand and pulled it to his lips before she could react.

Behind him, she could see Bill staring at them jealously.

Rebecca said a hurried goodbye and ran across the yard. She felt confused and unaccountably nervous. She had only just reached the trees beyond when the troopers came spilling out of the manor, buckling on helmets and harness, shouting for their horses. This was no ordinary ride, she thought. Where were they going? Again she wondered if Richard was right to trust Susannah. What if Oliver was going now, to hunt him down? Rebecca felt a sudden terrible dread stir inside her. But what, she thought, can I do?

Chapter Eight

WEDLOCK CAME QUIETLY. HE WAS wrapped in a grey cloak and at first all Richard saw was a shadow flitting through the trees. He stopped him about a hundred yards before he got to the mill.

'Ill met by moonlight, proud Tremaine.' Wedlock smiled impishly. 'Ye gods, you frequent strange lairs.' He dusted his cloak. 'You're damned fortunate I found you at all.'

Richard said nothing. In his hand he held a small pistol, cocked and loaded. He gestured with it amiably, and Wedlock's eyes fell on it for the first time.

'I say—' he began.

'This is a precaution.' Richard pressed the barrel firmly against Wedlock's chest so that he could feel the man's breathing and quickly frisked his left hand down his torso and thighs.

Wedlock's eyes twinkled. 'I didn't think you fellows went in for this sort of thing. What happens next?'

Richard nodded towards the river. 'We take a short boat ride.'

He led Wedlock away from the old mill to where a group of oaks hung out over the water. Beneath their twisted shadows, Richard had moored a small rowboat.

'Hop in.'

Wedlock obliged. Then Richard settled himself opposite and clunked the oars into place.

'You know I can't swim, Tremaine.'

Richard laughed. 'Then you can paddle. At mid-tide the water's less than two feet deep.'

He pulled easily on the oars and the boat turned and nosed out into the main stream. His oars sent little eddies of phosphorescence spinning across the flat, sullen waters. A heron glided across from bank to bank. Richard rowed gently for a minute or so, feeling the sting where Sarah's wound had not yet healed, then let his blades trail and the boat slowed to a sluggish drift.

He put the oars down gently.

'I'm sorry for this,' he explained, 'but we are safe here. Safer than on land.'

This was the plan he had mentioned to Sir Charles. The river was broad and shallow at this point, and the dense trees of the banks were a hundred yards away on either side. If Wedlock had brought friends with him, they could not take him unawares. In the dim starlight the water was grey and oily.

Wedlock smiled and clutched the side of the boat. 'Well, I hope it's worth it, Tremaine. I take it you have the assurances I seek?'

Richard nodded. 'Yes, I have letters from Sir Charles Roselyn and the Arundells.' He passed them across. Wedlock scanned them perfunctorily and handed them back.

'And you will guarantee my terms: ten per cent of whatever is recovered and an introduction to the King?'

'Yes.'

'Capital! Capital!' Wedlock slapped his knees, then touched his breast. 'May I?'

'Of course.'

Wedlock reached into his doublet and extracted some folded slips of paper.

'This,' he announced, 'is a letter of reference from Lord Willoughby, formerly of the King's Own Cavalry. I think it vouchsafes my credentials.'

In the weak light the black letters appeared indistinct

and blotchy, and Richard screwed up his eyes. Willoughby's commendations seemed genuine enough. He fingered the seal respectfully.

'This is a valuable document,' he said. 'If it fell into the wrong hands, it would ruin Willoughby.'

'Quite.' Wedlock retrieved the paper, folded it fastidiously, and tucked it back into his doublet.

'Now, the letter from the cavalry officer,' said Richard.

Wedlock smiled. Richard's hand was trembling slightly as he took it. It was a thin sliver of paper, crumpled, mottled and worn with time. Richard opened it gingerly as if he expected it to melt on the first breath of air. His eyes struggled to decipher the familiar spidery scrawl. It was his father's handwriting, he was sure. And there, at the bottom, were the words he had dreamed about.

'Michael Tremaine, Capt.'

So, had Wedlock found his father's body?

He looked up. Wedlock was studying his face intently.

'Go on,' he urged. 'Read the note.'

Then several things happened at once. There was a sudden flash from the south bank and the crack of a musket. Wedlock lurched and pitched forward over Richard's knees. There was another bang and the wood next to Richard's right hand blew apart. A splinter hit his face. His hand was numb. Wedlock was drawing hoarse, terrible breaths. Richard realised his knees and calves were wet. He levered the man up as best he could – he was a dead weight – and saw blood pulsing from the man's chest. There was another flash and bang. This time the bullet fell short and struck the water with a plash.

Frantically Richard scanned the bank. He could see

nothing. Wedlock's blood was slippery on his hands. They were sitting ducks. He struggled to fit the oars into place, but the port rowlock had been torn apart by the second shot, and he heaved uselessly on the one oar, sending the boat into a short, careening spiral. There were two more gunshots. The first smacked into the prow of the boat. The second hit him on the right arm. Richard dropped the oar as if he had been stung. He clasped the wound. Thick, hot blood was running through his fingers. He felt strangely light-headed. For a second he was struck with the patterns of the starlight on the crescents and eddies of water.

Then a cry snapped him back to his senses. Two horsemen appeared beside the mill and forced their horses into the water. The animals neighed and splashed, churning the water into loud foam as their riders urged them forwards.

Richard pushed Wedlock on to his back.

'Wedlock! Come on!' He slapped him about the face, forgetting his own pain, but Wedlock gazed blankly back.

'I can't move, Tremaine. Get the hell out of here.' He managed a pained smile. 'Besides, I can't swim.'

Richard stuffed his father's note into his shirt and dived overboard.

The river was colder than he expected. His arm was burning, but the shock of the water snatched away all sensation, then he felt his hands and knees slipping on the soft silt of the riverbed. He struggled to his feet, clutching the side of the boat. The water came up to his waist. Mud and water were plastered over his face. He wiped his eyes.

'Hoah!'

The first horseman was less than forty yards away, and Richard could recognize his hooked nose and mane of jet-black hair. It was Oliver Moreton. Oliver had seen him, too, for he pulled a pistol from his bandoleer and levelled it over his horse's head.

Richard threw himself back into the water. There was a splash just behind his right ear. He sprang up, took a deep breath and plunged beneath the surface. His clothes were heavy and cumbersome, but he forced his feet under him and managed to push himself away from the boat.

Just in time. Behind him he felt the water churn and tremble as the two horses stomped and staggered around the rowboat. He clawed his way desperately along the bottom, his fingers gouging the soft mud. His lungs were tearing inside him. He gave a final heave and shot to the surface.

A rush of noise! Suddenly the air was full of calls and splashing and the crackle of birds and wind in the trees. He gasped for breath and nearly lost his balance.

'There he is!'

He twisted round. He had covered less than ten yards. Oliver jerked his horse about and she pranced through the shallows towards him.

Richard ducked, snatching air into his lungs, and thrust to one side. Something passed within a few inches of his boots. He floundered backwards. This was hopeless. He kicked at his boots and they came off one after the other and floated away, and he flung himself back, through the water, until his air ran out. This time he felt the riverbed rise beneath him and he found that here the water was less than a foot deep. He crawled up like a beached seal and held his head above water.

Oliver and the other rider were dragging their horses around, trying to catch sight of him. He guessed that in the starlight he was probably hard to see, unless someone spotted his silhouette from the bank. Quickly, he fumbled his jacket off and pushed it away. That was better. His arms moved easily in the water now, and he cupped his hands and eased himself farther downstream. His right arm felt torn and weak, but the cold water had deadened the pain.

'There he is! To your left! There!'

He had covered only twenty yards. Oliver gave a cry and came ploughing through the water after him. Richard dived again and swam to the right. This time the water seemed to part easily for him and he felt himself glide across the mudbed. When he came up, Oliver had charged away to one side.

'Here! Here!'

They had spotted his jacket. Oliver skewered it with his sword, then, seeing it was empty, flicked it angrily away. Richard swam quietly. If he could keep moving he would eventually strike the main channel which would be too deep for the horses. He felt the current pull softly at his shirt.

'Where are you? Over here!'

Suddenly there were cries from the other side, the north bank. Horses were crashing through the trees. Richard stayed still and crouched low in the water. Oliver yelled across to them.

'Don't let him land!'

Richard struck out downstream. This was the only way open to him. But at that moment one of the men must have glimpsed him, for a rider launched himself from the north bank and came charging ferociously through the river, his sword outstretched like a lance. Richard tensed himself and watched him coming. On his other side, Oliver was less than fifty yards away.

Suddenly the man's horse lurched and stumbled, as if it had struck a pothole or hollow, and the rider went tumbling over its neck and into the water. Richard sprang up and waded towards him. The man came up choking and yelling. Oliver was forcing his way through the water behind him. The fallen horse struggled to its feet, thrashed through the water. It was neighing in pain. Richard hurled himself on top of the man and forced him down again. The man's thick coat and britches hindered him and his movements were leaden, unsteady. Richard elbowed him in the face, pinning him down, running his hands over the man's chest, searching for a hold, a grip, until his fingers felt the pommel of a knife in the man's belt. The man punched him in the stomach and the world went black for a moment. Then Richard plucked the knife from its scabbard and sank it clean through its owner's neck. The man made a startled, bubbling sound and clutched his throat. Blood was spurting through his fingers and he toppled backwards. Richard watched the dark waters for just a second, then Oliver's horse almost clubbed him over the head.

Richard threw himself into the water and felt something clip his shoulder blade. He realised later that this was the tip of Oliver's sword. Oliver's horse plunged forward, only inches away, and he felt its fetlocks chop the water by his hip and thought it would ride past, but Oliver held it, just there, obviously wary of the hole which had undone his companion. Then he leant down from the saddle and riddled the water with his blade. Richard squirmed and writhed desperately through the mud. The second thrust almost caught him and passed clean between the crook of his thigh and calf, then he came up gasping beneath the belly of the horse. He felt a sudden strain of muscle as the animal reared, its great mass lifting above him for a heartbeat, then it came crashing down over him and he scrambled through the space between its legs and dived into the mud on the far side. Oliver glimpsed him, and jabbed again and again. The sword stabbed the edge of his shirt and for a moment Richard was pinned on the riverbed like an insect. He fought against the blade, tearing the cloth. Oliver strained and twisted, sensing the resistance. There was the bang of a musket.

'Hold your fire, you idiot!' Oliver shouted. Richard took a deep breath and launched himself far across to the left. The water became suddenly deeper as at last he hit the main channel and he clawed his way downstream. When finally he was driven to the surface he was more than twelve yards away. Oliver was swearing at his companion and throwing his head around angrily, scanning the river. Richard took a deep breath and slipped back beneath the water, easing himself further downriver. When next he looked, Oliver was thirty yards away and cursing furiously.

Richard's arm was aching and he rubbed the wound between his fingers. What about Wedlock? He peered back upriver, but the rowboat had disappeared. Presumably Oliver's men had towed it under the trees.

Richard kept moving, going slowly this time, taking no chances. Oliver was still searching the river, but now Richard was too far away. Suddenly Oliver shouted and pointed. It was the soldier Richard had killed. His corpse broke surface and rolled aimlessly across the water. Richard took another stroke, then another, and another, and then he felt the current begin to drag him slowly but surely towards the estuary. He swam easily now, although in pain, and gradually left Oliver and his men far behind him. His arm throbbed, but still he did not dare come to land. At least he was, for the moment, safe.

He swung around a turn in the river and a wide stretch of water expanded in front of him. This was where the two rivers – the Truro and the Fal – ran together. He felt tired and was in two minds to struggle back towards the shore when he saw a large black shape looming before him.

It was a large barge, carrying goods upstream to Truro. The barge made slow, ox-like progress and its one sail hung heavily in the air. Richard struck out towards it, and had a sudden impression of its great bulk blotting out the silvery sky, then his palms were pressed against its hull, scrabbling for a hold, and his fingers snagged a loop of rope slung over its side for mooring.

The barge was only making a knot or so, but the rope was almost pulled from his grasp, and Richard realised his right arm was weaker than he expected. He snatched the loop with his left hand and hauled himself against the rough planking. Barnacles grated his knees.

'Help!' he called out.

'What in God's name?' came a voice from the top.

Richard called again, and was aware of a face appearing over the side. Then a strong arm snaked down and grabbed him by his collar.

'A drowned rat,' said the man.

Five minutes later Richard lay gasping on the deck, staring up at the endless stars. The man was smoking a pipe and watching him. He had bushy sideburns and a tanned face with thick, heavy cheeks.

'Thank you,' said Richard.

'On the run, are you?' The man eyed the wound on his arm.

Richard could see there was no point in lying. 'Are you for the King or for Cromwell?' he asked bluntly.

This seemed to amuse the man. 'Which one's for me?' he replied, and bent forwards slowly, his pipe smoking in his hands. 'I don't think either is going to bandage your arm for you, are they, boy? No,' he added, 'there's only one Lord who'll bind and dress your wounds.'

He threw an old piece of cloth at Richard. 'I'd guess you were for King, or else you wouldn't be running,' he said.

Richard tore his sleeve open. The bullet had passed across the top of his right biceps. He wrapped the cloth around it as best he could, and winced.

'Wait a minute.' The old man produced a flask of brandy and splashed it liberally over the wound. He laughed again when Richard swore. 'Now tie it up. Dare say you'll live.'

Richard smiled grimly. 'For a few hours more, at any rate.'

He looked at the sky. It was growing lighter in the east. Soon Susannah would be waiting for him at Tresillian Bridge, scared and anxious, and he would not be there.

Chapter Nine

THEY SIGHTED TRURO A FEW hours after dawn. The thought of Susannah had haunted Richard all morning, but he knew there was nothing he could do. How long would she wait for him? And when she realised he wasn't coming, would she curse him, or fret, or ride disconsolately back to Chynoon? He asked himself this time after time until eventually exhaustion overwhelmed him and he dozed fitfully on the scrubbed deck of the barge.

Jonah, the barge captain, poked him in the ribs as they neared the quays.

'Guess you'll be getting off here,' he said. Richard clasped his hand, but the man wouldn't listen to his thanks. 'Go in peace,' was all he said. 'Here,' he pulled out a battered and soiled cloak, 'put this on. How can I tell a brother to go in peace if he is naked and I do not clothe him?'

There were already several barges tied up, and the wharves were crowded with people. As they drew alongside, Richard saw that the quays were cluttered with a vast array of wares: barrels of salt, tubs of pitch and tallow, casks of brandy, wine and port, lengths of woollen cloth and linen and rope, ironmongery, candles, pottery and glassware, bundles of staves, crates of fruit. People were buying goods direct from the bargemen, haggling suspiciously and greedily. Others swarmed round the barges from curiosity. Then there were shouts and expletives and the squeal of horses and oxen as the carriers heaved their goods up the gangways, shoving through onlookers, and stacked them on the quay or loaded them into carts.

Richard was worried that Oliver might have the quays watched, and scanned the crowds for familiar faces. But he recognised no one, and heaving a side of salted port on to his shoulder, he marched up the gangplank, dropped his burden in the waiting cart, and let himself be absorbed into the throng. Many people had been in town since daybreak, but more were arriving all the time, and he drifted with the flow towards the main market, a large area of flat ground on the banks of the river. Several small boys pushed past him, laughing and calling. Most of the market-goers were ordinary countryfolk who had walked six, seven miles already that morning with their wives and their goods for sale – chickens, fruit, eggs, flitches of bacon and the like – and their clothes were drab browns and greys and maroons, the colour of the land in winter. Richard blended easily among them and realised his torn shirt and borrowed cloak were not so out of place. The gentry also had ridden in from their residences, and here and there were occasional flashes of their richly coloured costumes, of gaudy ribbons and flamboyant lace. Such clothes were always the badge of the cavaliers, and he guessed they were worn in defiance of the authorities, but seeing them mixed with the drabness of the ordinary people, they seemed strangely artificial and superfluous, like exotic fauna which had no real roots in the soil. Somehow they symbolised the failure of the royalist cause. Men of other persuasions were there too: sober-faced individuals with modest wives and short-cropped hair and simple black suits. It was men like these, stern, committed, who had crushed the flower of England's nobility underfoot and in place of the King had raised up Cromwell.

Richard could remember markets from his childhood, hectic, merry days of buffoonery and commerce. But today was a glum affair. The new authorities had prohibited beer and wine and entertainments on the site and the people appeared listless and bored. By this season, most farmers had already sold their crops, and the few wretched calves and sheep being penned and auctioned did not seem to merit the crowd's attention. Richard was tired and hungry, and with a few coins left in his britches, he gratefully bought some slabs of cold meat pie and settled down against the wheel of a cart to eat. It was while he was chewing the last of the crust that he remembered for the first time his father's note, and reached inside his shirt.

It had gone.

Cursing, he searched again, checking every fold, but it was not there. It was hardly surprising. His shirt was torn and rent. The note could so easily have slipped our during his escape, or simply dissolved in the water.

He leaned back with his eyes closed and considered the true seriousness of his plight. His mission was in tatters. Without the note, and with Wedlock dead or captured, he had no hope of discovering what had happened to his father, nor the whereabouts of the gold. And what of Susannah? He imagined her riding back to Chynoon alone. What would happen to her? Silently he cursed himself. They should have left for France immediately, together, and to hell with his duty. What was his duty but fulfilling the King's selfish ambitions?

He clenched his teeth angrily. I have failed myself, he thought. Failed my father. Failed Susannah. He pressed his back against the spokes of the cartwheel, wishing he was somehow removed from this.

'To your tents, O Israel!'

A man's voice, a strong, emotional plea, came to him

over the talk and mutterings of the people. He opened his eyes.

'To your tents, O Israel!'

The call rent the air a second time, and Richard stumbled to his feet. A little way off, beyond the remaining cattle, a small crowd had gathered, and it was from the middle of this group that the voice was coming. Richard drew nearer.

'. . . the time of trouble departed? Can we sink back into the life of ease and luxury in which our forebears wallowed like pigs? Nay, nay! For this very reason, their sin found them out and ruin was visited on them. Only think of that most sinful of men, Charles Stuart, proclaimed King by the pride of men, Charles Stuart, that man of blood! What was he but the living embodiment of our corruption? He was a foul and weeping boil, I say, who poisoned our very souls until at last its foul bile was cut out!'

A young man with short fair hair and a terrifyingly pale, almost bloodless face was declaiming with remarkable passion. He seemed to actually hurl the words out of his mouth. The veins on his neck bulged and strained with the force of his ejaculations. His eyes were bleak and clear blue and raked his audience like a flame of ice. Richard saw smiles and grimaces and roars leap across his face as he spoke, and the audience stood transfixed, craning their necks to get a better sight of the speaker, straining on tiptoe.

'To your tents, O Israel! Is our work done? Can our hands rest from the scythe? Many of your loved ones were led to their deaths by the sins of Charles Stuart, that vile contagion. But now the so-called King is dead, are we truly free? Has our blood been purified of sin? Think of the people of Israel, our spiritual forebears.

Had the Lord wished for them to be ruled by man or by the holy Law? By whim of man or the Law of God?'

The crowd responded. 'The Law! The Law!'

The speaker's face shone. 'Yes, truly, truly! And yet what did Israel do but refuse the Law of God and choose men, sinful, vain, proud men, to rule over them as Kings? Until at length the anger of the Lord broke out against them and swept them away like chaff.' He made a huge sweeping gesture. 'Yet have we acted differently? We have removed one tyrant only to welcome another in his place. For who rules England now, the Law of God or the whim of Cromwell?'

The crowd were becoming more animated. Richard suddenly realised this was no ordinary impromptu sermon. His blood quickened. What sort of message was this man proclaiming? And at that moment he recognised a face in the crowd. It was Jeremiah Brown, the youth he had met in the White Lamb when he was following Sarah Masters.

'Yes!' continued the preacher. 'Cromwell has set himself up as God. He has taken unto himself the very sins and foulness that were the King's.'

Several of the crowd began to murmur. One or two drifted away, with expressions of disgust or uneasiness, but many others shouted encouragement. Jeremiah in the meantime was working his way among them. Richard was fascinated by the speaker, yet he found the appearance of Jeremiah distracted him. There was something peculiar about the man's behaviour. He was staring stiffly at the preacher, but with none of the enthusiasm of the other bystanders. His hands were held oddly by his sides.

'In the Book of Daniel,' cried the preacher, 'it is written that there will be four kingdoms of men, and then the fifth and last kingdom of God the Monarch! When

will that fifth monarchy be? How can we hope for
that blessed kingdom, so long as Cromwell usurps the
crown for himself?'

Richard suddenly realised what Jeremiah was doing.

He was stealing the purse of the person in front of
him – a middle-aged merchant dressed in the dour
clothes of a presbyterian. A short blade glinted quickly
in Jeremiah's hand as he nicked the purse slung
through the man's belt. The bottom of the purse bellied
open and Jeremiah caught the coins expertly in the
palm of his hand and pocketed them without a down-
ward glance. So that was what happened to my purse,
Richard smiled grimly.

'Has any man the right to take what is God's for
himself?' demanded the preacher. 'Is that not
Cromwell's sin? Was that not the sin of Satan himself?'

The mood of the crowd changed abruptly. People
started yelling and shoving. A dense knot of black-
clothed men had barged their way into the middle. The
preacher saw them and sucked his lungs full of air. 'To
your tents, O Is—' At that moment a large, burly man
in a buff jacket knocked him to the ground. The
preacher lay gasping, winded. Someone from the crowd
ran forward and struck the preacher's assailant over
the head. The crowd roared in anger. The black-suited
men had formed a cordon around the preacher, two
pinned him to the ground. Richard guessed these were
Cromwell's men.

'Gentlemen!' cried one, an old man with a grey moustache. 'Order, please! This man speaks lies! Lies and
treason against our Lord Protector!'

A stone struck him on the forehead. He clutched his
eyes and the crowd rushed forward, ramming the
black-suited men aside. Someone heaved up the
preacher, still shouting, by the armpits, and Richard

275

thought the whole scene was going to erupt into chaos. Then there was a loud call, followed by the dull bang-bang-bang of muskets being discharged in quick succession. People screamed. A body of troopers had formed on the lip of the market and had fired a volley over the crowd. They began to reload. The fizz and whiff of smouldering matchcords wafted in the air. 'Peace! Order!' called an officer, brandishing his sword. The crowd faltered, people stared anxiously at the soldiers, one man ran forward, then, seeing he was on his own, stopped and ran back. Those at the rear of the crowd began to break away, clutching their children, and made for the shelter of the streets. Richard saw Jeremiah dart a glance at the soldiers, then disentangle himself from the mass of people and cut across to the right. Richard followed.

Behind him, the dark-suited men had seized the preacher again and forced him to the ground. Somewhere a woman was shrieking. Men were shouting, arguing, running noisily. Richard kept his eyes fixed on Jeremiah, as he snaked his way through the fleeing crowds and plunged into the web of lanes and streets beyond. Jeremiah was young and ran quickly. Richard's feet were bare and he jumped to avoid lumps of horse dung and pools of horse piss and stones and human excrement lying in the gutters. Jeremiah turned up a side alley and Richard thought he would lose him, but then he saw that Jeremiah had slowed to a respectable saunter and was entering the White Lamb at the end of the street. People were still staring up the street towards the disturbance at the marketplace, while others hurried nervously away and more soldiers came down the street at a slow trot, but Richard ignored them and went through the doors of the White Lamb.

Inside, the tavern was packed with drinkers, market-

goers, farmers and traders. Screwing his eyes against
the thick smoke, Richard angled his way through a
knot of farmers and made for the bar. Where was Jeremiah? A serving-girl came by swinging a huge tray of
tankards above her head, then he caught sight of Jeremiah's thick black hair. He had his back to Richard and
was helping one of the maids set a barrel on its side.
Richard watched carefully. Jeremiah must work here.
When he had finished, the girl brought him a quart of
ale and he stood hunched by the bar, drinking casually.
Richard waited until he had drained the tankard, then
he came up behind and slapped him on the shoulder.
Jeremiah spun round.

'Remember me?'

Jeremiah stared in surprise. He seemed to toy
momentarily with the idea of a greeting, then he shoved
past Richard and made a run for the back of the tavern.
Richard was thrown back, off-balance, into a group of
men, who swore angrily and would perhaps have come
to blows if Richard hadn't already leapt up, hurdling a
table, and raced after Jeremiah as he disappeared
through a door in the far wall. The door opened on to
the rear court, surrounded by stables, storerooms, but
Richard ran for the arch leading on to the back street.
Jeremiah was already through there, his feet ringing on
the ground. Richard pounded after him. The ale must
have blunted Jeremiah's wits for the next moment he
slipped on a stone and staggered. Richard was on him
in a second and hauled him by his collar into a side
alley, ignoring his screams. Jeremiah tried to struggle,
and Richard butted his head against the wall.

'Don't!' he hissed. 'I just want to talk.'

Jeremiah eyed him suspiciously.

'You stole my money.'

'What of it?' replied Jeremiah, with surprising

flippancy. 'I'll pay you back. Here.' He glanced towards a bulge in his jacket.

Richard rammed his head against the wall. 'I saw you steal that as well. Listen,' he came closer, so his lips were only inches from Jeremiah's own, 'I need help. You work at the White Lamb, don't you? One word from me and you'll be dragged before the magistrates. Understand?'

Jeremiah smiled hesitantly. 'Do you think they'll believe a word you say?'

'Do you want to risk it?' Richard stared at him coldly and tore the purse from his belt. 'You'll get this back later, agreed?'

Jeremiah squirmed against the wall and nodded his head.

'Good. I need some clothes and shoes and a means of transport out of here. I want to go east, up county. Can you arrange that?'

'Is that all?'

'That's all.' Richard released his grip and let Jeremiah slide down the wall.

'What are you on the run for?' Jeremiah grinned impudently.

'That's my business.'

'Have it your way.' Jeremiah reached up a sweaty palm and shook his hand. Richard didn't trust him, but he reckoned the simplest option for Jeremiah was to help him.

Together they walked back to the inn yard.

'I know someone who can take you to Lostwithiel,' Jeremiah announced. 'He's a carter, just brought in a load of logs to market.'

'That will do. Come back here once it's arranged.' With that, he left Jeremiah standing on the corner of the yard. Richard did not trust him enough to risk waiting at the White Lamb, though the thought of a square meal was sorely tempting. Instead he took up position across the street behind a stack of empty barrels. He was just becoming impatient when he saw Jeremiah come back out of the inn and stand sullenly on the corner. He seemed to be by himself, and in his hands he carried a parcel of clothes. Richard crossed the street quickly. Jeremiah gave him an ugly smile, and handed him a clean shirt and jacket and some rather worn but serviceable shoes. Richard put them on quickly.

'My friend's waiting round the side,' indicated Jeremiah. 'Hal's his name.'

Cautiously Richard walked with him. Sure enough, pulled up around the corner was a large lumber cart, with a young man squatting on the driving board. The youth had sandy straight hair matted down like a thatch. He grinned at Richard and revealed a mouth of rotting teeth. 'You're my passenger, eh?' There was something vaguely familiar about him, thought Richard.

'Don't I know you?' he asked.

Hal laughed. 'Hah, hah! I hope not! Not if you're a friend of Jem's.'

Richard pulled himself on to the cart and threw the purse back to Jeremiah, who pocketed it swiftly. Hal spat into the street and flicked the reins. The four nags shrugged irritably and lurched into a slow walk. Hal yelled obscenities at them, and fetched them a flick of his crop, then brayed loudly with amusement. 'Gee up, you bastards! Hup oah!'

The cart lumbered across the street, scattering a flock of geese and making their owner swear aggressively. Hal laughed back and thumbed his nose, and the cart pulled on to the main thoroughfare out of Truro, little more than a lane, which wound up the hill ahead. Richard leant back on the board and rested his feet. It was a little after midday, he judged, and it would take them the rest of the afternoon before they got near Caerleon, but at least this way he could rest and would be less conspicuous than on his own.

'What happened at the market?' he asked after a while.

Hal laughed. It was a stupid, braying sound, Richard decided. 'That was some to-do an' all, eh? They arrested some preacher, I heard, they caught 'un rousing the crowd.' He shook the reins briskly.

'Were many people hurt?'

'Five or six, that's all.'

'What did you think of his message?' asked Richard curiously.

Hal shrugged. 'Well,' he said, 'maybe the man had a point. All those people fought against the King an' for what? For another King?' He laughed again.

Richard smiled uneasily. 'I suppose your father fought, did he?'

'Yes. He was as stupid as the rest o' them. Marched off with his cousins and never came back. Died the first summer of a pike in the belly. That's all I know of the war. Load of lies!' he added with sudden spite. 'Nothing but a heap of lies!' Then he cast Richard a glance. 'You ain't caught up in that, are 'ee?'

Richard shook his head and stared at the road.

Hal began to whistle to himself, a shrill, tuneless whine. The cart creaked to the top of the hill, lurched in a huge rut, and then trundled down the other side. A valley stretched before them, fields bare and dull green, studded here and there with clusters of sheep, and at the bottom of the valley, where a stream ran, lay a thicket of oaks and hawthorns, their bare branches grey and sepia.

'Come on, hoah!' Hal goaded his horses into a fast walk down the slope and the cart shook violently.

Suddenly, over the racket, came the unmistakable rumble of hooves ahead. Richard tensed. A company of six horsemen appeared from between the trees and rode up the lane towards them. Hal began to yell at his horses to hold, and stood up and heaved on the reins. Richard pulled at the block-brake lever on the side of the cart.

At the head of the riders was Oliver Moreton.

And then, with a shock, Richard saw that just behind Oliver, on a sleek sorrel mare, rode Susannah. Her hair was pulled back demurely under her coif. As the riders galloped up the hill, he could make out the expression on her face. She seemed pale and sad. Her eyes were lowered. She can't have seen me yet, he thought, and tore his gaze away. Within seconds they would be alongside. Richard jumped down from the cart and pretended to fumble with the brake lever frantically. What was she doing here? Had Oliver found her at Tresillian? Why was he taking her to Truro?

Above him Hal was cursing loudly, and then Oliver pulled up in a clatter of hooves and dust.

'Get that godforsaken cart out of my way, you idiot!'

'I'm sorry, sir, it's the horses, they're old and stupid, sir,' whined Hal. He tugged at the reins. His horses stamped and did not move. Richard stayed bent over the brake, staring at his boots. Surely he would be recognised?

'I'll have your hide for this!' Oliver kicked his horse forward and glared at Hal. He raised his hand.

'No, Oliver, please!' It was Susannah. She cantered forward and smiled at him nervously. 'He's just a simpleton. We can ride around him.' She laid a hand on his arm. 'Come. We'll be late.'

Oliver swore.

Richard felt his jaw tighten with anger.

'You there! What are you doing skulking behind the cart?'

With a sickening jolt, Richard realised that Oliver was speaking to him.

He muffled his mouth with his hand and called up, 'The blasted brake's jammed, sir! I'm trying to fix 'un so we can move for you!'

There was a moment's silence. Richard didn't dare raise his head. Through the spokes of the wheels he could see Oliver's horse stamping in the dirt, until eventually he heard Oliver grunt, and shout: 'Come on! Move! Move!' The riders shook their reins and trotted on up the hill. Richard crouched by the hub while they passed, then hauled himself back on to the riding board.

Hal grinned. 'That brake ain't really jammed, is 'ee?'

'No.'

Hal burst out laughing and whipped the reins. 'Hah, hah! Well, you had me fooled there!' The cart jolted down the slope. Richard looked over his shoulder. Already the riders had disappeared over the breast of the hill.

'That Colonel Moreton's a right bastard,' said Hal with sudden feeling.

'Moreton?' asked Richard ingenuously.

'One of they parliament officers. Now he's lord of the manor I hear.' Hal cocked his head. 'That was his son Oliver who almost smacked me.'

'Roundheads have no respect,' muttered Richard. 'They killed the King, didn't they?'

'Aye.' Hal nodded and laughed again. 'But I've got something personal with the Colonel.'

'You have?'

'When my father died, I worked as a stableboy until that bastard sent us all packing.' He spat again. 'Not that this carting ain't better than cleaning muck for the lords and ladies.'

Realisation suddenly dawned on Richard.

'You're Harry Jenkins, aren't you?' he asked. 'You used to be a stableboy at Chynoon.'

Hal looked at him surprised. 'Harry? I ain't been called that since a boy.'

So this was the Harry Jenkins that Couch had told him about. The stableboy who had run an errand for his father on that last fateful night.

Richard felt strangely uneasy. He tapped Hal on the shoulder. 'I don't suppose you remember me. I'm Richard Tremaine.'

Hal looked stunned. 'No, that can't be—'

'Don't you remember? I had red hair. I was seventeen.' He stared into Hal's eyes, willing him to remember.

Hal's face suddenly darkened. 'What makes you think I'd be any friend of yours?' His laugh had a threatening edge to it and he slapped his knees. 'Hah! Look at 'ee now, begging lifts off the likes of me!'

Richard bit his lip. 'Things have changed, Hal.'

'Haven't they just? And how many favours did your father do me, eh?' He shook the reins violently.

'That was a long time ago.'

'He died, didn't he?'

Richard paused. 'Yes.'

'Well, good bloody riddance! He was the one got my father killed, and for what? Did he care a damn for us?' Hal's face grew red and blotchy. 'All bloody lies!'

Suddenly, Richard's feelings boiled over. 'Damn you!' He thrust Hal back over the riding board and they tumbled on to the flat of the open cart behind them. The horses plodded on regardless. The cart hit a stone and jolted sideways and Richard had a hand to Hal's throat and his knee on his chest. Hal bared his half-rotten teeth. Spittle collected between his lips.

'All right?' Richard pressed down his knee. He could no longer contain the anger and frustration which had been building within him. 'All right?'

Hal clutched Richard's fist. 'Yes, yes,' he whined. 'Let me go.'

Richard didn't loosen his grip. 'What happened on the night my father died? You brought him a note. Where had you come from? Where?'

Hal's eyes blinked pitifully. 'From Talbot's Farm, just the other side of Grampound.'

'Why? What were you doing?'

'Your father had sent me with a letter. I was bringing back her reply.'

'*Her* reply?'

'Talbot's wife: it was her I had to see.'

'Why? What did the note say?'

'I don't know, damn you!'

Richard got up. Hal wiped his mouth and glared at him spitefully.

'I'm glad you lost your home, Tremaine, you know that?' He laughed. 'Bowing and scraping to your flaming daddy! Pah!'

Richard felt something explode inside his head. He turned and punched Hal in the face. He hadn't realised how angry he was until he felt the man's lip burst apart in a welter of blood. Hal shrieked and clutched his mouth. Richard punched him again, and again. 'Damn you and your kind,' he yelled. 'My father fought for something he believed in. What do you believe in?'

'Please! No!' Hal was almost gibbering. His face was

a bloody pulp. Richard stood over him, fists clenched, face like thunder.

What am I doing? he thought. Suddenly he threw himself off the cart and ran down the lane.

He did not stop running until he had left the cart and his anger far behind. By then he stood on the final spur of hill, and the Tresillian river glistened like a broad silver ribbon below him. On his left, the houses of Tresillian were dotted along the riverbank.

He watched he scene until his breathing slowed and he felt his head clearing. He was trembling, though whether with weariness or emotion he could not – would not – tell. Eventually he wiped the sweat from his eyes and limped down the road towards the bridge. His shoes were ill-fitting and the run had blistered his feet badly.

Up on the right stood Tresillian Bridge. It was here that Hopton had surrendered the royalist army to General Fairfax, the commander of Parliament's forces, on 12th March 1646. And it was here that Susannah had waited for him this very morning, before Oliver took her into Truro.

His hand was aching where Sarah's knife had cut him. He realised in a daze that there was blood on his palms and knuckles – Hal's blood – and he wiped them quickly on his britches. A man sitting on an upturned barrel regarded him suspiciously. Richard straightened his jacket and walked on, falling into step with a large group of countryfolk heading back from market. They reached the bridge at the same time as a haywain and waited while the great carriage lumbered through.

On the far side of the bridge a woman was standing in the shadow of the trees. She wore a faded brown shawl and her arms were wrapped around herself for warmth. When she saw Richard, she stepped forward on to the road.

It was Rebecca.

Without thinking Richard pushed through the crowd of walkers and ran across the bridge. Rebecca was running towards him and he caught her in his arms, oblivious to the pain of his wounds. They clung to each other like lovers while the market-goers trudged by, until at last, reluctantly, he unwrapped her embrace.

'What are you doing here?' he whispered.

'Richard! I thought you were dead for sure!' Her face was strained with worry. 'What happened?' He didn't answer her immediately but led her away from the bridge and into the fields beyond. Here a path ran parallel to the river.

'I didn't expect to see you, Beckie.'

'I'm sorry,' she apologised reluctantly. 'I read your note.'

At another time he would have been angry, would have accused her of prying, but not now. Now, he sighed and sat down on the grass by the side of the path.

'Did you give it to Susannah?'

'Of course.'

'What did she say?'

Rebecca turned her face away. 'She thanked me for delivering it, that was all.' She paused.

'So why are you here? I don't understand.'

Briefly she told him about Oliver's appearance, and seeing the troop of cavalry ride out.

'I wanted to follow them, but that was impossible. So the only thing I could do was come here. I just couldn't go home, not knowing.'

'You've been here all night?'

She smiled seriously. 'Foolish, wasn't I?'

'But what about Susannah? Wasn't she here?'

'Don't you understand, Richard? That's what I was trying to tell you!' Her eyes flashed. 'Why do you think Oliver knew to come after you? She must have told him.'

'That's ridiculous,' he answered, suddenly angry.

'Richard, she never came here.' Rebecca was deliberately blunt. She stared at him furiously, willing him to believe her.

'She must have,' he began.

'I sat here all night waiting for you. Don't you think I'd notice if she turned up?'

'You had no right to read my note,' he said irritably. She started as if he had hit her.

'Aren't you glad I did?'

He was about to say something, but stopped himself. 'Of course I am,' he said. 'I didn't mean what I said.'

Rebecca's face softened. 'It's all right,' she said. 'I understand.'

'I saw Susannah about an hour ago,' he told her. 'Riding into Truro.'

'With Oliver? Yes, I saw them too.' Rebecca looked at him. In spite of her grim smile, she felt no joy in Susannah's behaviour. It merely confirmed her opinion of people. 'News travels fast, Richard. Everyone's heard about your fight at the mill. They say you killed a man.'

'I had no choice.'

She rested her hands on his chest. 'We all have a choice, Richard. You could have chosen not to be involved in this stupid duty of yours at all.'

'My father made that choice for me,' he replied. 'The day he disappeared.'

'So what will you do now?'

'I don't know. My mission's hopeless now. Once I've tied up a few loose ends I'll be gone.'

'And Susannah?'

'I can't just leave her, Beckie. It's not as simple as that. I need to talk to her.'

'Richard, she wasn't here!'

'So you say! But until I've talked to her, I won't rest. Perhaps she couldn't get out of the house. You must understand that.'

Yes, she thought bitterly, I do. I understand you love her, Richard, and you'll always make excuses for her. Just as I make them for you. She sighed. She could no longer feel anger. Anger was beyond her and beneath her.

Richard stood up and offered her his hand. Rebecca took it.

'You must be exhausted,' he said.

She managed a smile. 'I was too worried about you. I couldn't sleep anyway.'

'Thanks, Beckie. I can't tell you how good it is to see you.' There was an embarrassing pause, then he coughed and let her hand go. 'If you're not too tired, would you like to walk with me? There's someone I want to visit.'

Chapter Ten

BY THE TIME THEY REACHED Talbot Farm, the sky was filled with fat grey cloud, pressing down on them, stifling the colour of the landscape. A wretched mud track wound up from the lane. As they walked up, a dog started to bark, then another, ragged, angry barks. At the top the track opened on to a broad, filthy area, littered with animal waste and mire. On the left stood a ramshackle barn and, in front, the farmhouse itself. Talbot Farm was a small, slack-sided building, hunched in the shadow of five poor elms. Its thatch was sagged and stained by too many winters, its plastered walls were the shade of soiled sheets.

Richard glanced at Rebecca for reassurance, took a deep breath and marched up to the faded green door and knocked. Almost immediately there was the sound of movement inside, the door creaked open and a woman peered out of the gloom.

'Yes?' she began, but the word died on her lips. Her large hazel eyes were staring at him. 'Good God.' She turned and without another word stumbled back inside. Richard stayed where he was, bewildered. 'Go on!' hissed Rebecca, and he shook himself and stepped across the threshold.

Straight ahead stood a narrow staircase, to the right a cluttered storeroom. On the left a door opened into the main living room. The room was long and low and ribbed with sagging beams. The walls were lined with uneven shelves, cupboards and a dresser sporting a shabby collection of slipware – chipped, mottled. A small fire burnt fitfully in the hearth.

Mrs Talbot was standing at the far end of the room with her back to them. She was clutching the edge of the table and seemed to be gazing out of the window. 'Come in,' she said. 'Sit down.' She turned and caught sight of Rebecca standing in the doorway. 'I'm sorry,' she said, 'I didn't see you. Please, both of you, sit down.'

Richard was so taken aback he did as she suggested and pulled up a chair. Rebecca followed suit.

'Mrs Talbot?'

She looked at him then, and the thin grey light from the window revealed the lines etched beneath her eyes and down her cheeks. 'Yes,' she replied faintly. 'You can call me Mary.' She let go of the table and lifted her knuckles quickly to her lips. She appeared to be studying his face, intently, painfully. Rebecca said nothing. From the look on the woman's face, she could already sense the truth, and she felt for Mary Talbot and for Richard. She placed a hand on his forearm.

'It really is most uncanny,' Mary Talbot announced, then smiled, nervously, and her face shone. 'You know for a second I thought you were a ghost. Your father,' her words ran on, 'you look so much like your father. You've dyed your hair, haven't you?'

'You knew Michael Tremaine?' Richard felt his pulse quicken.

Mary took a step, then suddenly ran forward and threw her arms around him. She was crying and he held her tired body awkwardly and comforted her and wondered why. Eventually he felt her sobbing ease, and he lifted her face a little and she looked up and smiled painfully.

'I'm sorry,' she said. 'I just wanted to hold you for a

moment. You must be Richard. I always wanted to meet you.' She looked at Rebecca for sympathy. 'Please, I hope you will excuse me. You are Richard's betrothed?'

Rebecca looked away.

'This is Rebecca Penmarris,' replied Richard stiffly. 'She is a good friend of mine.'

'I see.' Mary Talbot appeared to study them both intently, as if judging the truth of his claim, then she looked down at her raw, chapped hands. 'Your father and I were lovers, when you were a boy.'

Rebecca glanced at Richard. He was not as shocked as she had expected. Somehow he had guessed something like this, ever since he heard Hal's dark, ugly laughter. Nevertheless the words hit him hard.

'You were?' His question was part accusation, part denial. He wanted her to suddenly break, crumble before his eyes, tell him it was all a cruel, bizarre joke, a mistake, anything. Suddenly he felt as if he did not want this new knowledge, and he was angry that this woman should have such power over him.

But instead of revelling in this power, Mary Talbot just sniffed and dried her eyes with the backs of her hands. Despite himself, Richard felt his heart torn by conflicting emotions. There was something in her actions and expression which seemed pathetic and touching, yet at the same time enraged and sickened him. He got up abruptly and stalked to the other end of the room.

'I'm sorry,' she said after him. 'He wanted to tell you, but there wasn't the time.'

Richard punched the wall next to the window. The plaster was soft and rotten and crumbled against his fist.

'Richard, don't!' Rebecca said crossly. There were tears in her voice. He stayed staring at the wall.

'You loved your father, didn't you?' Mary Talbot's voice was worn with emotion. He could feel her come close behind him. 'You're angry because you didn't know, aren't you?'

He didn't answer. His hand clenched and unclenched rhythmically.

'You don't have to love him any the less because he loved me,' she said.

'Richard! Please!'

'Do you mind,' he said quietly, 'if I have a few minutes on my own?'

Mary Talbot said nothing. She turned, took a pan of water, and placed it over the fire. With only the slightest glance at Rebecca, Richard walked out of the house. Rebecca did not follow. Mary spent the next few minutes feeding the fire with sticks, and Rebecca helped her. Richard's pain grieved her, but at the same time she found his behaviour embarrassing. He's so hot-headed, she thought.

'He's terribly upset,' she whispered to Mary. 'His father was everything to him.'

Mary smiled sadly. 'I know, child,' she replied. 'It's a shame he didn't know him better.' She paused. 'You both look famished.'

Outside the air was damp and grey. Richard sucked it deep into his lungs and glared at the wretched hedge and barn. A dog came running up to him and he kicked it away.

Was she right? That was a stupid question, of course she was right! He'd known it as soon as he set eyes on her.

He sifted through his memories, trying to think of his father, his mother. There was nothing, nothing in all he could recall, which gave any warning of this. He felt betrayed. Betrayed by the past. By Mary Talbot.

And yet, even as he thought that, Mary's face came back to him, wrought with insecurity, anxiety, sadness. The way she wiped her raw knuckles over her tired raw eyes.

Damn her! He stared out at the bare rolling fields beyond the farm. Damn! She had loved his father, that much was obvious. And she had mourned him ever since. Reluctantly, Richard felt his fury grow dull and numb. She's right, he thought. What is love that I should resent it? Except that love can corrupt even our best intentions, he replied. And he was pained to think that even Michael Tremaine had been corrupted.

'How did you meet my father?' Richard walked slowly back into the room. His voice was softer. He paused. 'I'm sorry for my reaction.'

Mary and Rebecca looked up. They were chopping vegetables at the table.

'You probably won't remember this.' Mary wiped her hands on her apron. 'But when the war broke out, Geoffrey, my husband, declared for Parliament. He rode off at the first news and fought for two years until he fell at Castledore. The King's men wanted to seize our farm, but your father protected me. He said the war wasn't women's business and I couldn't be accountable for my husband's betrayal.' She smiled proudly, as if some long-forgotten speech echoed in her mind. 'He was very eloquent, your father. When Geoffrey didn't return that autumn, we became close.'

'What about my mother? Had you no thought for her?' Richard asked, more roughly than he intended.

'Surely that was your father's responsibility, don't you think?' She stared back at him with a tired defiance. 'How do you think I felt, giving him up to her every night? Never knowing when he would come, or how

293

long he would stay. Do you think he loved her? Do you?'

'She was his wife!' Richard felt incensed. He came towards her. 'Have you no shame?'

Closer up, Mary Talbot looked suddenly old and beaten. 'You don't know, do you?' she asked. 'I had hoped you'd be more like him.' She looked at Rebecca for support. 'Your mother had been unfaithful, Richard.'

'Lies! Damn you!'

Throughout this, Rebecca had stood silently beside Mary. Now she spoke:

'Please, Richard, hear her out!'

'Why do you think she went to Lembury Castle?' asked Mary. 'Why did she leave you behind?' She saw him falter and continued ruthlessly: 'Your mother was having an affair with her cousin, Jack Melthorpe. She'd been seeing him for years, before she was married.'

He went to deny it, but checked himself. 'Then why didn't she marry him?'

She laughed wisely. 'You obviously didn't know Jack Melthorpe. He was a drunk, a waster, with no money of his own. But your mother always wanted to play the lady.'

'While you played the mistress,' he retorted, then wished he hadn't. He saw the pain on her face. 'I'm sorry,' he said in a hushed voice. 'I didn't mean that.'

'Yes, you did,' she answered. She crossed the room and began to feed more sticks into the fire. He looked at her thin back hunched over the hearth.

Pointedly, Rebecca refused to meet his gaze.

'Look,' he said at last. 'This is very . . . difficult for me. You must understand. What you're saying . . . It never occurred to me that my father and mother didn't love each other.'

'Was there really nothing you ever saw?' asked Rebecca suddenly.

He stared at her. 'What do you mean? You knew this as well?'

'Richard, you know I *care* for you.' She looked at him tenderly. 'I didn't know anything for certain. I was only a girl, what could I tell?'

'But you knew something?'

She swallowed. 'Why do you think your father spent so much time riding? Or when he was home he'd lock himself away in the library? Do you think it was just a love of books?'

Richard sank into a chair. 'Now I think of it, I can remember there were sometimes strained silences at meals, and I recall ... other things.' A brief image flashed in his mind of his mother running in from the orchard, her face flushed. Or was he now reading too much into the past? Time plays tricks with us all, he thought bitterly. Rebecca held his hand, willing him to understand. 'I never realised,' he mumbled. 'I just thought the relationship between my parents was normal. What child wouldn't?' He looked to them for support. 'Besides, when the war came my father was away so much.'

'Often he was with me.' Mary straightened up and looked at him. But there was no victory in her voice. 'He loved you, Richard, I know it grieved him that he couldn't tell you.'

'I'm sorry, Mary.'

Rebecca hugged him and he felt the desire to hug her back. Mary came closer. She was smiling, but tears sprang into her eyes. 'I feel we've got so much to talk about,' she said.

Over a bowl of vegetable broth, Richard learned a little of his parents' secret history. It was painful but, he realised, necessary. He was reminded of turning the apple over in the orchard and finding the underside all eaten and decayed, except he realised it was too simple to criticise his father's and his mother's choices without understanding them. The truth about people's lives was more complex than that, less certain. He would always consider his father had done wrong, undoubtedly, but perhaps this was only because he had always expected him to do right. His mother he could not condemn at all. He realised with a shock that whatever he heard, his mother would still remain a memory of soft misty beauty, a dream of innocence, incapable of fleshly sin. Whereas the woman sitting opposite him, with her worn face and lank strands of hair, seemed all too fallible. More than anything, he was glad Rebecca was with him.

'Michael told me so much about you,' Mary was saying. 'He was very proud of you, Richard.' She looked at him yearningly, and Richard felt deeply uncomfortable. I can't be a son to you, he almost said. He found her emotions and her obvious vulnerability somehow impolite, repellent, and looked away, ashamed.

'Yes,' agreed Rebecca. 'He was.'

'I always knew he'd come, eventually,' Mary told her. 'I don't know why.'

Richard chewed slowly. 'I only found out by the slightest chance,' he replied. 'I had no idea.'

Mary seemed hurt to be reminded of her irrelevance to his life so far, and dipped her head. Rebecca scowled at him and Richard felt suddenly guilty. He reached out and patted Mary's arm awkwardly.

'But I'm glad I found you, Mary. I really am.'

'Why are you here, anyway? You say it was only by the slightest chance.' Mary looked at him quizzically.

'I met the person who brought you a message from my father, the night he died,' he explained as gently as possible.

In the fading light of the afternoon, Mary's face seemed pale and waxen.

'I thought it would be the happiest day of my life,' she said softly. 'Michael had heard that your mother had died at Lembury. He had asked me to marry him.' She paused, and studied Richard's face. 'Yes, we were to be husband and wife.'

So soon after my mother's death, he thought, and felt a sharp, pungent bitterness creep through him.

Mary did not sense this. She touched his arm. 'You were going to be my family.' Richard said nothing, so she continued: 'That night, I was sleeping upstairs when I heard a racket at the door. I thought at first it was soldiers or robbers, but it was a young lad with a note from Michael.'

Richard nodded. 'That's the boy. Go on.'

Mary chewed her lip nervously. 'I still have that note.' She got up quickly and crossed to the dresser by the fireplace. From the drawer she pulled out a small leather pouch. Inside, folded tight, was a thin, yellowed slip of paper. 'Here, read it.' She handed it to Richard and stood watching him intently.

Richard's fingers were shaking. Quickly he flicked the paper open. It read:

My dear beloved,
The King's cause is, I fear, beyond repair. We are beaten by a cruel fate, our men are bereft of hope, valour, and even the commonest resources, and we must each look to our own lives. I will be with you shortly, God willing, if you would still be mine. Meet us at Tresillian, at dawn. Our men still

297

hold the bridge and we will be safe there. Bring clothes for a journey and what goods you need, but make haste! There is much to talk of. I fear all is not good, and there are some who question my intentions, although from what has befallen, does not every man doubt his own shadow? Who can judge me? Not you, beloved, you know too well. My son perhaps. *Divitias filius fulvo sibi congerat auro.* Let son count my worth even if another will not. Give him this for me, if I should not come, and tell him to mark it well and that I love him, and would have loved him more, if not for what has been. Tell him to count this letter as the last word. I will be with you soon, and for ever, your beloved servant, Michael.

Richard had a sudden vision of his father feverishly jotting this note on the library table, Hal Jenkins waiting patiently on the threshold, the candles flickering, the horses from the stable restless, dawn a few blood-red hours away. He gazed at the paper for a long time. When he met Mary's eyes, she saw a new tenderness there.

'You really loved him, didn't you?' he said gently.

'I never married again,' she replied. 'And I had suitors, many suitors after the war, but I would never forget your father, Richard. You know, I waited on that bridge until noon, with the soldiers marching by, and the dust hanging over the street. Then a little after midday, a lone officer rode in. Sir Ralph someone-or-other, he was a close friend of your father's and knew me.'

But Richard was looking at Rebecca. It is strange, disturbingly strange, how our lives echo those who have gone before us, he thought. And what of Susannah? Had she also waited for him there, in the same place, like Mary Talbot all those years before? Or was Rebecca right?

'He was caked in blood, and was wounded in the arm and leg,' Mary continued. 'The chirurgeons thought he was going to die, but he surprised them all.'

Richard wrenched his attention back to her account. 'Did he say what happened?'

'Sir Ralph said they'd been surprised coming through the copse above Chynoon.' She paused. 'He said your father died fighting bravely. But in the end they were overwhelmed by numbers.'

Richard frowned. Was that what Fielding had recounted at the Privy Council? He thought not, but he felt so tired he could not be sure. He jabbed at the carrots in the bottom of his bowl.

'And then?'

Mary's voice and expression were leaden. 'I came back here. What else could I do? I had no family, no friends to rely on. The King's cause was, as Michael said, hopeless, and I was already three months with child.'

Richard stared at her.

'You were pregnant?'

'Yes.' She met his gaze steadily. 'Michael was the father.' She broke off. 'That was why we wanted to marry.'

Richard stared at her incredulously.

'The baby was born six months later,' Mary went on. 'I christened him Michael.'

'What happened to him?' he asked cautiously. His heart was fluttering. He felt strangely dizzy.

'Since the war, things have not been easy for me. Without a husband to run the farm, I have had to hire men as best I can. I couldn't afford to keep Michael here.' She stared stubbornly at the table. 'Last year I sent him to work at Chynoon as a stableboy. That's ironic, isn't it?'

Richard was stunned. 'You mean he's alive?'

'Yes, Richard, you have a brother.'

Richard sat back in his chair. He had never anticipated this. Rebecca put her hand on his. And realisation dawned on him.

'Your son, what does he look like?'

'Slim, and with your father's hair, about so tall.' She indicated with her hand. Despite her sorrow, her face glimmered with pride. 'He's a handsome boy.'

There was only one boy with red hair at Chynoon, Richard thought. The boy he had seen fighting behind the yard, the one whom the others called 'whoreson' and 'bastard'.

'Why do you ask?' Mary looked at him proudly.

'No reason,' he replied. 'I was curious, that's all.' There is a terrible sadness in things, he thought, a terrible sadness and weariness in our lives when we have seen our hopes end in failure. He suddenly recalled his father reading a passage to him from Virgil when he was far too young to understand. What was the line?

'*Sunt lacrimae rerum et mentem mortalia tangunt,*' he muttered.

'What was that?' asked Mary.

'There are tears in our affairs and their mortality touches the heart,' said Rebecca, somewhat self-consciously. It seemed absurd to her that she, a peasant girl, should be translating Latin. Absurd and tragic. 'Virgil. His father's favourite.' Listening to Mary's tale she had felt the same sadness, the same defeat in the face of life.

300

Rebecca got up from the table and went to the door. 'I think I'll go outside for a while,' she said.

Richard watched her go.

'She loves you, you know,' said Mary.

'We are not meant for each other,' he replied quietly. 'It's strange how things never turn out as we expect.' What had Mary and his father expected together? He saw the note lying on the table and the disillusionment in her face. Emotions came prickling to the surface of his eyes and throat and yet his words, when he found them, were few and commonplace: 'I'm sorry, Mary. I'm sorry.'

He rose unsteadily from the table and they held each other for a long time, each thinking of a man who had died nine years ago, and each mourning the regrets of their own lives.

He found Rebecca sitting on the ruins of an old cart, in the shadow of the elms.

'How do you feel?' she asked, without looking up.

'Exhausted,' he replied. It was true. His only sleep was the few hours he had snatched on the river barge. He felt emotionally, physically drained. His whole body ached, from the inside out.

'You must rest, Richard.'

He sank on to the cart beside her. 'And so must you, Beckie.'

She nodded. She was tired, but for the first time in days she felt at peace – with herself, with Richard. Being with him now was as it should have been, she thought. If things had been different. She felt a tang of her old bitterness, sharpening her thoughts, but this time ignored it. She would not be hurt any more.

'Are you glad you came here, Richard?'

He sighed. 'Glad? Yes, I suppose I am. Though what I have heard has depressed me beyond belief.'

They lapsed into silence for a while.

'But this doesn't change anything, does it?' asked Rebecca eventually. 'When you leave here, what will you do?' In the past she would have asked this question accusingly. But after listening to Mary's tale, she felt strangely calm and indifferent, as if seeing the other woman's pain had cured her of her own.

'I . . . don't know,' he said. 'I shall leave for France as soon as I can. But before that, I will talk to Susannah.'

He began to pick at the soft wood of the cart.

'She didn't come to the bridge, Richard.'

'So you say.' He met the look in her eyes. 'I love her, Beckie.'

'I know.' She smiled gently. 'She is very lucky, Richard.'

Her words touched him. 'You will always be my friend, Beckie. You know that.'

'Yes.' At one time, his words would have wounded her. Friendship was less than she had wanted. But now, suddenly, it seemed the most important thing of all.

Slowly, wearily, Rebecca stood up and stretched herself. In the late-afternoon light she seemed somehow more delicate, almost transparent, thought Richard. But her face when she turned to him was firm and determined.

'I'm going home now,' she announced simply.

'No. Don't. Stay here.'

Previously she would have been only too ready to agree. She looked at him wisely. 'There's no point, Richard. I'm tired and need to get home. You obviously need to . . .' She stopped. 'You know where to find me.'

He lowered his eyes, to her rough, red hands.

'Thank you,' he said. 'I just wanted to say thank you. I don't know what I'd have done if you hadn't been here today.'

She smiled sceptically. 'Though you'd rather I had been Susannah, wouldn't you?' But there was no longer anger in her voice.

'Don't be ridiculous!' Richard felt emotions he did not want to recognise tumbling up inside him. She had no right to make these demands of him, he thought, not now. She was a friend. A friend.

But Rebecca had already turned and was walking to the house.

'Where are you going?'

She looked over her shoulder: 'To say goodbye to Mary.'

He stayed sitting on the cart until Rebecca came out again. He felt disappointed with himself, as if he had given her less than she deserved, but he knew he could do or say no more without destroying their new-found peace. She almost turned towards him, but he saw her check herself and start down the track, her slim body held proud and erect.

Then, slowly, painfully, he got to his feet and made his way back inside.

Mary was waiting for him.

'Don't worry,' she said. 'You don't have to say a thing.'

He looked at her dumbly. 'I feel exhausted.'

She smiled briefly, in sympathy. 'I'm not surprised.' She showed him upstairs, where a large, battered mattress nestled under the eaves.

He collapsed gratefully on to the mattress as if he had been struck from behind. All he wanted was oblivion for a few hours.

When he woke, it was to the same crushing sense of sorrow, but he forced himself to his feet and the smell of stewed chicken enticed him from the kitchen.

'I thought you'd be hungry.' Mary smiled proudly and wiped the hair from her eyes.

'Yes. Thank you.' He sat down at the table. Outside the night seemed black and impenetrable. 'I'll have to leave soon. It's not safe here.'

Mary looked concerned. 'Will you be all right?'

He managed a ragged grin. 'Who knows? I'm headed for France. There's nothing for me here.'

'You could ask for a pardon,' she suggested.

'What? Is that what my father would have done, do you think?' His voice recovered some of its old fire.

'Your father would have wanted you to be safe and well.'

'Perhaps that just isn't possible.' He looked at her. 'You're saying this because of Rebecca, aren't you?'

Mary ignored his suggestion and placed a platter of chicken and gravy and vegetables in front of him. 'I'd like you to stay, Richard. You'd always be welcome here.'

Richard looked at her, though not unkindly, and she fell quiet.

As he ate, she began to hum to herself. It was an old tune, a sad, mournful ballad he remembered from his childhood, and Mary's voice seemed to inflect each syllable with a fresh poignancy:

> O where has my true love gone?
> He's flown away at the break of day
> And left me here alone.
>
> The horse has loosed its stable rope
> The boat has slipped its anchor rope,
> And left me here without hope,
> For where has my true love gone?

The bird cries in the morning light,
The gull cries in the clear day light,
The crow cries in the evening light,
For where has my true love gone?

I went to the beach and called his name,
I sang to the sea and called his name,
I cried to the wind and called his name,
But my true love he has gone.

She stopped singing and looked at him. 'I couldn't believe I would never see him again. For months after, whenever I heard a tap at the door, or a scratch at the window, I thought it would be him.'

Richard took a drink of water.

'I haven't heard that song since I was a boy,' he said. 'My nurse used to sing it to me.'

Mary smiled weakly. 'Your nurse was Mary Chalmers, wasn't she? Her mother was my nurse too, many years before. I remember she would sing to me just before I went to sleep. There were other songs, in the old tongue, which I forget now.'

Richard smiled too. By the old tongue, Mary meant the old Cornish language, the speech of the Celts. The farmhands had still spoken it in his grandfather's time, but now east of Truro it was a forgotten thing, like a faded dream. Everything we hold dear passes away, he thought. The only person he had known who spoke it was Jacob Sawle.

Suddenly he realised what that meant.

Jacob Sawle had come from the West of Cornwall and had served Michael Tremaine for thirty years, but he still only spoke English with difficulty. He remembered the man frowning and muttering to himself in the thick, lilting language. What was it he had said to

Sedge on the hillside, as he lay dying? *Our prince is in Avalon*. The words had struck Richard as incongruous. And now he realised why.

Jacob Sawle had not been speaking English.

Close to death, he would have used the language of his birth, of his blood. Richard racked his mind. He looked up. The weariness of a few moments ago had vanished. 'Mary, do you know any of the old tongue?'

She looked startled and laughed. 'Hah! Maggie used to teach me the names of things until my father forbade her.'

'If I said to you *our prince*,' he began, 'could that mean anything in Cornish, do you think?'

It took a second for Mary to understand what he meant, then she shook her head. 'I don't know,' she said, 'it's so long ago, and Maggie never taught me properly.'

'How about *avalon*?' he continued. 'Did she ever use the word *avalon*?' Or anything which sounded like it?'

Mary thought for a moment. 'I remember her saying that an apple was called *aval*.' Then her face lit up: 'Yes, and our orchard was called the *avallon*.'

Orchard. Richard suddenly remembered the apple trees at Chynoon. Our prince is in orchard, he thought sceptically. What did that mean?

'And, you know,' she continued, 'I can't be certain, but I've got a feeling she called my mother's wedding ring *owr*.'

'*Owr*?'

'*Owr* – gold,' she went on eagerly. '*Owr pryns*, the golden prince.'

Richard frowned. 'The golden prince? That doesn't make sense.'

'Or the prince's gold,' she smiled. 'Does that help?'

Richard repeated the words to himself silently.

Owr pryns yn avallon.

'*Yn* – that means in, doesn't it?'

She nodded.

Owr pryns yn avallon. The prince's gold is in the orchard.

He felt a sudden rush inside his chest. Of course.

The first time he had returned to the orchard, he had remembered dropping stones in the old well with his sister. And now he realised the old well was no longer there. It must have been filled in or covered. But that was what Jacob meant. The Prince's gold is in the orchard well. He recalled the deep, dank silence, and then the plunk-plunk of their pebbles hitting the bottom.

'What is it?' asked Mary, somewhat bewildered.

Richard laughed gently. 'Something which has been playing on my mind, that's all.' He squeezed her shoulders.

She looked at him thoughtfully. 'This business of the King's, Richard, it's not dangerous, is it?'

He was touched by the look on her face. It was strange, but perhaps she had been right: it did feel as if he had known her for a long time, as if there had been something of her in his father, or vice versa, like an imprint which did not fade.

He got up from the chair and saw his father's note still lying on the table.

Divitias filius fulvo sibi congerat auro. Those words again. Let my son gather riches in yellow gold. It was uncanny, almost as if his father had known he would die and that Richard would come after him. And what else had he said? 'I fear all is not good, and there are some who question my intentions, although from what has befallen, does not every man doubt his own shadow?' and 'if I should not come'. Was his father worried about being attacked by enemy troops? Or had he anticipated a more personal threat? Again, there was something in Sir Ralph's account which did not make sense.

'Take it,' she said. 'He wanted you to have it.'

She took the note from between his fingers, replaced it in its pouch and handed it back to him. He tucked it inside his britches.

'I'd better go,' he said. 'While it's still dark.'

Outside the night was thick and chill. There was a breeze in the air, and the elms rippled. Richard sniffed the scent of damp leaves and fresh mud from the doorway.

'You know,' he said, 'I don't think this storm has played itself out yet.'

Mary looked at him.

'You're taller than your father,' she said. She reached up, and pulled his cloak about him.

'Take care of yourself, Richard. May the Lord bless you.'

He bent and kissed her on the forehead. 'Thank you,' he said.

'For what?'

'For loving my father all these years.'

He saw her eyes start to mist, and turned to leave. As he trudged down the track the image of Mary Talbot stayed with him, a bruised and tender woman, dressed in grey, and with nothing left to live for but an eight-year-old son who was the butt of other children's jokes.

Chapter Eleven

'GOOD LORD, TREMAINE! WHAT ARE you doing here?' Sir Charles Roselyn's cheeks were blotched and pinched. He looked past Richard at the pelting wind and blustering trees outlined against the night sky.

'It's a long story, sir.' Richard slumped against the door jamb. He had walked from Talbot's Farm without stopping, and his feet were swollen and blistered.

'Well, don't just stand there—' Sir Charles ushered him inside and peered out into the blackness again. 'You weren't followed, were you?'

Richard went through to the library and poured himself a glass of port. He downed the glass in one, then gasped gratefully and wiped his lips. 'Excuse me, please. There were times when I didn't think I'd get back here again.'

'The country's rife with rumours! One of the ploughmen said Oliver Moreton had caught some delinquents on the river. I thought you were dead for sure.' Sir Charles stared at him anxiously. 'I hear you killed one of them.'

Richard nodded silently.

'Fellow was the brother of one of my maids,' Sir Charles elaborated. 'But can't say I blame you.' He paused. 'So, did you meet your man?'

Briefly, Richard recounted the events – Wedlock's letter, the attack, his escape. When he mentioned his arrival in Truro, Sir Charles looked surprised. 'Did you see the troubles, then?'

'You mean the preacher?'

Sir Charles cleared his throat theatrically. 'Preacher be damned! I heard they had to send troops up from Pendennis. Fellow's being held at the castle now.'

Richard sighed wearily. 'The man seemed to have a point.' He reached for the bottle.

'Once you let people interpret religion for themselves, there's no end to the evil they will do,' pronounced Sir Charles.

'He was preaching against Cromwell, not the Church. Surely you'd agree with that?'

Sir Charles curled his lip dismissively. 'These fellows preach against any sort of authority; how could I condone that? Why, they know no shame, they have no respect for tradition or morality. I've heard they delight in fornication, and copulate openly, and indulge in the most shameless passions and lusts, all in the name of freedom! Freedom be damned!'

Richard looked at him sceptically.

'Sir, with respect, I think that accusation has been made of every religious group since the time of the Crucifixion.' He placed his glass on the table. 'Anyway, be that as it may, I think I know where the gold is.'

'You do? You said you lost your father's note.' Sir Charles seemed more anxious than pleased.

That night Sir Charles held a conference with the other royalists. They too greeted the news with mixed emotions.

'So how deep is this well?' asked Sir John Grenville. 'Can we pull it out? Will we need ladders?'

'Twenty feet at most,' replied Richard.

'But can you be sure it's there?' asked Sir Charles for the third or fourth time. His face had assumed a dull, leaden hue. 'What proof do you have?'

Yet again, Richard patiently took them through his reasoning: Jacob Sawle's dying words, his own memory of the well, Henry Couch's statement that the men rode out with no baggage. 'The apples of the Hesperides,' he concluded, 'were of solid gold. Maybe the inscription on the sundial gave my father the idea for the hiding-place.' His voice flared at the end: 'Are you convinced?'

'Yes, yes,' said Sir John Arundell brusquely. 'I think we're all agreed, Tremaine. The question is, how do we break this damn well open with that fellow Moreton in residence? It's no easy task.'

'Or do we leave it there?' suggested Sir Charles. 'I mean, are we sure the money will be of use?' he added defensively.

Richard gritted his teeth. 'Sir, I have been charged by His Majesty with finding this gold and restoring it to his cause.' He flexed his hands expressively. 'My father gave his life for it, damn it.'

Sir Charles fixed him with a surprisingly penetrating look. 'I understand, Tremaine, but just because your father died for it does not mean we should do the same.' Richard was about to reply, but Sir Charles hushed him with an outstretched palm. 'No, please, I meant no offence, Richard. You want to retrieve this gold, which is right and commendable, but isn't it more to do with your father's memory than your devotion to the Crown?'

Richard felt a powerful desire to demand an apology from Sir Charles there and then, but something in the old man's gaze restrained him. In a way he knew Sir Charles was right.

'But does that matter?' Sir John Grenville interceded. 'My father also gave his life. If Tremaine fights to avenge his father, what is wrong in that?' He nodded at Richard sympathetically.

'So, are we supposed to creep around this garden like common thieves?' asked Sir Charles.

'What do you think?' Sir John nodded at Richard Arundell.

'If the gold is there, it could take us all night to get it out. We're bound to be spotted,' said Arundell flatly.

'Well? There aren't that many staying at Chynoon. Couldn't we overpower them?' asked Richard.

'What? Fight?' Sir Charles looked aghast.

'No. There would be no need for that.' Richard made a quick calculation. 'There's ... William and Oliver Moreton, Dr Masters, a preacher. There's a guest, Hugh Lovelace, the grooms and so on. If we were let into the house while they're asleep, we could hold them until we've finished.'

'Break into the house? Is that feasible?'

'No, not break in, *let* in. I ... know someone who would open the door for us.' The idea had come to him in a flash.

'What about these soldiers you saw Oliver Moreton with, won't they be there?' asked Sir John.

Richard frowned. 'I don't know. Moreton does have a sort of barracks.'

'He's very friendly with Captain Standish at Fowey,' mentioned Sir Charles. 'Perhaps they were his.'

Sir John muttered something about Captain Standish.

'But if they're not there on the night,' Richard persisted, 'don't you agree we could surprise the manor?'

'This person who will unlock the doors for us,' asked Sir John Grenville, 'can you trust him?'

'Her,' corrected Richard. 'Yes, of course I can.'

Chapter Twelve

IT WAS STILL EARLY WHEN Susannah swung herself into the saddle and urged her mare out of the yard.

Oliver had already left on his business, she thought with a strange feeling of dread, and she threw her horse into a canter as soon as she was clear of the manor.

What had happened? She remembered the triumphant look on Oliver's face as he had strode into the Great Hall. 'He was skulking in the river like a drowned rat,' he had gloated. She felt her stomach turn. Was it her fault? Should he have come back for her? And yet, she knew she had the right to demand that of him. She had given herself to him. And now he might be dead. She felt a pit open in her stomach. Oliver said they had found a body ...

She gripped the reins tightly. And I must survive as best I can, she thought. On my own, as I always have.

Below her the beach opened up, bleak and white in the fresh morning air. And there at the far end stood a lone figure, tall and dark and graceful. Susannah halted. The maid Bridget had said she might find her here. This woman knew enough to ruin her. She guided her horse across the sand.

'Rebecca! Is that you?'

The woman was hugging herself and staring out to sea. Slowly she turned round.

And as Rebecca turned, her heart sank. She had come here for peace. The woman called Susannah Tremaine was the last person she wanted to see.

'Rebecca!'

313

Susannah's hair was streaming and flaming in the
wind. She looked down from her horse and smiled
confidently. Rebecca's smile was more like a grimace.

'Good morning, Miss Tremaine!'

'Lovely weather for a ride!' announced Susannah,
clutching her hat and laughing as lightly as she could.
'I wanted to see you,' she added in an undertone.

Rebecca tried to avoid her gaze.

'It's about Richard Ferrers,' explained Susannah, and
Rebecca felt her back stiffen.

'I hardly know him, miss. He just found me in the
fields and told me to give you that note. Was it important?' Her lips were trembling and she hoped Susannah
would think it was with cold. But Susannah didn't
notice. She too felt her emotions were naked and
exposed and shielded her eyes as if against the harsh
glare of the sea.

'He means no more to you than that?'

'No, miss. He was a merchant, wasn't he?' Rebecca
felt herself growing more apprehensive.

'Oh, well . . .' Susannah trailed off, as if lost for
words.

What's she trying to say? thought Rebecca. 'Miss?'

'I just wanted you to know that I also . . . hardly
knew him.' Susannah steadied her horse with her hand.
'I don't know why he tried to contact me. It was most
embarrassing. If my fiancé ever found out . . .' She
looked at Rebecca significantly, and Rebecca
understood.

'Oh no, I never speak to Master Moreton. He won't
hear anything from me, miss.' Rebecca spoke deferentially to Susannah as custom demanded, but the word
'miss' still stuck in her throat.

Susannah smiled gratefully. Her cheeks glowed.

'Thank you, Rebecca.'

'What happened to him, miss? Have you heard?' Rebecca asked casually, and saw Susannah's studied cheerfulness almost fall apart, then Susannah regained her composure and said:

'Master Moreton thinks he drowned in the river. They pulled a body out yesterday.'

'Richard's body?'

Susannah shook her head. 'I don't know. Oliver's gone to Truro to see.' She cupped her hand over her face, as if now the wind stung her eyes. 'But as I said, I really didn't know him.'

'No, nor I.' Rebecca cast her eyes to the sand.

'Lovely weather for a ride,' repeated Susannah suddenly, and pulled herself upright in her saddle. 'I really must be going. Goodbye, Rebecca.'

'Goodbye, Miss Tremaine.'

Susannah briskly flicked her reins and set off up the hill above the beach. Rebecca watched her go.

Why do you trust her, Richard? she thought. Why? Yet even Rebecca could not deny the look of genuine concern on Susannah's face when she had asked about Richard. She does care for you, she thought. Perhaps I should know that more than anyone.

Susannah also had her thoughts. She had a worrying intuition that Rebecca Penmarris knew more about Richard than she claimed. But unlike Rebecca, her own feelings were too confused and painful for her to worry about anyone else's. Was that Richard's body? She wouldn't know until Oliver returned from Truro, yet she could hardly bear to find out.

As soon as she reached the crest, she kicked into a gallop and rode hard down the next hill until she felt her blood pounding in her temples and her breath hoarse and dry.

Damn him! Damn him!

315

She reached the edge of the wood and instinctively reined in her horse. The mare nosed its way underneath the trees and they descended slowly to the stream at the bottom of the vale, then splashed through the water and up the other side. A handful of crows took wing, clattering through the trees.

'Susannah!'

The voice startled her. She twisted to the right.

Richard had stepped from behind a tree. He was smiling.

Susannah felt her chest leap and threw herself out of the saddle and stumbled through the leaves towards him. Then he caught her in his arms and she burst into tears and laughter all at once.

The tears cut Richard to the quick. He had thought all night and all this morning about what they would say to each other. Now, she was sobbing in his arms, and all he could do was hold her as tenderly and tightly as he could. Then her tears passed and she didn't bother to dry her eyes.

'So, pleased to see me?' he asked gently.

'Oliver told me they'd found a body. I was so worried. I waited for you at Tresillian and you didn't come—' Her words tumbled out in a rush and then she stopped, catching the look in his eyes.

'Rebecca was there as well. She said she didn't see you.' He made his voice as brutal as possible, so the words bludgeoned her. But inside he could feel his heart racing painfully.

'That's not true!' Tears, of anger this time, started in her eyes. 'I was there! God knows, I waited and waited! I thought you'd been killed!'

'So why didn't she see you?'

'What's Rebecca to you, Richard?' She regarded him

316

suspiciously. 'Why was she there at all? I saw her this morning. She said she hardly knows you.'

Richard felt himself redden. He turned away.

'What are you keeping from me, Richard? You were supposed to plan our escape, and now I hear you were involved in a fight with Oliver.'

He glowered at her.

'I can't tell you, Susannah. You'll have to trust me!'

'Then trust me too, Richard! I was there, at Tresillian, from five in the morning. Of course Rebecca didn't see me. The bridge was too exposed. I waited in the woods on the south bank. I stayed until about eight, I think.'

'Then what happened?' He looked at her piercingly.

'Then?' Susannah gave her answer slowly, cautiously. 'Then I went home. I couldn't afford to make anyone suspicious. I thought you'd left me. But on the way I ran into Oliver, riding to Truro.'

'Why?'

'Why do you think, Richard? He was furious! He told me you'd killed Roger Keast. He was going to the Committee in Truro to report the murder. Oliver insisted I came with him; after all, I am his fiancée,' she added defensively. 'I could hardly refuse.'

'Has he ... tried anything with you?'

'No.' She glared at him, a mixture of anger and tenderness. 'He has promised to leave me alone.'

'I'm sorry.' He hugged her closer. 'I get so jealous when I think of him.'

'Well, don't.' She placed her fingers reassuringly on the collar of his jacket. 'You know I love you.'

She stared into his eyes with such longing.

'I love you too.'

She kissed him and he felt himself wanting her desperately. He began to run his fingers down her back.

'No, Richard. Don't!' She twisted against his grip.

317

She looked flushed, uncertain, and his throat went dry with desire.

'Come here,' he whispered.

'No,' she said, but with no conviction. He squeezed her against him, letting his torso explore every inch of her figure. 'Don't . . .' Her voice trailed off. She was breathing heavily. 'Not here . . .'

'Where then?'

'The hollow,' she murmured. She turned to walk up the slope, but he caught her wrist and spun her round.

'Or what?' he asked, enjoying himself now. 'What if I want to make love to you here? Now?'

She pouted her lips in defiance. 'Dare me.'

'All right.' He began to pull the dress off her shoulders, roughly, forcing the material down over her arms. She gasped. Then her breasts were free, and he bent over them like a starving man. She felt her body seethe within her.

'Come on.' She tore herself away and struggled up the slope. He let her reach the lip of the hollow, then he grabbed her and they went tumbling over, scattering leaves in all directions.

'I've been dreaming about you, every night,' he murmured breathlessly. 'I've missed you.' His hand was on her legs, forcing them apart, rucking up her skirt.

'Richard! Please!'

His other arm enfolded her and he kissed her again, passionately, hungrily. She felt his tongue penetrating her mouth and seeking her out, and her thighs melted against his.

'I'm so glad you're alive,' she whispered, and the very words inflamed her. She writhed against him, feeling his hard, muscular frame. His hand stroked the inside of her legs, gentle, teasing, insistent. Susannah opened her eyes and saw the naked branches of the trees against the soft white clouds, and felt him lift her skirts, gently, reverentially, and run his fingers up and down her thighs, easing back the fine layers of fabric until she was naked to his touch.

'I need you,' he whispered, and dipped his head.

Weakly, desperately, she opened herself to him, and felt his tongue, greedily, ravenously, seek her out. A flame was working its way up between her legs, caressing her, licking her very core into a hot swollen burst. She gasped and tasted moist leaf and lichen in the air and pressed deeper into the bed of leaves.

'Please,' she moaned. 'Stop.'

But he didn't obey her for the longest, most exquisite ten minutes of her life until eventually he raised himself and gazed down on her soft, frantic body.

'I love you,' he said.

How like a man, she thought. She reached up and quickly unbuckled his belt and tore his britches down. He closed his eyes and groaned as she took him in her hands, squeezing him, holding him, feeling the life throbbing inside him.

'Richard!' She ran her hand up over his stomach, as flat as a blade, feeling the soft fur of his hair, tawny and bronzed. He bent and kissed her breasts feverishly and then she was pulling his hips down between her legs. She saw the look of pleasure in his eyes. Her flesh quivered expectantly. She needed this. She needed him to prove to her she was his. He paused for a second, gazing into her soul, then thrust and she felt herself open to consume him.

'I love you,' he whispered again, and began to move very slowly backwards and forwards, deeply in, and out, with such a slow, firm pace that she felt him sliding against every fibre of her being. In. In. Her breaths came in time with his movements. She closed her eyes and felt the cool air caressing her. He lifted her up and plunged deeper into her, grunting with satisfaction, adjusting the angle of his penetration, rubbing himself against the very lip of her and then sinking deep inside, and she bucked against the incessant pleasure of his loins, writhed against him. Then suddenly his breath came in rasps and he was plunging like a wild, ferocious animal, thrusting into her, driving, with a desperate frenzy. Her body, her feelings became a blur of hot sweet flesh. Her breath came in long, weak gasps. She pushed herself against him, matching thrust to thrust, pushing, twisting, writhing, until everything – the ground, the sun, the sky, the trees – exploded.

Gradually the trees and sky returned to normal. The world, momentarily kaleidoscopic, reassembled itself and they lay spent and exhausted in each other's arms.

Very gently he ran a finger up her stomach and over the tips of her breasts. She shivered and opened her eyes.

'So,' she said afterwards, 'have you come to sweep me off my feet? Is a swift ship straining at its anchor for us?'

'I wish.' He nibbled her lips ravenously. 'I wish all this were finished.'

'All what?' She bit him back, gently, inquisitively.

But he ignored her. 'Do you really want to come away with me? Truly?'

She looked hurt. 'You still don't think I waited on the bridge, do you?'

'That doesn't matter.' He caressed the soft, pink flesh of her breasts, and then his fingers plucked at the slim silver pendant nestling between them. 'There's a question I have to ask.'

'What's that?'

Richard stared into her eyes.

'Who are you?'

She froze. Suddenly his touch seemed hard, menacing. 'How do you mean?'

'I was a childhood friend of Richard Tremaine's,' he said. 'I visited Chynoon several times. I met the real Susannah. I know you're not her. The only real thing about you is this.' He held up the pendant so it flashed in the light.

She hesitated.

'Well?' he whispered, and began to lick the outlines of her nipples. Instinctively, she cupped his head in her hands.

'Why didn't you say anything when we met?'

'What? And me a guest in your house? Besides, you meant nothing to me then.'

She swallowed. 'But you ask now?'

He paused and gazed at her fondly. 'I love you, Susannah. I don't mind what the truth is. But I must know.'

She touched the pendant thoughtfully.

'You're right. I'm not the real Susannah Tremaine. My father was a glovemaker in Leicestershire,' she explained. 'I was his youngest daughter, youngest of six, and when I came of age he found me a position as a lady's companion. My first job was to accompany Mistress Tremaine when she arrived at Lembury. Her daughter Susannah was there too. Everyone said how much we looked alike.'

Yes, he thought, I can imagine that. 'So what happened?'

'The siege of Lembury was terrible, Richard. Captain Falkirk refused to surrender and when the Roundheads stormed the castle they offered no quarter. In the last assault a mortar struck our chambers. I was in the next room. When I came round, I crawled back through

321

the debris. Both Mistress Tremaine and Susannah were dead.' A shadow passed across her face and she clung to him. 'I have never been so scared. Never. The Roundheads had broken through the gates and our soldiers were being butchered. The building was on fire and women were screaming. I knew that if they found me they would . . .' She closed her eyes. 'I saw them with one of the kitchen maids. They had her out in the courtyard. Six men took her, one after the other, right there in the dirt and the filth, then the seventh slit her throat.'

He touched her gently. She was shaking. 'So what did you do?'

'What could I do? I knew that if they thought I was a gentlewoman, I would be safe, so I took this' – she fingered the pendant – 'and put on one of Susannah's dresses.'

'And the real Susannah?'

'I said was me, Jennifer Turner.' She shuddered. 'My plan worked. Of the whole garrison I was the only woman who . . . went unscathed.' She closed her eyes as if in silent prayer. 'All the men were killed. At first I thought I would keep up the charade for just a few days until I got home. But the Roundheads held me for longer than I thought – almost six months – because my new father was an important royalist, it seemed. By the time we discovered he was dead, I realised there was no need to stop pretending. I looked like Susannah Tremaine and no one in the area had known her. Besides I was, in theory, the heiress to the estate.'

'If you came away with me, you'd have to leave all that behind,' he pointed out. He said this to see how much the manor meant to her, and what she would think if she knew his identity.

She laughed without a second's pause. 'So?' she

asked. 'Now you know the truth, do you still want me?'

He breathed in deeply, smelling the rich, moist aromas of earth and loam on her body.

'Of course I do.'

'Do you think I care about Chynoon, Richard? The only way I can inherit it is if I marry Oliver.' She saw the look on his face and smiled. 'Whether you want me as Susannah Tremaine or plain Jennifer Turner, I'm yours.'

He raised himself on one elbow so he could kiss her lips.

'I'm sorry,' he said, 'for making you relive that. It must have been terrible.'

She shivered. 'You could have no idea. That girl's screams, the looks on those men's faces . . . I will never forget them.'

'You're safe with me.' He smiled. 'I can still call you Susannah?'

She wrapped her arms around him.

'You can call me whatever you like,' and she whispered something in his ear which made him want her again.

'When you were at Lembury, did you notice a man called Melthorpe?' he asked. 'Jack Melthorpe?'

'I think so.' Then she grinned. 'Rutting Melthorpe, they used to call him. He was quite a ladies' man.'

His face darkened. 'Was he close to Mistress Tremaine?' he asked, then decided he didn't want to know. What good would it serve?

Susannah studied him intently. 'What does it matter to you, Richard?'

'Susannah,' he leaned forward. 'I have something to tell you as well. I'm not really a merchant's clerk.'

'I know that.' Her eyes gleamed. 'You're far too interesting.'

'I'm here on the King's business, does that surprise you?'

'The King?' She sounded breathless.

'Will you help me?'

Her eyes flickered with indecision for only a moment, then her face hardened: 'Yes. I will.'

'There is something at Chynoon which I need to recover for the Crown. Once I've done that we can leave.' He squeezed her hand. 'Are there soldiers staying at the manor?'

She shook her head. 'They left yesterday.'

'Tonight, I want you to let us in. No one will be hurt, I promise. We'll hold everyone for an hour or so, then we'll be gone.'

Susannah wrapped her arms around him, feeling the warmth of his body. 'You will take me with you?'

'Of course.' His hand brushed the side of her leg. 'I'll come just after midnight. I'll rap twice on the door.'

'Will you be on your own?'

'No. There'll be others. Don't worry.'

She looked at him earnestly. 'Richard, you won't leave me, will you? Even if you didn't need me to help you, you would come back for me?'

'You know I would.' He kissed her gently, warmly, then looked up at the trees shaking in the wind. 'I'd better be getting back.'

He doesn't care about me, she thought, and felt a sudden surge of insecurity. Then she pulled his face down to hers and kissed him again until she was sure.

Susannah left Richard in the woods and rode back towards the manor. Her body was warm and aching pleasurably from their lovemaking, and she sighed impatiently.

Storm Within

It won't be long, she thought, just until tonight.
And then it will be over.

Chapter Thirteen

THEY SET OUT AT TEN o'clock that evening: Richard, Sir Charles Roselyn and the others. They were ten in all. Sir John Arundell had brought four retainers, dour, heavy men who said little, and Sir John Grenville was accompanied by the biggest man Richard had ever seen. Thomas Payne stood at least seven feet tall and possessed a thick, trunk-like body with limbs like branches. The men rode in silence, each deep in his private thoughts, their horses bulging with spades, shovels, rope and empty saddlebags. They approached Chynoon along the byways, so they met no one and the cottages they passed were few and sunk in darkness. Overhead the wind plained and keened in the trees and the clouds spun across the sky like blown leaves.

Eventually they breasted the final hill and cut down the side of a steep, wooded valley. Beneath the trees the night became dark, the going wet, and they slowed to a walk. Richard began to feel unsettled and yet strangely exhilarated. Several times he felt the reassuring butt of the pistol in his breast pocket. His chest seemed tight and at the same time fiery, tense. His vision prickled and he felt as if he could see every twig, every leaf, every bead of dew. It would not be long now.

'Ho! Sirrah! Will you trot by?'

A loud cry echoed from the hedge next to them and a wild, misshapen man leapt into view. One of the riders swore and pulled his sword.

'No!' shouted Richard, and urged his horse forward.

'Careful! Careful! You may hurt someone!' cried Poor Tom and cowered down at his feet. 'I know you, don't I?' he said to Richard.

'Is this true?' asked Sir Charles disdainfully.

'He guided me to Caerleon.'

'Heaven help you,' said Richard Arundell.

Richard swung himself down and patted Tom on the shoulder. 'Are you well, Tom?'

'Are any of us?' asked Tom intensely. 'How could I be well when the devils ride abroad? Do you think they sleep?'

'Leave him, Tremaine,' ordered Sir Charles. 'Let's get this over and done with.'

'Wait a minute.' Richard bent closer to Tom, ignoring the odour of unwashed cloth and flesh. 'The devils ride abroad, do they? What is it, Tom? Have you seen anyone?'

Poor Tom pursed his lips together as if he was about to spit a pip, then suddenly babbled: 'A dozen or so of the metal-capped ones came riding through here tonight, singing hey nonny nonny and a clippety clop.' His voice was shrill, lilting.

The riders fell silent.

'Metal-capped ones . . .' muttered one of the men.

'Have you seen soldiers?' asked Richard. 'Soldiers?'

'Yes! Yes! The devil's own, galloping down to the big house.' Tom lifted the two fingers of his right hand and made a prancing, riding movement through the mud.

'What do you think?' asked John Arundell.

'Could be a trap,' said Grenville. 'What's your opinion, Tremaine?'

Richard was aware of their eyes fixed on him. 'I don't see how it could be,' he began. 'No one knows our plan apart from my contact.'

'But can you trust her, man?'

327

Richard felt his mouth go dry. Their lives were in his hands, he knew.

'Come with me through the trees,' he told them. 'I'll go to the manor alone. If it's a trap, you can escape.'

'But what about you?' asked Grenville. 'You won't stand a chance.'

Richard glanced down at Poor Tom. 'Should that concern you? As you said, maybe I'm doing this for my own reasons.'

There was an awkward silence. Then Sir Charles coughed grimly. 'Right,' he announced, 'we'd better move forward, eh?'

'You can't escape your destiny,' cried Tom. 'No matter how you dally with that whore Fortune!'

Richard swung back on to his horse.

And what are my reasons? he thought. Really, he knew, he was not doing this for his King, or even his father, but for Susannah. He had said he would come for her, and so he would. More than anything, he needed to prove that he trusted her.

'Follow me,' he said.

Behind them they could hear Tom calling to the wind, his voice a wild, chilling cry.

'Beware! Beware! The fiends ride out! And the dog of the devil will devour us all!'

No one said anything. Richard led the way now and took their horses across the hill to the left until they stood in the woods overlooking the orchard and herb garden and the rear of the house.

Chynoon seemed quiet and brooding, its walls sunk in darkness. The moon hung balefully over the out-houses, and cast a silver sheen over the ivy on the North Tower. Their horses' breath steamed in the air.

Richard dismounted and passed the reins to Sir Charles.

'Watch me,' he said. 'If everything's all right, I'll come back myself. If I don't come back, or if you see anyone, ride out.'

'Take care, sir,' muttered Sir John Arundell.

'Hah!' Richard laughed ironically and made his way down through the trees. It did not take him long to reach the stables and he paused for a moment, scanning the house, searching for clues, the slightest sound or chink of light, to tell him all was not well. Nothing. All he could hear was the thick rasp of his lungs and the beating of his heart. As he skirted the wall of the house, each step sent the gravel skittering in all directions. The brickwork felt warm and grainy.

He reached the door. Susannah would be on the other side of it, he knew. All he had to do was knock.

He took a deep breath and looked around once more. Everything was quiet. He tapped lightly, twice.

'Richard?'

He heard her voice, soft, sweet, like a promise.

'Is that you?'

He pushed slightly and suddenly the door sprang open.

Susannah was staring at him aghast. Behind her Oliver Moreton levelled a pistol at his chest. Other men were moving, dark in the shadow of the corridor. There was the clink of steel on steel and the fizz of matchcord.

'Don't move an inch, Tremaine,' Oliver commanded. 'If you want to live.'

Tremaine, he thought. He knows who I am.

But by then it was too late.

PART THREE

STORM WITHIN

Chapter One

THE NEXT FEW MINUTES PASSED in a blur. Men sprang from the doorway and seized him. Susannah was screaming and struggling in Oliver's grasp. Oliver pushed her aside and smashed the butt of his pistol into Richard's face. The sky spun.

'Where are the others?' he hissed and brought his face eye to eye with Richard.

'What others?' Richard ejected a mouthful of blood and spittle on to Oliver's cheek.

Oliver struck him again.

Richard felt his knees buckle. Men ran past them and took up positions across the yard against the wall of the herb garden. They were quick, quiet as shadows, stern-faced. Richard strained round, hoping Sir Charles and the others were already pulling back.

Oliver grabbed him by the throat, hauled him upright. 'What is it, Tremaine? Your friends won't rescue you now.'

Richard caught his eye. 'Go to Hell.'

Oliver's face was black with anger. He was silent for a moment and then he reached across to Susannah and kissed her full on the lips. She struggled and squirmed under his embrace. Richard felt his anger building inside and clenched his teeth, forcing himself not to react. By his side, two of Oliver's servants grinned lasciviously and trained their pistols on him. Eventually Oliver turned back, a dry smile playing on his face. Susannah was breathless, flushed, angry.

'Richard!' she called. Their eyes met, just for an instant. 'I love you! I didn't betray—'

'Take him to the cellar,' Oliver interrupted. 'Of course you did, Susannah. You've played Richard false from the start.'

'No! That's a lie, Richard!'

The two men were already forcing Richard down the corridor. He fought against their arms, wanting to believe her.

'Richard!'

Susannah threw one last, desperate look at him, then he was dragged into the Great Hall.

'So, Tremaine, you came back.' William Moreton's huge frame blocked the doorway in front of them. His heavy eyes glimmered with amusement. 'As a dog returns to his vomit.' He stood close as his son had done. 'I should have known from the first. You'd have your revenge on me, would you?'

'I don't know what you're talking about,' Richard replied. He noticed that behind Moreton stood another man, shrouded in shadow. Moreton leaned forward. Richard braced himself for a blow, but Moreton raised his eyebrows sardonically.

'There'll be time for that later,' he said, his voice thick like treacle, then strode off towards the yard.

Richard now got a clear view of the other man for the first time.

The man was wearing a leather mask which completely obscured his face from the forehead to the jaw. It was the kind of mask often worn by travellers in the winter months and was a smooth sheet of leather, dull red and featureless apart from narrow eyeslits and a gash for a mouth. The mask paused and studied Richard for an instant, and between the slits, Richard imagined his eyes flickering. Then the man walked quickly away after William Moreton.

Richard strained after him, but his two guards jerked him round and marched him through the Hall then down the steps to the cellar. The noise of its door swinging on its hinges was sickeningly familiar. A reek of decay and damp hit him and then he was shoved down and manacled as before, the tight iron pinching his wrists.

'So we meet again?'

The voice startled him, and he realised with a jolt there was another body slumped on the flagstones next to him.

'Wedlock! Is that you?'

'Nay, but a poor shadow of myself.' There was the clank of chains.

'I thought you were dead.'

Wedlock laughed at that, but soon the laugh turned painful and gritty and he cleared his throat of sputum. 'I fear I may soon be altogether more grave, if you will pardon the expression.' He sat up. 'My wound looked worse than it was. Moreton pulled the bullet out himself, said it would help me understand my sins. He enjoyed delving in my flesh,' he added darkly.

'But why? What did they want with you?'

'There is much you don't know.' Wedlock breathed heavily. 'Unfortunately, they will not believe you until you have suffered much.'

Richard shut his eyes. Susannah, what did you say to them? Did they hurt you?

There was a grating noise and the door swung open. Oliver Moreton ducked his head and entered. With him was the man in the mask Richard had seen a few moments before.

'Enjoying our hospitality, Tremaine?'

335

Richard did not answer.

'What's that? Cat's got your tongue?' Oliver prodded him with the toe of his boot. Richard pushed his foot away.

'What do you want, Moreton? Who's your friend?' He jerked his eyes towards the other man.

'What do I want? I want to know what you were hoping to find in our house.'

Oliver's boot caught him just under the chin. His head was smashed back against the wall. His jaw shouted with pain, his head was fizzing, bursting with pain.

Oliver stood over him, his foot pressed on to his right forearm. The other foot toyed with his face.

'What were you looking for?'

Richard went to reply, but realised dully that his mouth wouldn't obey his commands. It was thick and dead. He tried to spit and felt his mouth blocked.

Oliver swung his boot backwards.

'Leave him alone!' cried Wedlock. 'He knows nothing.'

'So why did you come here?' Oliver regarded him as he would a snail in his path.

'I wanted to free Wedlock,' mumbled Richard.

'You were looking for something.'

'Who told you that? Susannah?' Richard regained some of his fire.

Oliver smiled. 'Did you really think she would help *you*, her wretched failure of a brother? Look at you, Tremaine! You have no hope, no faith, no purpose in life, do you? You have nothing. You are an empty bag blown about by the wind. I could crush you now.' He kicked Richard savagely in the stomach.

Richard had tensed his stomach muscles, but the boot tore into him, sending foul ruptures of pain through his abdomen. He gasped and vomited on to the floor beside him.

'See? Nothing.' Oliver picked him up by the hair and wiped his face in the contents of his stomach.

'Make it easy on yourself, boy.' The stranger's voice was indistinct and muffled by his mask. And yet, thought Richard, there was something familiar about it. He blinked. The man coughed. 'Tell us why you're here, Tremaine. It will be easier for you.'

Oliver Moreton wiped his hands on his britches. 'Trust us.' He grinned cruelly.

Richard willed his head to clear. 'I know you, don't I?' He frowned up at the man in the mask. 'I know you!'

The man hesitated and turned to Oliver.

Oliver gazed down at Richard. His eyes were dancing. Then abruptly he turned on his heel and marched towards the door with his companion. 'We'll be back later, Tremaine. In the meantime, think of me interrogating Susannah.' As he pulled the door to, he chuckled softly.

'Are you all right?' Wedlock crawled across, breathing painfully, and raised Richard's head.

'What is happening?' asked Richard. 'Who's the other man?'

'I don't know. He only arrived a day ago.'

Richard pressed his fingers against his mouth and flinched. 'Damn him!' He spat again, and pulled himself up against the wall. Its cold and damp seeped into his spine.

Wedlock nudged him on the shoulder. 'Sleep,' he said. 'There is hope yet.'

'Hope?' asked Richard incredulously.

'We shall see,' replied Wedlock, and coughed unpleasantly. 'Damn this moisture!'

*

Somehow Richard fell into a hard and fitful sleep. When he opened his eyes he found he was outside the manor, walking through the cold, damp grass. It was night and a dark wind was blowing and made him ache uncomfortably, and he guessed dully that he was dreaming. He came to the orchard and there, white with apple blossom, his father stood.

'Father,' he said simply, 'I had not expected to see you here.'

'I don't go far these days,' replied Michael Tremaine, and smiled out of the corner of his mouth. He bent down, still smirking, and tugged at the grass. A great disc of earth lifted off in his hands and revealed a perfectly circular shaft descending into the ground.

'See,' he explained, 'these weeds get everywhere these days.'

Richard peered into the hole but could see nothing but blackness so thick it seemed to be a material thing.

Michael Tremaine stooped over and began to pull things out of the hole. They were white and smooth in the moonlight and then Richard realised they were naked bodies, curled up like grubs. Michael Tremaine stretched them out on the grass beside him and they shone palely. Richard looked and suddenly they had the faces of people he knew.

His mother was there, serene and beautiful, with Ursula Moreton, dressed in a pretty blue necklace, and beside her Sarah Masters, rich and fecund but quite, quite dead. He looked at her closely and her lips and breasts were crimson. Then up came his sister, his real sister, fresh as a pea, and his father popped her down on the grass, but she wasn't his sister, it was Susannah.

'Father, what are they doing here?' he asked, and his voice was nervous.

But his father was grunting over a great heavy object. His back strained as he lugged it into the moonlight. It was Rebecca. Why was she so heavy? Richard wondered. Her hair hung down in wet black tresses.

'Wake up, boy!' He was thrown against the wall and woke with a bang.

Richard opened his eyes and stared in horror at something with no face. Then he realised it was the leather mask.

'What in God's—'

'I want to talk! We haven't got much time,' the voice hissed, and jerked a thumb to where Wedlock had been. The floor was empty.

'Where have you taken him?'

The man bent down and set his candle firmly on a flagstone. By its pale flickering light, Richard could just make out the dozens of huge casks and barrels stacked against the wall of the cellar. 'Listen. Moreton will send for you soon. He will torture you to see what you know. I can save you some pain.'

Richard felt his stomach race. 'Why should you?'

'Needless pain never helped anyone, boy.' The voice was wooden and dead. 'Tell them you returned to England to foment an uprising for the King. They'll believe that.'

'I know you, don't I?'

The man bent over him, searching his face, then breathed out heavily.

'Yes,' he said. 'You do.'

He reached up and unlatched his mask.

It was Sir Ralph Fielding.

Richard stared at him.

Fielding squatted stiffly on his haunches. He looked older and grimmer than when Richard had last seen him

339

in Cologne. His smile was tired. 'I'm not a young man any more, Tremaine.' He wiped his hand over his beard.

Richard felt suddenly angry. 'You've betrayed the King, haven't you?'

'Betrayed?' Fielding turned the word over in his mouth as if it were a pebble. 'The King was betrayed at Marston Moor and on the field at Naseby,' he flashed. 'We were betrayed by blind brute pride and incompetence! Don't talk to me about betrayal. I gave everything to follow the King's flag – family, home – and for what? Some minor position in a Privy Council which can't even pay for its chambers!' His voice was thick with anger.

Richard glared. 'So, my mission's been doomed from the start.'

'I'm afraid so.'

Richard had a memory of Samuel Dowles' empty house and scattered books.

'But why? Why after all this time?' But even as he spoke, he guessed the truth. 'It's the gold, isn't it? You know where the chests are hidden.'

Fielding's face tightened almost imperceptibly.

'So the last thing you wanted was for me to find it. I suppose it's been your nest egg all these years,' Richard snarled. 'But what about Wedlock? Hasn't he told them where it is?'

'Him?' Fielding snorted. 'He's more a fool than you are. He knows nothing. God knows they tried to break him.' There was something in his voice which made Richard shudder.

'And they'll do the same to me, no doubt.'

'What do you know, boy?'

Richard realised with chilling clarity that if Fielding guessed he knew the gold was in the well, his life would be worthless.

'Nothing. Wedlock told me nothing before they attacked us.'

Fielding pressed his lips together. 'Then tell them everything, about the King, the people who were helping you, everything.' He got up to leave.

'Wait,' said Richard. 'There's something I need to know.'

Fielding halted.

'Was everything you said in the Privy Council lies? What about my father?'

Fielding took a deep breath.

'You don't understand, do you?' He gazed deep into Richard's eyes. His voice when it came was just a whisper. 'I killed your father.'

Richard stared at him.

Fielding tightened his lips into a grimace. 'I have never forgiven myself.'

'Why?'

'Hah! Why indeed?' Fielding crouched down again so he was only a foot away. 'Let me tell you what really happened that night.'

Blindly Richard fought back the tide of shock and anger and disbelief, and forced himself to be still. He felt as if the slightest movement would break the spell which hung in the air between them.

'I told the truth about our retreat from Bodmin,' Fielding began. 'I still don't know how your father kept us going. I think the others would have given up and deserted at once. But I lied about the timing of the cavalry attack. An advance party got us before we ever reached Chynoon, as we were coming through the woods below the moors. By the time we got here there were only four of us left: myself, your father, and two of the men, Jacob something-or-other and Tobias Jewell. Jacob was wounded.' Fielding wetted his lips. 'We buried the gold on the way and patched ourselves up here as best we could. We were too tired to go any further. You might think we'd have slept like dogs, but a little after two, I was woken by a noise, I forget what now, and thinking it might be the enemy, I went downstairs.

'It was your father. He was outside in the yard talking to someone. He'd left a candle burning in the library and when I looked in, I saw there were quills and ink and something written in code.'

'Code?'

'Yes, numbers, a cipher of some sort. I was trying to make it out when your father came in. I asked him who he was talking to, and he slammed his books shut and demanded to know what I was doing creeping round his house in the middle of the night.' The timbre of Sir Ralph's voice changed. 'We were tired and we argued and I went back to my room. But I couldn't sleep. I didn't dare. There was only one explanation for your father's behaviour. He was in contact with the enemy.'

'That's ridiculous!' Richard's anger bubbled to the surface.

'Is it?' Sir Ralph's eyebrows arched. 'In those last few days half the King's army were in negotiations with General Fairfax. I sat up all the rest of the night wondering what I should do.'

'What happened?'

'We set out the next morning for Tresillian. Poor Jacob could barely sit in his saddle, but he insisted on coming with us. Once we were over the first hill, I confronted your father.' Sir Ralph's face was grave. 'He pulled his sword on me, Richard, as soon as I spoke!' He banged his hand against his open palm. 'It was stupid! Stupid! He should have told me. I would have understood!' His voice was sharp, bitter.

'So what happened?'

'I had a loaded pistol in my breast pocket. When he swung at me, I shot him. There was nothing else I could do.'

'Did you kill him?'

'Of course I did! I hit him in the head at point-blank range,' he added bluntly, but in the way in which a man will recall something of great personal pain. 'Then Tobias attacked me. He wouldn't listen.' He looked down at his hands. 'I killed him too.'

'And Jacob?'

'Jacob was already dying. I left him in the field with your father.'

Richard closed his eyes and tried to imagine the scene. But what had Sedge told him? When he found Jacob Sawle, Michael Tremaine's body had not been there.

Sir Ralph breathed hoarsely. 'Well, there you have it.' He pressed his palms on his knees and levered himself upright. 'I can honestly say that scarcely a night has passed when I haven't thought of your father and regretted what I did.'

'I don't believe you,' said Richard stubbornly. 'Why didn't you mention this before? Why didn't you simply tell the King that my father was a . . .' His voice stuck in his throat.

Fielding looked thoughtful. 'Your father and I were friends, Richard. He had a good name. I did not want to dishonour it.'

Richard did not know what to say.

'You ask why I betrayed you,' continued Sir Ralph. 'It is ironic, don't you think, that you are trying to find the gold your father intended to betray to Parliament.'

'You are wrong,' said Richard simply. 'My father

wrote a letter that night to his mistress, that was all.
He probably did not want to admit as much to you.'

Fielding stared at him sadly.

'I only wish it were true, Richard. I would rather
think I killed your father needlessly than know that, at
the end, he betrayed the cause we fought for. But I
saw the look in his face – you didn't. That knowledge
has eaten away at me all those years until at last I
realised I believed in nothing either.'

Richard shifted awkwardly in his chains.

'Why are you telling me this?'

Fielding scratched his beard. 'Because you trouble
me, Tremaine. Now I have your blood on my hands as
well as your father's. I wanted neither, in all honesty.'

'I don't care for your honesty. What's to stop me
telling them everything you've told me?'

Sir Ralph laughed. 'Do you think they'll believe you?
Or will they care?' His voice flamed into life. 'You don't
understand who Moreton is, do you? The man is a law
unto himself. Have you heard of the Fifth Monarchy?'
He stared at Richard.

'No, what is it?'

'The Kingdom of the Blessed, that's what it is.'

Richard shook his head. Then something the preacher
in Truro had said came back to him. 'Is that what
Moreton is involved with? Insurrection? Against
Cromwell?' He felt confused and disorientated.

Fielding laughed humourlessly. 'You'd better ask *him*
that.' He nodded at the space vacated by Wedlock.
'He's Cromwell's man.'

Richard nodded. So, Wedlock worked for Cromwell.
He had suspected as much.

Fielding snorted. 'These followers of Cromwell are
as bad as the King's. All planning and paperwork, no
blood and spirit, none of them. When I heard what

Moreton is going to do, I threw in my lot. At least these men believe in something.'

Just then the door grated and lamplight washed into the room.

'Come on, Tremaine.' Two guards tugged him roughly to his feet.

Fielding caught his gaze one final time. 'Remember, Richard, tell them everything.'

Chapter Two

THE GREAT HALL WAS CROWDED with people. William Moreton was enthroned on his great seat before the blazing fire. By his side stood Oliver, then Dr Masters and Sarah, then the man Richard recognised as Hugh Courtney, the Quartermaster General, and several others, Gregory Clement and Captain Standish among them. Hugh Lovelace was lurking in the shadows talking to a cavalry officer. In addition there were almost a dozen troopers in full uniform, and maids and servants. Richard saw Bridget and Daisy among them. The great fire roared in its bed and sent huge red flames leaping and flaring across the walls.

Richard was led into the centre of the Hall and forced to his knees a mere two feet in front of William Moreton. Red flames danced on Moreton's head and crowned his skull. His dark, lambent eyes bore down on Richard. Richard tried to catch Sarah Masters' gaze but she turned awkwardly away. People were muttering to each other but as soon as William raised his hand they fell quiet.

'So,' he announced, 'we would have the truth now.' He ran his tongue over the edge of his lips and grinned slightly.

Richard said nothing and Moreton continued: 'This storm which spat you on to my coast, it was no accident, was it?'

This puzzled Richard. 'How do you mean?'

Moreton leaned forward and swiped the back of his hand across Richard's face. Richard felt a huge bang and for a second everything, even the searing flames, went black. The man's hand was like a shovel. His face was numbed, stinging.

'It was a storm, an accident. I was supposed to be put ashore farther down the coast,' he managed.

'Hmm.' Moreton's eyes were like a salamander's, thought Richard. They were filled with the hot flames of the hearth. 'And what were you to do?'

'The King wanted me to lay plans for an uprising.'

Moreton laughed. 'What, the royalists capable of an uprising? Pah!' The gathering chuckled obsequiously in agreement. Then he drew his head closer. 'Do you realise that to confess as much carries the death penalty?'

'Yes.'

Moreton raised his eyebrows. 'Captain Standish here will see that due sentence is carried out.'

Richard shrugged. 'As you wish.'

But Moreton's gaze did not waver. 'You disguise you feelings well, Tremaine. They are a credit to your shabby King. But that is not all, is it? I have heard you seek something else, something hidden here. What is it?'

Richard studied Moreton's face. What does he know? he thought. Suddenly in the shadows he caught sight of Sir Ralph Fielding. Why should I protect your gold? he thought bitterly. Moreton punched him.

Richard's head was thrown back. He felt his mouth well with blood and let it dribble down his chin. He felt sick. But somehow, stubbornly, he could not bring himself to talk, though it was more for hatred of the man in front of him than for any lingering sense of duty.

'I was trying to find documents belonging to my father,' he replied.

This time Moreton hit him harder.

When he next had thought, he was staring up at Moreton's great domed skull. He felt violently dizzy. His head screamed. The two guards levered him upright.

'You lie! It is the King's gold, isn't it? The love of gold.'

'I've told you, there is no gold!' said Fielding suddenly.

'Silence!' Moreton raised his hand angrily. 'Would you prefer to join your former colleague?'

Fielding blanched and said nothing.

'Look.' Moreton seized Richard's jaw and forced his head to the left. Susannah was standing about six feet away, clad in a white slip, a guard on each arm. As soon as he saw her, he felt his heart twist with misgiving. She went to say something, and stopped herself anxiously.

'Doctor, will you assist?'

Dr Masters stepped forward, smiling thinly. He slowly took off his jacket, handed it to his wife and rolled up his sleeves. His forearms were thick, like hams, and covered in coarse black hair. Then he conjured from his belt a long, glinting razor and walked towards Susannah.

Richard froze. Susannah caught sight of the blade. Her mouth dropped open and she tried to step back, but the guards held her firm. Her body was trembling uncontrollably.

'Great God, what are you doing?' Richard shouted.

Masters said nothing. Then he reached up and with a snap plucked out one of her hairs. Susannah gasped. He held the strand so it glinted like copper in the firelight. Then, very carefully, he carved it in half with his blade. Susannah's face was white now, the fine shapes of her cheekbones pressed up against her skin, white and skull-like. The shift clung to her body. She glanced at Richard, at Oliver.

'What is this, Moreton?' demanded Richard. He tried to get to his feet but the guards forced him down.

'Silence!'

Dr Masters reached up again and wound his fingers deep in Susannah's hair.

'No! Please!' Susannah gave a strangled scream and he twisted her head back, exposing her long white throat. Then, very carefully, he pressed the flat of the blade against her skin. Oliver Moreton clenched his teeth but did nothing.

'Now,' said Moreton. 'You did well, very well, to treat your sister as a stranger when you arrived. Why, my son even thought you were her lover.' He cast a cruel glance at Oliver. 'But now the truth is out.' He leaned closer so his dry breath burned on Richard's cheek. 'Tell us where the King's gold is, Tremaine, or the good Doctor will cut your sister's throat.'

'Thomas, no!' Sarah Masters suddenly ran across the Hall, grabbing her husband's arm.

'Get away!' Masters roared, and slapped her angrily across the face.

With a sob she was flung to the ground. 'Please!'

Susannah stared at her, hoping desperately, not daring to speak. Through the pressure of the blade, she could feel the Doctor's arm twitching with fury. 'Do not disobey me, woman! Submit – to – our – cause.'

Her hair straggling across her face, Sarah struggled to her feet. None of the onlookers had moved or said anything. She looked frantically from one to another, searching for support, but found none. William Moreton glared.

Richard felt his chest tremble. His mind was a jumble of thoughts and emotions. Susannah was straining backwards against Masters' grip as if she could some-how distance herself from the cool edge of the razor which dimpled her flesh. Her eyes implored him. Help me, he could feel her say. Help me.

Richard swallowed with difficulty. His whole body was shaking.

'Well, Tremaine?' William Moreton grinned into his face. Susannah let a faint cry whisper between her teeth. Richard cursed himself. Can I trust you? he thought. Did you betray me? Yet he knew that even if she had, even if she would always betray him, he would save her anyway. But how?

He cleared his throat and spoke slowly. 'Dr Masters can do what he wants,' he said. 'She is not my sister.'

There was an intense silence in the Hall. Richard could hear each breath that issued from Susannah's lips. She was panting. He wanted to hold her, take her. Masters stood poised, glancing impatiently at William for the sign. Above them all, unseen, the nymphs and cherubs gazed down.

'Well?' asked the Doctor. He flexed his arm.

William Moreton was staring into Richard's face. A tic beat angrily under his right eye.

'Is this true?'

'Of course it's true. I'd never seen her before I came here.' He looked at Oliver tauntingly. 'Ask her.'

William Moreton's breath blew over him like a sweet perfume of decay. Richard felt giddy. Then slowly the man withdrew.

'Well?' asked Masters, peevishly.

Moreton made an ugly guttural noise. 'Let her be,' he announced, and Richard felt the tension in the air snap. He sagged against his guards' hands. Thank God.

Masters hesitated for a moment then abruptly snap-ped his fingers open and Susannah tumbled to the floor.

Defiantly Sarah ran forward to comfort her. Masters turned away, his face like thunder.

'Tell me, Doctor,' said Richard loudly, looking at Sarah, 'the first loyalty of a wife should be to her husband, should it not?'

His question caught the room unawares. All eyes focused on Masters as he picked his jacket from the floor.

'Of course,' he replied slowly and began meticulously to unfurl his cuffs. Sarah was kneeling over Susannah.

'Then why do you allow her to play the whore with Colonel Moreton?'

Only the logs in the fire made a sound. Sarah Masters did not look up. The great muscles on the sides of the Doctor's neck bulged with suppressed anger. William Moreton's eyes scorched him.

'These are sacred mysteries,' replied Moreton. 'They are not for the ears of the profane.'

'But you are fucking his wife, aren't you?' replied Richard, his voice as blunt, as provocative as he could make it.

Moreton glanced at the Doctor. 'Why don't you answer this whelp, Thomas?'

Dr Masters strode up to Richard, still clutching his razor. His face was glistening with sweat.

'It would be so easy,' he whispered, 'to do with you now.' And then he smiled. 'Have you not understood the least of my words? Do you not have ears to hear?' He clenched his teeth together. 'Can God's elect sin? Can they commit adultery?' His words spattered across the room like the flicker of the fire. 'Of course not. Only the damned sin because they cling to their bodies and the foul sins of their flesh. Among us, everything is permissible, for we are freed of our flesh. We are all one flesh!' His eyes flashed. 'Do you think I care if my

351

wife gives sport to my master? Is that not what she is
for?' He strode wildly across the room and seized Sarah
by the hair and forced her round to face the assembly.
'Does she not sleep in the contriving of lust? Down
from the waist she is a centaur!'

Tears sprang in Sarah's eyes, she writhed against her
husband's grip.

'Shame on you!' roared William Moreton at Richard.
'Cease, good Doctor! Do you not see how he seeks to
drive a wedge between us? If only you knew, boy' –
he placed a finger underneath Richard's chin and lifted
his face – 'for us what sweet delights there are.' His
eyebrows quivered.

Masters let go of his wife. The back of his shirt was
stained with sweat. Sarah fell sobbing on the floor next
to Susannah.

'Enough!' William Moreton clapped his hands
together. 'We have had enough of an exhibition this
evening.' He glanced at Richard. 'Do you still desire to
slit her throat, Doctor?' His voice was slick, casual, and
Richard felt his blood chill.

'Indeed.'

'Good.' Moreton placed his fingers on his lips. 'You
have six hours, Tremaine, in which to contemplate your
sin. Tell me where the gold is and I shall let Miss
Tremaine live. If not . . .'

'I've already told you, she is not my sister.'

'In that case,' replied William, 'why should you
worry what we do with her?'

Susannah stared at Richard in horror. 'Richard!
Please!'

William smiled. 'Escort Master Tremaine back to his
chamber. We will talk with him later.'

Richard was hoisted to his feet.

'Richard!' Susannah was frantic. She ran towards him

but Oliver caught her in his arms and held her. Tears were streaming down her face.

'Susannah!' Richard twisted against his guards, but they dug their fingers into his arms and hauled him out of the door.

'Six hours!' roared William.

And then the door slammed behind him and he could see her no more.

Chapter Three

THE CELLAR WAS STILL EMPTY WHEN Richard was brought back. He wondered dimly where Wedlock was and what they were doing to him. A few hours later, or so he guessed, the door was flung open and Wedlock was dragged senseless to his manacles. His fine beard was torn and bloodied and his face was horribly crushed. Richard crawled over and felt his neck. He was still breathing.

Sir Ralph Fielding came to see him shortly after that. His face was heavy and swollen, as if bloated with his own self-disgust.

'What are you going to say to them?' he enquired anxiously.

'Nothing that need worry your precious gold,' replied Richard. He noticed that in his belt, Sir Ralph carried a knife. Would he dare kill me? he wondered. But perhaps the love of gold had burned in Sir Ralph for so long that he would do anything. It was his only love left. 'I don't know where it is, remember?'

Sir Ralph pondered his words carefully. 'This is bad, Richard. Bad.'

Richard looked him in the eye. 'You could save her, Fielding. Tell Moreton and he will spare her.'

'No.' Fielding turned away. 'He will kill her anyway.'

'And you would watch? What kind of person are you?' asked Richard angrily. His mouth was stinging from his injuries.

Sir Ralph got slowly to his feet and glanced at Wed-

354

lock's outstretched body. 'The kind that would stay alive,' he replied.

Wedlock had still not moved by the time the guards returned for Richard.

'Well,' whispered Oliver to him on the way up the stairs. 'Have you made up your mind?'

Richard grinned at him disdainfully. It seemed that everyone was hanging on his decision with bated breath.

'What does it matter to you?' he asked.

'If you don't tell, my father will have Susannah killed,' replied Oliver. 'Do you want that?'

Richard said nothing. If Oliver really cared for her, he wondered, would he even let his father threaten her? He reminded himself that William Moreton commanded blind obedience among his followers. If Dr Masters would willingly give him his wife, presumably Oliver would give up Susannah. Richard no longer felt afraid, just tired and sickened.

William Moreton was waiting in the Hall, with Fielding, Masters and Captain Standish. Beside them stood Susannah, clad in the same white shift. As soon as she saw him, she gave a little cry. Her eyes bored into his very soul. Through the windows the bleak rays of morning cast the room in a grey lifeless light.

Did you betray me? he wondered, searching her face. Susannah's lips quivered.

'Well, Tremaine? Have you wrestled with your conscience?' asked William sardonically.

No, thought Richard. He had known what he would say from the very first.

'If I show you where the gold is, do I have your word you will not harm her?' he asked, and saw Sir Ralph flinch.

'What if I do not choose to give it?' asked Moreton toyingly.

'Then you will have to break me if you can. And if I die first, you will never know.'

This amused Moreton. He smiled. 'A man after my own heart,' he muttered. 'Very well, you have my word. We will not kill her.' He glanced across at Susannah. Her face was washed with relief.

Richard took a deep breath. 'It's in the orchard. There's an old well.' He saw with satisfaction the look on Fielding's face.

Moreton smiled faintly. 'Show us.'

Richard led them out across the yard and into the orchard. Overhead the trees tossed in the air. Birds swirled. It was cold, and Susannah was shivering. Oliver lent her his coat. Gratefully she took it and slung it over her shoulders. Richard looked at her stonily. His father had died for this gold and he was betraying it for her. But ever since Fielding's confession, his mind had been made up. Hadn't enough people died already? He no longer cared for the King's duty or even his father's memory, just the warm, precious life before him.

It took him three attempts with a shovel before he heard the ground give a hollow thud. As he had guessed, the mouth of the old well had been sealed with a large slate slab, then covered with earth. When they levered the slate off, a whiff of stale, bitter air rushed out to meet them and then dissolved in the breeze.

Oliver dropped a stone over the edge and heard the splash.

'Is the water deep?' he asked.

'A few feet, that's all.' Richard stared thoughtfully into the black hole.

Moreton's servants lowered down a man on a rope. There were a few minutes of splashing around and muttering, then they heard him give a great cry. Despite himself, Richard felt his heart jump. He smiled grimly at Fielding.

William stooped over the shaft. 'What is it, Hicks, what have you found?'

'Three chests, Colonel! Heavy as sin!'

A suitable phrase, thought Richard.

Hicks strapped the chests together then clambered to the top. He was gasping and covered in mud. The others ignored him and began to strain on the ropes and gradually hauled the chests up. Moreton barked encouragement at them. His thick, heavy features had become animated. Oliver licked his lips excitedly. Richard watched them with a strange feeling of contempt. The chests were bulky and snagged several times on the rough walls of the well, and each time the men heaved and swore and the chests came free and banged loudly. 'Careful, damn you!' roared William, then suddenly: 'They're here! They're here now!' He bent down and with one almost effortless gesture, hoisted them over the lip of the well. His face was shining.

Three servants rushed forward and manhandled the chests across the grass away from the edge. They lay there, brown and leathery with water and mud.

My father died for these, thought Richard. And the others too. He looked at Fielding.

'Open them,' instructed William.

Jumping forward, Oliver pushed the others away and began to work at one of the locks with his knife. The men stood in a semicircle. No one said anything. All eyes were riveted on the chests. Even Susannah was staring, her danger forgotten, her face thrilled.

Then Oliver gave a grunt of satisfaction and the lid sprang back.

The chest was full of rocks.

For a moment, everyone stared at the chest, then Oliver kicked it on its side. The rocks tumbled on to the grass, glistening and slimy. He tore at the lids of the other two chests and they emptied up their contents. Rocks.

A terrible silence buzzed in the air. Richard smiled to himself, almost burst out laughing. So his father had had the last joke, after all. Sir Ralph Fielding had gone white. 'Great God,' he muttered.

Oliver stared around furiously. His eyes glittered. He picked up one of the rocks and hurled it between the trees. 'Lies!' he cried. 'Lies!' He leapt on Richard.

'No!' William commanded. 'Leave him.' He strode towards Richard. 'You see the folly of putting your faith in gold, Tremaine? Which moth and rust corrupts and the thief breaks in and steals.'

Richard managed a smile. 'I couldn't agree with you more. We've all been fools, have we not?'

'You could have done well, Tremaine, had you not tied yourself to the King.'

Richard shrugged. 'But I have.'

'Indeed.' Moreton grinned and stabbed at the rocks with his feet. 'So, you die for nothing.'

'Maybe,' replied Richard. 'What about Susannah?'

William looked at him. 'You kept your word, Tremaine. I'll keep mine. For now.' He gestured to his men. 'Take him back to the cellar.'

Richard looked at Susannah one last time. There, his eyes said to her, I've done what I can.

Susannah met his gaze. She did not cry. Her face was calm and determined. She would survive.

358

As Richard was brought into the cellar, Wedlock stirred and looked up.

Thank God, thought Richard. He's still alive.

'What did they do to you?' he asked as soon as they were alone.

Wedlock grimaced. 'Nothing you couldn't guess.' He closed his eyes as a wave of pain rolled within him. 'How about you?'

Richard told him.

Wedlock laughed painfully. 'Hah, didn't they realise, there is no gold!'

Not soon enough, thought Richard. There was a stamp of feet on the steps outside and the door yawed open. It was Oliver.

'I thought I'd find you skulking here,' he quipped and strutted across to them. 'Getting to feel like home, isn't it, Tremaine?'

'What do you want, Moreton?'

'My father has just decided. You and your companion will be hanged tomorrow morning. I thought I'd tell you personally.'

'My companion?' Richard felt a rush of apprehension.

'Mr Wedlock,' Oliver explained. 'Don't worry, Tremaine, I've got other plans for your *sister*.' He pulled his lips into a smirk.

Richard clenched his fists but said nothing.

Oliver waited, savouring the moment, then abruptly spun on his heel.

'Well, see you tomorrow,' he said. 'Shall we say about seven o'clock?'

Chapter Four

REBECCA WAS TRYING TO SLEEP when the sound of the horse outside the cottage startled her. Thinking it might be Richard, she got up and ran to the door before Elizabeth could wake.

Oliver Moreton stared down from his saddle. His eyes glittered like stones.

'Did you think I'd forgotten you so easily?' he asked, admiring the slim lines of her body through her smock.

'I don't know what you mean.' Clutching her arms round her, she backed towards the door, willing herself to be calm.

'You should call me sir.' He swung down from his horse and stepped lightly towards her. His hand was raised.

'Are you going to hit me, like you did Billy?'

'No. Not unless you want me to.' He grinned and ran the tip of his finger down her cheek. He was annoyed when she did not flinch.

'Don't,' she whispered with all the dignity she could muster. But inside she was screaming with fear. If he persisted she knew there was nothing she could do. Richard! Where are you?

In the trees beyond the cottage, the wind quickened.

'So,' said Wedlock at last. 'Perhaps this is a good time to make our peace with the Lord.' In the darkness of the cellar, his words sounded particularly poignant. 'Do you have a God, Tremaine?'

Richard did not know how to answer. 'My father

fought for the rights of the bishops,' he said, 'and the Church of England.'

'That's not what I mean,' replied Wedlock. 'Men will kill for their God but they will not always live for Him. Killing is always easier than living.'

Richard coughed. 'I did not expect—'

'What? You did not expect me to have a God?' Wedlock wiped a smile off his face. 'Who else is the living God for but those who live life to the full? Do you think God only wants to be worshipped by lily-skinned clerks? By this time tomorrow our flesh will be empty and you and I shall be face to face with our Maker.'

They fell silent for a time, sharing a strange, sombre companionship neither had felt before.

Richard was reminded of what Sir Ralph had said earlier. 'You're one of Cromwell's agents, aren't you?' he asked.

'If you had lived in England longer, you would know you should never ask that question,' answered Wedlock, drily. 'But, yes, for the sake of argument, I am.'

'Why are you here?'

Wedlock gestured towards the dark mass of barrels on the far wall. 'What do you think is in those? Flour? Brandy? He chuckled. 'There is enough powder here to start a small war.' Richard stared at him. 'You have lived in Moreton's household, you have talked to the man,' continued Wedlock. 'What would you say drives him?'

'I don't know,' Richard shrugged, then admitted: 'I have never met anyone like him.'

'Have you not?' queried Wedlock. 'Then you are fortunate indeed.' He sighed. 'Sometimes I wonder why we killed the King. Ever since then we've been plagued with madmen who think they can create heaven on

361

earth. Don't people ever learn? We are infested with plots and riots and schemes.'

'And what is Moreton plotting?'

But Wedlock snorted. 'I do not wish to spend my last hours talking about William Moreton and his brood. I have said enough. Soon we will sleep and when we wake we will die. In the intervening time I would rather make my peace.' He winced and turned away, and although so many unanswered questions echoed in his head, Richard did not wish to disturb him.

Richard leaned back wearily against the wall. Wedlock was right. What did it matter? He thought of Susannah coming to him in the cellar – it seemed like a lifetime ago – and the taste of her soft, sweet flesh. What was she doing now? Would she be safe, as Moreton had promised? He felt emotions quickening inside him, choking him and he wished above all else that he could see her once more, talk to her, tell her he loved her, as if somehow just saying that would set his heart at rest for the darkness which was to come. He closed his eyes. Susannah. She had a funny way of smiling, he recalled, which made her eyes dazzle. He pressed his back harder against the wall. This was ridiculous. By an effort of will he forced himself to think of other, earlier times in which Susannah's bittersweet face had not tormented him. He remembered his mother and father walking with him to church on Sunday mornings. He remembered sun-kissed days spent running in the meadows through a foam of buttercups. He remembered clambering down the cliffs to the sea and feeling the wet salt-breath on his skin. The memories fell gently over him like flower petals blown from a tree. They soothed him like a balm.

The click of the door opening and closing jolted him from his dreams. There was the soft rustle of skirts and a woman's scent wafted over him. Beside him Wedlock snored faintly. How long he had been asleep he didn't know.

'Susannah!' he murmured, and raised himself on his elbows.

It was Sarah Masters.

Richard shook himself. 'What are you—' he began, but she hushed him.

'Quick!' she hissed. 'I haven't got much time. If they find out . . .' She hoisted up her skirts, and Richard had a sudden glimpse of leg, then he realised with a shock that she had plucked a knife from her garter.

'This was all I could find,' she told him, and pressed it into his hand.

He stared at her dumbly. 'I don't understand.'

'Don't you, Richard? Don't you?' Sarah's voice broke into life. 'You were cruel to talk of me in the Hall. I hated you,' she added viciously.

'Then why—'

'Because I hate my husband more,' she snapped. 'He humiliated me.'

Richard waited for her to continue.

'Love, Richard. Thomas told me we were a brotherhood of love. Everything was to be shared between us, even our bodies, in the name of love.' She was trembling with emotion. 'Do you think I wanted to be called a slut and a whore like that? He doesn't love me, he never has. All this talk of our cause was just selfish lies.'

Richard clenched the knife tightly in his hands.

'So why have you come here?'

She stared at him. 'You love Susannah, don't you? You did your best to save her.' Her voice was almost envious. 'And you could have killed me at Tregony, Richard. I won't forget that.'

She got up quickly. 'I must go back before they

363

notice.' She turned at the door. 'The guard has the keys to your chains. He's on his own.'

'Sarah,' Richard whispered after her. 'Thank you.'

She smiled nervously. 'Don't thank me, Richard.'

'Sarah,' his throat contracted, 'there's one final thing: Susannah, is she all right?'

Sarah stood poised on the threshold. She parted her lips indecisively.

'Sarah!'

But she shut the door and was gone.

Why hadn't she answered him? He ground his teeth furiously, nervously. Where was Susannah? What had happened to her? 'Wedlock?' he whispered, but the only reply was the sound of gentle snoring.

Reluctantly Richard forced himself to wait for what he guessed was half an hour, although in the pitch blackness of the cellar, time had lost all meaning. Then he sent up as loud a cry as he could.

Wedlock grumbled and twisted round.

'What on earth, man?'

'Hulloah! Loah!' Richard ignored him and yelled again and again. His voice rang on the cold stones of the cellar and he roared until his throat was hoarse.

'Quiet! Peace!' Wedlock crawled over. 'Are you unhinged?'

Wedlock scrabbled on to him and tried to stop his mouth with his hand.

'No!' Richard bit savagely and the man cursed. 'Help! Hoah!'

At that moment the door flew open. The guard was mouthing, 'Shut your blasted—' then he saw Wedlock on top of Richard and ran towards them, a look of anxiety on his face.

'If either of you devils . . .' he muttered, and shoved Wedlock violently aside.

'Help.' Richard flopped back against the floor.

'There's nothing—' snapped Wedlock.

'Quiet! Are you all right?' The guard stooped over and prodded Richard.

Before the man could move, Richard threw an arm round him and stabbed the dagger hard into his chest. The knife snagged on a bone, and for one moment Richard thought it would stick, then he screwed the blade and it plunged deep into flesh. The man's eyes bulged in shock. He made a horrible choking noise in the back of his throat, his cheeks puffed as if he was about to vomit. Then a great gout of blood spurted through his lips. Richard felt violently sick. Blood was spattering over him. His head was hammering. He clenched the guard tighter as if he were a lover and pressed with all his might on the blade. The man squealed and clasped him with the last terrible strength of a dying man, then he sank limply to one side. A low bubbling noise trickled from his mouth. Richard shuddered. His right hand and arm were slick with blood; already it was drying and sticking on his fingers.

'Great God,' whispered Wedlock.

Richard pushed the guard on to his back and rifled through his pockets. His hands were feverish. The key must be here somewhere. The man was warm. He smelt of sweat and urine. Then Richard's fingers found the key in his pocket, fumbled and dropped it, picked it up again.

Forcing back the violent nausea he felt building inside him, he jabbed the key into his wristlock and twisted. The key stuck and he felt his pulse leap, then suddenly there was a satisfying click and the lock flipped open. He shook it to the floor with a clatter and undid the other.

All this time Wedlock had been staring at him in surprise. 'Quick, Tremaine.' He raised his wrists.

Richard hesitated. Wedlock was injured, sick. Would he make it?

'Hurry, man!'

Richard tossed him the key. 'You're on your own,' he said. 'I have things to do.' Already he was bounding up the stairs two at a time.

He half expected Oliver Moreton to be waiting for him at the top, but he felt too angry to care. If that was the way it was, so be it.

He reached the corridor and halted, sniffing the air like a dog. Nothing stirred. Behind him he could hear Wedlock undoing his chains. He crept down the passage and inched open the door to the Hall. The room was still redolent with the scents of burning wood and tobacco smoke and the tang of stale breath and bodies. He crossed quickly, stealthily, gained the far door and listened again. He peered into the rear corridor.

Abruptly there were voices to the right, from the library. He froze. He recognised William Moreton's rich, gruff tones. Someone else was talking quickly, reasonably. Others muttered. He caught the odd word: 'Catholics', 'element', 'token'. Meaningless. Already he was tiptoeing away and up the staircase. He paused on the halfway landing. From here he could view the rear yard. It was empty.

The the door from the kitchen opened below him and two serving-girls crossed to the Great Hall. Richard froze. They were only ten feet away, but neither looked up. He realised with a shock it was not as late as he had thought.

He carried on up the stairs. Wedlock momentarily intruded into his thoughts but he shook himself free. He would have to fend for himself. He reached the first

floor, past the room where Ursula had lain, then up a
further flight of stairs until he was outside Susannah's
room. An odd stifling smell hung in the air and he
shook his head as if to clear it. His heart was beating
in his throat. He pressed against the oak panelling.

He paused for a second. His breath seemed imposs-
ibly loud.

Cautiously, he squeezed the handle down. The door
clicked loose, and taking the weight on his hands, he
eased it ajar. It didn't creak and he breathed out
thankfully.

The sound of her voice startled him. It was soft and
tremulous, almost a sigh. She sighed again and again,
then there was another, heavier sound. He pushed the
door open.

Susannah's bed lay to his left. On it, she was naked
and on all fours, with her back to the door.

And she was being entered by Oliver Moreton.

Richard stared in disbelief. Oliver had her by the
waist and the muscles stood out across his shoulders.
Susannah had arched her neck, her hair was tumbling
across her back. Oliver's buttocks tensed and thrust
and Susannah's whole frame shuddered under the
impact. Her breaths came in short, hot sighs.

Richard strangled the anger welling up in his throat.
A desire seized him to attack them there, to plunge the
dagger into Oliver's neck, to hack, stab, maim. He was
trembling violently. He couldn't breathe.

Oblivious to the man standing behind him, Oliver
thrust more quickly, more enthusiastically. Susannah
groaned, bent her head farther back.

Richard stumbled out of the room like a blind man.
Somehow he pulled the door shut and fetched up
against the far wall.

His mind was black with ... He couldn't think. He

clenched his fists as if the knuckles would burst and then forced himself down the hallway, away from that room. The hall lurched drunkenly. The air seemed suddenly contagioned with the sweet sickly smell of sex and semen. He made himself breathe through his nose, slow, steady breaths.

Susannah.

He saw her riding through the fields with him. Her cheeks glowing. Smiles dancing.

He should have known all along, the very first time he saw her with . . . His mind went blank again and he struggled to control himself. He would destroy . . .

'Is that a horse?'

William Moreton was calling out of the library door. His voice rose starkly up the staircase.

Richard's mind cleared.

He had to get out of here.

Suddenly he realised that all he wanted was to be away from this place. Even though the thought of Susannah made his senses churn, he forced himself to be still until he heard William Moreton step back into the library and close the door.

Then, hardly daring to breathe, he stepped back down the stairs. He reached the bottom, and strode casually down the deserted corridor as if he were merely a guest. He reached the door, yanked it open and stepped into the yard.

A buffet of wind struck him and he was stunned momentarily by the roar in the trees.

The air seemed intensely fresh. He sucked in a great lungful and steadied himself against the jamb. The same voices rose and fell from the library. Someone coughed loudly. He scanned the yard. Empty and sunk in gloom. He hugged the side of the house and walked quickly to the far corner, and then plunged across the open space into the trees beyond. He half expected someone to cry out, or a dog to bark, but there was nothing but the howl of the wind and the rustle of a bird through leaves. He dived under a bush of holly, ignoring the scrape of its leaves, and lay panting.

Now for a moment he allowed himself to give way to the grief and pain he had denied inside. He lay staring into the sky. All he saw was blackness.

So she had betrayed him.

His insides felt torn and bruised. She had lied from the beginning! He rocked his head from side to side in anger. How could he have been so stupid? Why hadn't he listened to Rebecca? Blind lust, he realised. He should have known the very first time he saw her with Oliver. And yet, he told himself, she had freed him from the cellar. She had given herself to him, wantonly, joyously . . . He squeezed his eyes shut. He didn't understand. Overhead the trees creaked like a ship at sea.

He hauled himself to his feet. His legs were weary, shaky. His bones ached. Now, as his blood cooled, his injuries became painfully real.

Through the thump of the wind, there was the muffled trudge of hooves on the driveway and a man's voice, sharp, swearing. He shrank back beneath the bushes. At the head of the drive a line of packhorses emerged, led by half a dozen sailors and flanked with troopers. The horses were laden with tubs and caskets like those in the cellar.

As soon as the men took these goods to the cellar, the alarm would be sounded.

Richard crept away through the bush and on the far side broke into a run, stumbling through the wood and then out across the fields, huge and empty in the sparse moonlight. Here he was exposed to the gale without mercy and the full flat hand of the wind smacked against him and shook the breath from him. Running, breathing became harder, and he thrust his head down. He was tired sooner than he expected, and several times he dived behind hedges to catch his breath before pressing on. He was chilled to the bone. His fingers and feet were horribly numb. All the while his ears strained for sounds of the alarm, the baying of dogs, but he heard nothing. Why hadn't they spotted he was gone?

He passed into a wood, wading through a mire of mud and loose brambles and rotting tree-stumps, skinning shins and palms, and clambered up the rise on the far side under the shadow of the oaks.

Rebecca's cottage was not far.

If he could get there, she would help him. She had to.

He ignored the trembling in his legs and forced himself up the hill and through the soft ploughed field, and finally fell against the door of the cottage.

The door swung loose and he toppled straight into the living room.

He expected someone to shout or startle, but the room was deathly quiet.

'Rebecca!' he called. 'Elizabeth!'

The same whiff of burned almonds. He stumbled to his knees and twisted his head this way and that. The wind had jumped into the room behind him and everything was a mad, roaring chaos until he slammed the door shut. The cottage was in a shambles. Everything – the pots, the chests, the bedding – had been ransacked or upended or destroyed. The strength drained out of him.

Who could have done this?

Then the realisation hit him. Only one person knew there was any connection between him and Rebecca.

Susannah.

The word burned him. He spat, as if it were somehow lodged in his mouth.

Rebecca's mattress lay gutted on the floor. Richard sank on to the mess of stuffing. The wind flung itself against the cottage, the door groaned on its latch.

Underneath his foot he felt something. Reaching down, he saw it was Rebecca's shawl. Then overhead the clouds groaned and throbbed with wrath. A vast rumble bellied across the heavens. The sky heaved, strained, and split apart.

Richard got up, threw back the shutters and stared out into the face of the storm. Clouds were being crammed inland by the relentless onslaught of the wind. Now they were panicking and stampeding, it seemed, and the air shrieked with their cries. A great lance of lightning stood on the hillside before him. A tree flashed and popped like a spitting log. And the thunder rolled down like a wave on the beach, washing all before it.

Now he saw with a new precision.

The first streaks of rain lashed his face through the window. He felt suddenly calmed by their iciness. He bent down. In a smashed crock he found the remains of half a chicken and in another pot a clout of honeycomb. He gorged himself on this, and felt his nerves tingle.

Amid the debris, something glinted. It was a short carving knife, six inches long, and he slipped it into his belt. Then, slinging a tattered cloak over his shoulders, he stalked out into the teeth of the storm and back towards Chynoon.

He saw now that he had created this.

By returning to his home, by searching for the ghost of his father, he had brought all this to pass as surely as if he had laid a curse upon them. He had condemned Rebecca the day she saw him. And why? Because all he had cared about was himself. He cursed himself ruthlessly and with each step he took towards the manor he felt angrier, stronger, as if the storm itself bore him forward.

He entered the woods which ran down to the manor drive. They roared with the storm and he fought his way through crazed undergrowth. It was not much farther now. He stumbled over roots.

Suddenly the bushes behind him crashed apart. A great black dog leapt towards him. Richard had a fleeting glimpse of a great fanged mouth and huge burning eyes before he threw himself to the ground. The beast soared over his head without stopping. It hit the leaves with a rush and plunged into the undergrowth beyond.

Richard picked himself up and then followed it down towards the house.

Chapter Five

RICHARD ARRIVED AT CHYNOON JUST as a squadron of cavalry was preparing to ride out. Great flanks of rain drifted horizontally into the house and the horses flattened their ears and neighed. One of the riders – their leader – was leaning down, talking to Oliver Moreton. Richard felt his stomach tighten. The wind hammered against them, then the riders tugged at their horses and swept around the side of the building and along the drive. He wondered if they were looking for him. Of the packhorses and their cargo there was no sign. Richard guessed it must be late now, perhaps two or three in the morning, though the clouds were so dense it was hard to tell.

Richard worked his way around to the front of the house and waited until he was sure the way was clear. Then, taking a deep breath, he ran lightly across the open space and came to rest underneath the big bay window of the Great Hall. Through a chink in the shutters, he could see that the fire was still lit and, above the din of the storm, the odd word or shout arose. He crept towards the north wing, keeping low, until he reached the broad mass of ivy running up the corner of the tower. He tested the thick stalks. They seemed resilient, but it was ten years since he had last done this. Checking round one final time, he dug his fingers into the ivy and hoisted himself up. His feet scraped for ledges in the corner and he felt the bunches of his shoulder muscles strain painfully. He must move quickly, keep his rhythm. He swung for a higher root, clutched it, pulled and sprang for another. His right arm stabbed with pain where he had been shot. The toe of his boot bit into a gap where the mortar had crumbled away and he kicked himself higher. Breaths came in gasps. His arms worked like a spider's legs across the face of the wall. Reaching, testing, and taking his weight first on the left, then on the right.

He was ten, twelve feet off the ground now. Another three feet, agonisingly slow, and he found himself hanging below the window of William Moreton's chamber. The ivy cracked in his hands and feeling his right arm give way, he swung himself up and grasped the ledge. If Moreton were in his room, he had no hope but, as he expected, the room was unoccupied. Richard perched precariously on the rim of the sill, feeling the fifteen feet of empty space behind him. Then he snatched at the lip of the casement and prised it open and tumbled into the room.

An overpowering odour assailed him, a warm, lactic stench which reminded him of curdled milk or fetid whey. He coughed and pressed his hand over his mouth. The smell seemed almost to blind him and he took in the surroundings only dully, as if through a fog. He sprang back to the window and flung it wide. The cold, fresh wind bounded into the room and shook the tapestries on the walls, scattered loose papers.

Richard surveyed the room. Moreton's study had almost the impression of a curio shop. Stuffed monkeys eyed him from huge ornate bookcases. Rugs of burgundy, cinnamon and puce littered the floor. A vast oak desk was piled high with volumes, manuscripts, documents fluttering in the gusts, a black-bound Bible, thick with tags and markers. A globe of the world crafted from brown leather stood in the corner, and a brass telescope, and a set of navigator's tools, and a huge bullet-proofed cuirass. Richard sniffed the air. The rancid scent remained. It hummed, reverberated, in the air, in his thoughts.

It was the scent of evil.

Richard had the sudden intuition that he had stumbled into the very core of the darkness which clotted the atmosphere of the manor like an almost tangible thing, thick and luscious. Although there was no fire in the grate, the room was almost insufferably warm and close, even with the window open and the storm raging. He crossed to the door, bolted it, and returned to the desk.

His mind was racing. Rebecca had not been in the cellar – where had they put her? Not here, evidently. Perhaps somewhere in the south wing, he guessed, but could he be sure? What if she wasn't here at all? Frantically he scanned the room, searching for a clue, anything.

He didn't have much time. He was terribly aware that any delay could cost Rebecca her life. Yet his eyes lingered on the books, the personal objects, and he was aware of his own fascination with William Moreton himself. Surely here, in Moreton's lair, there must be a key to the man *himself*! He had to know. Richard skimmed the books lying on the desk. They seemed to be religious tracts, statements of accounts, estate records, nothing of relevance.

He tried the drawer of the desk. It was locked, but he shattered the lock by brute force and spilled its contents on the floor. There was a powder horn, a quire of loose papers, and a leather-wrapped book, about eight inches long. Sensing something, Richard picked the book up and flipped it open.

It was a journal, containing plain sheets of paper, neatly trimmed, about two-thirds of which were covered in a thick, angular script. Richard turned to the front of the book and read: 'Volume VI, April 1654'. The first entry followed:

'6th: A great shadow moved over my soul today. I was reminded of the shadow a boat casts on the seabed. Men do not understand that without this shadow there would be no light. Look into the sun and see the shadow at its heart.

'7th: My desire grew today. I consumed it.

'8th: How much longer must I wait for a sign? My flesh craves action. The dragon sits in Babylon. There is talk of election to Parliament. Another farce, rigged for Cromwell's cronies! That is not the way of God's *elect*. Meeting: CCC tonight. L in Babel.'

This was the man's very heart.

Richard turned the pages feverishly, counting the seconds. Under May 14th, he read:

'The new maid balked at our requests. I educated her. Damnation!'

Under June 6th: 'Buried the body under the yews. Let the worm gnaw what the mistress denied. So all our passions. Free at last. This house is a petty kingdom for the Spirit which dwells within me. I rage and fret. Carew writes from London. The new committee is composed of unworthy vessels. C says they are strawheads to be reaped. Cpn S a true sword, and others.'

Cpn S? Captain Standish, Richard guessed.

He peered at the script. Sometimes the ink became so dense that words and phrases could not be read. One entry which disturbed him said simply: 'I'll cut her mother's dugs and slit . . .' the next three words indecipherable.

Other records were more factual, such as: 'Rec'd 3 ankers musket powder. Rec'd 6 barrels' and Richard guessed they referred to the shipments which arrived by packhorse.

Many references were to politics and meetings and these became more prominent with each day.

'Aug 3rd: Meeting Tregony. All attended. I think they are agreed. My soul burns within me and will not be relieved.

'Aug 21st: HC reports well from Bristol. CC agree.'

Again these letters reminded him of the ones scribbled in Samuel Dowles' journal: CCCL. Were they the same?

Richard pored over the text, flicking from page to page until the sensation made him dizzy.

He could imagine William Moreton inscribing these daily records here on the desk, but he baulked to imagine the thoughts which pulsed inside that head. As the months progressed, several things became apparent: Moreton was indeed moving towards some sort of plan, for the records of meetings and deliveries became more frequent, his comments more assured; secondly, Moreton's mental, or spiritual, state was deteriorating rapidly. An entry for September 1st was scrawled: 'All devouring flesh, all deflowering flesh.' Under September 11th Richard found a passage in which Moreton seemed to be rationalising his thoughts. It read: 'In the beginning Adam rejected his birthright and was rejected from his birthplace. Now we must reclaim our home from the serpent. We must take mankind home and kill those who have usurped Eden. We must show no mercy. Let us fill the gutters with their corpses and hang the suitors in the square. None shall live save those whose names are written *here*. We cannot fail.'

Richard's hands were trembling. Hungrily he turned the pages. Here it was.

'Oct 15th: Visited Samuel Dowles. The poor man whimpered. We cut his finger before he talked. He had no will.'

The next entry read:

'Oct 16th: Caught the boat on the rocks. Killed all save one, a merchant's son. Should I have listened to her?'

Richard stared at the words, trying to understand their significance. *Should I have listened to her?* Had this saved his life?

He read on, compulsively.

'Talked with him today. He is an innocent, I am sure. But that is nothing new. The strength of a cause is determined by the innocence of those who will die for it.'

Was I an innocent? Richard wondered.

'Oct 17th: Oliver returns. My own soul returns to me. And with him L. We have reached perfection, in our plans at any rate. I argue for the 5th, for patriotic reasons.

'Oct 19th: Ursula dead. Beloved wife. She was in such pain and begged me to comfort her. I gave her such comfort as my strength afforded, oh dear dear wife. You would have been my companion. Masters tells me it is a sign to make us strong. I rejoice at her joy in the Lord yet I am troubled. Why must she die now? Masters says we must bear it in silence. I let my body relieve itself with the others but find no joy therein.

'Oct 20th: The innocent one strikes our bosom! Oliver found him abusing her corpse. The filthy serpent. I shall crush him with my heel. Even as I write he skulks in the cellar, but I shall have him out. I foretold this would happen if we traded with the devil.

'Oct 21st: Stolen from me? There is a traitor. Moyle says he took S and has buried himself in the old mines.

'Oct 22nd: S returns. Praise be for that, though I wonder why we continue with this farce. We have no need of her, though Oliver seems enslaved. He should free himself as I and Masters have done. Devotion to one body is devotion to sin. When will he learn to free his *self*? I fear the worst if even our own followers cannot rid themselves of this *need*.'

As Richard read it, it seemed that William Moreton bared his soul before him, and he began to understand the strange logic which impelled him.

To William Moreton, he realised, everyone was damned unless they belonged to his cult of the elect. Cult: the word had a strange, pagan feel to it. He shook himself. And Moreton was planning something, something so significant that he could regard everything else, including murder and the torture of Cromwell's agent, as mere details. But what was he planning? With chilling clarity, Richard realised that William Moreton was capable of *anything*. We are only limited by our sense of self, he thought, and Moreton lost that long ago.

One thing puzzled him. He had assumed Moreton killed Ursula, yet the journal gave no indication of it. Far from it: Moreton clearly regarded him, Richard, as guilty. *The filthy serpent*, he had said.

He turned to the last entry. Moreton had written:

'Nov 1st: L is ready to fly. CCC ready. We wait. Now let us purify ourselves with the blood of the unnecessary. The innocents.'

The *unnecessary*? People like Rebecca, Elizabeth, he realised. Those who were not needed. Richard put the book down. His hands were shaking. He must find Rebecca before it was too late. If she was still alive . . . No, he wouldn't think of that.

He drew his knife. He crossed to the door, listened,

then slipped the bolt. The door led to an antechamber, which opened on to the corridor. He peered out. The passageway was empty, dark. Richard crept to the top of the stairs. From the ground floor, there came the sound of voices raised in anger. Someone was barking orders. Footsteps hurried. Doors slammed. Richard edged down the first few steps. Someone was sobbing and he heard the door to the Great Hall close.

Damn.

If Rebecca was in the cellar, then his only route, through the Hall, was blocked. He hesitated, then descended to the halfway landing. The door on his right was unlocked, although it creaked so ferociously that he was sure someone would hear it, but no sound of alarm came from the Hall and he went in.

The door led into the minstrels' gallery. From here musicians would serenade guests while they dined. But the gallery had not been used since his father's time and the room was rank with dust. He closed the door behind him and crossed quietly to the balcony overlooking the Hall.

At first he could not recognise the figures below him. The sparse red flames from the fire cast them into grotesque relief and left most of their bodies and the Hall sunk in great pools of darkness. From what he could see, two men were standing in front of the fire. They were holding a woman on her knees between them.

Who was it? He gripped the edge of the balcony.

Then William Moreton stepped out of the shadows beside the hearth.

'You have betrayed us, Sarah. Betrayed us all.' His voice was vast, monstrous. It filled the room like a strong, pungent odour.

Sarah Masters was struggling and twisted her head,

then the two men pushed her down so her face was pressed against the floor.

'Don't let her move!'

Of course, that voice! Richard realised with a shock that the speaker was Dr Masters himself. The Doctor strode forward and stood next to William Moreton.

'See! She does not deny it!' said Masters.

Moreton said nothing. He crossed to the two men holding Sarah.

'Lift her up!'

They jerked her roughly to her feet. Richard could see her shaking and twisting, but her two captors were far too strong. He wondered why she didn't speak or call out.

Then Moreton reached up and there was a flash of blade and Richard's heart jumped, then what he realised had been a gag was cut from her head and Sarah gasped for air.

'I didn't—'

'Silence!' Moreton struck her with the flat of his hand. There was a sudden flash of lightning and for an instant the figures were caught in a frozen tableau of white light. Sarah's head was flung to one side. William Moreton stood over her, his great bug eyes staring, his tongue protruding slightly between his lips. Dr Masters glowered at her, his face as tight as a knot of muscle. Richard saw that the two men holding her were Oliver Moreton and Captain Standish. Then a roll of thunder drowned the room in blackness.

'. . . can dupe us, whore?' Moreton was yelling. 'Doctor, show her as she truly is!'

Masters' short, dense body seemed particularly solid in the dancing flames.

What was he going to do? Richard's pulse hammered

in his temples, in his wrists, in the taut drum of his chest.

Masters gripped the front of his wife's bodice, and very slowly tore it apart. Sarah screamed and twisted, but with brutal efficiency the Doctor stripped off her bodice and sleeves and Richard saw her creamy back and full, rounded breasts exposed. Helplessly she tried to cover her breasts with her arms. Beneath the groans of the storm outside he could hear her sobbing.

'Hold her arms!' commanded Masters. Then staring into her eyes, he ripped the thin fabric of her skirt away. Her clothes lay in a crumpled heap on the edge of the firelight.

Richard felt his stomach tighten.

'See! See how she is a fiend! A centaur below!' Moreton's face was almost bursting with emotion. 'Fie! Fie!'

'Please,' implored Sarah. 'I didn't let them out!'

'Look, even now this Cleopatra would honey us with more lies,' said Moreton. 'When your own good husband caught you with the key.'

Masters glowered at her, his face a mask of hatred.

'Please!' she whispered. There was another flash. Blue light shattered the gloom and then darkness thundered in behind it. The whole house seemed to shake.

'Good God! What are you doing?'

Everyone was looking towards the door. Sir Ralph Fielding strode into view. He held his right arm out in a gesture of entreaty.

'She has been caught in sin,' replied Moreton simply.

Fielding muttered something Richard couldn't catch and walked up to Sarah. She bowed her head beneath his gaze.

'But she's naked! This is no way to treat a lady! She's your wife, dammit!' he shouted at Masters.

Masters walked impassively towards him.

'My only bride is my cause, sir. As yours should be.' He folded his arms across his chest. 'If you have no stomach for justice, don't dine at our table.'

Fielding paused. He glanced around. 'Oliver! Standish! This can't be right!'

No one replied. Then William Moreton laid a hand on Fielding's shoulder. 'Stay,' he ordered, 'and watch.' He pushed Fielding to the side of the hearth. Then he drew himself up to his full height. Sarah seemed to shrink before him.

Richard ground his teeth together. His eyes scanned the Hall desperately for an idea, a means of stopping them, but there was nothing. Nothing! This is my fault, he realised. She did this to help me.

'So, will you confess your complicity, my child?' Moreton gazed down at her. The fingers of his left hand grazed her skin, and Richard saw her try to twist away and then stop and hang limply from the men's hands as if she had resigned herself to her fate.

'Yes,' she whispered.

'Why?'

'Because I . . .' she stammered, searching for the words. 'Because I hate what you've done to us!' she suddenly blurted. 'I hate what you've done to my husband. To Ursu—'

'Enough!' Moreton swatted her as he would a repellent insect. 'See!' he crowed. 'She is consumed within by the worm!' He reached down and placed his hand between her legs. Richard closed his eyes.

'There's hell, there is darkness, there is the sulphurous pit!' Moreton's teeth were clenched tightly together. Richard could only guess what he was doing with his fingers. Sarah Masters screamed. Her body writhed.

'Good God!' whispered Fielding. 'In the name of God!'

A ragged smile played across Moreton's face. 'Do you confess all?' His voice was thick, evil beyond belief.

'Yes, please . . .'

Moreton stepped back and unbuckled his trousers. Richard felt physically sick. He saw Fielding blanch, then march abruptly from the Hall.

Tears were bursting at the edge of Richard's eyes. His throat was sick with bile. If there was anything, anything . . . he thought. But there wasn't.

For an instant he thought he would also, like Fielding, turn away. But then he realised that would do no good whatsoever. If we do not face up to the evil men do, how can we overcome it? he thought. Somehow he knew he must not turn away from Moreton's actions, if he was going to have the strength to confront the man himself.

Against every nerve of his body, Richard forced his eyes to watch.

He would never forget what happened next.

Oliver Moreton and Captain Standish each held one of Sarah's legs and forced them apart. All the time Sarah was screaming and jerking her body every way she could. Sweat was glistening on William Moreton's head, Richard saw very clearly. Then the muscles on his neck tensed and he thrust into her. Sarah shrieked – a soft, piercing sound – then suddenly some will to resist snapped and she slumped against him. Brutally, mechanically, William Moreton pumped his body into hers. His face bore a strange expression of indifference and disdain, as if he were performing some unpleasant but necessary task. It was, Richard realised, a task of violence, nothing other than that. Then after a few seconds Moreton grunted and emptied his seed into her.

'Release her,' he told her captors and wiped his hands

on his britches. Then he turned to the Doctor, and Richard saw that Masters had stripped to his shirtsleeves.

'Cut her throat,' Moreton's command was so casual that for a moment Richard did not understand what he had said.

Masters stooped over his wife, grabbed her by the hair and yanked her head back. She whimpered, in a daze, not comprehending. Masters put his right hand down and jerked it back and the hearth was struck by a thick, ragged arc of blood. Sarah emitted a breathless gasp that choked before it was out of her mouth. Blood spurted across the floor, splashed on to the boards. Richard felt his stomach heave. Masters let go of her hair and her head hit the ground with a thud.

No. No. Richard stumbled backwards. He felt he was choking. The stench of blood seemed to fill the room. William Moreton said something to Masters, but Richard could no longer hear. He staggered away from the balcony and flung the door open into the stairway. For an instant, he didn't care whether he was seen or not, but then he realised with a jolt that the same would happen to Rebecca unless he saved her. Rebecca! He had a sudden vision of Dr Masters looming over her.

Where was she? Damn them all! Gripping his knife, he made his way back upstairs. There was one person who would know.

Sir Ralph Fielding opened the door on his second knock. He paused for a second when he saw Richard's knife, but he made no effort to resist and swung the door wide.

'You'd better come in,' he muttered. His face was a sickly grey. His eyes were tired. He looked as if he hadn't slept for days.

Richard entered, still wielding the knife, but sensing

it was somehow unnecessary. In the near corner of the room stood Fielding's sword. Fielding made no attempt to reach it and walked over to the window. Rain slapped against the glass.

'Don't make a sound!' hissed Richard, but Fielding only chuckled. It was a dry, eerie noise.

'Do you think I care any more? After what they did tonight...' He gazed into the night.

'I... saw it.'

'Did you?' Fielding spun round and faced him. 'Tell me, Richard, why did you come here?'

'To find Rebecca Penmarris. She is here, isn't she?' He looked anxiously at Fielding.

Sir Ralph smiled cynically. 'Then you have a chance, Richard, and do you know why? Because you care for her, don't you? She means something to you, something deep – here.' He stabbed his finger against his chest. His beard bristled.

Richard hesitated, unsure how to respond.

'I can see it in your face,' prompted Fielding. 'Listen, Richard, what I mean is this: if you care for this girl, if you have a real passion for her, then you might just have enough' – he groped for the word – '*will* to save her. Will, that's right.'

'How do you mean?' asked Richard impatiently. Yet there was something in Fielding's words which held him captive.

'Do you remember the King's council at Cologne?' Sir Ralph's eyes glittered. 'Why did you agree to come here? To serve the King?' His tone was mocking, sceptical.

'Originally I came for my father's sake,' answered Richard.

Fielding caught the look in his eyes. 'Well, you know

my part in it,' he replied. 'If you want to kill me for it, go ahead.'

Richard did nothing. Rain beat on the window.

'I fought for the King for years,' said Fielding. 'And at the time they called me ruthless. Ruthless!' He hooted bitterly. 'In these last few days I have seen *ruthless* for the first time. I have never done anything with a fraction of the *feeling* of these people.' He clenched his hand into a ball. 'You've seen what they are capable of? Do you really understand?'

'Yes.' Richard stared him straight in the eye.

'Good,' replied Fielding. 'It is a mark of weakness – the weakness of good mediocre men – to refuse to see what their enemy is capable of. Mediocre men think that evil is also mediocre.' He snorted violently. 'They think the devil does not exist!'

'I came here to find Rebecca,' reminded Richard.

Fielding ignored him. He had started to speak and now he could not stop himself. 'Do you know what Moreton is planning?' he demanded. 'Do you know why he is prepared to butcher women and men?'

At that moment there came a shuffle of footsteps on the floorboards outside. Fielding crossed quietly to the door and listened. The wind rattled in the eaves. After a few minutes Fielding breathed out and straightened himself.

'Remember Hugh Lovelace, that spineless clerk from London?' he continued, more carefully now. 'What no one told you is that he is one of the personal secretaries to the Lord Protector Cromwell.' Fielding watched the surprise register in Richard's face. 'This morning he will return to London. What's the date today?'

Richard thought. 'November the first, I think.'

'On the fifth, Hugh Lovelace will assassinate Cromwell.' Sir Ralph smiled grimly. 'Does the date surprise you? The anniversary of Guy Fawkes' plot to kill King James.'

'But why is that important?'

'Lovelace won't survive the assassination. But if he kills Cromwell on November the fifth, and says his lines properly, who will everyone blame?'

Richard understood. 'The Roman Catholics.'

'Exactly!'

'But surely,' ventured Richard, 'if he kills Cromwell, won't he be helping the King?'

'Do you really think so? Why have none of the royalists' plots ever succeeded? Will, Richard! They lack will! We think we can wave a sword in the air and the people will come flocking, but what does the King offer the people?' Fielding laughed. 'Oh, if Cromwell is killed, I'm sure a few royalists will try to clamber on to the stage, but who do you think will really seize control? A few noblemen with feathers in their hats? Or maybe the dull, mediocre presbyterians?' Fielding laughed dismissively. 'Or a band of people who know they are absolutely destined to impose the Kingdom of the Elect? A people with such will they can sacrifice wives, lovers, friends, anything, to achieve their goal? Is that what you want, Richard?'

Richard shook his head.

'Great God!' said Fielding. 'I was attracted to them, I admit. In place of so much doubt and failure, they offered me certainties, conviction! Success!' He sighed. 'I wish I had stayed in France and accepted failure.'

Richard coughed impatiently. 'Rebecca. Where is she?'

Fielding didn't look up. 'In the old laundry, I think, in the south wing.'

'And her mother?'

'I don't know.'

Richard hesitated. Sir Ralph had told him the truth, he felt. But could he leave him alive? He felt the knife in his palm, and thought of his father. No, he could not. Moreton had taught him that much. He must kill him now, while he was off guard.

There was a sharp knock on the door.

Fielding's head snapped up. He glanced at Richard, motioned him to be still. 'Who is it?' he called.

'Fielding, it's me. Piers Standish.'

Sir Ralph swore under his breath and indicated his sword. 'Take it,' he mouthed. Richard slipped the blade from its scabbard.

'Coming,' called Sir Ralph. He pretended to fiddle with the lock. 'Blasted key!' Richard went behind the door. The sword was heavy in his hand. Fielding flicked his fingers at Richard – 'Give me the knife' – Richard hesitated for only a second, then passed it over. Sir Ralph took a deep breath. 'That's it!' He pulled the door open.

'Fielding! The Colonel sent me to see if you were all right.'

'Yes, come in. Is he still in the Hall?'

Sir Ralph turned away and Standish followed him into the room.

'No. He and the others have retired for th—'

Standish's word stopped abruptly. Sir Ralph had turned back casually and clamped a hand over the captain's mouth, ramming him against the wall. As if by magic, the other hand appeared on Standish's chest, clutching the haft of the knife. Its blade, Richard knew, was already buried deep.

Standish's eyes bulged, he tried to speak. Sir Ralph stared impassively into his face and twisted the blade home. Blood began to seep between his fingers pressed over the man's mouth. Richard shut the door quickly.

Standish was still dying, slowly, wretchedly. He gave a few small desperate kicks. But Fielding was too strong and kept him pinned to the wall. The expression of concentration on his face was almost tender. The kicks became more feeble until something seemed to flicker out and Standish stopped moving altogether. Fielding held him for a few seconds longer, then gently let him down to the floor.

'We must be quick,' he said. 'The barracks are full of troops. There's more in the rooms beyond the library.'

Their eyes met.

'If I'm going to die,' said Fielding pointedly, 'I'd rather do it for some reason.' He opened the door quietly and together they went down the stairs.

Fielding paused outside the Great Hall. He was panting. 'Damn nerves,' he muttered. 'Are you ready?'

Richard nodded.

Fielding put his ear to the door then, hearing nothing, turned the handle. The Hall was dark. A heavy, malign odour hung in the air. A smell of sweat and fear and stale sex, thought Richard bitterly. A dark, ugly pool glistened in the dying embers of the fire. There was no sign of Sarah's body.

Richard led the way across the Hall and into the corridor beyond. Behind him the Hall seemed empty, menacing. What he did not see was that in the minstrels' gallery, where he had watched only a short while before, a figure stirred.

'I'll watch the door here,' whispered Fielding.

The old laundry lay along the corridor on his right. Richard ran down the passageway and didn't see the guard coming round the corner.

The man snorted with surprise, then Richard cannoned into him, and they toppled over, hitting the cold flagstones together. The man was in his forties, heavily

built, with thick, short limbs. Richard felt him brace his
legs and then was punched bodily back against the
wall, his lungs gasping. The man grunted, raised his
fist. Richard struggled upright and plunged his sword
into the man's abdomen. The force of the man's charge
drove the blade deep. He squealed and tried to clutch
the sword. In a panic, Richard jerked it up and cut
clean through the man's hand. Blood was everywhere.
The man was thrashing about, retching blood in great
ugly gouts. And then the blade touched something vital
and the man sagged against him. Richard staggered
under his weight. He heaved the body back on to the
floor. He was drenched in the man's blood.

'Are you all right?' hissed Fielding.

'Yes,' Richard was rifling through the man's clothes.
There was a bunch of keys on the belt. Then he was at
the laundry door, working through the keys. The third
one fitted and the door swung back. The laundry was
cold and bare.

'Richard! Is that you?'

Rebecca was kneeling against the wall, less than five
feet away, her wrists chained. Richard saw her white
smock was torn and hung open. She clutched it round
her.

'Are you all right?' He felt a rush of anxiety and
struggled over, clutching her in his arms. 'I was worried
about you.'

'Yes. Yes.' She looked nervously into his face. Her
eyes were swollen and raw and he could see she had
been crying. Suddenly she seemed indescribably precious. 'You came back for me, didn't you?'

He hugged her closer, feeling her warm body against
his. 'It's all right,' he whispered. 'I won't let you go,
Beckie.' Then he realised she was alone. 'Where's
Elizabeth?'

In one awful moment he guessed the truth.

'What happened?'

'She wouldn't come with them.' Her voice was grey and bloodless. She had cried until there was nothing left, he thought.

He kissed her gently on the cheek. 'I'm sorry.' He pulled gently away from her. Her smock was stained red from his shirt. He took in the torn cloth grimly. 'Did they touch you?'

She looked at him fiercely. 'No.' Her lip quivered.

Quickly, efficiently, he began to try the keys in the locks which bound her chains.

'Come on!' Rebecca began to panic and tug at the chains. Then he felt the lock click and the chains fell away. He gripped her by the wrist and helped her to her feet. As he did, something sparkled in the dim light of the cellar.

'This is beautiful,' he said. 'Where did you get this?' For the first time he noticed that on her third finger she wore a fine gold ring, exquisitely engraved.

'No time for that now.' She pulled her hand away. 'Come on!'

They ran back along the corridor to the Hall. There was no one at the door.

'Fielding! Where are you?'

'Over here!'

Richard sighed in relief.

'I caught this lad skulking around.' Fielding smiled. Strung up by the collar, a small, skinny boy was struggling in his grip. It was Stephen Moreton. The boy blinked at them pathetically.

'Please,' he implored. 'I saw you from the gallery. I want to help.'

Fielding tightened his hold. 'Killing children's not my idea of war,' he muttered. 'What do we do?'

'The boy's father would have no such scruples,' Richard remarked.

Stephen's face was pinched with fear. 'I won't tell my father,' he whispered, then grew suddenly hysterical. 'He killed my stepmother, you know! I hate him! Hate him!'

'Come on, Tremaine, let's get out of here,' Fielding snapped impatiently. 'You're coming with us,' he told Stephen and, still clutching him by the collar, set off across the Hall. He was about halfway across when the far door opened.

A soldier, holding a chunk of bread in one hand, appeared in the doorway and stared at them for one dreadful moment. Silence hung in the air. The bread dropped from the soldier's hand. Richard opened his mouth to speak. Then the soldier caught sight of Rebecca and let out a yell and drew his sword.

Fielding swore and pushed Stephen away. The boy fell against a chair with a clunk. The soldier shouted again and ran forward, his sword poised, ready. Sir Ralph only had Richard's dagger.

'Fielding! No!' But it was too late. Sir Ralph leapt at the man. The soldier dodged his lunge easily and thrust with his sword. Richard saw Fielding shudder, as if he had fallen into a cold pool of water, then the blade appeared through the middle of his back.

'No!' he called.

Fielding grunted and reached forward and smashed his dagger into the man's face, again and again and again until the man collapsed in a welter of blood. Fielding staggered against the table, one hand to his stomach. His face was very pink. He coughed and blood tumbled from his mouth.

Richard ran to his side.

'You stupid—'

'Get out – now!' Fielding ordered. His eyes were already bleary. 'I wanted to die, don't you see? Now maybe your father will leave me in—'

He slumped forward, breathing thickly. The front of his tunic was dark with blood.

'No, don't...' Richard clutched Fielding's thick, broad shoulders and forced him upright.

Rebecca pulled at his arm. He ignored her.

Fielding tried to say something but his lips sagged uselessly.

'Don't worry,' said Richard. 'You did the right...' But then he realised Fielding could no longer hear and let him slip to the floor.

Where had Stephen Moreton gone? Richard scanned the Hall. His mind was a jumble of thoughts.

Rebecca tugged his arm again.

'Quick! Richard! Quick!'

Then two more soldiers stumbled through the door, wielding swords, blocking their escape. Richard suddenly reacted. Grabbing Rebecca, he went to run back across the Hall, but the first soldier intercepted him, his sword flashing wildly.

'Stop! Collins, stop!' A voice rang out. The soldier stopped in his tracks.

Richard also stopped and turned.

Oliver Moreton stood in the doorway, clad in his shirt and britches. His hair was swept back from his face. His eyes glittered.

'Stay!' he commanded the soldiers. He drew his own sword and felt its balance in his hands. 'I see Sir Ralph did not make it.'

Richard gritted his teeth.

Oliver strode forward. He was light on the balls of his feet. His legs were like coiled springs, waiting to be released. He grinned.

'Why did you kill her, Oliver?'

'Who? Sarah?' He arched his eyebrows, suddenly resembling his father. 'Do you need to ask?'

Richard came forward a pace.

'Richard, no!' Rebecca's voice seemed particularly plaintive. He had hoped to save her, if no one else.

'What happens if I win, Oliver, like last time?'

Oliver's face became angry. 'You won't win.'

'But if I do? Will your men kill me anyway?'

Oliver laughed. 'Of course they'll kill you.'

Richard gripped his sword tighter. The wound in his right arm had started to throb.

'What about Rebecca? Tell them to let her go.'

Oliver did not reply. He sprang across the floor and launched a blow at Richard's chest. Rebecca screamed. Richard jumped to one side, felt the sword pierce the air beside him. He had a sudden whiff of Oliver's warm sweat, then lunged forward, but Oliver knocked his aim away. They jumped apart, swords quivering, probing, circling each other. Oliver's eyes were straining with concentration. The skin over his cheeks, nose, throat, was taut. Far above them, someone was ringing the bell and its chimes echoed through the Hall.

Richard felt the boards beneath his feet. His back was cold, wet with sweat. Oliver's eyes narrowed and Richard pounced, catching Oliver's sword early in its lunge. The blades rang. Richard's wound stung with pain and Oliver beat his sword down and drove forward. Richard ducked. Oliver jerked his blade down and Richard rolled to his right, then over, over, as Oliver's sword struck the boards behind him, then he was back on his feet, hearing the soldiers running towards him.

'Leave him!' snarled Oliver, then attacked again. Richard parried and Oliver fought him back across the floor. Richard had a sudden glimpse of Rebecca, pressed against the wall, her face white. Then he swerved, deflected, parried again. They were both breathing heavily. Richard met Oliver's next blow and as their swords locked, they clashed together, faces inches apart. Oliver grunted and spat in Richard's eyes. Rebecca shouted something. Richard stumbled back, half-blinded.

Let Oliver think I can't see.

Oliver laughed breathlessly and swung at Richard's neck.

Richard jumped clear, banged his sword down on to Oliver's and knocked it out of his hand. The sword clattered against the floor and lay still. By that time Richard had the tip of his blade prodding Oliver's throat.

'No one move!' he yelled. Sweat was running down his forehead. He was shaking.

Oliver stared at him furiously.

'Well, go on then. Kill me.'

Richard tasted blood in his mouth. He steadied himself and jabbed the sword forward a little, keeping Oliver off balance.

Could we escape? he wondered. He tried to think.

'Richard! No!' It was Susannah. She was wearing a sheer white nightgown and came running into the Hall. Behind her was William Moreton and with him more soldiers. Richard turned, suddenly distracted.

There was a sudden blow to his leg and he staggered back. Oliver held a slim red hunting knife in his hand. It was covered in blood and Richard realised his leg was bleeding profusely. He clasped his fingers over the wound. It hurt like the devil.

'Hah!' Oliver jumped away and before Richard could

move, he had crossed the Hall and seized Rebecca by the arm. Rebecca was struggling wildly.

'No!'

Oliver flicked his knife up and pinned it against her throat. He glanced across at his father triumphantly.

Richard froze.

'Oliver! Don't!' This was Susannah. 'You don't have to—'

'Quiet!' he roared. He was panting wildly. He levelled his gaze at Richard, then barked an order: 'Kill him!'

Was that smoke? Richard sniffed and shook his head. It didn't matter.

The four soldiers grinned nervously and advanced. Richard kept his left hand clamped over his leg, trying to staunch the flow. He hobbled backwards.

'May you burn in hell, Moreton!' he shouted.

William Moreton's face was swollen with hatred. 'You have cost me much,' he said. He snapped his head at his son. 'Kill the girl. Let him see her die.'

Did Oliver hesitate? For even a fraction of a second did he hesitate? Richard never knew, for suddenly everything happened at once.

The first soldier leapt at him, and Richard jumped backwards. The door that led into the south wing was still open, and he had some vague, hopeless notion of getting that far. Then suddenly someone was shouting: 'The house is on fire! Fire!'

Richard saw his attacker falter and sprang forward, stabbing him through the arm so he dropped his sword. The man yelled, and dropped back.

Rebecca! Richard turned to find her. But the next man attacked, stabbing wildly.

'Fire! Fire!'

'In the name of God,' bellowed William Moreton. 'The cellar is on fire!'

Richard noticed the air was full of a black sour smell. A lunge caught the edge of his shoulder and he sank to his knees just in time. Where was the door? He slashed savagely at his assailant, forcing him back, then turned and ran for the door. The soldiers were inches behind.

'Forget him! The cellar! The cellar!'

Thick smoke was streaming out of the corridor in front of him. There was a sudden bang and a man gasped. Richard gained the threshold and turned, knocking the soldiers back.

Sedge! High up in the minstrels' gallery, on the other side of the Hall, the old man was clutching a flintlock.

'Rebecca! Save Rebecca!'

Richard shouted but he didn't know if Sedge had heard. Where was she? Somewhere a woman screamed. Black smoke was suddenly all around him. The soldiers were charging the door. Richard retreated, hacking right, left, down the narrow corridor, one pace at a time. His leg was weakening. A man in a helmet sprang forward, and Richard tripped, fell against the side of the corridor, somehow missed the blade and stumbled away. He reached the top of the cellar steps, the stairway was clogged with smoke. Richard threw himself past the opening and the soldiers paused, then dived down the stairs.

Richard backed along the corridor and round the corner.

Confused shouts came from the cellar. Men were running down the steps. Strangely, Richard found himself forgotten. His heart was pounding. He put his fingers to his leg and winced, but the bleeding seemed to have slowed. There were more shouts. Gunshots. Sedge? Richard gripped his sword. Should he go back? He staggered against the side of the corridor.

'You cannot cheat death.'

The voice caught him by surprise.

It was Dr Masters, clutching a pistol, standing five feet behind him. His beady eyes shone with suppressed fury.

Richard turned to face him. He thought desperately for something to say, and then the whole world exploded.

Chapter Six

Rebecca! her face came to him before he opened his eyes.

Where was she? Was she hurt?

He shook himself angrily and realised he couldn't move, opened his eyes and was almost blinded by sharp, stinging dust. What had happened? Something was crushing him. He sucked air. Hot dust clogged his mouth, his throat; he was unbearably hot. He struggled, trying to free himself. What...? Dr Masters. Sedge. Rebecca. His mind was a confusion of images. Bright red lights were flickering over him. Something was rustling, like papers being crumpled.

What had happened?

He remembered an explosion, a great flash of smoke, and white, red. Men shouting, screaming. Or did he dream that? He flexed his arms again and realised they were pinned by a fallen beam. The house must have collapsed. He suddenly recognised the rustling sound.

Chynoon was on fire!

He tried to fight back a wave of panic. His heart raced, he strained against the beam, and pain rippled down his chest, across his stomach. He groaned, and for the first time he was afraid he was badly injured and would die here, failed and wretched, in this hell of heat and dust. He was panting heavily, panting thick, dusty air. Be calm, he told himself, calm! And lay there counting his breaths.

Rebecca. Was she still alive? He had a sudden vivid

memory of her pressed against the wall, Oliver's knife to her throat. Don't panic. Breathe. Breathe.

Red light was flickering and crackling. There was a sudden crack and a sharp wrenching noise, then a rush, like shingle on a beach, as a welter of slates tumbled off the roof.

Richard strained at the beam. It was too heavy. He realised he couldn't move because his arms were packed around with mortar and plaster and brickwork. He cursed. Slowly, methodically, he squirmed his hands back and forward, back and forward. His face was caked with dust, sweat dribbled into his eyes, his mouth. Thick, sour smoke choked his nose. His right hand worked a space for itself. He strained against a chunk of smashed masonry and wormed his right arm free. He lay panting gratefully for a second, then worked on his left. This seemed to be jammed by a spike or something, and he feared for a moment the bone was broken, then he managed to force the beam back with his right arm and his left came free. The smoke was scorching, getting thicker and heavier; his head swam. He tore at the beam, prised his torso and then his hips then finally his legs out of the rubble. He lurched to his feet and staggered as if he were on board a ship. Where was Masters? People were shouting somewhere. The whole corridor seemed to career to one side, then he straightened himself and waited till his head stopped spinning.

Where had everyone gone? Dr Masters had been standing right there. Now there was a huge pile of rubble where one of the arches had collapsed. Something black protruded. He bent down. It was Masters' black felt hat. Beside it lay an unfired pistol. Richard picked up the pistol and stuffed it into his shirt.

The house cracked. Suddenly a ball of fire billowed

from the room to his left. Richard blundered back down the corridor. As he passed the cellar stairs a wall of such intense heat struck his face that he almost fell. The very air seemed seared from his lungs. He tumbled into the Great Hall beyond. Servants were staring at him, their faces white and drawn. Men were running up with buckets.

In their midst, the great unmoving frame of Sir Ralph Fielding still sat propped against the table. He looked strangely imperious.

'Moreton! The others! Where have they gone?' he roared.

The man nearest him dropped his bucket, spilling the precious water over the boards. Richard realised he was covered in blood from head to foot. 'Where are they?'

The man choked. 'Gone! They rode out. I don't know where!' he said quickly, as Richard lunged forward then past him towards the far door. His leg gave out on him and he stumbled against the table, swore, and reached the door. More servants came running in – Bridget, Daisy – and he turned and grabbed Bridget roughly. She screamed.

'Did he take Rebecca with him? Did he?'

'I don't know, sir!' She stared at him wild-eyed and he threw her aside.

Where had they gone?

He reached the rear door and stared across the yard. The wind raged overhead and he was momentarily stunned by its onslaught. Was it still night? The yard was thick with darkness. It seemed this night would never end. He peered towards the east and saw pale cream light washing the hem of the sky.

The stable door banged wildly in the wind. He limped across. Two horses were neighing and he peered inside. All the others had gone. Richard tore a saddle and harness off the wall and strapped them to the first horse. The animal was uneasy and stamped and snorted, and he had to settle her with his hand before he could fasten the buckle and lead her outside. The wind was ragged in the trees above. He heaved himself into the saddle, feeling his ribs sting, and set off.

Moreton would not have fled unless he had to, thought Richard. But the fire had destroyed everything. Would Lovelace still attempt the assassination? Richard didn't know and didn't care. If Rebecca was still alive, she would be with Moreton, she had to be. But where would he go? Inland? Across country? He would be too conspicuous. The sea. Of course! The sea was his only chance.

Richard kicked his horse into a gallop and clattered down the drive.

Moreton had gone to Porthcarrick.

Chapter Seven

RICHARD REACHED THE CLIFF OVERLOOKING the village just as dawn was breaking, wet and ragged in the sky behind him. But overhead the clouds were massed so densely that the air was still black and thick. Rain lashed his face and he shielded his eyes from the wind as he strained to make out the dim, murky shapes moving among the cottages. Horses. He could see horses, and men running down towards the sea. He followed their direction. In the lee of the harbour, a small pinnace was riding and bucking at its moorings. The sea was frothing and heaving and looked like ink. He realised with a shock that the sailors were actually attempting to hoist the foresail, and the canvas was snapping savagely in the wind.

It would be madness to sail.

A small jolly boat struggled across the harbour to the ship's side and he saw people clambering into the frigate. Was that a white smock? He felt his throat tighten.

Throwing himself out of the saddle, he began to climb down the sheer flank of the valley. This was a dangerous time, for the bare rockface offered him no cover. He was about halfway down when a man came out of a cottage and seemed to stare up at him, and he froze, unable to move, while the rain beat upon him and the wind burst overhead. But after a few seconds, the man turned and walked down to the cove. Several other men were gathered at the water's edge. Amongst the group, Richard saw the glint of helmets. After that, he went as quickly as he could, scrabbling from root to ledge, outcrop to root. The rock was covered with loose shale, sodden and treacherous, and he slipped several times, skinning his palms, before he reached the bottom.

Was he too late?

Richard fetched up behind the rough granite wall of a cottage. He listened but there was no sound but the wind and the crash of the sea. He waited until his breathing slowed. He felt tired, leaden, and forced himself upright. Was he too late? He peered round the corner. The row of grim, pinched cottages were shuttered tight against the storm, and revealed nothing. Hunched over, he crept along the side and crossed to the cottages. From here a path ran down to the storehouses and two more dwellings, then curved left to the beach.

At that moment the door of the nearest cottage swung open and a fisherman stepped out. He was a short, stocky man in middle age, with an unshaven face.

Richard caught him by the collar and knocked him back against the open door. The man was going to call out, then he saw the expression on Richard's face and stopped.

'You're not with the others, are you?' he asked. He looked frightened.

'Are they here?' asked Richard. 'The Moretons?'

The man hesitated. 'Father and son. They've six men with them. They say we're to cast off within the hour.' He snorted. 'Damned murder, to go out in this weather.'

'Then why are you going?'

'Do you think we have a choice? We take 'em or they kill us.' The man glowered. 'My son's one of the crew.'

Richard glanced quickly down the path, and seeing no one, let go of the man.

'I can help, do you understand? Were there any women with them?'

The man shrugged. 'I don't know. I didn't see them arrive.' Then: 'Yes, there was, I think, in the rowboat, a woman.'

'Only one? What did she look like?'

The man shrugged again. 'Maybe she had dark hair.'

Dark hair! Richard felt his heart leap. 'Are you sure?'

'No, maybe I'm wrong,' muttered the man. 'What the hell does it matter?'

Rebecca had dark hair. But was it her? What of Susannah? A terrible impression came to him, of Rebecca already lying in a ditch, her throat slashed, her body mutilated, but he forced himself to deny this. She must be on the boat, he told himself. She had to be.

He stared at the man.

'What's your name?'

'Thomas Webb.'

'I need to get to the boat and stop them. Will you help me?'

Webb hesitated. Richard spoke close to his face. 'If they sail, do you think your son will come back?'

Thomas Webb sighed. 'All right.'

'Can you get me to the ship?'

Webb led the way down the path. Out of the shelter of the cottages the wind hit them with new force. Richard looked down at the cove. Two rowboats were pulled up on the shingle. The other men had gone, presumably out to the ship.

Just then the door of one of the cottages across the village opened and three men stepped out. Richard recognised Dr Masters' squat, muscular frame immediately. So he had escaped the explosion. Richard dipped his head, his hand fingering his sword. If they glanced in this direction ... Thomas Webb continued down the path. Masters didn't look at them as he crossed the path and disappeared into one of the storerooms. The two soldiers followed.

Richard smiled to himself. This meant there were only three men with Oliver and William.

'They must be waiting for Jem to row them over,' muttered Webb.

Sure enough, a fourth man, a fisherman, came out of the cottage and stood hunched in the rain. He saw Webb and nodded dourly.

Webb nodded back and led Richard down on to the beach, which was littered with rough grey shingle, sleek and glistening in the rain. Their feet crunched loudly.

Webb took the first boat they came to and they lugged it down to the water's edge as fast as they could, its keel grating on the stones, and then they were away, Webb heaving on the oars.

Even in the harbour, the force of the wind was unspeakable. The waters were rucked into waves, scagged with white, and splashed over the prow. Richard could see the pockets of wind moving across the water, chopping and darkening its skin. Whenever a clump of wind hit them the whole boat shivered as if it were struck by some physical thing. Webb strained at the oars. The boat struggled forward.

Come on, damn you! Faster!

Richard peered across the water towards the ship. The rain had thinned slightly and fat single drops stung his eyes.

Ahead, now only forty feet away, rose the dark bulk of the pinnace, lurching and creaking at its anchor chain, its rigging silvered by the first rays of sunlight.

The sailors had abandoned their attempt to hoist the foresail and were squatting in front of the stern cabin.

'Hullo! John! Is that you?'

A soldier appeared at the side of the ship. He waved across. Richard waved back. Webb grunted and pulled harder. The boat shouldered its way through the waves, landing with a smack on the sea. Water leapt over the prow.

'Hulloah! John?'

Ten feet away now.

Surely he must recognise me, thought Richard, then realised that the face of the sea was black and lightless.

The boat knocked into the ship. Richard scrambled to the side, clutching his pistol. A wave hit the boat and lifted it against the wooden side, and Richard stumbled. Webb swore and grabbed a shroud. 'Quick! Damn you!' he muttered.

'John?'

The soldier was leaning over the side. Richard saw the man's head briefly silhouetted against the sky, took aim, and pulled the trigger. There was a click. The powder's wet, he thought. And then the pistol fizzed and fired. The man suddenly disappeared from view.

Damn.

Throwing the pistol down, Richard grabbed the shrouds and clawed his way up the side. He reached the top, got a hand to the rail, expecting a sword to strike any second, and heaved himself over. The soldier was sprawled on his back, his head shattered. Richard lurched to his feet. He scanned the deck. The sailors had jumped up, were scattering. One soldier was on the right, by the prow, the other . . .

The other attacked from the left, his sword catching the cuff of Richard's jacket before he whipped his hand back. He was a big man, yellow-haired, with large gaps in his teeth. He grinned with excitement, fear maybe.

Richard jumped back, deflected his next blow. The man staggered under the lurch of the ship, steadied himself on the rail, and came on. He's swinging wildly, thought Richard. He parried, again, again. But the man was fresh and afraid and forced him back across the deck. Where was the other soldier?

The man bared his teeth, sensing Richard's uncertainty.

'Behind you,' he jeered.

Richard jumped aside, glanced over his shoulder. The man lunged at him. The deck was empty. Richard stumbled, dodged the blade. But what he had seen was the face of the water rucked by a squall. He parried, braced himself.

Then the squall banged into the side of the boat, tipped it like a plank. The man staggered, wrong-footed, and Richard thrust his sword into his chest. He saw a glint of shock in the man's eyes. Then Richard got a foot to his groin, knocked him down and finished him. He sprang round. Where *was* the other soldier?

The sailors were standing in a knot by the prow. They were struggling with someone and Richard suddenly saw the soldier pitch over the side and disappear. The ship was bucking and lurching so wildly he didn't hear the splash.

They must be below deck.

Richard gripped his sword tightly. Had they heard the pistol shot?

The door to the cabins stood beneath the stern-deck. He crossed the seesawing deck at a run. He reached the door, kicked it open and flung himself inside.

For a second everything was blackness. A man struck at him, missed. He heaved his sword and the boat

lurched to one side and he was thrown against the far
wall, came up with a thud in the face, a brief impression
of wood, grain, salt, and then rolled to one side. Oliver
Moreton spun round, his sword raised, and Richard
had a clear view of his face, pale, hollow-cheeked,
strangely handsome; a lantern was swinging wildly,
then Richard hacked him down. Oliver screamed.
Richard kicked his sword away.

'Don't touch him!'

He had known William Moreton would be here, but
even so the bellow of the man's voice caught him by
surprise. By the yellow dance of the lantern, Richard
saw the Colonel slumped against a pillar.

Richard started. He did not believe how the man
could have changed so much in the last few hours.

William Moreton's face had been drained of flesh.
His thick, sallow skin seemed to hang from his skull.
Great hollows rimmed his eyes. His mouth was cur-
tained by thick, heavy lines.

In his hand he held a pistol, cocked and loaded.

'Are you all right, son?'

Oliver groaned. His breathing was hoarse, ragged,
blood was oozing through his shirt. The boat lurched
to one side, then swung wildly back again. Below deck
the plunge and heave seemed even more violent.
William steadied himself against the pillar.

'I knew you would follow us, Tremaine.'

'I came for Rebecca.'

William snorted. 'Did you really?' His eyes had lost
none of their fire. He stared at Richard in such a way
that Richard felt suddenly unsure. 'Don't lie to yourself.
You came because of your anger. You wanted to kill us.
Admit it.'

'Are you going to shoot? Shoot!'

'You've always been angry, haven't you, Tremaine?

Angry with me for taking your house, angry with Oliver for taking your lover. Did you ever stop to think that maybe we were right?'

Richard seethed inside. 'Where is Rebecca? Is she still alive?'

Moreton looked tired. 'Do you really want Charles Stuart to lord it over you? Do you really need another man to tell you how to live? I did once, a long time ago, on the battlefield. Then I realised what fools we were. Man doesn't nee—' His last words were drowned in a surge of wind.

'That's lies, Moreton! Kill me, or give me Rebecca!'

'Don't want to listen, eh? See,' Moreton smiled horribly, 'I am a broken man now, the spirit has abandoned me. But I fought for a cause.'

Richard thought of Sarah Masters. 'You killed innocent people.'

Moreton sighed. 'Yes, I did. But how many did Charles Stuart send to their deaths at Marston Moor? Naseby? How many did the Lord Protector slaughter? At Dunbar? At Drogheda? At Worcester? Our killings were pinpricks in comparison. And for what? To establish a true, equal parliament, where each citizen would have the freedom to vote, for the government of his choice. Is democracy such a bad thing?' Moreton took careful aim. 'But it was not to be. Our new Jerusalem must wait, it seems . . .'

Richard tensed, waiting.

Suddenly, Moreton's mouth jerked open. Surprise flickered across his face and he toppled forward. The pistol fell from his hand. Behind him stood Susannah Tremaine. She was holding a long red knife.

Richard stared at her.

'Surprised, Richard?' She smiled at him, a painful, weary smile which made his heart twist. She looked at the knife and the smile faded. She threw it on to the floor in revulsion.

Oliver groaned. Richard snatched up the pistol.

'I don't understand,' he said. 'Why kill him? Why kill him now?'

She looked at him sympathetically. 'Because he has served his use,' she replied. 'As he said, he had nothing left to live for.' She steadied herself against another wave. 'Did you really think I was just a glovemaker's daughter?'

No, he thought, but I wanted to.

'You're one of Cromwell's agents, aren't you?'

She nodded. 'I'm sorry,' she said. 'I tried to warn you.'

'I thought you loved me.'

'I do, Richard! I do!' Susannah looked genuinely distraught. 'I'm so relieved you're alive! Now this is over, we can . . .'

'Where's Rebecca? Is she here?'

But she ignored him. 'I was doing my duty, Richard. But I love you!'

He felt himself grow angry. 'You were fucking him!' He knelt over Oliver's body, pulling his head up by the hair. Oliver gasped with pain. 'Was all that duty as well?'

'I had no choice, Richard! You disowned me, remember? Masters would have slit my throat.'

Richard braced the pistol against Oliver's temple.

'Where's Rebecca, damn you?' Oliver stared at him contemptuously. Richard pressed the pistol harder. 'Is she dead?'

Susannah faltered. 'Don't kill him, Richard! We need him!'

'Is she dead?' He glared at her.

412

'Probably.' She stopped. 'William left her behind with Dr Masters.'

Masters! He had let him go . . .

Richard pulled the trigger and shot Oliver through the head. Susannah screamed, but he was already running across the deck. Webb! Where was Webb?

Chapter Eight

THOMAS MASTERS HITCHED HIS BRITCHES under his belt and grinned unpleasantly. Then he stretched out a thick, muscular hand and stroked the side of her face. Rebecca twisted away.

'Don't be proud, girl,' he whispered and let his lips curl into a grin. 'Won't be long now, damn you!' He motioned to the two soldiers and they dragged her out of the storeroom. Jem Roberts, the boatman, was stamping impatiently on the path. The wind momentarily blinded Masters and he pulled the collar of his coat higher.

'Damn this weather!'

'Where do you want her, sir?' asked one of the soldiers. He ran his hand down over Rebecca's back. 'Shall we have her here?'

Rebecca clenched her teeth. I will not scream, she thought. They will not make me scream. The soldier's fingers reached the top of her buttocks and paused. She forced herself to ignore them and stepped forward.

'Come on,' she insisted. 'Where are you going to take me?'

She would not care any more. She set her face into the face of the wind.

Masters chuckled softly and followed her gaze out across the harbour.

That was strange. A rowboat was moored against the gunwales of the ship.

The leer left his face and he squinted through the rain. Curse his eyes!

'Can you see anything, John?' he asked the soldier next to Rebecca. 'What's happening?'

The man shrugged.

'Do you still want me to take you out?' asked Jem. He scowled. He felt for this girl in front of him. 'Wind's dying, so it is.'

Masters ignored him and strode down towards the water. Something was not right.

The two soldiers would have dragged Rebecca after him, but she walked down of her own accord. I can do this, she told herself. I will not lose my dignity.

Masters was standing on the shore. His thick, heavy body was impervious to the wind when even the rocks and stones seemed to shudder.

'Something's wrong,' he muttered.

One of the soldiers peered up at the hills towering over the village. They seemed menacing, ominous. 'Is there anyone there?' he asked.

'Trust in the Lord, boy,' answered Masters mechanically. In the teeth of the wind, he unbuttoned his coat and handed it to Jem.

'Hold her.' Quickly, dextrously, he flicked his cuffs up. He stared out at the grey mass of water, battened by the wind. The rowboat had not moved, perhaps he was worrying for nothing. And yet . . .

'I'm afraid this will be quicker than I would have liked, but we must go.' He glanced at her briskly, like a doctor considering a patient.

He only let her see the razor for a second, then he held it behind his back. He had found that the thought was enough to unhinge most of his victims. Most of them broke down and whimpered, begging him to have mercy on them, before the end.

Rebecca trembled despite herself. Will it hurt? She

tried not to imagine the pain, the sensation. This is not happening. This is not, she told herself.

Try to think of ...

The two soldiers forced her to her knees. She heard the one on the right suck in his breath sharply. The one on her left was shaking more than she was.

I will ...

Masters bent over her. His frame suddenly blotted out the wind, the light. She suddenly felt very warm. His breath kissed her cheek.

Then Richard arose from the sea before them.

He saw Masters raise his arm, the blade caught the only hint of sunlight in the air and made of it something almost beautiful.

The soldier on his right saw him, opened his mouth to speak.

Beautiful. Rebecca.

They were dead before they could utter even a prayer.

He kicked them aside. Rebecca was covered with blood. Her eyes flickered. She recognised him, he clutched her to him, butting Masters' severed trunk aside.

'Rebecca! I didn't ... I didn't leave you!' His words were choked with tears.

She smiled weakly. 'Don't worry. I know you didn't, I know.'

He kissed her, not caring about the taste of blood which clung to her lips. I love you. I have always.

She pushed him away. He stared at her stupidly and her smile burst into laughter. 'Don't you ever do that to me again!' She propped herself up on her elbows. 'Look at me, I'm covered ...'

He realised her laughter was hysterical, but in spite of himself, he grinned back. He stood up and went to help her to her feet, and she knocked his hand away and tottered down to the water's edge. Her smock was violently red. She let herself fall into the cold, grey water, and lay there, suddenly careless of the biting cold. He sagged down beside her.

'I didn't think I'd make it,' he said.

She rubbed the water over her breasts, stomach, arms. 'I feel . . . sick,' she announced suddenly, and retched into the water beside her.

He laid a hand on her shoulder. She was trembling and cold. 'Are you all right?'

'I think so.' Her face became serious. 'You know, back at the manor I really thought Oliver was going to kill me, but he didn't. I don't know why.' She paused. 'Then there was the explosion. I thought I heard my father calling. Men were screaming. There was smoke everywhere and Oliver dragged me to the stables. I was so—' She checked herself, regaining composure. Her lip quivered. 'Is my father all right?'

He shrugged. 'The last I saw, he was on the balcony.'

'And what about Susannah? Have you seen her, Richard?'

He got painfully to his feet. He was so tired he could hardly stand.

'I don't want to think about her any more. I came here for you, Beckie.'

She looked away.

'It's true, Beckie!' She heard the edge in his voice and turned back. The wind had made her eyes sting with tears. Richard offered her his hand. 'I should have come back for you nine years ago.'

Don't say that, she thought. It's what I want to hear.

Jem Roberts had watched from the edge of the beach. Now he came towards them. He did not look Richard in the eye.

'Have you clothes for the lady?' Richard asked. Both he and Rebecca were shaking with cold. He wrapped his arms around her and they clung to each other.

When they looked up, they saw that people had appeared at the doors of the cottages – women, children, old men – and were staring in relief and shock. One of the women came down with a blanket and folded it around Rebecca. 'I'm sorry,' she murmured. 'All of us are.'

Richard turned back and gazed over the grey rucked waves to where the ship still rode at anchor. Slowly, Thomas Webb pushed his boat off from the side and pulled through the waters towards them. In the prow sat a woman, her blood-red hair streaming in the wind.

Chapter Nine

THEY SMELT THE BURNING BEFORE they reached the manor. The harsh, bitter scent infected the air and clouded their thoughts. They hurried their horses up through the last of the trees and across the field.

At the crest of the hill they stopped. From here they could see the old house streaming with thick white smoke. The fumes rose in fat clusters, then drifted northwards and were scattered by the wind. Richard felt his heart quicken. Then he saw that amid the smoke, people were moving, ant-like at this distance, and there came faint shouts through the moist autumn air. Overhead, the storm had cleared with the day. The fields, woods and buildings were bathed in a gentle lemon light which gilded the smoke and made it into something faintly beautiful and gossamer.

He looked at Rebecca. She seemed pensive, her eyes fixed on the scene before them. In the soft, clear light, she was particularly beautiful, he thought, and reached across and kissed her on the cheek. She smiled back, perhaps a little melancholy.

'How do you feel?'

She glanced at the ruined manor. 'How do you?'

Without speaking, they rode down the last field. As they drew closer, Richard saw the south wing was almost completely destroyed. The roof seemed to have been peeled open and reeking timbers, like a charred and ruptured ribcage, jutted through the smoke. Mercifully, the fire had halted on the edge of the Great Hall, and the library, kitchens and north wing were unscathed. The servants had formed a chain and were passing buckets up from the well and into the house. Other servants were shovelling soil on to the smouldering remains. Richard noticed that among the serving-men and women were soldiers and cavalry troops. Where the sunlight pierced the smoke, it glinted on their cuirasses and helmets. He wondered vaguely if he should be alarmed, but he was now too tired to care. As they rode across the yard the servants stopped working and stared at them.

Sitting by the main door and sporting a brilliant white bandage was a man with a crisp grey moustache and beard. He smiled when he saw them and doffed his hat with a flourish.

Richard grinned back.

'So, you made your escape!'

Wedlock tut-tutted in mock seriousness. 'You left us quite a mess, Master Tremaine.' He winked at Rebecca. 'And who is this fine lady?'

'Rebecca Penmarris,' she replied, before Richard could. 'I assume you are another of the Lord Protector's agents, Mr..?'

'Wedlock. Just Wedlock.' He looked at Richard as if sharing a private joke.

'Well?' asked Richard irritably.

Wedlock patted himself on the chest. 'Reckon I'll live, in case you're worried.'

Richard scowled at him. 'So what are you going to do, arrest me?'

'Goodness, no. There's plenty of time for that later, Tremaine. Don't forget' – Wedlock coughed flamboyantly – 'I owe you my life.'

Richard swung himself out of his saddle. He reached up and helped Rebecca down. His hands around her waist felt good.

Wedlock coughed. 'Well, at least you have me to thank for saving your mansion.' He nodded at the work gangs, but Richard felt nothing other than a great, weary indifference.

'Tell me later. I'm exhausted.'

'Wait, sir!' Rebecca's voice was urgent. 'In the house, did you find the . . . an old man with a beard?'

Wedlock considered her carefully. 'Was he your father, Miss Penmarris?'

She nodded. She couldn't speak.

Wedlock sighed. 'No. I can't say we did.'

Rebecca shut her eyes but her face was still very pale. Richard took her by the hand and went to walk into the house. Wedlock laid a hand on his chest.

'Richard. Is it settled, this business?'

'Yes, it is over.' Richard saw him relax. 'Send your men to Porthcarrick. They'll find what they want there.'

'And Susannah?'

Richard lifted Wedlock's hand away. 'She's alive,' he muttered, and walked on.

Inside, the Great Hall was stained and reeking with smoke. The floor was covered with shattered plaster, shards of wood, debris. Richard felt something crack underfoot and looking down saw the fractured limbs of a cherub. Rebecca gripped his hand tighter.

'Come on,' he said. Two soldiers were sweeping the floor and stepped aside to let them pass. Richard took her up the stairs and into the first room he came to, and closed the door behind them.

He stopped and studied Rebecca's face intently. Her face looked proud and drawn and beautiful. He ran a hand down her cheek, and winced when she pulled away.

'I need to sleep, Rebecca, more than anything else in the world. Will you stay with me?'

'Richard, you know how much there is between us.'

'Yes.' His voice was dry. She was so beautiful.

'I don't need to be with you for my sake,' she said proudly. 'What of Susannah? I thought you loved her.' Only her eyes betrayed the terrible vulnerability she felt.

'There is no one else.' His voice was soft, pleading. 'Rebecca, I need you.'

They looked at each other for a long time until everything which words could not express had passed between them.

'I love you, Rebecca. I always have done.'

There. He had said it, and Richard Tremaine was finally revealed to her.

Only then did Rebecca allow herself a faint, wistful smile.

'You are a stubborn, stupid man, Richard Tremaine. You have caused me such pain.'

'I know that too.'

In a silence as tender as a bruise, they began to undress until they stood tired and naked before each other.

She winced when she saw the ragged wounds across his chest, his arm, his leg. She touched him, gently, with the very tips of her fingers, and saw his skin redden to her touch. He breathed out sharply.

'Are you all right, Richard?'

He almost laughed with joy, for the concern in her voice. 'If you promise to look after me.'

And she knew he was right.

There in the room Rebecca suddenly felt a great joyous innocence before him. She was pleased he saw her like this, and she him, naked, wounded. Without the distortions of passion, without lust, but with an acceptance as clear and delicate as the early light of day which washed over them, washed them clean.

Then she took him in her arms and held him gently and led him to the bed they both longed for.

Chapter Ten

Richard awoke a little after noon to the sound of hammering from outside. Rebecca still slept, nestled in the crook between his arm and chest, her black hair spread across the bolster. He stared at her for some minutes as if surprised at how good he felt. His body was sore and painful and he screwed his face against the pain, but somehow this did not matter. He waited until he was sure she would not wake, then eased himself out of bed.

On the chair a servant had laid out clean clothes for them both. He dressed quickly and quietly. He was just about to leave when he remembered something and searched frantically through his pile of tattered rags bundled on the floor. The leather pouch which Mary Talbot had given him, with the letter from his father, was still there, tucked inside the remains of his britches. He mouthed a word of thanks, slipped it in his jacket, and went downstairs.

He could not believe how much had changed in six hours.

The Hall was now clean and tidied, although a haze of dust and the scent of burning still hung in the air. From the kitchen came the smell of bread baking and beef crisping and the familiar clang of pots and cutlery. Hammers rang across the yard from where a group of workmen were constructing a wooden buttress to brace, by the look of it, the west wall of the house where the roof had collapsed. Richard stood on the steps and watched them, letting his head clear in the warm afternoon. Soldiers sat round in desultory knots of two or three, smoking or talking or taking their ease.

Richard heard a tap on the window behind him and turning around saw Wedlock beckoning from the library.

With him was Susannah.

He felt himself stiffen as he entered. He stared at her coldly. She was standing by the window, her face downcast, and he could see by her swollen cheeks and eyes that she had been crying. Despite himself, he felt a great tenderness come over him.

'Take a seat.' Wedlock extended a hand. 'You slept well?'

Richard smiled grimly, and Wedlock went to the door and leant into the corridor: 'Bridget, could you fetch us some brandy, please? Quick now!' He came back. 'Your father had a fine collection of books, I see.'

Richard said nothing. He felt oppressed by Susannah's presence. He kept his eyes fixed on the dark oak of the table. He heard her dress rustle. Wedlock began to leaf through a volume of Caesar's *Commentaries*. The only sounds were those from the workmen and the kitchen, and the crisp turning of the pages.

'Fascinating, fascinating,' Wedlock announced at length. 'You know there are many who would compare our own Lord Protector with Caesar – a flattering comparison, don't you think?'

'Moreton did,' replied Richard. 'Caesar was assassinated, wasn't he?'

'Yes, indeed.' Wedlock shut the book with a bang. 'But poor Mr Lovelace will not, I think, get that far.'

There was a knock on the door and Bridget brought in a tray of brandy and glasses. Richard saw Susannah glance at him awkwardly, then look away.

Wedlock poured the brandy generously. 'Susannah

has told me what happened, what you did, I mean. You did well.'

Richard did not feel in the mood for thanks. 'I acted for myself, that is all. Doubtless she has also told you how she consorted with the enemy.' To his own ears, his words sounded bitter and angry, and he hated himself. He saw her wince.

'Miss Tremaine is a loyal servant of the government,' replied Wedlock evenly. 'We are very proud of her.' He considered Susannah, saw the expression on her face. 'Perhaps you could leave us for a while, Susannah?'

Richard thought for a moment she would object, but then she walked quickly out, looking straight ahead.

They listened to her footsteps retreating down the corridor. Wedlock passed him a glass.

'You know she's not my sister, don't you?' asked Richard, staring into the brandy. 'Her real name is Jennifer Turner.'

'But doesn't *Susannah* suit her more?' Wedlock wiped his lips in satisfaction. 'Susannah enabled us to observe Moreton . . . intimately, so to speak.'

Richard scowled. 'So her betrothal to Oliver, everything, was a ruse from the beginning?'

'Yes. Yes.'

'And what about her feelings for me, were they all part of the scheme?'

Wedlock looked at him with a surprising degree of sympathy. 'You'll have to ask Susannah. In that, she is a free person.'

Richard felt his voice thicken. 'When we got out of the cellar, I went to look for her . . .' he faltered. 'How do you know she didn't betray you to Moreton? She was happy enough to leave you to die.'

'You know,' replied Wedlock, 'you might be right. Perhaps Susannah was seduced, just for an instant, by

Moreton's rhetoric. He *was* very persuasive. After all, weren't you almost tempted by what he said?' He studied Richard intently.

'No.' Richard shook his head in disgust.

'But what else could she do?' asked Wedlock. 'Look what happened to Mrs Masters. She had to survive to warn the authorities.'

Richard looked sceptical. Did Wedlock really believe that?

'She will have her . . . uses,' added Wedlock, as if reading his mind. 'People like her always do.'

His tone angered Richard.

'Like me, as well, you mean? I suppose we all just have our uses!' He smacked his hand on the table. 'But that's what I don't understand. You wrote to the King, saying you had discovered his missing gold, yet all the time you were working for Cromwell.'

'A cunning device, was it not?' Wedlock grinned sheepishly and tweaked the end of his moustache. 'I'm afraid the gold was my idea too. We guessed some had gone astray during the retreat – gold has a habit of going astray – and poor Charles Stuart is so strapped, he'll believe anything.' The grin broke into a sudden hoot of laughter. 'You should have seen your face in the Three Lords!'

Richard stifled his anger. 'But what was the point of this *game*?'

Wedlock straightened his face. 'It was bait, that's all.'

'But why?'

'The royalists are always scheming, but can we convict them? Never! We thought this ruse would make them play their hands.' Wedlock pursed his lips. 'I tell you, these royalist gentlemen are a cancer! If we don't cut them out, they will keep on rebelling, and who will die? It will be the common folk who swing from the

gallows, not the gentry. Those introductions you gave
me on the river would have been the beginning. It's a
pity I lost them.' He looked at Richard mischievously.
'I don't suppose you'd attest to a few names in court?
No, I thought not.' He paused. 'You know, my plan
went wrong from the moment they decided to send
you, Richard Tremaine, of all people! And then your
blasted ship got wrecked! The next thing I know is
you're a guest at Chynoon, thanks to my agent's over-
zealous concern. If it had been me, I'd have let you go
down with the others, I'm afraid. Moreton, you see,
was an altogether more serious character. People of
belief always are. His plot might actually have worked.'

'So where did Fielding fit into this?'

'Fielding had been helping us for years. Which
member of Charles' entourage isn't? How do you think
they pay their bills?' added Wedlock wryly. 'We'd
promised him a free pardon – eventually – but when
he thought his precious gold was in danger, he threw
in his lot with Moreton. And look at his gold! Stones
and mud!'

'I think Sir Ralph Fielding was a soldier looking for
something to believe in,' said Richard.

'Aren't we all?' replied Wedlock.

Richard finished his brandy. It burnt his throat pleas-
antly. 'I no longer want to follow anyone.'

'If only more people felt like that,' Wedlock nodded.
'You know, I *like* you, Tremaine.'

Richard did not respond. Other thoughts troubled
him. 'Have you read Moreton's journal?'

'Lies. Lies and rantings.'

'In the journal there were names, and letters. CCCL.'

'Yes.' Wedlock smiled. 'CCCL. Carew, Courtney,
Clement and Lovelace. Lovelace would have done the
dirty work. John Carew and Gregory Clement both

signed the King's execution. They hated Cromwell just as much. I think they saw themselves as Brutus and Cassius, ridding the country of a would-be king,' he explained. 'Hugh Courtney would have delivered the Army in the West.'

'They had that much influence?'

'The Fifth Monarchy of Christ is a powerful movement.' Wedlock pointed to the window. 'Look around you. How many men and women are happy with their lot? Are things really better now the King is dead? Moreton and his type can offer them something altogether new. After all, it was people like him who won the war for us. Conviction, Tremaine! Blind conviction!' He gazed up at the picture of the Crucifixion over the fireplace. 'And to think our God is a God of peace and forgiveness. Why do the people listen to Messiahs of war and destruction? Do you think your King is any different? If he returns will he forgive the men who slaughtered his father?'

'I am a servant of the King.'

'Are you? Are you really?' Wedlock stared at him, then lowered his gaze. 'There is something I must tell you. When we cleared out the Hall, we found the body of an elderly man, a retainer apparently. I believe he may be Miss Penmarris's father?'

Sedge. Richard felt his heart sink.

'You knew this morning, didn't you, when she asked.'

'Yes.' Wedlock looked up. 'Would you like to tell her?'

Richard sighed. 'Of course. I am to blame, I suppose.'

'No,' said Wedlock. 'You're not to blame. It's too complicated for that.'

But Richard was not persuaded.

Rebecca was still sleeping when he got back to the

room. She looked so peaceful, he thought, and stayed his hand in mid-air. Then he braced himself and shook her gently.

She stirred, stretched lazily, and opened her eyes.

'It's you,' she said simply and gave him a sleepy smile. 'Have I slept long?'

'Yes,' he kissed her. 'I love you.'

'I love you too.' She looked at him. 'What's wrong, Richard?'

Richard breathed slowly. He kissed her again. And then he told her as simply and gently as he could.

He tried to hold her but Rebecca pushed him clumsily away and stumbled out of bed.

'Don't! Please. Don't!' Her eyes were blinking rapidly.

He spoke to her several times. 'Rebecca . . . I'm sorry . . . I love you.' But she batted him away with her hands.

'Don't say anything, Richard. Whatever you say I will hate you more.' She struggled to maintain her composure. 'I have to be alone.'

She saw the fresh clothes laid out for her on the chair and pulled them on, awkwardly, ungainly, holding her head proudly all the while, teeth clenched, eyes fixed straight ahead, and willed Richard not to interfere.

He stood and watched her, feeling an infinite distance between them.

'Rebecca!' he said at last. 'Please let me help!'

She was right. Whatever he said . . . She levelled her gaze at him. 'I think you've helped enough already, haven't you, Richard? If you hadn't—' She stopped herself abruptly. Such outbursts belittled her. She struggled into her bodice. 'I'm going out now. I must be alone.'

'Wait! Will I see you later?'

She stared at him with sudden intensity, then slammed the door behind her.

Richard punched the bolster as hard as he could. He was still staring at the imprint of his fist when he heard the door creak open. He looked up, hopefully.

It was Susannah. Wedlock had been right – the name did suit her.

She was in the room before he could say anything. He stared at her. He felt that perhaps for the first time he was seeing her as she really was. Her vitality, her vivid self-assurance had gone. In their place was a frightened, sensitive woman, with wounded eyes, whose hair was tangled and whose skirt was torn. She noticed his gaze, for she began to smooth down the ruffles with her palms.

'I had to see you,' she explained, almost as an apology.

He did not reply.

She stared at him with such a look of longing and pain that he felt his heart stir against his will. Susannah saw the expression on his face. 'I'm sorry,' she said, 'I never wanted to deceive you like this.' She lowered her eyes. 'I never lied about what I felt for you.'

'I understand that,' he said. 'I lied to you as well, don't forget.'

There was a silence. Outside the hammering had started again.

'Then why leave me like this?' she began.

Richard got up and went to her. Susannah smiled.

'You killed Ursula, didn't you?' he asked bluntly.

Susannah looked stunned and was about to deny it when she stopped herself.

'Yes,' she replied. 'I did.'

He turned away.

'Wait!' she cried. 'Aren't you going to ask why?'

'Will that make it any better?' he asked angrily.

She blanched. 'You don't understand, do you? We were all in danger here. I couldn't afford for anyone to discover who I really was, or who you were.' She looked at him pointedly. 'Oh, yes, I knew you were the King's agent before you even set foot on board the *Marguerite*. Why do you think William saved you from the wreck? On a whim?' She laughed, though without any humour. 'I had to use every ounce of influence. When you told me you'd received a note, I knew it must be from Ursula.'

That note. *Meet me in the orchard . . .*

'But why kill her?'

'Do I have to spell it out?' Her eyes flashed. 'Ursula was unhappy with Moreton's plans, she had a roving eye. Could I allow that? What if she realised you were not Richard Ferrers? Or if Moreton found out? We were so close.'

Richard said nothing. He remembered the sparkle in Ursula's eye. Her love of life.

'But why did William conceal her murder? He must have known she'd been killed.'

Susannah grimaced slightly. 'He need never have suspected anything. I . . . I used poison.'

'Poison? But there were marks on her neck!'

Susannah looked at him blankly. 'You must have been mistaken, Richard. She was not strangled.'

Then Richard understood the significance of those words in Moreton's journal. 'She was in such pain and begged me to comfort her. I gave her such comfort as my strength afforded, oh dear dear wife.' Oh dear God, he thought.

'You have done an evil thing, Susannah.'

'It was my duty,' she replied. 'If that is my sin, damn me.' She flashed at him: 'Tell me, if I were a man, would

you judge me so harshly? Would you?' She lifted up
her hands and clutched at the air. 'Don't you think I
hated what I had to do? Can't you love a woman who
can do that?'

Richard stared at her. The soft afternoon sun fell on
her tangled hair and rippled it with flame. She was
beautiful, strikingly beautiful, and angry. He wished he
could go to her now and hold her and forget what had
happened. But we are too old for that, he thought. This
world is too old.

'You're going to take her with you, aren't you?' she
said, half mocking, half accusing.

He didn't reply.

'You don't love her, Richard. You might think you
do, but you don't. You care for her because she was an
innocent in our world, but you don't love her.' She
stared into his eyes. Her lips were parted, swollen. 'In
spite of all this, you love me, Richard. I saved your life,
damn you!'

'No,' he replied. 'I thought I loved you, I wanted to
love you. But you said yourself, you saved me out of
duty.'

'Wait.' She grabbed his shoulders, pressing herself
against him. Her body was lithe, strong. 'Please.' She
raised her lips to his mouth. But the storm which had
been within them both had died and suddenly he
realised that he felt nothing, only a sadness for what
was no more.

Chapter Eleven

RICHARD LEFT THE MANOR BEHIND HIM and walked across the fields to the church. Rebecca was sitting on the grass and rearranging the white flowers she had once brought to Ursula's grave. They had yellowed and started to rot.

She looked up.

'I knew you'd come here,' she told him.

He knelt beside her and took the flowers out of her hands.

'I'm sorry for running away,' she went on. 'I needed to be on my own.' She folded her hands over her knees. 'I expect you'll be leaving soon.'

He nodded and she looked away towards the grey mass of the church.

'I will never forgive you for coming back, Richard Tremaine. Never.'

'I had no choice. It was my duty. But I never wanted to hurt you, Beckie.' He wrapped his arm round her shoulder, but she remained stiff and unyielding.

'I will never forgive you, Richard. Know that. But also, know that I will always, always love you.' Then she looked at him. 'I have nothing here, now. Nothing. Take me with you and marry me. You owe me that much.'

Her broad, straight lips hesitated into a smile.

Richard bent his head and kissed her softly, then she wrapped her arms around him and they held each other until some of the pain and tenderness had eased.

'When I said I loved you earlier, didn't you believe me?' she asked.

He looked at her. 'You realise I have nothing, don't you? No money, no inheritance. Not even a cause I believe in.'

'Well,' she smiled back, 'you can read and write and you seem strong enough to me. Perhaps you could try working for a living.' She got up and offered him a hand. 'I'm not going to ask you again, Richard.'

He took her hand gratefully.

'Then, my lady, I suppose I had better accept.'

His eyes fell on the gold ring she wore on her third finger. He saw now that the design traced on the band was of apples and pomegranates intertwined. Rebecca caught the look in his eye and smiled.

'Mary Talbot gave it to me when I went to say good-bye,' she explained. 'She said your father gave it to her when they were betrothed.'

'But I told her we were only friends,' he replied, somewhat self-consciously.

Rebecca's smile became mocking and teasing and slightly more beautiful. 'Yes! And didn't that hurt! You know, you can be the most stubborn, insensitive, witless fool I've ever met.'

'But then why did she—'

'Mary *knew*, Richard, as soon as she saw us together.' She gave him a look which was proud and knowing and happy. 'She also realised how stupid you were. She told me to be patient.'

He realised he was blushing. Him! *Blushing!* He kissed her gently on the cheek.

'Thank you for waiting, Beckie.'

They walked back to the manor hand in hand. If loving alone will make us happy, he thought, we will be happy.

They parted at the edge of the yard. Rebecca wanted to return to her cottage one final time, alone, she insisted, and collect her belongings.

Richard went to find Wedlock.

Wedlock was still in the library. With him was Stephen Moreton. The boy blinked at Richard nervously. Wedlock smiled. 'Thank you, Stephen, you can go now,' he whispered, and the boy darted out and closed the door behind him. Wedlock leaned back in his chair and regarded Richard with some satisfaction. 'I suppose you're going to plead for your freedom, Tremaine?'

'So, are you going to let me go?'

Wedlock scratched his nose. 'Do you know,' he asked, 'who started the fire in the cellar?' Richard said nothing, so he answered himself. 'Stephen Moreton, that's who. Does that surprise you? And do you know why? The poor boy was devoted to Ursula. He couldn't forgive Moreton for killing her.'

'Moreton didn't really kill her, did he?'

Wedlock shrugged. 'I was his father's prisoner – what else could I tell him? It saved your neck in particular,' he added pointedly.

Richard scowled. 'So what will happen to the boy now? How many more lies will you feed him?'

'Lies? Lies?' Wedlock arched his brows, as if momentarily offended. 'Well, I suppose he will be squire of Chynoon when he is older. Not that he is particularly blessed with wits, I grant you.'

Now it was Richard's turn to look offended. 'This was my family's home.'

'Exactly,' replied Wedlock. Then his face burst into a brilliant, impish smile. 'Reclaim it.'

Richard stared at him in amazement.

'Our country needs more people like you,' Wedlock

continued. 'People who don't believe in ideals. People who just want to live their lives and let others do the same. Reclaim your inheritance. I'll see you get a full pardon.' He smiled. 'Fielding would have got at least as much.' Then he added: 'Your father would have got a lot more.'

Richard understood the look in his eyes. So Fielding had been right all along.

Richard went over to the mantelpiece.

'Would you mind,' he said, 'leaving me alone for a while?'

Wedlock got to his feet. 'If you don't accept my offer,' he said, 'I'll see you're free to go.'

Richard stared at the wall. Everything Fielding had said had been true. He gripped the mantelpiece in anger. How could he not have known?

What more surprises do you have in store for me, Father? he thought.

He remembered the letter Mary Talbot had given him and felt in his jacket for the leather pouch. The letter was moist, and the ink had run, and he had trouble making out the words, but he could still read: 'Who can judge me? Not you, beloved, you know too well. My son perhaps.'

Was this his father's confession? Not to Mary, but to him, Richard? 'My son.'

Richard read on: '*Divitias filius fulvo sibi congerat auro.* Let son count my worth even if another will not. Give him this for me, if I should not come, and tell him to mark it well and that I love him . . . Tell him to count this letter as the last word.'

No. This was not a confession at all.

Richard scanned the bookcases. Where had it been? A slim red volume jutted out slightly and he plucked it down. This was it. The poems of Tibullus.

437

There in the front of the book was the same quotation as in the letter. *Divitias filius fulvo sibi congerat auro.*

Only it wasn't a quotation.

Richard turned to the first line of the first poem in the collection and read:

'*Divitias alius fulvo sibi congerat auro.*' Let *another* gather riches in yellow gold.

Richard studied the letter again. 'Let son count my worth even if another will not . . . Tell him to count this letter as the last word.'

Let son count my worth. Son. Count this letter as the last word.

Filius, the Latin for son, had six letters. *Alius*, another, had five.

Richard counted down six lines of the poem. The last word of the sixth line was *focus*: '*Dum meus adsiduo luceat igne focus*': 'So long as my hearth gleams with constant fire'. *Focus* was the Latin for hearth.

Focus. It was almost as if the word itself was a pun.

But then, if Michael Tremaine had hidden the gold, he would have had to hide it somewhere close by, somewhere almost obvious.

Where had Fielding seen him?

Here. In the library.

Richard stooped down and peered up into the chimney. It was filthy with soot. He squatted in the hearth and reached up inside. The chimney breast swelled out above the mantelpiece and formed a small ledge, no more than eight inches deep. Running his fingers along this, he found it crammed with leather bags, heavy and full.

He drew his hand out quickly, wiping it on his britches, checking his sleeve for marks.

Five thousand pounds.

A fortune. Enough to rebuild Chynoon and more

besides. Gold which, as far as anyone else knew, did not exist.

He found Wedlock in the yard.

'Well?'

He smiled. 'It seems I have no choice. I accept your offer.'

'Capital!' Wedlock clapped his hands together, then added: 'Of course, we may have . . . work for you, from time to time.'

Richard looked at him. 'Duties, you mean? Like my father?'

Wedlock was about to say something when he caught sight of Rebecca coming round the side of the building. In her hand she carried a pathetically small bundle of belongings.

She went up to Richard and kissed him.

'Do we go soon?'

He caught her arms and pulled her closer. She felt warm and loving and he knew that she really would be happy to come with him to France, knowing he had no money, no prospects.

Forgetting Wedlock he picked her up and whirled her in his arms.

She screamed and giggled.

'I've missed you,' he whispered, grinning wolfishly. He took the bundle out of her hands and threw it away. 'How I've missed you.'

Her eyebrows knotted in mock seriousness. 'Richard Tremaine . . .' she began.

But he was already laughing out loud.

Endpiece

THE SUNLIGHT WHICH FELL THAT DAY brought with it a new peace to the world. The clouds had finally been blown away and the sky was light, clear.

Under the curve of a hedgerow, huddled and twisted in his rags, slept Poor Tom, until, some little time after noon, the gentle sunlight kissed his eyelids and he woke. He sat up, scratched, and rubbed the side of his head. The wound was still painful after all these years, but today its pain was fresher, sharper, as if the pure, clean rain had washed deep inside and made it clean. And with the pain, a new realisation came to him.

I am not Poor Tom, he thought.

I am Michael. Michael Tremaine.

He stretched, and his joints and sinews cracked joyfully. Something like a bad dream had departed from him and for a moment he lay on his back and laughed out loud. He was free! He felt his legs, his arms, his stomach, his chest, marvelling at their sensation, as if they were long-lost friends.

Where have I been? What have I done?

Images came to him, of fire, of blood, and abject hunger, but they were no longer real.

Then, with a sudden sense of haste, he sprang to his feet and began to trot down the hill.

Chynoon lay on the other side of the woods. Soon he would be home.

Voices began to chatter in his head again, but this time he ignored them like the twittering of sparrows.

I am Michael Tremaine. I will not forget again.

Rebecca and Richard were resting in the shade of the apple trees when he found them. He started to run towards them and felt his feet labouring through the long grass, and then his eyes were blinded with tears and he stumbled. My tears are like molten lead, he thought.

When he looked up, their warm, anxious faces were above his. Then Richard grabbed his hand, his poor shredded hand, and pulled him to his feet. Suddenly they were smiling and crying and laughing. Servants were running from the house. The dogs were barking. The sunlight was almost dazzling.

And that was perhaps the happiest hour of his life.

Other bestselling Wa   titles available by mail:

☐	Half Hidden	Emma Blair	£5.99
☐	Flower of Scotland	Emma Blair	£5.99
☐	The Conquest	Elizabeth Chadwick	£5.99
☐	The Champion	Elizabeth Chadwick	£5.99
☐	The Italian House	Teresa Crane	£5.99
☐	Siena Summer	Teresa Crane	£5.99
☐	The Dancing Stone	Evelyn Hood	£5.99
☐	All That She Wants	Maeve Haran	£5.99
☐	Soft Touch	Maeve Haran	£5.99

The prices shown above are correct at time of going to press. However, the publishers reserve the right to increase prices on covers from those previously advertised without prior notice.

WARNER BOOKS

WARNER BOOKS
Cash Sales Department, P.O. Box 11, Falmouth, Cornwall, TR10 9EN
Tel: +44 (0) 1326 569777, Fax: +44 (0) 1326 569555
Email: books@barni.avel.co.uk

POST AND PACKING:
Payments can be made as follows: cheque, postal order (payable to Warner Books) or by credit cards. Do not send cash or currency.

All U.K. Orders	**FREE OF CHARGE**
E.E.C. & Overseas	25% of order value

Name (Block Letters) _____

Address_____

_____

Post/zip code:_____

☐ Please keep me in touch with future Warner publications

☐ I enclose my remittance £_____

☐ I wish to pay by Visa/Access/Mastercard/Eurocard

Card Expiry Date
